"You have not heard of me?"

His question made her hesitate. "Should I have?"

"If you have not by now, you will tomorrow when I win."

She had heard braggarts many times, but his tone was different. He was not boasting so much as stating a fact. "What will I hear?"

His eyes seemed even more engulfed in shadow. "Something that will not be in my favor."

Strange that he would admit that. "Will it be true?"

He answered like a witness giving evidence in the king's court. "Partly, I expect, but not the whole truth."

"What is the whole truth?"

His deep voice softened again. "That would take some time to explain." He came nearer.

She could not seem to think or even breathe, everything else subverted by the new and wondrous excitement and curiosity this man created within her.

Other AVON ROMANCES

MARGARET MOORE

THE Maiden AND HER Knight

AVON BOOKS
An Imprint of HarperCollinsPublishers

This is a work of fiction. Names, characters, places, and incidents are products of the author's imagination or are used fictitiously and are not to be construed as real. Any resemblance to actual events, locales, organizations, or persons, living or dead, is entirely coincidental.

AVON BOOKS
An Imprint of HarperCollins*Publishers*
10 East 53rd Street
New York, New York 10022-5299

Copyright © 2001 by Margaret Wilkins
ISBN: 0-380-81336-X
www.avonromance.com

First Avon Books paperback printing: October 2001

Avon Trademark Reg. U.S. Pat. Off. and in Other Countries, Marca Registrada, Hecho en U.S.A.
HarperCollins ® is a trademark of HarperCollins Publishers Inc.

Printed in the U.S.A.

10 9 8 7 6 5 4 3 2 1

For Mom

Chapter 1

He did not belong there.

Seated in the shadows cast by the pillars of her father's hall, the man's unfamiliar, stern face flickered in the light of the torch above him as if he were more spirit than mortal, and sent to sit in judgment on them all.

Who was he to come to Montclair Castle and regard them thus? Lady Allis wondered. He was no great and powerful nobleman, or he would not be alone, with no squire or page to serve him. He was not wealthy, for his clothing was plain, made of wool and leather, not fine silks, brocades and damasks. Most strange of all, he wore his long, dark hair loose about his shoulders like some kind of savage.

He moved his head to look at the high table, and Allis quickly turned toward her father, the earl of Montclair. He sat motionless, staring down at the untouched trencher before him. He said nothing, noted nothing, ate and drank nothing, when she had so hoped hosting this tournament would rally him and restore something of his former vitality.

"Again you do the honors well as the lady of Montclair Castle," Rennick DeFrouchette murmured beside her, his voice smooth and slick as oil.

Although he was tall, lean, rich and good-looking, the baron's handsome features could not disguise the greed that gleamed in his cold blue eyes, or the cruelty in the scornful curl of his lip when he regarded all those he considered beneath him, in status or in wealth.

He lifted her hand to his lips and pressed an unwelcome kiss upon it, while his gaze flicked to her breasts. "Your father is very proud of you."

"I hope so, Baron," she replied with a small smile, playing this game because she must.

Turning away, she surveyed the many trestle tables set up in the hall and covered with white linen, candles blazing in holders upon them, or in stands near the walls. In the hearth, a fire burned, providing light and warmth against the April evening's chill.

"You are a most dutiful daughter."

She smiled once more and fought the urge to tell him exactly what she thought of him. She had heard of his harsh punishments for the least offence on his estate and the danger of being a maidservant in his household.

Even sitting this close to him was enough to rob her of her appetite.

"Yet surely every woman longs to be an equally dutiful wife in her own home," the baron continued, toying with the jeweled rings on his left hand, "especially one such as a man like myself can provide. I would see that your father is well cared for, too."

Watched over as if he were a prisoner, as she would be, and her brother and sister, as well.

Once more hiding her disgust, her gaze wandered to the silent man who studied those around him as if he had never seen Normans before. He must have, or he would not be here.

Judging by the breadth of his shoulders and chest, as well as his muscular arms, this man made his living by fighting.

He must not be very successful. He was older than most of the knights gathered here. A man his age should have earned an estate by now, or at least found a place in a lord's service, unless he preferred the freedom of a life unbound by daily duties and responsibilities. He was free to go where he would, and do as he wished. If she were free, she would tell DeFrouchette to go to the devil.

Merva, full figured and of middle years, her brown hair possessing the color and gloss of chestnuts, sauntered into view. She headed toward a group of young knights closest to the stranger.

Merva was not pretty, but she was frank, earthy and loved to jest with the young men. She liked to do more with the young men, too, and as long as that didn't interfere with her duties, Allis turned a blind eye.

The maidservant laughed, a deep, throaty gurgle that drew the stranger's attention. He smiled a small, secretive little smile that lit his formerly grim visage.

Allis wished she had been the one to inspire that smile, to be like Merva for just a little while—bold and carefree, making suggestive remarks with a wink and a smile, all but demanding what she wanted. She would walk right up to that stranger and ask him if he thought he was Samson to have such hair. Perhaps he would smile and suggest she be his Delilah. They would laugh and look meaningfully at each other, and share more banter and maybe he would maneuver her into that dark corner and try to steal a kiss—playfully, of course, and yet how her blood would race . . . just as it was now as she imagined being in his arms.

Baron DeFrouchette squeezed her hand, hard enough to hurt. "My lady, I fear you are ignoring me."

She gently extricated her hand from his grasp. "I was looking for my brother."

"He is listening to the squires boast."

She followed the baron's gesture and spotted twelve-year-old Edmond with the young men who were in a knight's service until they themselves were knighted. Not surprisingly, her brother had a rapturous expression on his face. Nothing would please him more than to be a squire and then a knight.

"Your sister is likewise enjoying herself."

He nodded toward Isabelle, who sat nearby, surreptitiously watching the squires. Her fifteen-year-old sister wore her finest gown of rich emerald-green cendal that shone in the flickering lights, and her most precious jewelry, a pendant of gold and emeralds that had been their mother's. Her long blond hair, a shade darker than Allis's, was woven into two braids, and the ends encased in pointed silver casings. In deference to her age and station as chatelaine, Allis wore her hair coiled close about her head and covered with a white silk scarf held in place by a thin band of gold. A barbette, also of white silk, went beneath her chin. Unlike Isabelle, she did not sport her best gown; nevertheless, the one she wore had been costly enough, for it was made of ruby-red brocade, shot through with gold. About her waist she wore a girdle of gilded leather.

"A pretty woman, your sister," DeFrouchette observed.

"She is more child than woman yet."

"It will be only a little while before your father receives requests for her hand in marriage. She should make a good match."

Fetch a good price, he seemed to be saying. "Perhaps."

"I would think as her elder sister, you would want to be married first," the baron said, his long fingers wrapping around his silver goblet. It was easy to imagine those fingers wrapped around her throat, strangling her. She shivered at the thought and crossed her arms for warmth, as well as to shield herself from his lascivious gaze.

"I always thought it was considered impolite to remind a lady of her age."

"I meant no offense, my lady. I confess I grow weary of waiting. Your father agrees it is time you were married."

If he were in a melancholy mood, as he usually was, her father would agree with almost anything.

But she didn't say that.

She knew the trap was closing on her, and she had no escape. As much as the idea repelled her, as a woman she had few alternatives. Any choice but marriage to the baron could mean she would have to live far away. At least the baron's estate was close to home. Therefore, if marriage to the baron was the only way she would be able to remain nearby and protect her family, that is what she would do.

"I appreciate your patience, Baron," she said as she looked about the hall—her home and her cage—then toward Merva, who still laughed and joked with the knights.

The stranger now sat leaning against the wall with his arms crossed, watching the wench and the knights with genial amusement.

Despite his apparent lack of interest, Merva had obviously set her sights on the aloof stranger. If she had, she would quite probably get what she wanted. Merva did not often take no for an answer, and did not often get refused, either.

What would he be like with a woman? Would he be as fierce with his passion as she suspected he would be upon the battlefield? Would he take a woman swiftly, with virile demand, or would he be slow, meting out pleasure until a woman begged for more?

"I have taken the liberty of claiming the *heriot* from the widow of the charcoal burner," DeFrouchette said, drawing her attention yet again.

At least he was not pressing her more on the subject of a betrothal.

"It is not much of a cow, unfortunately."

"It was my understanding they had but one."

"Yes."

"Did you not hear Brother Jonathan say that their youngest child was sickly and would need fresh milk?"

Obviously unconcerned by the hardship his enforcement of the lord's right would cause, the baron dipped his fingers in the basin near his left elbow. "Then I suppose they had better buy another cow."

"The widow is too poor. We don't need their only beast."

DeFrouchette frowned as he wiped his fingers one

by one on a linen napkin. "It is your father's right to claim the best animal from the widow of his tenant. It is not my fault the fellow had but one."

"I would rather you had consulted with us first."

DeFrouchette's frown became a patronizing smile. "I assure you, he would have agreed, even if you do not. This is why women do not run estates. They are too tenderhearted."

"While some men apparently have no heart," she muttered under her breath.

At that precise moment, the unknown knight stopped watching Merva and looked at the high table. At her.

Their gazes met and held—and in that instant, she suddenly felt that she had no secrets from him, that he knew her innermost feelings. That he could see into her lonely, hopeless heart.

She tore her gaze from him and stared down at the table, just like her father. Surely she was imagining things. She was fatigued, tired after a long day and worried about her family. There could be no way under heaven that a man she had never met could comprehend her feelings.

Nevertheless, she abruptly shoved back her heavy chair and got to her feet. The hound nearby scrounging for scraps from the table yipped with surprise, and the baron looked equally startled.

"If you will excuse me, my lord, I believe I should see to the preparations for Lord Oswald's arrival tomorrow. He sent word he will be here after the noon, and I should make certain all is ready now. Tomorrow morning I may not have time."

"Very well," the baron replied. He was obviously annoyed, but she was already leaving.

She took a moment to pause beside her father and press a kiss upon his cheek. He merely nodded and continued to stare down at his untouched food.

O'r annwyl, Connor thought in Welsh as he watched the lady hurry away. She loathes the man who was sitting beside her to the core of her heart, just as she loves her ailing father dear.

The love for a father he could easily understand, for he had loved his own and mourned his death yet. But the loathing—that was interesting, considering that the fellow was seated between the lady and her father in a place of great honor that would lead one to suspect a betrothal was imminent.

If that were so, the man would do well to reconsider. Not only did the earl's daughter hate him, she didn't look the kind to be easily persuaded to a change of mind. He had seen that expression often enough on his sister's face to know that it bespoke an independence of thought not considered proper in well-bred ladies.

He could just imagine what Cordelia would say if she were forced to sit beside a man who inspired such a look of disgust. Obviously, Lady Allis was more polite, or perhaps less stubborn.

Still, he couldn't blame the fellow for wanting the lady. She was lovely, with dark eyes beneath shapely brows, her skin smooth and pinkly flushed either from excitement or the heat of the hall, and her lips full and inviting. The plain white scarf that covered her hair seemed somewhat austere, as if she were a novice in a convent—but the rich, red gown belied that impression, as did the proud carriage of her head. No humble bride of Christ she.

Yet she was not simply the spoiled, pampered daughter of a wealthy man. He had not been long in the hall before he realized who ruled the servants and the household, although Lady Allis looked no more than twenty.

Nearby, a group of young knights laughed raucously, interrupting his musings.

Connor regarded them indulgently, as he might a gaggle of children. They were obviously noblemen's sons who came to play at battle when they were not drinking themselves into a stupor or trying to seduce the servants. So he had been in the days of his youth—a lifetime ago.

He was not here for mere sport, as they were. He was here to win, for the object of this sort of event was to capture one's opponent and demand a ransom. In this way a landless knight could earn a living, and hopefully more than that.

Once more he glanced at the high table, and studied the wealthy man seated beside the earl. While he had a breadth of shoulder that was impressive, the older man's flesh was too soft to have spent much time engaged in actual fighting, or even tournaments. He would likely have finer equipment, yet in all other matters such as skill and training and especially experience, Connor was sure he was his better. He was also certain he had a better mount, for Demetrius was as battle-hardened as his master.

The buxom, middle-aged serving wench came again to fill the goblets of the young knights. She laughed lustily and it was clear by her bright eyes that she was enjoying their attention. He would not be surprised to learn she would welcome one of those young knights into her bed tonight. Maybe even two.

"You're a quiet one, I must say," she noted, coming

toward him with her hips swaying seductively. "I don't know but that the quiet ones are the best after all. Save their vitality for something other than talking, they do."

That elicited another hoot of laughter.

Connor smiled and crooked his finger, indicating that he wanted to speak with her.

Merva grinned and leaned down so far, he had an excellent view of nearly the whole of her breasts. "Yes, sir knight?"

"Who is that seated beside the earl of Montclair?"

"Oh, that's Baron DeFrouchette," she replied, coy and helpful. "I'm surprised you haven't heard of him."

"I do not recognize him from court."

"Not getting there much these past few years. His estate borders Montclair and he's stayed close by to help Lord Montclair. A very kind neighbor, the baron."

"I could tell he is an honored guest."

"As well he should be. Who knows what might have happened to the estate if he hadn't been such a good friend?"

And no wonder he was so interested in the earl's daughter. He would surely be enlarging his own estate if he married her, as well as obtaining a very beautiful and desirable bride—provided he could overcome the lady's animosity.

"I gather his reward will not be long in coming."

"Reward?"

"Lord Montclair's daughter."

Merva grinned. "And ain't she the lucky one? I tell you, I would have married him years ago if I were in her shoes." She gave him a wink. "I'd have hopped into his bed years ago, too, if he'd ever asked me."

He didn't doubt it. "I am surprised, then, that they

are not already wed. Was there another man she preferred?"

"No, and not likely to be, neither. Any woman with eyes and a brain in her head would see that De-Frouchette's a prize—rich, handsome and a baron to boot. She's just been waiting for her father to get better."

"What ails him?"

"He's grief-stricken over his wife's death."

"That was recent, then?"

Merva grew grave and shook her head. "Six years ago. He loved her dear—we all did—but we thought his grief would pass eventually." She glanced at the high table and sighed. "Not rallying and getting worse, I fear. It will be better for the whole family when Lady Allis marries."

Better for the whole family indeed—if that was what she wanted.

As Merva prepared to refill his goblet, he covered it with his hand and shook his head.

"What, no more wine?"

Her surprised exclamation drew the attention of the young knights, who were giggling like sots well in their cups.

"No. I prefer to keep my wits sharp, and drink will only befuddle them. And tempting though other things may be, I am saving my vitality to use against my opponents on the field."

Merva brayed a raucous guffaw, then made an exaggerated pout. "If you say so. A serious competitor, are you?"

"Very."

The young men stopped laughing.

"He has to be. He's got nothing else," one of them sneered.

Connor's good humor disintegrated as he glared at the young man barely past his youth. His dark brown hair was trimmed around his head in the Norman style and he wore a long velvet tunic of rather bilious green stained with dribbled wine, and he was very drunk.

"You know me?" Connor inquired evenly, in a tone that would have served as a warning to a sober man.

"You are Sir Connor of Llanstephan, are you not?" The young knight turned to his companions. "That's in *Wales*."

His tone implied that Wales was a dung heap.

"I am," Connor calmly admitted. "And you are?"

"I am Sir Auberan de Beaumartre, eldest son of the earl of Beaumartre. *You* were sent home in disgrace from the Holy Land by King Richard himself. You have no land, and no honor."

Smiling a smile that had struck fear into men's hearts for many a time before this, Connor slowly got to his feet.

"Yes, I am Sir Connor of Llanstephan," he declared, "whose forebears were Welsh kings, whose mother was a princess. I am the second son of a Norman baron, a knight of the realm and formerly of the king's retinue, one who went with him to try to wrest Jerusalem from the hands of the infidel. You must forgive me if I cannot recall seeing you among my fellow crusaders."

Auberan flushed.

"Oh, you did not take up the Cross and accompany your sovereign lord? You did not rush to fight against the Saracens? You chose to pay the scutage to the king's coffers and stayed safely here at home to drink another man's wine and chase another man's servants, to be warm and well fed while other, better men were dying in a sacred cause?"

Connor splayed his strong, callused hands upon the table and leaned closer, making his opponent flinch. "Tell me, then, sir knight, how it is that I, who did those things and who suffered for them, that I, who fought the infidel at my king's side and yes, was sent home because I could not countenance his command to massacre prisoners at Acre, how is it that *I* have no honor? I shall see you on the tourney field tomorrow, Sir Lickspittle, and we shall decide which provides the better education in the arts of war, battle against the infidel or charming tournaments at home."

With that, Connor turned and strode from the hall, not caring a whit if people stared at him.

Let them. Let them all stare. This was nothing compared to his departure from the king's presence. That silence had seemed eternal, his shame likewise.

But it was as Connor had said, and he would still say the same should Richard appear before him now. To kill unarmed prisoners, even Saracens, was unchivalrous, the action of a barbarian and not a Christian king.

He hurried out into the cool night air, away from the noise and the smoke from the candles and torches, and especially those preening, bragging young fools as once again the screams of the unarmed, dying Saracens—twenty-seven hundred of them all roped together like animals—filled his ears. The glorious Crusade, fought in the name of God.

He spit the bile from his mouth and leaned against the cool stones of the inner curtain wall. His eyes closed, he waited for the sick feeling to pass.

He was in England, not the Holy Land. He had a job to do. He would think of the tournament, not the past.

He slowly climbed the stone steps to the wall walk. Paying no heed to the sentry, he surveyed the field where the melee would take place tomorrow, a seemingly level field of grass kept short by sheep. Two lines of men, determined by their loyalties, the location of their lands and, in his case, by who he wished to capture, would face each other. Then, at a given signal, they would fight until some were captured and others the victors.

At dawn, while the rest of the participants still slumbered, he would make a foray onto this field. He would find out if the ground was soft or hard. There might be small rises and gullies, or even holes that would cause a charging horse to stumble with disastrous results for beast and rider.

He sniffed the air for signs of rain, but caught no scent of damp on the wind. That was a pity. Rain would likely disgruntle and upset his fine opponents, whereas it didn't trouble him a bit. Nor did it bother his horse.

The moonlight shone on the river flowing through the valley and illuminated the road leading through the village to the bridge over the moat and the well-fortified barbican, the gatehouse in the outer curtain wall. He had ridden beneath a giant portcullis, the grille made of wood cut into points at the bottom. It slid through grooves cut in the stone, ready to crash down to prevent invaders from entering. Further inside the barbican was the solid, bossed oaken door, with a smaller door for foot traffic called a wicket, cut into it. Above these two gates was the murder hole. If enemies became trapped between the outer portcullis and inner door, defenders could pour boiling oil or hurl stones from above to kill them.

Square towers dominated each corner of the massive walls and overlooked the whole of the castle, village and valley. From their tops there was probably not a foot of Lord Montclair's land that could not be watched.

He looked past the village to a small plateau, where a large cathedral was being built. Now it was little more than a pile of stones and masons' materials, but the foundation was sufficiently finished to tell him it would be a most impressive building.

Hopefully there would be true men of God to lead it, men who were more concerned with men's souls than enriching their purses.

His gaze roved over the outer curtain wall and the large, grass-covered outer ward, where he was encamped along with many of the guests and their pages and squires, then the inner curtain wall and enormous courtyard befitting a lord of power and considerable personal wealth which came from being overlord to a prosperous valley. He noted the huge, round donjon, the keep which would have been the first fortification the lord of Montclair built when he took this land from the Saxons the century before.

All in all, rarely had he seen such an impregnable, impressive fortress in England. It made his family's castle overlooking a Welsh valley seem like a hovel. As for their land, it supported sheep and cattle, but little else.

With a sigh, Connor trotted down the steps to the courtyard. He would retire and sleep, to wake early and refreshed tomorrow.

As he headed toward the gate in the inner wall, a door suddenly banged open, the sound making him instinctively shrink back into the nearest shadowed alcove. He was just realizing his back was against a door when Merva came into view, walking in his direction and looking about as if searching for someone.

Perhaps she was looking for him. Unfortunately— or fortunately, if he was in the mood—women had been wanting him since he was fifteen, and Merva did not seem the sort to let a man go quietly on his way if she was attracted to him.

He had no desire to be with this woman tonight, or any night. While he had enjoyed her earthy banter in the hall, he wanted to rest, and she didn't excite him in the least.

Not like her mistress.

The moment Lady Allis had first appeared in the hall, lovely and serene, he felt the years, and all their sorrows, drop away. He was again a youthful knight smitten by the sight of a beautiful maiden, one who seemed angelic in her quiet peace.

But then there had been that moment when he had met her gaze, and he knew that while she might have the form of an angel, a passionate woman inhabited that shapely frame.

Serene or not, passionate or not, she was still as far above him as the angels.

Still, he wasn't pleased that Merva continued to head directly for him. Maybe she could smell a man from fifty paces, like a hound on the scent. Maybe she could see in the dark as well as a cat. Either way, he wasn't about to be caught.

Reaching behind for the latch of the door, Connor stealthily made his escape.

Chapter 2

"**Y**ou would all be better off if I were dead," the earl of Montclair mumbled as Allis tidied up the few articles on the table in his bedchamber.

"No, we would not be better off without you," she said gently as she tucked the fine silk coverlet about his chest and fought back the dismay his oft-voiced litany always invoked. "Please, Father, don't say that."

She had helped him to bed after seeing that the chamber at the top of the south tower was prepared for Lord Oswald of Darrelby, an important man in this part of England. Then she had gone to the kitchen for the warm broth her father sometimes drank before he went to sleep.

Avoiding the baron, she had waited until she was sure her father had retired from the hall and taken the broth to him. Tonight, he had not wanted it, so now she did the few small tasks yet remaining before bidding him good night.

"I must be a great burden to you all."

She patted his hand and smiled to reassure him. Again. "You are not. You are the earl of Montclair, and the people need you. Edmond, Isabelle and I need you."

"I am a useless old man."

She went to his painted wooden chest and lifted the lid. "What would you like to wear for the tournament tomorrow?"

He turned his head to face the wall. "I don't care. Anything."

The familiar ache returned. There was a time her father had been so fastidious about his personal appearance, her mother had teased that he was the most vain person in the family. "We wouldn't want it said the earl of Montclair had become unkempt. Perhaps your fine blue velvet tunic and cloak with ermine trim, if it is cool."

"Whatever you think best. I do not want to trouble you. Perhaps it would be better if I didn't go into the field."

"You must, Father," she insisted, clinging to the hope that this tournament would rally his spirits. "You are the host, and it is your duty to give the signal for the melee to begin."

He closed his eyes. "Ah, yes, my duty."

"So you will go into the field? Two foot soldiers will be with you. You won't have to stand. We shall have a chair brought out for you, and if it looks like rain, a canopy will be put over it." She had tried to think of every contingency, so that he would not be uncomfortable.

"If it is not too much trouble."

"It won't be, I assure you. You will give the signal?"

"I will do it."

She sighed with relief as she closed the lid to the chest. "Wonderful! And Lord Oswald will be arriving tomorrow, after the noon. You will be happy to see him, I'm sure. You were always great friends."

In better spirits herself, she finished tidying, and then realized he had finally fallen asleep. Praying he would have a peaceful night, she softly kissed his forehead and quietly left his chamber.

Once again avoiding the hall, and the baron, she made her way along a side passage to a door leading into the rose garden her mother had set out before her death. A redbrick walk in a herringbone pattern weaved its way through the beds, and the stalks of climbing roses trailed over a trellis above and the walls around. The scent of the roses, dew-damp ground and fertile earth refreshed her, and was blessedly welcome after the close confines of her father's chamber, or the smoke of the great hall. A half moon provided enough illumination for her to avoid treading in the beds, or stumbling into the wooden benches set along the walk.

As she drew near the door in the wall leading into the courtyard, she took off her circlet, scarf and barbette, and set them on a nearby bench. She tugged the pin from her hair and let it tumble about her shoulders. Rubbing her scalp and rotating her neck, she sought to lessen the tension.

"My lady?"

She jumped and whirled around as the unexpected sound of a deep male voice invaded her peaceful solitude. "Who is it?"

A man stood in the shadows near the garden gate,

as if he were a part of them. Her anxious gaze darted to the surrounding battlements, seeking the sentry who should be patrolling there. "I warn you, I have but to scream—"

"There is no need to cry out, my lady. Not wishing to cause you any harm, me."

His gentle, deep voice seemed a part of the night, and the peace she had found for a few brief moments. He did not sound like a Norman. There was an accent to his words that she thought sounded Welsh. "Then come into the moonlight and show yourself."

The handsome stranger from the hall sauntered out of the shadows. The man who knew her heart.

No, that was impossible. He could know nothing about her except her name and station. "What do you want?"

"To thank you for a fine meal and your generous hospitality." He strolled closer, and his movements had that special grace men skilled at arms sometimes possessed, a lithe suppleness of the limbs despite their obvious strength.

Up close in the moonlight, he was darkly handsome, with his hair black as a crow's wing waving about his angular face, his eyes pools of mysterious shadow, and his exquisitely shaped lips compelling even in stillness. "You might have done that in the hall, or waited until tomorrow."

"The hall was too crowded, and I think you have many cares when you are there." He smiled that secretive little smile of his and warmth spread along her limbs, a warmth unfamiliar, strange—and yet strangely welcome, too. "Besides, tomorrow, I may be the worse for battle."

An alarm sounded in her mind, and in her heart. She must not be alone with him—or any man except her father. "So now you have thanked me and now you may go."

"I fear I must prevail upon you a little longer, for I confess I am trying to avoid someone."

"Who?"

"A woman."

It was ridiculous to feel envious. "What woman? As chatelaine of Montclair, I should know if a woman is annoying a guest."

"Her name is Merva."

Of course. Who else could it be? She should have thought of Merva at once. She was clearly more tired than she supposed.

"I would not call her attention annoying—simply something I would rather avoid and she seems the persistent sort," he said with a wry self-mockery in his tone that was very different from the way every other man addressed her. He spoke to her like a companion, not a person seeking to impress or command. "A wise man learns when to stand and when to leave the field, and this time, I thought it better to flee."

Alone in the moonlight in her mother's garden with this smiling stranger, all her duties and responsibilities and worries suddenly seemed far away, and a light hearted euphoria stole over her. "Merva is not often disappointed. I'm sure she would be heartbroken to discover you are hiding from her."

His low laugh sent delicious trills of delight along her spine. "Her disappointment would be short-lived, I think."

"Probably. We have many guests."

"Not fussy, is she?"

She frowned. Perhaps she should leave the merry banter to Merva, after all. "I am sorry to wound your feelings."

"Oh, you haven't. It's a relief."

His smile and tone told her he was not offended, and she smiled. "You usually have to hide from women? You are that constantly pursued?"

He laughed again, a low, delightful chuckle this time that seemed to well up from his broad chest, pleasant and joyful—yet utterly virile. "Not constantly. As I told your maidservant, I am saving myself."

"For any particular woman?"

"No, for the tournament. Mustn't be too fatigued."

The moonlight, the garden, their solitude, his laughter . . . all combined to embolden her. Why not be like Merva, just this once? "I wondered if you believed you are like Samson and that if you cut your hair, you would lose your strength."

He grinned, slowly and speculatively and oh, so very attractively. "If I thought it would help, I'd grow it to my ankles. But I assure you, my lady," he continued, lowering his voice to one of confidential intimacy, "my strength is not in my hair."

Her throat suddenly dry, her heart suddenly thudding in her chest, she swallowed hard—and reminded herself that she was the daughter of the earl of Montclair merely enjoying a moment of banter with a knight.

In a moonlit garden, where they were all alone.

She should leave, her conscience commanded.

But not before he answered the question that had troubled her ever since she had noticed him in her father's hall, her heart decreed. "Then why do you wear your hair so long?"

"Practicality."

That was an unexpected answer. "How is that practical?"

"Extra padding on my neck for the base of my helmet," he explained. "It rubs there, you see," he said, pressing his hand to the back of his neck, "and if I use straw, it tickles."

"You are ticklish?"

"Only in certain places." He crossed the space between them. "What about you?"

That strange, seductive warmth coursed through her body. She could almost feel his muscular arms around her, his fingers brushing over her heated skin, perhaps to tickle . . . perhaps for another, more exciting purpose. Her lips parted of their own accord, as if anticipating his passionate kiss. . . .

Gracious God, what in the name of the saints was she thinking? Her imagination was running wild and she must constrain it, for she was a lady, the daughter of an earl, not a simple maidservant to be so thrilled and excited by a knight of no particular importance. "I am not ticklish," she snapped.

"Not at all?" Still smiling, he eyed her speculatively, in a way that made her wonder if her gown had somehow become transparent in the moonlight—a thought that should not make her feel as it did. She should be angry, not . . . not . . . curious.

There was only one thing to be done about this bizarre situation, and his bold, impertinent smiles. "Good evening, Sir . . . ?"

She had not even asked his name.

"I am Sir Connor of Llanstephan."

She turned to go. "Good luck tomorrow, Sir Connor."

"You have not heard of me?"

His question made her hesitate and all her former curiosity revived. "Should I have?"

"If you have not by now, you will tomorrow when I win."

She had heard braggarts many times, but his tone was different. He was not boasting so much as stating a fact. "What will I hear?"

His eyes seemed even more engulfed in shadow. "Something that will not be in my favor."

Strange that he would admit that. "Will it be true?"

He answered like a witness giving evidence in the king's court. "Partly, I expect, but not the whole truth."

"What is the whole truth?"

His deep voice softened again. "That would take some time to explain." He came nearer.

She could not seem to think or even breathe, everything else subverted by the new and wondrous excitement and curiosity this man created within her. He roused a part of her to life that she had not even known existed.

Still he came closer, and as before, she could practically feel him pulling her into his embrace. Part of her yearned for him to do just that, but her mind urged caution.

What did she really know of him, after all, but that he was a guest in her father's hall, a knight here to take part in the tournament? And he was poor, while she was not.

Perhaps, despite his gentle words, he was as motivated by lust and greed as the baron. While Sir Connor of Llanstephan was certainly outwardly more attractive to her than Rennick DeFrouchette, maybe he was simply better at hiding his true nature.

She was no naive girl to be swayed into sympathy

for a handsome man who might ultimately have all too common designs. Indeed, she had allowed him too much liberty already. "I regret your story will have to wait for another day, Sir Connor."

She began to leave, but he put his hand on her arm to stop her. "There is no need to flee."

"I am not running away," Allis retorted as she lifted his long, lean fingers from her forearm. "I have many things to do."

"I am sure you do, for I could see that you are the chatelaine here. It must be a heavy burden for one so young."

His wistful tone threatened to soften her resolve, but the knowledge that he could be like Rennick strengthened her. "I thank you for your concern, but we all have burdens to bear."

"Some more than others."

He spoke sincerely, as if he knew all too well about the heavy burden of duty and responsibility and had not the freedom she assumed he possessed. That in his own way, he was as imprisoned as she. "God tests us all."

"In many ways," he agreed with no hint of self-pity, but rather merely acknowledging that it must be so.

"Have you been tested?"

He studied the nearest trellis. "I believe so, yes."

His new reticence might be just another ruse to encourage her sympathy. If so, it was very effective. "Did you succeed or fail?"

"My time of trial continues."

Despite her suspicions, she could not quell the compassion his words aroused. "I am sorry to hear that."

"Are you, or is this but a polite response a chatelaine makes to a guest?" He waited with tense expectancy, as if her next remark would seal his fate.

How could that be? She did not know him, had never met him before, yet she could not rid herself of this powerful notion. Confused, uncertain as to his purpose, she took what had to be the wiser course and turned toward the door into the hall. "Yes, I am sorry. Now I give you good night, sir."

"Good night, my lady."

Before she could move away, he took her hand in his callused one, but he did not kiss it. He brushed his lips over the rise of her knuckles, then slowly turned it over. He did not kiss her palm, either, which would have been a shocking enough intimacy.

He pressed his warm, soft mouth to her wrist.

Heat surged through her arm, to her chest, her face and that most intimate of places between her thighs. Never had she imagined a man's lips could make her feel this way—overwhelmed and overheated and yet disappointed.

What might she feel if he pressed those lips against hers?

What might she feel should he do more?

That thought was enough to make her stumble backward, away from this stranger with those eyes and those lips, that smile and that virile body, that deep, compelling voice . . . the very personification of all risk and all danger, the living temptation to cast aside duty and honor for one hour of passion in his arms.

She feared Sir Connor then, more than even Baron DeFrouchette. And so she turned and fled.

Chapter 3

Rennick DeFrouchette swatted the head of his squire as Percival tried to pull off his master's scarlet leather boot. "Well, who is he?"

"His name's Connor," the thin, auburn-haired youth panted as he finally got the baron's boot off. Red-faced from the effort, he wiped beads of perspiration from his upper lip.

Rennick frowned, and the glimmering light of the candle made him look demonic, despite the luxurious surroundings. This private chamber was second only to the earl's in terms of size and furnishings, as befitted an honored and important guest. Rennick had made certain it was so, ordering the servants to provide him with the earl's finest linens and furnishings while he visited, which was often. After all, the grieving earl needed his advice on so many things.

"Connor? What kind of barbaric name is that?" he asked.

"Welsh, my lord," Percival replied as he straddled the baron's leg and made ready to remove the other boot. "His family holds land in the march. He's Sir Connor of Llanstephan, second son of a baron. His father was Norman, his mother Welsh."

"Second son, eh?" The baron put his stockinged foot against the thin young man's backside and pushed.

"Aye, my lord," Percival cried as he fell forward, boot in hand, his red hair flying. He nearly crashed into the carved bedpost. "He was in the Holy Land with the king."

A muscle in Rennick's jaw twitched as Percival straightened. "Ah. One of the chosen, was he?"

"Yes, my lord, and very well regarded by King Richard, too, until they quarreled. Richard cast him out of his retinue and sent him back to England."

The baron reached for the silver goblet containing some of the earl of Montclair's excellent wine. "Cast out, was he? Like Lucifer from heaven." He raised the goblet to his lips. "What was the nature of the quarrel?"

"Seems he told King Richard he had acted unchivalrously."

Rennick swallowed his wine so quickly, he nearly choked. "I can imagine how Richard took that. The fool's lucky our illustrious and martial sovereign didn't cut off his head." He took another sip of wine. "So he was sent home. Is that all?"

"No, my lord," Percival replied as he stood waiting for further commands. "His family is seriously behind in the payment of their taxes."

"Ah." A knowing grin spread across Rennick's face. "So he is poor. No wonder he kept looking at me. He likely thinks to capture me in the tournament tomorrow."

"I would if—" Percival fell silent.

"You would if you were he? Of course you would, for I will be the richest man on the field." Rennick eyed his squire again. "And you would emulate me in other matters, too, eh, Percival? How goes the wooing of the fair young Isabelle?"

Percival flushed and didn't meet his gaze.

"She is pretty and comes from a good family, so why should you not try to win her affections?"

The relief on the youth's face was pathetic.

"Does she seem to reciprocate?"

"No, my lord," Percival admitted.

"Pity," he lied. The last thing he wanted was for this oaf—albeit a highborn one—related to him in marriage. "I wish you success. Perhaps a victory in the squires' melee will improve matters."

Just as he hoped a victory in tomorrow's tournament would make Allis appreciate him more. "How is Sir Connor on the field?"

"Very good."

"He does lose?"

"Yes, my lord, he does . . . occasionally."

"I see." Rennick twisted the stem of the goblet in his long fingers while Percival shifted nervously.

"My lord?"

Rennick glanced at him.

"My lord, you told me to watch Lady Allis and I did. After she left the hall, she went to the kitchen, and to her father's chamber."

"I thought as much. And then she retired."

"No, my lord. Then she went into the rose garden, and she was not alone."

Rennick sat up abruptly. "Who else was there?"

"Sir Connor, my lord. I saw him leave."

Rennick set his goblet down on the arm of the chair so hard, he bent the base of it. "Did he see you?"

"No, my lord."

He stared at the stone floor, scowling. He had been more than patient waiting for Allis to see that he and he alone was a worthy match for her.

Unfortunately, he had lived long enough to know that for most women, it wouldn't matter that Connor of Llanstephan had no more money than a pauper at the castle gates, or that he had been cast out of the king's retinue. He was good-looking, young and virile, and had probably seduced scores of women who had less to offer than Allis. He was likely well aware of the large dowry that awaited the man who married Allis of Montclair and would use every means and skill he possessed to woo and win her.

It was not enough for this Welsh dog to be among the king's chosen. Now this dishonored whelp wanted Allis, too?

If that were so, Connor of Llanstephan was as good as dead. He had not waited and planned and schemed and put up with Lord Montclair all these years for some impoverished knight to swoop in and steal what he deserved. *He* was going to wed and bed Allis, and he was not about to let Allis—and her dowry and the power of being the earl's son-in-law—slip away from him.

"He was there but a little while, my lord," Percival stammered, his face pale. "I am sure the lady did nothing unseemly. She is a very model of propriety, my lord."

"You are not sorry you told me this, are you, Percival?" Rennick inquired, his emotions once more restrained.

"No-no, my lord."

"Good. You were following orders, as a squire should if he is to be knighted. And I quite agree. Lady Allis is above reproach."

The young man's slender shoulders slumped with relief. "Yes, my lord."

"The Welshman is a different matter. Sometimes, Percival, it falls to us to remind these rebellious upstarts of their place."

The next morning, Allis stood in the storeroom checking the amount of clean linen available when Isabelle and Edmond burst in, quarreling yet again. She set the napkins she had been counting on the nearest shelf and prayed for patience.

"It isn't fair!" Isabelle cried. Her hands balled into fists as if she was considering hitting Edmond, which had been known to happen. "I don't understand why I can't watch the melee from the battlements, too."

Allis crossed her arms. "Because a lady does not watch a tournament. A knight doesn't stick out his tongue, either," she chided Edmond, having caught him in the act.

"A lady doesn't get to have any fun," Isabelle mumbled. She picked at the hem of her long cuffed sleeve and pouted.

This was also a frequent complaint. "If you mean watching grown men ride at one another like a pack of dogs and bash each other, no, we don't."

"You're just jealous!" Edmond declared, his feet wide apart, and his arms crossed in unconscious imitation of his elder sister.

"I still think we should be allowed to watch. I'm going to ask Father—"

"No, you won't pester Father about this," she interrupted sternly. "No ladies of rank watch tournaments, and you are a lady of rank. As such, you enjoy certain privileges, and as such, you have a duty to behave as you should."

As Isabelle flushed, Allis was very glad Isabelle didn't know about her sister's meeting with the knight in the garden last night.

She should have commanded him to leave the garden at once, and not let herself be drawn in by his good looks, his gentle humor, or his wonderful rich voice. Whatever he said, it was best forgotten, and she should not spend another restless night thinking of him, or imagining being in his passionate embrace, his strong arms around her and his lips upon hers, kissing her as she could easily envision a man like that could kiss.

She had acted very inappropriately, and was justly ashamed of herself, which explained why she felt so warm even now. After all, she was not Merva, but the daughter of the earl of Montclair, no matter how much she wished it could be otherwise. "Besides, I could use some help in the tent for the wounded."

"You will let me do that?" Isabelle asked, her eyes widening with eager excitement.

"Yes, I think you are old enough not to swoon at the sight of bloody noses and broken limbs."

Isabelle turned to her brother and stuck out her tongue.

"Isabelle, I will need a helper, not a girl who needs looking after herself."

"I'll do whatever you ask of me," she promised.

"See that you do—and don't spend all your time talking with the handsome young fellows who get hurt, tempting though that may be." As she well knew.

Isabelle blushed. "I won't."

"So off you go, Edmond, to the wall walk. Don't shout or do anything that might distract our guests. You are there to watch and learn, not cheer."

"Yes, Allis," her towheaded brother called out as he ran off.

"When do we go to the tent for the wounded?"

"They are only gathering now. It will be a little while before the melee begins."

Isabelle sighed and leaned against the large chest holding various linens. "I think being a lady is generally very boring."

Allis picked up the dozen napkins she had put on the shelf and closed the lid. "But we can do things others cannot. For instance, if I feel a need to ensure that Lord Oswald's chamber is in good order—again—and should I decide to linger there, no one will tell me I cannot. And if I happen to glance out the loophole toward the field where the melee is about to begin—"

"You can see the tournament!" Isabelle finished with sudden, enthusiastic understanding.

"Or as much of it as I care to," Allis agreed, smiling. "Truly, I don't have any great desire to see men hurting each other, but the first charge is generally very exciting. As soon as the first charge is over, though, we must go to the tent for the wounded."

"Aren't there servants enough for that?"

"It is our duty to see that our guests are well cared for." Allis assumed a guileless expression. "Of course, if you don't think those young men will be filled with admiration for a girl gently tending to their aches and cuts—provided she does not encourage any impropriety . . ." She let her words trail off suggestively.

"Allis," Isabelle said with a giggle, "if you were not my sister, I would say you were a wicked creature very well versed in how to attract a husband."

Allis instantly sobered. "I don't want a husband. It is enough for me to look after our father and Edmond." *And you*, she finished inwardly.

With an apologetic look, Isabelle patted her sister's arm. "I'm sorry. I didn't mean to upset you. Besides, you're practically betrothed as it is."

If only Isabelle knew how that remark dismayed her! But she would not burden Isabelle yet with all that duty and responsibility might demand of a woman nobly born. "Come along, Isabelle. And whatever you do, do *not* tell anyone we watched."

Fortunately, they didn't meet anybody except Merva as they hurried to the south tower, and she was too busy sweeping out the hearth to pay any heed to them. She looked exhausted, too. No doubt she had had a busy night.

With whom did not matter. Indeed, if she had been with Sir Connor, that should be nothing to her except that it would prove he had come into the garden intending to seduce her, either for sport or gain.

She remembered how he had stepped out of the shadows, as if her lonely heart had conjured him up. How long had it been since she had felt as carefree as she had for those few brief moments when she had asked about his hair? Six years, before her mother's death had forever changed her world.

Perhaps it was no wonder, then, that she had been so drawn to him. His banter had taken her back to a happy time, and made her feel a girl again.

No, not a girl. Some of the emotions he inspired had nothing of girlish innocence about them.

Why, even now, even here in the stairwell of the castle, tendrils of heat curled and danced through her body as if those passionate thoughts roused by him could never be completely controlled, or forgotten.

He was a dangerous man indeed, and one she suspected she would never forget, because he had let a little light of joy into the deep places of her heart, where she stored her secret pain.

They entered the round room at the top of the south tower. Usually it was used for storage, but during a tournament or feast days when Montclair Castle was full of guests, it was pressed into service as accommodation. Now, a large rope bed stood across from the door, the featherbed covered with fresh clean linen and a satin cover. Beside it was a bronze candlestand holding six beeswax candles. Near the door was a washstand with a basin and jug of fresh water, and several small pieces of linen. In deference to Lord Oswald's status, they had hung tapestries on the wall to both brighten and keep the room warm against the chill of the early mornings. Two small, narrow windows, intended for archers rather than to let in light, provided some illumination in the daytime, yet it was like being in the dim, silent chapel when no one else was there.

"This is perfect!" Isabelle whispered as she joined

Allis at the loophole that overlooked the tournament field. "We can see everything from here."

Two groups of mounted men faced each other across the field. At the midpoint, to the side and out of their way sat their father, two soldiers flanking him.

In the past, he would have been walking up and down the lines of waiting participants, making jokes and recalling past victories. And disasters, too. When she was Isabelle's age, she had despaired every time he told the story about the fish his friend had hidden in the padding of his helmet and how it had smelled for weeks afterward; now, she would give almost anything to hear him tell it again.

"Don't they all look splendid?" Isabelle said with another blissful sigh.

With the sun glinting on their armor, and their colorful surcoats, they did look wonderful—the might and power of Norman England arrayed before them.

Her gaze was drawn to one man wearing a white surcoat embroidered with a red dragon rampant and, above his heart, a cross that marked him as one of those who had traveled to the Holy Land with King Richard. He was seated on a magnificent black war horse that stood so still, it might have been a statue.

So might its master, for he was equally motionless. He did not fidget, or talk to anyone near him. Alone and aloof, he sat upon his horse as if he were there to pass judgment upon them here, too, and she was quite sure that beneath his helmet—padded with his long, dark hair—his penetrating glance had already marked out his prey.

What could she hear against Sir Connor of Llanstephan? Why did he mention that at all, except to create sympathy?

Perhaps it was sympathy he deserved, and not merely a seducer's tactic.

"Did you hurt yourself? You're rubbing your wrist."

"No." She shoved her hand into her dangling sleeve. "I get a bit nervous waiting for them to charge."

Fortunately, Isabelle was no longer watching her, but gazing steadily out the window. "There's the baron and Percival. Percival is going to participate in the squires' melee tomorrow. He even asked . . ."

Isabelle's sudden hesitation caused Allis to give her sister a wary, sidelong glance. "What did he ask?"

Isabelle tossed her blond head. "He asked to wear one of my scarves, but I refused."

Isabelle was growing up and she was pretty, so it was inevitable that some youth was likely to make such a request, yet her sister's vain response troubled her. "Had someone else already asked you?"

"No."

"Then why?"

"Because he's a ninny!" Isabelle's gaze faltered and the defiant manner deserted her. "Really, Allis, it would have been wrong of me to encourage him, don't you think? He might believe I cared for him, and I don't. Not in that way."

Allis didn't reply. What could she say, that Isabelle should play the hypocrite like her sister? "I believe they're about to begin."

"The baron's wearing your scarf, I suppose?"

"Yes," she muttered, hating herself for agreeing to his request made the forenoon before.

And yet, if Rennick DeFrouchette had his way, soon she would be enslaved as his wife.

Chapter 4

Mounted on his destrier, Connor patiently waited for the charge to begin. Demetrius, likewise used to battle, also waited patiently, with only the flicking of his ears to betray any anxiety or excitement.

Despite his seeming unconcern, Connor was aware of many things, not the least of which was the weight of his weapons and armor. His helm alone weighed ten pounds, his chain mail hauberk considerably more. His dull tournament broadsword dragged at the belt about his waist and slapped his thigh. His long, bossed shield covered his left arm and side, and he held the reins in that hand, leaving his right free to control the heavy, unwieldy lance. Made with a blunted tip, it pointed upward, and he rested the arm holding it against his body.

He mentally ran through everything to remember

about a charge with a lance. The two most important
were grip hard with his knees and maintain his balance. Once Demetrius was galloping toward the op-
posing line, staying seated and maintaining his
equilibrium must be his focus. If he lost his balance by
leaning too far forward or back, he could fall from his
horse without even touching an opponent.

He scanned the men preparing on the opposite side
of the field and spotted the Baron DeFrouchette wearing a scarlet surcoat embroidered with a gold griffin,
making him an easy target.

Then he turned his head toward Lord Montclair, for
his helmet blocked his peripheral vision, and he
wanted to urge Demetrius forward the moment the
lord's arm lowered. He didn't want to be at the back of
the pack with the anxious and excited younger knights
in front of him. They would charge at anyone they saw,
and he had no desire to be caught in such confusion.

The old man sat in a large, ornately carved oaken
chair at the side of the field. The morning promised to
be a fine one, and warm for spring, yet the earl was
dressed in a heavy cloak with ermine trim, long, blue
tunic, thick boots and gloves. He was flanked by two
soldiers standing attentively at his side.

But the man's heart did not seem to be in it. Like last
night, he looked downward, as if studying the grass at
his feet.

Had his father been like that, not caring about anything, when his mother had died? He had lived but
days longer, and Caradoc had said grief had killed
him—grief and disappointment over a disgraced son.

He would not think about that, not before a tournament. He would think of something pleasant . . . like
the Lady Allis.

He had thought her lovely in the hall, where she presided with grace and calm smiles, although she was not as serene as one might suppose, not when one caught that flash of spirit in her eyes. In the garden, the sight of her glorious unbound hair had been enough to transfix him. Then, when she sighed, he realized how lonely and sad she seemed. Strange thoughts for him to have about the beautiful daughter of a rich and powerful man, but so it was.

He decided the least he could do was to thank her. Then he had been tempted to make her smile—and been rewarded. She had been unexpectedly warm, amusing, fascinating. She had awakened feelings in him long dulled by hardship and the pain of loss, something youthful and joyous, like the delight he had felt years ago with his first lover, a giddy, silly girl, he realized with the wisdom of age, but pretty and appealing and very, very generous with her favors.

Now, seated on the steadfast Demetrius as he readied himself for battle one more time, it came to him that what he had felt in his youth—the heady excitement, the burning desire, the bliss when a girl let him caress her—paled to insignificance when he remembered how his whole body flushed with yearning at the sight of Lady Allis with her hair unbound. Simply kissing her wrist had inflamed him far more than even making love with other women had.

Despite the feelings Lady Allis inspired, he never should have touched her. He was who he was, and she was the daughter of the earl of Montclair.

For a long time after he had left her, he expected to hear the booted feet of soldiers marching toward his tent, sent by the earl of Montclair to tell him he was no longer welcome and that he must depart at first light.

Surprisingly, they had not come, which told him the lady had kept their meeting a secret. While that thought pleased him, he didn't dare risk speaking to her alone again. Last night, she might have been attracted to him, or in a mood to play at love, but once she learned about him, that would change.

To think he himself had almost told her what he had done, and why, intending that she hear his side of things. But for what purpose? Even if she sympathized, as she seemed to do last night, there could never be anything serious between a landless knight and the heiress of a great household, not even if her quick pulse throbbing, her glowing eyes, the rapid rise and fall of her breasts and her parted lips told him she felt something for him, too. And no matter if she intrigued him as no woman ever had, or possessed the most beautiful, soft hands he had ever seen or touched.

Long, slender, supple fingers. Soft palms. A grace in the wrists that made him want to see her dance almost as much as he wanted to feel those hands on his body.

If she had not gasped and pulled away when his lips brushed her wrist, he would have slid his lips lower and kissed her palm. Then her fingertips one by one. He would have gently tugged her into his arms and taken her mouth with sure purpose until she relaxed against him, weak with yearning. As their bodies touched and heat bloomed between them, he would have tenderly kissed and caressed her, keeping a rein on his passion until hers blossomed beneath his touch.

Aroused by his thoughts, he shifted in the saddle, and Demetrius started to prance. He quickly gripped his horse tighter with his knees and commanded himself to stop thinking about Lady Allis and anything else except what he had to do this morning: capture Baron DeFrouchette and get a large ransom.

The earl of Montclair slowly raised his trembling arm. His arm pressed against his side for stability, Connor lowered his lance. He would loosen his grip during the charge and hold his weapon out slightly from his body. That way, his arm would be better able to absorb the impact. If he were too tense or held the lance too close to his body, he could be pushed off his horse upon contact with an opponent's shield.

Lord Montclair's arm fell, and in that moment, Connor dug his heels into Demetrius. His horse leaped forward and broke into a gallop, ahead of the rest of the men on his side.

With a sound like distant thunder, the huge beasts of all the knights in the melee galloped forward across the space between them.

There was the baron, easy to see in his scarlet surcoat, his lance wavering. Likely his arm was too weak to effectively control his weapon. Hunched down, his gaze straight ahead, Connor moved his shield toward the middle of his body and aimed his lance directly at the baron's shield.

His lance struck the shield—and split, the separate pieces shattering like so much tinder.

He couldn't believe it. His lance was oak, the hardest wood in England. It shouldn't have—

The baron's weapon plowed into his shield, his arm and shoulder taking the full force of the collision. He tumbled off Demetrius and fell hard onto the ground. Stunned, the wind knocked from him, it felt as if his left arm had been torn off at the shoulder.

No, still there . . . but the pain . . .   .

Ignoring the agony and the noise of the horses, men

grunting, lances striking shields, as well as the clang of
sword on sword, he struggled to get to his feet lest he
be trampled by the huge hooves of the baron's horse
and those of other combatants. At the sound of a
sword being drawn from its scabbard, he crouched
and looked up to see the Baron DeFrouchette looming
above him. His left arm numb and useless, his shield
fell to the ground—but by then he held his sword in
his right.

He heard a different sound and whirled around just
as another knight in a royal blue surcoat embroidered
with a silver eagle brought his blunted sword down on
his injured shoulder. The blow and the pain brought
him to his knees.

"Get off the field, you Welsh pauper, and leave it to
more worthy men," Baron DeFrouchette taunted.

His pride fierce, his resolve fiercer, Connor staggered to his feet. "I can still take you," he growled, his
teeth clenched as he blinked back the hot tears of pain
that filled his eyes.

"You heard him, Welshman," the other knight said
in the noble drawl of Sir Auberan de Beaumartre. "Get
off the field."

"Damn you! I'll take you both!"

"Oh, I think not," the baron sneered. "Here come
the nursemaids to tend to the unfortunate wounded.
Shall I call them over to you, Welshman? They can
carry you from the field."

Both men laughed as they turned their horses back
toward the melee, which had moved off toward higher
ground.

Gritting his teeth, he started after them, determined
to fight, the blood of battle throbbing in his ears, the desire to beat them pounding through his body. Sweat

poured down his face and into his eyes, stinging and momentarily blinding him. He went to yank off his helmet with his left hand and again fell to his knees as pain like the curse of hell shot through his left shoulder.

He remembered what he had said to Lady Allis last night, about knowing when to quit the field, and uttered the most profane and colorful Welsh curse he knew, because today, that time was now.

Struggling to his feet, he spied a rotund little man in a black ecclesiastical robe trotting toward him. With him were two men, bareheaded but clad in the padded *gambeson* of foot soldiers, carrying a litter.

He waved them away. He was not going to add to his humiliation by being carried from the field. He would make it to the tent for the wounded on his own, or swoon trying.

Allis paced impatiently inside the tent set up at the south of the large field. There the sunlight would shine all day, warming the interior and providing illumination. The wounded would be brought here first to be assessed by Brother Jonathan and tended to as necessary. Five cots were ready for those who were unable to walk. A trestle table for Brother Jonathan's medicines, linens and some basins for washing had been set up, and a large barrel full of fresh water was nearby. The floor beneath them was grass, kept short by the sheep that usually pastured there.

After seeing Sir Connor's lance shatter against the baron's shield and his tumble from his horse, she had rushed from the tower room afraid for his life, Isabelle right behind. Her anxiety increasing with every passing moment, she had immediately sent Bob and Harry, two of their strongest, fastest soldiers who had been assigned to help carry the injured, with a litter to find the wounded knight in the white surcoat embroidered with a red dragon rampant and return with him and Brother Jonathan, who had gone to the field to watch the start of the melee.

"Perhaps he wasn't hurt," Isabelle suggested hopefully. "Or not much. They do wear chain mail, after all. Bob and Harry haven't brought him yet, have they? If he were seriously hurt, they would have come back with him on the run."

She tried to take heart at her sister's words, but the litter bearers might not hurry if their burden was a dead body.

Out of the corner of her eye, she saw the flap at the entrance to the tent move. She whirled around, but it wasn't Bob and Harry or even Brother Jonathan.

Wearing a white surcoat with a red dragon rampant, Sir Connor of Llanstephan stood holding his left arm against his body with his right, his helmet in the crook of his left elbow. Although his long hair was damp from perspiration and his face pale, relief poured through her. "You're not dead!"

"Not yet," he replied with the merest hint of a smile as he entered. He wore his chain mail as if it weighed almost nothing and moved as if he had been born in it. Only a strong man who had worn it daily for a long time carried it so easily. "But needing some help, I am."

Of course he was, and she had just sounded like a fool. "Your arm has been hurt?"

"Yes."

Trying to recover her dignity, she walked briskly toward him. "I'm glad it is only an injury. My father and I would be very distraught had one of our guests been killed."

"Your father, too, is it?" His eyes flicked up and down her body, while her heart . . . fluttered. That was the only word to describe the sensation.

She couldn't allow her heart to flutter. She couldn't be near a man who could smile when he was in pain, who could make her body warm as if in an oven when he took her hand, who had insolently kissed her wrist and robbed her of sleep. She knew her future, and it didn't involve such sensations. Her future was a marriage she didn't want to a man she didn't love because she had no other choice.

"I would have been upset, too," Isabelle added eagerly, staring at Sir Connor with unabashed interest. "Is your arm broken?"

He smiled at Isabelle, too. "It's not my arm. It's my shoulder. Would you be so kind as to ask someone to find my horse? I don't know where he went after I fell."

Isabelle nodded and hurried out of the tent, obviously keen to be of assistance.

Allis tried to decide what to do. By rights, and as her previous behavior and the sensations swirling within her now cautioned, she should not be alone with this man. Her wrist still felt as if it had been branded with his kiss, marked forever by the passionate heat of his lips. Yet he was wounded and she had come to help attend to the wounded.

She went to the tent flap and looked out. "I don't see Brother Jonathan. He must have seen you and realized you were injured. He's a physician."

"Is he a short fellow running about with two soldiers carrying a litter?"

"Yes."

"I saw him and waved him off. Perhaps he tends to

others more seriously hurt. I can wait." His grin looked more like a grimace of pain and there was discomfort in his brown eyes.

She was here to nurse the injured, not consider her wayward emotions. "May I at least take your helmet?"

"Since I don't see anybody else."

Despite her resolve, she approached him as she might a skittish horse. If he noticed her awkwardness, his expression did not betray it, although it could be that he was too enveloped by pain to pay much heed to her at all.

As she lifted the helmet from his elbow, she pulled upward on his left arm. A foreign word exploded from his lips so loud and unexpected, she nearly dropped the helmet.

With his right hand, he grabbed her arm to steady her. "Forgive me, my lady."

She shied away, taken aback by both his strength and the surge of blatant excitement within her. "You are in a great deal of pain, aren't you?"

"Not the worst I've felt."

She put his helmet onto the cot behind him. "You should have told me how much your shoulder hurt. I would have been more gentle. Can you move your arm away from your body at all?"

"I don't think so."

"Can you touch your right shoulder with your left hand?"

He tried, but when she saw how pale he went, she stopped him and said, "I had better examine it more closely. We must remove your garments."

His eyes narrowed, but in the dark depths of his brown eyes, another emotion flared. "We?"

The sparks kindled something in her, too, that must and would be controlled. "I don't think you'll be able to do it by yourself."

Accepting what she said, the fire in his eyes diminished. He shrugged, and winced. "Very well, my lady."

Although she had little choice, her fingers trembled as she unbuckled his sword belt. She could tell that beneath the chain mail and padding, his belly was flat, the muscles taut from years of training and warfare. His hips were narrow, and she could guess the breadth and strength of his thighs.

Despite his pain, he stood perfectly still, which was a mercy. She could pretend he was a statue, not a man of flesh and blood, bone and sinew.

"Since I am at your tender mercy, my lady, I think it would be wise to apologize for any offense I may have caused last night. I was impetuous, I know. I have often been chastised for that."

Was it some sort of trick he had mastered, to sound both amused and sincere? She didn't dare look at his face. Just the notion of raising her eyes past his virile chest to his strong chin, to encounter his tempting mouth and intense eyes, was enough to keep her gaze firmly focused on his buckle. "Now you have apologized, so you may be quiet and still."

Her task was accomplished at last and, stifling the urge to fan herself, she laid the belt and sword on the bed beside his helmet.

"If I crouch, you can lift my surcoat over my head," he suggested. He did just that, so that his face was level with her breasts, his lips a mere finger's length away.

Her breath caught in her throat. *Remember who you are. Remember what must be.*

She repeated the words over and over in her mind, an insistent chant to strengthen her resolve to pay as little heed as possible to the man in front of her who had no smirk on his face, or lust in his eyes. In fact, he was very pale and clearly in some considerable pain.

"Tell me if I am hurting you." Biting her lip with determination, she took hold of his surcoat and eased it over his arms and shoulders as carefully as she could, then drew it off.

He must have strong legs to be able to crouch for so long when he wore a hauberk. A frisson of excitement skittered along her limbs, making her feel soft and pliant, vulnerable and gladly so.

Which was wrong. She could not afford to be vulnerable. She must be strong, for herself and for her family's sake.

At last she got the heavy and cumbersome mail off him, and much to her relief, he straightened.

Next came his padded *gambeson*. As she began to unbuckle it, she made a discovery that made a mockery of her determination to ignore him save as merely another wounded man to tend. "You are not wearing a camise or even *just-au-corps*?"

"They tickle me, too. At this time of year, it is hot enough with the *gambeson*, hauberk and surcoat."

Heat. Tickling. Never before had such simple words created such a reaction within her—or the sight of a man's naked chest. She stared at the contours of his muscles, as defined as if they were chiseled out of marble. Hairs, dark and curling as those on his head, spread across his bronzed skin that glistened with the virile sheen of perspiration. More encircled the dark aureoles of his nipples, while others formed a line below his navel and disappeared into his leather breeches.

"I did not expect to be wounded, or I would have worn a shirt."

An unwelcome flush of embarrassment crept up her face. "You are that vain of your skill?"

"I was that sure my opponents would have less."

She began to ease off his *gambeson*, attempting to touch him as little as possible. "You underestimated them."

"No, I did not."

"Given that you are here and they are not—" She gasped as his bare left shoulder appeared. It was very swollen and bruising to a dark, ugly shade of purple.

Connor bit back another Welsh curse at the sight of it, then nearly jumped out of his skin when Lady Allis touched him there. A strange sensation of pleasure mixed with pain roiled through him, even stronger than when she had helped him disrobe.

O'r annwyl, when he had lowered himself before her, eyes to perfect breasts, only the agony of his injury had conquered the stirring in his loins, despite his resolution to remember their respective stations. Now, half naked and still in pain, he could not subdue the desire she brought flaring into life, or the wish that these circumstances were different, especially when she stared at him after removing his *gambeson*.

He clenched his teeth and tried to keep his mind focused on something—anything—other than her fingertips moving over his naked skin, down the front of his shoulder and around it.

"Forgive me, but I must be sure that the injury is what I suspect."

Her he could easily forgive, because he could admire and respect a highborn lady who cared for wounded men. And, if he were being honest, because he found her fascinating.

To take his mind from the pain, he stared at her face and focused on the little wrinkle of concentration between her blond brows, a shade darker than her hair, which was covered by a light blue silk scarf held in place with a narrow circlet of gold.

Mercifully, she stopped feeling his shoulder. Then she took his left hand in hers, putting her fingers on his wrist. He knew the gentle pressure was a medical necessity, but as pain radiated from his shoulder, so waves of pleasure rippled outward from her touch, although not enough to triumph over the agony.

Her brows knit with concern, and her mouth tightened.

"What is it? Is there something very wrong?"

She shook her head, and his dread diminished.

She placed her fingers on his right wrist. "I feel no difference, which is good. Sometimes there can be damage inside. Can you make a fist with your left hand?"

He did, and she gave him a small smile that made him feel his wound was not so very bad. "Excellent. Now you may sit down."

Weak, and with the pain gaining upon him, he was glad to obey.

She folded her hands and regarded him with a tranquil steadiness that was comforting. "You've pulled the bone from the socket in your shoulder. I will have to put it back immediately, before more damage is done."

Stunned, he stared at her.

"The bone is out of the socket. I must put it back," she repeated slowly.

"I heard you." Aye, so he had, but to think she could be so calm, so matter-of-fact . . .

He did not see the sympathy lurking in her soft brown eyes, only the grim set to her full lips, the very lips he had wanted so much to kiss. "*You* are going to put it back?"

"Yes. I have done it before, when the miller had the same injury. Brother Jonathan showed me how. It takes not strength, but skill. And it is going to hurt."

As if he needed to be told that. As if he were a boy who had not been to war and seen all manner of wounds and sickness.

"Do it, then, and be quick."

Chapter 5

Allis recognized the look in Sir Connor's eyes—
the resolute refusal to let pain dominate him, the
summoning of strength and the courage to accept
whatever a physician must do.

True bravery did not always manifest itself in the
charge of men and horses, but rather at such times as
these, when a man's enemy was his own flesh and
blood and bone.

"I have often helped Brother Jonathan," she assured
him as she hurried to the long trestle table. She picked
up a vial and poured some of its contents in a cup, then
brought it to him. "Drink this. It will ease the pain."

He studied the cup and sniffed its contents.

"It's not poison. It's made from poppies."

"Yes, I've smelled it before. In the Holy Land." He
downed it in a gulp. "Do it now."

"It takes time for the potion to—"

"Now!" he growled, his burning, agonized eyes searing her heart. "It will hurt either way and waiting makes it worse."

He had no idea how much pain he was inviting. "Sir knight, please—"

He grabbed her arm with his good right hand. "Do it!"

He could order armies with that voice.

She planted her feet, took hold of his left arm and followed his command.

Sir Connor didn't shout or curse or scream as the bone popped back into place. No sound at all escaped him as he squeezed his lips together, closed his eyes tight and clenched his jaw, yet he went so white, he was the color of his surcoat.

"I'm sorry, but there is no other way and you would not wait."

Taking a deep, shuddering breath and slowly letting it out, he opened his eyes. "The worst is over, is it?"

"Yes."

"Thanks be to God for that." His gaze fastened onto hers and he inched closer. "And thanks be to you, my lady, for your help."

She didn't back away. She couldn't. She had heard of men who could tame horses or dogs with only their eyes, and he might be one of them, so powerless did she feel to turn away.

Nor did she wish to, as she stared into the dark brown depths, seeing pain and sorrow and something that took her a moment to comprehend. It was true gratitude.

"My lady!" Brother Jonathan exclaimed.

She gasped and looked toward the entrance of the

tent, feeling as guilty as if she had been caught in a passionate embrace. Brother Jonathan was just inside the entrance and Bob and Harry stood behind him, craning to see past the plump holy man. Bob, the taller of the two, was the first to close his mouth, while Harry ran his hand through his tousled black hair.

"You should have told me you were hurt," Brother Jonathan chastised Sir Connor as he hurried toward them, his hazel eyes snapping with as much ire as she had ever seen him express. "I saw him on the field," he continued, addressing her, "but he walked away as if he weren't hurt."

"So I understand, Brother Jonathan. He is the kind to suffer in silence, even though his shoulder was out of joint."

"If I had known my injury was as bad as that, I would have asked for help."

She slid the half-naked knight a glance, not believing that for a moment. He was a proud warrior and probably would have swooned rather than let himself be carried from the field.

Brother Jonathan examined Sir Connor's shoulder and checked his pulse and his grip, as she had done. "Excellent, excellent," he mumbled, but exactly who he was addressing wasn't clear.

Nevertheless, she took that as a sign that she had done well, and Sir Connor's shoulder was correctly repaired. "I gave him a draft to ease the pain."

"Good. It will be sore for a day or two yet," Brother Jonathan said to him, "and for some time afterward. It must be wrapped and kept still. Soon you can begin to work the muscle, but slowly and gradually. You don't want to weaken the joint, or it will pop again."

"Again?"Sir Connor looked and sounded a bit nauseous.

"Yes, and more easily. Over time, that could wear the joint and you would be in constant agony."

"Then I shall do as you say."

"Excellent. Now if Lady Allis will assist, I will prepare some bandages for wrapping your shoulder. Lie back and rest, sir, until we are ready."

Sir Connor nodded and did as he was told. She hoped the potion was taking effect, for he must be in considerable pain, certainly far more than he was showing.

"Put salve on these, if you will, my lady. It will ease the ache."

She nodded and tried to keep her attention on her task and not the questions the two soldiers proceeded to ask Sir Connor.

"Been in a lot of tournaments, have you?" Bob inquired.

"A few."

"And battles with the infidel, eh?" Harry asked, nodding at the cross on Sir Connor's surcoat.

"More than a few."

Bob whistled. "With the king?"

"Yes. I was on Crusade with Richard."

"Now there's a man!" Harry said with obvious approval.

She happened to glance at Sir Connor at that moment. He was in the process of covering his face with his right arm, but before he did, she saw that he did not share that sentiment.

Most men of arms admired the king, and it was strange that he did not.

"What's Richard like, really?" Bob asked. "I mean,

we hear all sorts of things. Do women really faint when they see him?"

The tent flap opened, and two more soldiers appeared, assisting a man who moaned with every step they took. His leg was twisted at an odd angle, obviously broken.

"God's heavenly heart, I don't like the looks of that," Brother Jonathan cried, shoving bandages at her. "My lady, would you mind wrapping Sir Connor's shoulder? I really should tend to this man."

"But Brother Jonathan—"

He had already bustled off, so there was nothing else to do but wrap Sir Connor's shoulder.

Remembering far too well the feel of his warm skin and especially the feelings touching him invoked, and very aware that they were no longer alone, she took the bandages and approached Sir Connor. "Bob, Harry, help him up."

"I don't need any help," Sir Connor protested genially as he struggled to sit while keeping his left arm immobile.

Realizing the potion was most definitely affecting him, she nodded to Bob and Harry, who quickly stepped in and eased him upright.

"That's a humiliating experience for a man, that is," Sir Connor observed with a lopsided grin.

She didn't need any help now. It would be better, in fact, if Bob and Harry were out of earshot. A man in this state might reveal . . . might say almost anything.

It would be best of all, perhaps, if they didn't watch, either. She might blush, or her hands tremble again, and she didn't want them to see such evidence of a temporary, foolish, girlish weakness. Who could say what two gossiping foot soldiers might make of it?

"Bob, Harry, why don't you see if there are other wounded on the field?"

Dismissed, they bowed and departed, leaving Allis, Sir Connor, Brother Jonathan and his moaning patient in the tent.

Commanding herself to concentrate and get this over with as quickly as possible so that her heartbeat would settle and her breathing return to normal, she began to wrap the salved bandages around Sir Connor's shoulder and chest to keep the joint as immobile as she could.

He suddenly sucked in his breath. "Not wanting to insult you, my lady, but I've had gentler nursing from the man who tended the king's horses."

"I'm sorry." She went a little slower, and with more caution.

"If I didn't know any better, I'd say you'd been talking to Caradoc," he reflected with preternatural calm. "My brother, that is. He would enjoy doing that, but he wouldn't be as delicate as you. Oh, he'd be rough! Nothing more than I deserved, he would tell me." He smiled, obviously not realizing he was grinning like a drunken fool. His Welsh accent seemed to grow stronger with every utterance, too. "I'm glad he's not. You're much prettier, you are. I don't know many other beautiful and wealthy ladies would tend to wounded as you do.

"Look you, wanting to rip that scarf off your head, me, and see your lovely hair again," he continued, his words slurring. "Like gold it is, molten gold. It was your hair first made me stay in the garden, where I knew I shouldn't be." He leaned closer and a tendril of titillation slid along her spine. "Aye, knowing that I ought to go, I was, but when I saw you looking so sad and lonely . . . like I have been so many times . . . I wanted to make you smile a little. And I did, didn't I?"

She tried to fight the excitement igniting and flaming into being within her as he continued. The feelings he roused in her must be put to death swiftly. Completely.

But the need he awakened proved too strong and too powerful to stifle. She could not find it in her to tell him to be quiet, especially when he caressed her cheek with his callused hand. His warm, rough palm felt so gentle and so good against her skin.

She nervously glanced over her shoulder. Brother Jonathan was still busily attending to his patient.

"Different you were in the garden with me," Sir Connor whispered. His deep, musical voice seemed to weave a spell around her, as if they were once more alone in the moonlight with the soft scent of roses about them. "Friendlier. Sweeter. I should have kissed you on your lovely rosy lips, I'm thinking." His thumb brushed over her mouth. "But I could not."

Totally entranced, her hands still, she bent closer, until her mouth was mere inches from his. "Why not?"

"Because I am . . . who I am."

A strange and unexpected answer. "Who are you?"

He swayed slightly, as if he were drunk. "Why, Sir Connor of Llanstephan, of course!"

Then he laughed, a great raucous rumble of hilarity that seemed like a slap in the face, so loud and unexpected it was.

She looked over her shoulder again, to see Brother Jonathan and his patient staring at them.

"The potion," she reminded the holy man, who went back to his task as Sir Connor continued to chuckle like a demented fool.

That was what she got for asking questions of a man who had drunk that potion. Pleasant and exciting though they were, she should pay the mutterings of a drugged man no mind. "Enough talking, sir knight. Lie down. You should sleep."

He slowly reclined upon the cot. "Will you join me?"

Her response was an indignant, "No!"

"Very proper answer, my lady, but I know these games." He tried to waggle his right forefinger at her, reminding her that he was drug-addled, and she had been mistaken to take his invitation seriously.

"You want me. You wanted me last night, as much as I wanted you. I should have kissed you on your lovely lips, I should. I should have caressed your soft skin and confessed how much I admire your grace. I should have made love with you right there in the garden. I should have slowly, slowly showed you how you make me feel when I look at you, like there might indeed be a hope for happiness and contentment on this earth for me."

More unexpected words from this unusual man. If he were in his right mind, her heart would be tenderly touched by what he was saying. As it was, his words could be dismissed as easily as Bob and Harry.

Or if not just as easily, they would be at last. They must be.

He smiled dreamily, with a hint of the charming young rogue she could easily believe he had been. "Or maybe we would not have had the patience to take our time."

He took her hand, his closing around hers, and she let him, guiltily indulging herself for one brief moment. There never would and never could be anything more between them. Perhaps it was because of that, or because Brother Jonathan was busy, or because he made her feel like a beautiful and desirable young woman and not the price for a family's security, that a sly, mischievous spirit stole upon her. "Why, I hardly know you, Sir Connor."

His grin, even lopsided, was charm personified. "You would have known me better by the finish."

He limply gestured for her to lean closer. "Would you do something for me?"

Looking around and seeing that Brother Jonathan was still occupied, she bent down. She was so close, she could feel his breath on her cheek.

"When you see the man you despise," he whispered, "please tell him I am going to kill him."

She reared back as violence and the baron intruded into her stolen moment of peace, for she knew exactly who he meant. Last night in the hall, Sir Connor had caught her unguarded expression and whatever else he interpreted from that, he had rightly guessed her opinion of the man she must marry.

Sir Connor continued slowly, as if he were speaking in his sleep, which in a way, he was. "He tried to kill me first. My lance . . . my lance should not have shattered like that."

At the time of the collision she had been too concerned about his fall to consider exactly how it had happened. Was it possible he was right? Could he have been the victim of foul play?

That seemed impossible. Every man in the tournament was duly licensed by the king's court, having paid for the privilege of participating in tournaments throughout England. Surely no dishonest man would be allowed . . .

Yet, would the king's court, always so short of funds because of Richard's penchant for war, be so particular, or would the ability to pay be the only requirement?

To be sure, she had never seen a lance demolished in that way—but then, she had not seen very many melees, either.

She opened her mouth to question him more, but his eyes closed, his jaw went slack, and his chest began to rise and fall with his slow, even breathing. He was asleep.

More injured men straggled in, obviously not seriously hurt as they casually waited for Brother Jonathan and discussed the melee, so she took a moment to contemplate Sir Connor's serious accusation. Had De-Frouchette really tried to kill him? And if so, why?

DeFrouchette would certainly act out of malice; of that she was certain. He would do all he could to ensure an enemy's defeat, and not honestly, if necessary.

Sir Connor was no threat to him . . . unless they had been seen together in the garden. No one else had been there, nor had she noticed anybody close to the door when she returned to the hall. There had been no guard on the wall walk nearby. Of that she was very sure, for she had looked for one when Sir Connor had first spoken to her.

But she had not kept watch on the gate leading from the garden into the courtyard where Sir Connor had entered. Someone could have been there, watching in the shadows.

Yet what would anybody have seen to report to the baron? A short conversation, a kiss on the wrist. Her body warmed and she blushed to think of that—but was it so terrible, really? Was it enough to try to cause serious injury, perhaps even death? Even for De-Frouchette?

Or maybe it had nothing to do with her, and everything to do with the fact that the baron might fear a well-trained knight upon the tournament field.

Perhaps it wasn't the baron at all. She didn't think there was any other man in the tournament who might be so ruthless, but there could be, she supposed.

As if summoned by her tumultuous thoughts, Rennick DeFrouchette sauntered into the tent as if he were the master of all he surveyed. When he spied her, he surveyed her with the same insolent presumption.

She wanted to march right up to him and accuse him of cheating, but caution, so long her guide in all things, held her back. Sir Connor had spoken in a drug-induced haze, and even if he truly believed what he had said, he must have evidence to prove it. Otherwise, his accusation would only earn the enmity of a merciless, powerful man.

As for the baron's possible motive, if he had done such a dishonest and dishonorable act, she had best ensure that he understood there was nothing between herself and Sir Connor except a brief conversation and a simple kiss on her wrist. And she would do well to see that it was so.

She put a smile on her face as she approached the baron. "Is the melee over?"

"Yes. Sir Auberan owes me fifty marks," he bragged before he glanced over at Sir Connor. "I see you've been looking after the Welshman. I trust I didn't injure him fatally."

"You did that?" she asked, feigning ignorance to try to gauge his feelings.

"Yes. Breeding shows itself in many ways, you know. He was doomed from the start."

"It is a serious wound. He cannot travel for some days."

Rennick frowned. "You would have him stay at Montclair?"

"Any who are hurt and unable to travel must stay. We can do no less."

"The expense—"

"My father is the host, so until he informs me otherwise, they will all stay until they are well enough to travel."

Rennick's eyes narrowed, and again she reminded herself of the dangerous path she trod. Any misstep—like last night—could have serious consequences. "It has always been so."

"Come, my lady," he commanded.

"My place is here, until all the injured have been seen to."

"You do not look overly busy."

Unfortunately, he was right. "Very well." She moved away before he could take her arm. "I will come outside a few moments."

They went around the tent away from the tournament field, closer to the river and the willows that lined the bank.

"I see no reason for all the injured to remain in Montclair, eating your father's food and drinking his wine," he said as they stopped in the shadow of the trees.

You do, she wanted to point out. "We would not want it said that the earl of Montclair lacks hospitality."

"As long as the earl and his daughter take care to whom they are hospitable. That Welshman, for instance. It would be better for him to be on his way."

Her heartbeat quickened, both with tension as she wondered if he was going to speak of last night and the hope that if he did not, she would get some answers to the multitude of questions she had about Sir Connor. "Why?"

"He is dishonored, cast out of Richard's retinue by the king himself."

"Why was he cast out?"

"They quarreled. He is fortunate he was only sent home, and not arrested for treason."

From what she had heard of Richard, she thought so, too, even as she wondered what the quarrel had been about. "You read all the licenses of the attendant knights, and apparently saw nothing amiss. Therefore, I assume there was no objection raised when he paid his fee to the court to participate in tournaments, and so is entitled to enter any he wishes. Perhaps he left the king of his own accord. Or have you made an error?"

Rennick's heavy, dark brown brows pulled together as he frowned. "You question me close, my lady. Is this the gratitude I get for helping your father?"

"Naturally I am grateful, Baron," she lied, quickly forcing another bogus smile onto her face. "It is just that I am trying to understand how this man came to be here if he is unworthy."

"I didn't know about his past until recently."

"Who told you?"

"Do you doubt what I say?"

"No. I am simply trying to grasp why he was worthy yesterday, but is not today and why, although he has every right to participate in the tournament, you believe it would be better for my father to risk being considered an ungracious and miserly host than to allow the man to stay a few days until his wound is mended."

"There are more things to consider than that, my lady." His knuckles grazed her cheek, but she felt no tingle of pleasure. She saw only his fist. "I suppose I cannot expect a woman to understand, beautiful and clever though she may be."

She gazed up into the baron's face, felt his breath hot upon her and saw the lust shining in his blue eyes. How she wanted to spit into his face! To tell him exactly what she thought of him. But she couldn't—he had too much power over them.

So she must be a hypocrite. "Forgive me if I have inadvertently insulted you, Rennick. I thought my future husband would want to maintain the good opinion of the nobles of the realm. I didn't mean for you to be angry with me."

With an eager, hungry expression, he roughly tugged her to him, and his voice seethed with lechery. "When you beg my forgiveness, how can I be angry?"

He could have spouted poetry like a minstrel of the king's court, and she would still be disgusted by his desire. As for being in his arms, a snake's embrace would be more appealing. She splayed her hands on Rennick's chest and subtly tried to back out of his hold. "We might be seen."

"So what of that?" he muttered as he bent down to kiss her. She turned her face so that his mouth met her cheek. He pulled back and glared at her.

She feared he was going to strike her, but whatever burst of heat his anger unleashed seemed to cool. "Stop this coyness, Allis. Everyone knows you will be mine one day. Our estates join, and so should we. I will protect you, and your family." He smiled as his grip tightened. "I've waited long enough for you. I can't wait much longer." His gaze intensified, and she saw the rage surging within him, strong enough perhaps to overcome his patience, and his lust. "You make me mad with jealousy."

Despair, like a dark cloud of fog coming down the river valley, began to blight the small blossom of happiness she had dared to feel when she was with Sir Connor. Worse, this could be the confirmation that they had been seen in the garden. If so, more than she and her family were in danger of suffering Rennick's wrath; now she must protect Sir Connor, too, the man who had wanted to make her smile.

She knew how, and although her very soul rebelled against the method, there was no alternative. "A lady likes to be pursued, and not have her affections taken for granted, Rennick," she purred as she wound her arms about his neck, "otherwise she might do something to ensure that she is appreciated."

His eyes widened with surprise, then flared again with carnal craving. "It was a game, Allis? If so, you play a dangerous one."

"You amaze me, Rennick." She toyed with the hair around his ugly ears and banished from her mind any comparison of his brown, straight hair cut in the Norman style with Sir Connor's long, thick and waving locks. "I would think a man in your position would have nothing to fear from anyone."

"Only losing you."

Only losing his grasp on Montclair, she mentally amended as he again swooped down to kiss her. She quickly cupped his face in her hands, preventing that. As she did, his frigid blue eyes locked onto hers. His arms tightened around her as if he would squeeze the very breath from her body.

The time had come. She had put it off as long as

possible, yet she could not make Rennick wait any longer. The tournament had not rallied her father and, despite all her efforts, he continued to weaken day by day. Edmond was too young to rule Montclair, and one day soon, Rennick would surely go to the king, if he was in England, or to Richard's justiciar, and tell them that someone—some *man*—must be put in charge of Montclair until Edmond came of age. She didn't doubt Rennick would paint himself the most suitable and logical candidate, and probably offer money to ensure that they agreed.

If Rennick had to pay, his anger and bitterness would never end. But if she became his wife—if she gave him the body he so obviously craved—that might satisfy him for a time, and as his wife, she would be able to keep close watch on him.

Yet even though she accepted the necessity, the words did not come easily. But come they did. "I *have* kept you waiting long enough, Rennick. If you still wish to marry me, I agree."

Chapter 6

"**A**t last," Rennick said, as his whole face shone with triumph and satisfaction.

Allis wanted to scream with despair, but she submitted to his embrace and endured his mouth plundering hers, seeking only the gratification of his own lust.

She choked back a sob, and he did not hear it.

She must be strong. She must endure. She must—

"Rennick!" she cried, shoving him away when he roughly grabbed her breast.

Righteous, furious anger at his impertinent action energized her. She might have to be his wife and eventually have to submit to his pawing, but not yet. By the saints, not yet!

But she must not give Rennick cause to doubt her sincerity. She breathed deeply and put her hands on his arms that did not have the hard curves of Sir Connor's. "You have been patient so far, Rennick, and that has impressed me. Do not spoil it now."

He grabbed her around the waist. "I *have* been patient and am eager for my reward."

"Which you will have soon enough. Name the day you would have me for your wife."

Her words had the effect she hoped. Again he smiled, while she felt anything but happy. "I would marry you today, but there are important people who should be invited to our wedding."

Any delay would be welcome, but she tried not to show that, either. "I will leave the actual day up to your best judgment, my lord, as long as we have at least a fortnight to prepare. These important, influential people must be entertained as befits their station, and yours."

It would be at least a fortnight before Sir Connor would be healed enough to leave, but she must put that from her mind.

Rennick inclined his head in agreement.

She should be pleased to see such evidence that she could influence her husband-to-be, but that discovery did nothing to lift her spirit from the deep well of bleak despair.

But, as always, she could not wallow in that gloomy pit. She had her father to take care of, and Isabelle and Edmond. She must not burden them with her sorrow. Their mother's death and father's illness were enough for her brother and sister to bear, and her father must not be upset. So they must all believe her happy in her choice, just as Rennick must. "I also think it would be wise to suggest a date to those you consider most important, and only when you are certain they can attend, announce it formally. That way, you will not offend anyone."

"You are indeed as intelligent as you are beautiful."

He pulled her to him and kissed her again, hard and forceful, with nothing of love or affection, or even lascivious desire. It was all power and domination.

He let go and his gaze raked her face and figure. "I trust you will be worth the wait, my lady."

She would never show him fear, or let him believe he could intimidate her. She would give him her hand and her body, but not her pride. "As I hope you will be, my lord."

She stepped away before he could embrace her again. "Now I must return to my duties. I have left Brother Jonathan long enough. I would not have it said that the lady of Montclair is remiss, either."

"Very well, my lady. After all, soon enough you will be my dutiful wife."

Allis didn't trust herself to speak as she hurried back into the tent where Sir Connor slept on, oblivious.

Outside the earl's solar that night, clouds scudded across the moon and a low wind moaned, threatening rain. In this chamber, however, where three men sat in chairs of dark, aged oak, richly carved with vines and grapes, and the seats softened by bright, silk-covered cushions, all was warm, bright and comfortable. Thick tapestries depicting the nobility at leisure hung upon the walls, illuminated by several expensive candles whose scent filled the room. A gleaming silver carafe of excellent French wine stood ready and matched the equally shiny goblets the men held.

"I don't want to have anything to do with him,"

Auberan de Beaumartre muttered, his gaze darting between the baron near the window and the portly figure across from him.

Fingering the bottom of his goblet, Rennick glanced at Lord Oswald, then smiled at Auberan. "Because he's part Welsh?"

"Yes! They're all savages."

"Savages who have no love for Norman kings or their taxes. Savages who can fight," Lord Oswald said, his voice a low murmur, but firm and strong and very confident. "And this particular one has even more personal reasons for hating Richard."

Oswald leaned forward so that his jowled face moved into the flickering candlelight. "He was once as loyal to the king as it is possible for a man to be, but given what happened . . ." He shrugged and sat back.

"What exactly did happen?" Rennick inquired. "Lovers' spat?"

"No, and I would keep such suggestions to yourself. Those rumors about the king's habits are just that—rumors," Oswald said firmly.

Oswald of Darrelby was the most ruthless person Rennick had ever met or heard of; Auberan, however, was apparently as ignorant of Lord Oswald's true reputation as the earl of Montclair, for he disregarded the older man's obvious wish to leave that subject. "Those 'rumors' have been going around since Richard was fourteen, so there must be something to them."

If Auberan wasn't careful, Oswald would toss him off the battlements with no more thought than another man would flick a fly from his hand.

"That is not important," Oswald rumbled. "What is important—and what most of the nobles will agree upon—is that we don't want to pay the exorbitant taxes Richard raises to fight in foreign lands. That is what will unite the different factions, not his personal tastes. Besides, he's not the only one at court with such tendencies, so condemning him for them may work against us."

"Nor is he the only one who feels it justified to raise an army and go to the ends of the world to fight," Rennick pointed out. "Richard had plenty of support for the Crusade."

"Until the first stories of what was happening came home." Oswald ticked off the reasons on his plump fingers. "Starvation, camp fever, massacres of unarmed prisoners. Worst of all, he failed to capture Jerusalem, yet the fool still thinks he's the hero of the ballads sung about him by minstrels and other dolts who don't know the truth."

"He's never even spent an entire year here in the whole of his reign," Auberan added, "whereas Prince John has rarely left."

"Because he's been trying to wrest England from Richard's rule," Oswald replied.

"He will be a better ruler than his brother," Auberan declared.

"He will be more easily intimidated," Rennick said. "That is what is important to know about John. The barons and other nobles will find it easier to control him, and therefore the taxes will be kept low."

Oswald nodded. "And that is the point we should make to our Welsh friend."

"He's not my friend," Auberan mumbled. He eyed the baron. "And I don't think he's yours, either. Didn't you see the way he looked at Lady Allis?"

Rennick smiled a small, cool smile. "Let him look."

Auberan eyed him doubtfully.

"She was playing a woman's game with me," Rennick explained, lust filling him as he remembered Allis in his arms. Soon, there would be no more toying with him. Soon, she would be his, in every way. Soon she would discover who was truly the master of Montclair. "She has agreed to be my wife and we will be married before the summer is over."

"I thought you were jealous," Auberan said, "and Sir Connor's 'accident' a warning to keep away from her."

"His lance shattered, that's all."

Oswald's mouth tightened with mounting impatience. "Be that as it may, we should try to win him to our cause. His Norman father was very well regarded by the Welsh as well as the men of the court. Edgar was a very clever fellow—married a Welsh princess and was lax in enforcing the king's laws, so naturally those barbarians liked him. Now his sons have inherited their loyalty, if no money, and the other Welsh nobles will listen to them. By winning Connor to our side, we will have allies in Wales."

"We don't need allies in Wales. What are the Welsh to us?" Auberan protested. "Just a thorn in our side."

"I am beginning to think we don't need you, Auberan," Oswald said in a way that made Rennick's blood run cold. Auberan might come from a powerful family, but he was an annoying, stupid fellow. The ground at the bottom of the battlements could be the best place for him—another accident, of course.

"How difficult is it to comprehend that the more we have on our side from all parts of Britain, the more likely we are to avoid a charge of treason when Richard is dead?" Oswald demanded. "God's wounds, man, have you forgotten what happened when that oaf

William Rufus was assassinated? No one challenged
the story that his death was an accident even though
the man who shot him was the finest archer in England, because every single man in England—Norman
or Saxon—wanted William Rufus dead."

Auberan paled. "Are you planning to assassinate
the king?"

"What did you think we were planning? A feast?"
Oswald snapped.

"I thought . . . I assumed . . ."

At a glance from Oswald, Rennick rose and grabbed
Auberan's tunic, hauling him to his feet. "Are you
with us, or not?"

"I . . . of course I am with you, if it can be done as
you say, with no repercussions."

Rennick let him go and Auberan fell back into his
chair. "Do you think we would do this if we could not
be sure of success? We are going to be cautious and
careful, because anything else will be disaster for us
all."

"What about Percival? Does he—?"

"The lad is my squire and does what he is told. That
is all he needs to know, for the time being. Later, if we
think him worthy, we may invite him to join us in our
cause."

"Regardless of whether or not we have the earl of
L'Ouisseaux and his son on our side, we must have
more support from the nobility in Wales, and Ireland
and the Scots," Oswald said. He smiled indulgently.
"But rest assured, Auberan, you don't have to be
friendly to Sir Connor if you do not wish to be." He
slanted a glance at Rennick. "Nor you, Rennick. Not
after you both took pains to insult him. Leave him to
me. He knew my brother." Oswald's voice hardened

and his black eyes glittered in the candlelight. "He was with Osric when he died in the Holy Land. For the present, caution must be our watchword, and what we have discussed goes no further. Are we agreed?"

They both nodded.

"Good. Leave us, Auberan. I have another matter to discuss with Rennick."

Auberan hesitated.

"Leave us!" Oswald repeated sternly, and this time, Auberan did not stand upon the order of his going.

When Auberan had closed the heavy door behind him, Rennick eyed Oswald. "Must we include that dolt in our plans?"

"His father will keep him in check, and even that fool knows he puts himself at risk if he talks too much."

"You truly believe we must woo the Welshman to our cause?"

"Yes, and thus I would have been most annoyed if he had died."

Rennick kept his face a blank mask.

"I would also be very upset if one of my friends is found to have done or ordered any tampering with lances."

"Naturally."

Oswald steepled his fat fingers. He wore no jewels, yet he was far wealthier than Rennick, and far, far richer than the king. "As long as you understand me, Rennick. I don't want this Welshman harmed, at least for the time being, or suspicion about his accident to fall upon you. If he proves resistant to our request to join us, then I shall not care what fate befalls him and you can do what you like."

Rennick nodded, knowing full well that if Oswald considered him a liability, his climb to power would be thwarted, utterly and completely—and his life likely ended, too. "Yes, my lord."

"So, you have finally brought the lady to heel, eh? Or should I say, to bed?"

"To heel, but not yet to bed."

"Given how you feel about her, I should not be surprised you are so willing to wait, but I confess your patience astonishes me." The mask of jovial friendliness disappeared. "But now that you have *finally* succeeded, Rennick, you had better wed and bed her soon. We need your alliance with her father and what that will say to others who hesitate to ally themselves with us. They will take your marriage as a sign of approval from a most respected man, and join us at last. Then we can move."

As if putting his words into action, Oswald heaved himself out of his chair and poured himself some more wine, while Rennick struggled to contain his anger at being chastised like a child and reminded that he did not command much respect among the nobility of England.

However, he was indeed a patient man, and he could wait to have his vengeance on Oswald. Until then, he would be content to be second to Oswald— which meant that should disaster befall, there would be someone above him to blame.

After taking a sip of wine, Oswald said, "Prince John makes Auberan look like a prodigy. John has already done many stupid things another king would have had him executed for long ago. We must move soon, and I want you firmly allied to Montclair before we do." He gave Rennick a knowing smirk. "Why, come to think of it, when news of your betrothal to Allis of Montclair reaches our sovereign's ears, Richard might even wonder if he misjudged you when he did not select you to be in his retinue."

Rennick didn't answer as Oswald set down his goblet. "Now I bid you good night, Rennick. It grows late, and my journey here has wearied me."

Rennick watched Oswald stroll from the solar. Then he slowly surveyed the luxuriously appointed chamber. One day soon, all this would be his. He would be rich, he would be powerful, and he would have the woman he had desired for so long.

He would be respected.

And Richard would be dead.

Chapter 7

Connor moaned. His mouth was as dry as the dust of the desert and his head ached like a punishment for his sins. As he opened his eyes, a pain like the devil's pitchfork pierced his left shoulder.

Drawing in a quivering breath, he surveyed his surroundings. Although it was dark, he could make out his bossed wooden chest that normally contained his armor and few personal possessions. His three-legged camp stool was near the small basket of apples he kept for Demetrius. His hauberk, *gambeson* and surcoat were neatly folded and placed upon the stool, with his helmet, sword and belt on top of the pile.

He had no memory of being brought to his tent and put on his cot. Somebody must have carried him here. Those two soldiers who had questioned him about Richard, perhaps.

He looked around, trying to gauge the time of day. The east side of his tent was brighter, which told him it was dawn, or shortly after. He had slept through the afternoon and the night, so he had not eaten since yesterday morning.

Closing his eyes, he heard again the bone-jarring crunch as his lance shattered and relived the instant anguish of the collision. His eyes still shut as if fearing what he might see, he raised his right hand to gingerly feel the bandages and sling around his left shoulder.

He remembered the flare of recognition in Lady Allis's brilliant brown eyes when he had entered the tent, and his relief that she seemed more concerned for him than angry. He recalled the way she had undressed him. He could scarce draw breath as she started to undo his sword belt, and it was not just because of his physical pain.

Later, the agony overwhelmed every other sensation, until the draft she gave him took effect. After that, his memories became disjointed . . . vague . . . like the Welsh mountains in the mist.

Her gentle, graceful hands. The little wrinkle of concentration between her shapely brows. Her soft lips pressed together, then parting, as if opening for him in anticipation of his kiss. Then the dreams. Incredible, exciting, tantalizingly vivid dreams.

He had told Lady Allis how much he admired her hair, and how he had wanted to make her smile. Her response had been a slow, seductive smile of pleasure and wonder, as if she had been waiting years for a man to say such a thing.

Half afraid of her rebuke, yet inspired by that smile, he had dared to lean close to her and brush his lips over hers. Softly, gently he kissed her, tasting the merest hint of wine and honey on her mouth. Miraculously, she did not protest, but slid her arms about his neck and drew him closer.

Warmth had turned quickly to heat as their kiss deepened. He could not say at whose insistence it began to change, nor did he care. All he knew was that now they were kissing with unbridled, fervent passion. Mouth upon mouth, tongues entwining, he had never known such intoxicating kisses.

He held her so close, her breasts, her hips, all of her seemed pressed against him as if they were as good as naked.

Then, suddenly, they were. His whole body trembled as her desire-hardened nipples touched his bare chest, and his arousal met the tousled hair between her thighs. With a sigh, she arched back, and he wound his hand in the glorious mane of her blond hair before trailing a row of heated kisses down the curve of her chin, her neck, her collarbone. Cupping one luscious breast, then the other, he swirled his tongue about the peaks, the soft sounds of her excitement adding to his own.

They said no words, and needed none as the tension of their need and desire grew. She pushed him back and he fell onto a bed—a wondrous strange bed, round and soft, covered in silken sheets of rich ruby-red shot through with golden threads. Pillows of royal blue and cream cushioned his fall. Above, a canopy of white silk so thin it was almost transparent moved in the breeze scented with roses and spices. Around the bed were fine lamps of burnished gold, their flickering flames lighting marble pillars and tall vases covered in intricate patterns of bold, bright colors. A carpet covered the mottled marble floor and a door nearby opened to the starry night. It was as if they were in the palace of Saladin himself, as he had so often imagined it when the nights of his journey were long and lonely.

More beautiful than the room and the stars, though, was Allis. Her long blond hair waved about her perfect body as she stood in the lamplight, watching him.

He held out his hand and she took it, her long, graceful fingers curving around his broad, callused ones. Lithe and supple as a cat, she crawled upon the amazing bed and stretched out beside him.

Carefully, slowly, as if she were made of the most rare and precious glass and one false move could shatter her or send her fleeing from him, he touched her. She smiled, but her body trembled, too, as if she were both willing and afraid.

"I will not harm you, my lady," he murmured as he leaned upon his elbow and looked down at her, his shoulder no longer painful. "I will never harm you."

"I know." She brushed a lock of his hair back from his shoulder. "My Samson."

Her arm curved about his neck and she drew him down, closer and closer, until they kissed again, mouths parted and tongues lightly teasing, tasting, touching.

He moved down to once more pleasure her breasts. "I want to love you. I want to excite you. I want to pleasure you."

"Yes," she sighed, her breath coming in short and swift gasps. She writhed as he flicked his tongue over her pebbled nipples. His hands roved over her hips and between her thighs, readying her. Arousing her. He would be easy and gentle, tender and yet as passionate as ever he had been in his life.

Instinctively she parted her legs, and in the next instant, he was somehow between them, raised on his hands and looking into her face. Her eyes closed, her lips parted, she might have been asleep, except that her body undulated like a reed upon a wave.

"May I love you, Allis?" he whispered, his whole being crying out to do just that, but part of him fearful that she would not want him. That she would open her eyes and in them he would see a look of revulsion that would remind him that he was disgraced and cast out.

She did open her eyes—and there he saw not just passion and desire, but need and understanding, as if she knew all that he was and had done, and accepted him nonetheless.

"Allis, I will love you as no man has ever loved you," he vowed as he began to gently push inside her warm moistness. "With my heart and my body, with all that I am or ever will be."

She surrounded him and welcomed him. She accepted him and loved him. Their bodies united, he was made whole again.

Then he felt the ropes of his cot through the thin straw mattress beneath him.

His eyes fluttered open. There was no oriental canopy of silk above him, but only the fabric of his tent. He lay not on silken sheets and cushions, but on a straw mattress and worn pillow.

He sat up. He must have nodded off, to dream again of loving Allis of Montclair.

As joy had washed over him in his dream, so despair came upon him now. It was as if God had given him a vision of heaven, only to allow him to awake in hell, and one of his own making.

Because once, he could have aspired to gain the love and hand of such a woman, before his pride and vanity, and that of his king, had brought about his downfall.

He ran his hand over his perspiring brow and tried to dismiss the notion that those dreams were deliberately sent to torment him and remind him of what he had lost. More likely they were caused by the potion she had given him.

He frowned. At least he thought all those disjointed memories were only the products of a drug-induced sleep. Telling her about her hair and wanting to make her smile . . . that seemed different. More real, much less a dream.

No, they were all dreams. They had to be.

He rolled over on his right side and got to his feet. Dizzy, he swayed a moment, then sat heavily. Dreams or not, coming to Montclair was a mistake. Yes, there were rich men here, and great potential for ransom. Yes, he needed money because he had vowed that he would earn a sum equal to all that his father had spent to send him on the Crusade and then some, enough to get his family's estate out of debt and provide a good dowry for Cordelia—but now look where he was. His left arm all but useless, his lance shattered, and a fascinating woman perhaps thinking him some kind of beast.

He should pack up his things and depart at once, to let his arm heal . . . somewhere else. Not home. Never home, until he came laden with silver and gold to show Caradoc that his time in the Holy Land had had some benefit, after all.

Thinking of his heated words to his brother before he had left Wales two years ago reminded him of the thin state of his own purse at present. He would have to be careful with what money he had, and he had to buy another lance.

Ignoring the persistent images of Lady Allis, naked and willing, lingering in his mind, he thought about the way his lance had splintered. His weapon might have had some damage he had missed and it was old, but he had examined it the day before and seen nothing amiss. He should have checked it again the morning of the tournament, though—a mistake he would never make again.

These things would explain a broken lance, not one shattering into pieces. There was one way that could happen, and it would mean his weapon had been tampered with.

Every instinct told him the man who had sat beside the Lady Allis at the feast was the culprit. Given the attention the baron paid to Lady Allis, it was clear he was more than a mere friend, or hoped he was. It could well be he knew or suspected that the lady did not share his affections.

Jealousy could make a man do evil things. The baron had ridden straight for him, although he had probably not fought in years. A man determined to prove something, or to rid himself of a rival might do that, especially if he knew his opponent posed no real threat.

Yet if somebody had seen him and Lady Allis in the garden, what exactly would they have observed? Some banter, a kiss on her wrist. Nothing so very impertinent or intimate. The impertinence and the intimacy were all in his mind, and the passion, too, perhaps. Even if she seemed to share it, there had been no words to that effect, and no actions on her part.

There was Sir Auberan, too. They had exchanged angry words, and that might be enough to make him want revenge. Yet even if Auberan had the knowledge, he doubted that young man possessed the resolve and the skill.

Whoever did the deed, when could it have been done? While he slept? While he joined the others in the hall to break the fast before the melee? His weapons had been unattended then.

The first thing he must do was discover if there had indeed been foul play, and to do that he should study the pieces of his lance and look for signs of tampering.

Before he did anything else, though, he should find Demetrius. Demetrius was like a friend, a comrade-in-arms who had been his companion through some of the worst moments of his life.

Moving slowly and more cautiously, Connor again got to his feet. He was less dizzy this time, thank the Lord, and his aching head was getting better, too.

Now, to dress himself. That proved no easy task, but he managed it and with only a minimum of cursing. Once attired in a clean shirt and tunic, his belt around his waist, his scabbard against his thigh and his arm again in the sling, he went outside. The cool air of early morning greeted him, and the grass was damp with dew. Beyond, the massed tents of the other knights, their squires, pages and servants stretched toward the castle wall. Pennants flapped in the breeze, and in the sky above, thin white clouds moved swiftly past. Several servants were already up and about, scurrying about the tents like so many busy bees.

With a grin he spotted Demetrius tethered a few yards away, quietly munching on the grass. The de-

strier lifted his head, stamped his foreleg and whinnied a greeting.

"Good day to you, too." He ran his right hand over
his horse's back and examined his body and legs for
any wounds. "A better day than mine, at any rate. Not
a scratch on you, my friend."

Out of the corner of his eye, he saw something
move. Alert for danger, he whirled around, biting back
a Welsh obscenity at the jolt of pain as he reached
across his body with his right hand to draw his sword.

A blond-haired, well-dressed lad of about twelve
years old stared back at him. Judging by his hair and
features, he was a relative of Lady Allis, a brother or
cousin.

His left shoulder throbbing, Connor sheathed his
sword. "Who might you be?"

"I am . . ." The boy took a deep breath and drew
himself up. "I am Edmond, the son of the earl of
Montclair."

And a proud young Norman lord in the making, as
evidenced by the bravado in his green eyes. Connor
smiled, for he had been full of bravado, too, when he
was that age.

"That is a very fine horse," the boy said, hurling the
words as if he half expected Connor to disagree.

"Demetrius is indeed a fine horse. What makes *you*
say so?"

"He's . . . he's big."

"Yes."

"He's strong. You can tell by his haunches."

Connor nodded. "Very strong."

The boy chewed his lip and looked worried.

"Come closer and look at his eyes."

Edmond did and Demetrius raised his head to study him.

"See how bright and shrewd they are? Plenty of big, strong horses there are, my lordling, but rare indeed is one as clever as mine, or as patient."

"What can he do?"

"Tricks, you mean?"

Edmond nodded.

"Not a one."

The boy's face fell with disappointment.

"Tricks are not going to do you much good in a battle."

"How do you know he's clever, then?" the lad demanded.

"He learns fast. But cleverness is not as important as patience."

Edmond looked skeptical.

"He will not move until he's told." *Unless his master is having lustful thoughts about a woman and shifts unexpectedly.* "And when he does move, he's steady."

"Steady?"

"Aye, like a rock beneath me. And trust me, young sir, when you are wearing eighty pounds of armor and rushing at your enemy, you want to feel as if you are sitting on something as strong and steady as a rock."

Edmond regarded Demetrius with new respect. "Was he with you on the Crusade?"

"Yes, and I would have died more than once but for him. Smarter than me, he is sometimes, moving to avoid a blow."

"What battles were you in? Did you kill any Saracens? Are they as fierce as they say?"

Ah, so here it was—the reason this boy had ventured forth in the chill of dawn to see him. The reason many young men and boys sought him out, aye, and women, too. They wanted to hear about the Crusade and, inevitably, Richard.

He didn't want to talk about either one. "Does your family know you are in the ward?"

"They won't miss me until mass." He pointed at Connor's sling. "My sister told us what happened to you. Yours is the worst injury," he noted, as if that should be a great comfort.

Connor bowed in acknowledgment of his superior harm.

"All the wounded must stay here until they are well again."

"Until we are well?"

Edmond nodded. "It's our duty as hosts, and Allis says you must always do your duty. Without complaint," he added as a grudging afterthought.

Connor suppressed a sympathetic grin.

"Edmond?"

They both turned to see Lady Allis marching toward them, her plain, pale blue gown whipping about her ankles with her brisk pace. A simple leather girdle around her slender waist was her only ornament, and she wore no scarf or wimple; her bountiful hair was drawn back in a single, long braid. Despite her simple attire, she still looked astonishingly lovely and very regal, as if she were a princess masquerading as a commoner.

His chest tightened. Had he spoken aloud his praise of her hair? Was that why she had not covered it—and if so, what did that mean? Or was this a mere coincidence?

"Is it time for mass?" Edmond asked as his sister came to a halt.

Allis kept her attention on Edmond and not on the tall, handsome man beside him. "Not yet. You should have told Merva or one of the other servants where you had gone."

When she had discovered that Edmond was not in his chamber, she had guessed that speaking with a man who had been on Crusade had been too tempting to resist.

Edmond slid his toe back and forth over the dew-damp ground. "I'm sorry, Allis."

"He wants to know about the Crusades, like a good many other people," Sir Connor said. He turned to Edmond. "I have an apple in my tent for my horse, his usual reward after a melee whether I win or not. Would you like to feed it to him before you go?"

Edmond nodded eagerly and went to fetch it.

She told herself that there was no reason she should be afraid to look at Sir Connor. She had seen him half naked, after all, and she had pledged herself to another. That should strengthen her against Sir Connor's potent fascination, which should not be so strong when he was simply standing in the ward waiting for her brother—to whom he spoke with such genial good humor, although she could tell he was still in pain. "How is your shoulder this morning?"

"It aches, but not so bad as yesterday."

And surely it was only right that she examine him. By touch. "May I?" Without waiting for his answer, she put her fingertips on the wrist of his left hand. His blood pulsed beneath her fingertips and his flesh was warm and strong. Like him.

She must control these wayward thoughts and concentrate on her task.

Despite her inward admonitions, she envisioned his naked chest. The small scars, the muscles, the dark hairs circling his taut nipples.

She then took his right hand and pressed her fingers to that wrist. The pulse beat beneath her fingertips as vibrantly as the other. How tempted she was to let her fingers linger there, feeling the life force within his virile body.

"My lady?" he queried softly.

So would his deep voice sound if they were alone in the same bed, whispering after a night of passionate intimacy.

God help her restrain these wicked thoughts, these sinful longings! She belonged to Rennick De-Frouchette by her own decree, and to have such thoughts about another man was wrong.

She let go of his hand as if it burned hot with the flames of hell itself. "They are both the same still. That is good."

"My head aches a little, from that medicine, I think."

"Yes, it can do that."

"I had some very strange dreams," he continued, and his brown eyes, as deep and intriguing as his voice, studied her intently.

She warmed beneath his steadfast regard, for there was more gentleness and kind concern than had ever been in Rennick's hard blue eyes. "That is not unusual."

"They were very . . . vivid."

She took a step back. "The potion can have that effect."

Edmond came out of the tent holding an apple. He went toward the huge horse, which lifted its head and whinnied.

She had been alone with Sir Connor only a few moments, but she felt as if she had experienced a lifetime of emotions, both thrilling and sad.

"Demetrius will be his friend for life now."

If Sir Connor sensed her mood, he did not show it. He stood and spoke as if they had merely exchanged meaningless pleasantries while Edmond was gone. Perhaps, in his mind, that had been all they had done.

That realization added to her sorrow, until he turned to her. Then she saw, in the brown depths of his eyes, a spark of true respect and even affection that lifted her from the depths of her despair. Yes, it was wrong of her to feel as she did when she looked at him thus, but oh, how good it was! And yet because of that look, she had to tell him that she was not free. Because of that look, he deserved nothing less.

She settled her features into the familiar mask of calm dignity that was so easy to assume with Rennick.

Gesturing for Sir Connor to follow, she walked away from her brother and the horse. When they were far enough from Edmond that he couldn't hear, she said, "I believe you may be under the mistaken impression that I do not care for Baron DeFrouchette, the man to whom I became betrothed yesterday and will soon marry. At times he does annoy me a little, but what couple does not have their little spats?"

She watched Sir Connor's face, seeking some sign of the effect of her words, but if she had assumed a public mask, so had he, and she found no answers there.

"I wonder why you did not tell me this before."

"I am not in the habit of telling everyone my business. I would have, if I had known you were going to kiss me."

"On the wrist only."

"Yes, but you shouldn't have done that."

He made a little bow. "Forgive me."

How cold and aloof he sounded, and so very proper. And how she silently mourned the change, which was necessary and inevitable, yet agonizing all the same. She was tempted to leave, but she had another reason for coming here. He had made a serious accusation yesterday when he was under the influence of Brother Jonathan's draft, and she had to know if he still had the same suspicions. "Yesterday you implied that you suspected someone of foul play."

Standing as stiffly as a solder, he inclined his head in affirmation. "That is true. My lance should not have split and shattered that way."

"It was made of wood, Sir Connor."

"Oak, my lady. Hard and strong. To split along its length is unusual, but not unheard of, if a chisel is driven into the shaft at the base just above the hand guard and along the grain. Then the gouge is filled with colored clay to hide it."

"Can you prove this?"

"Perhaps, if I have the pieces."

"They were all gathered up and taken to the armory in the keep. You may examine them later."

"I shall."

"You believe the baron did this?"

"I think he might have reason."

"What reason?"

"Can you not guess, my lady?"

She looked away from his accusing eyes and enticing lips toward her young brother, so happy and innocent of the ways of the world. So few things he did could have serious consequences, while she . . . "The baron has no cause to be jealous."

"Then I am wrong and I shall have to try to discover who else might cheat."

She glanced at Sir Connor once more, and this time their gazes met and held, as they had that first night. She saw no harsh accusation, but a longing that seemed to meet and touch her own lonely soul, as if his hands reached out to save her as she teetered on the brink of a dark and bottomless chasm.

"Don't accuse Baron DeFrouchette even if you have proof."

Chapter 8

Connor drew backed abruptly, as if she had hit him. Her words had been as sharp and firm as if they had been a blow, another shock in a morning of confusion. No woman had ever raised such a tumult inside him, of joy and anguish, hope and despair. One moment, he was sure she shared his desire, the next she was calmly telling him she was betrothed to another.

"He has powerful friends and allies. He will not hesitate to destroy you if you become his enemy."

She spoke quietly, presumably so that her brother wouldn't hear, but to him she sounded as she would nestled against him, sharing his bed.

He had guessed she was unhappy, but this hinted at something far worse. "He is the sort of man who threatens people who oppose him?"

"Just believe me."

So he would—and there was the reason she would look with loathing at the man, yet become his wife. Lady Allis was the sort of woman who would do whatever she must to protect her family. She would never ask a man like him for help or protection, and he was in no position to offer it unasked, but as she had no call to warn him about DeFrouchette, he would let her know that she had an ally, if she so desired. "You do not have to explain to me. I have met his sort before."

She faced him squarely, as one warrior to another, although they fought different battles, with different weapons. "Let the matter rest. You will heal and live to fight in other tournaments, against other wealthy men. As a knight, I'm sure you understand duty and know how to accept it—as do I."

"Yes, I understand duty and sacrifice very well, as I know you do, my lady," he said softly, but not with pity. Pity would be an insult to her, as it would be to him.

Then he saw her sister standing awkwardly by the tents, a large basket in her hand. She looked very young and fresh as the dew in her pretty lavender gown, as Lady Allis must have when she was that age, before the years and responsibility had brought out her womanly beauty.

"Isabelle, what are you doing here?" Allis demanded, caught off guard again.

Since meeting Sir Connor in the garden, it seemed as if the very ground beneath her feet had become as unstable and unsteady as sand, and the most disconcerting thing of all was not the desire he aroused in her, powerful and undeniable though it was. It was his sympathetic understanding, offered not with pity, but with respect, as he might a comrade-in-arms.

"I thought Sir Connor might need some refreshment," Isabelle murmured, blushing and looking at the ground.

Isabelle was right, and Allis wished she had thought of that.

"How kind of you to remember me, my lady," Sir Connor said, giving Isabelle a warm smile. "However, I feel capable of walking to the hall, if I may have the pleasure of your company."

His good-natured, deep voice stirred the embers of desire Allis hadn't been able to extinguish. Excitement, hot and turbulent, simmered anew.

And she was not the only one affected, for Isabelle beamed and blushed even more. "You will join us for mass, too?"

"Thank you, but I prefer to sit near the door of the chapel. The scent of incense . . ." He paused, then began again. "The scent of incense can be a little overpowering."

Thank God for small mercies, Allis thought, telling herself she was glad. She didn't need the complication of Sir Connor near them in the chapel. "Edmond, it is time to go to mass."

He reluctantly left the horse and came to stand beside her. "You don't have a squire, do you?" he asked Sir Connor.

"No, I don't."

"I could be your squire."

"Edmond!" she cried, aghast at his bold request.

"Flattered as I am by your offer," Sir Connor replied without condescension as he addressed Edmond, "I cannot afford a squire."

Edmond's eyes flashed indignantly. "A squire doesn't get paid."

"Edmond, you are too young."

Her brother ignored her. "I could be your page."

Had Edmond taken leave of his senses, or forgotten she spoke for their father? Or was it that Sir Connor made him also feel the world was upside down and the young could disobey their elders. "No, you could not."

"There are pages here as young as Edmond," Isabelle pointed out, smiling at Sir Connor. "I think it would be wonderful for Edmond to be Sir Connor's page."

"Much as I would welcome his assistance, and proud as I am that the heir of Montclair wishes to serve me," Sir Connor said before Allis could reply and quell this sibling mutiny, "I cannot provide for another. Besides, there are others of higher rank for Edmond to serve, as befits his station."

"But you were on the Crusade," Edmond protested. "I saw the cross on your surcoat. Nobody else here has been on Crusade."

Allis put her hands on her hips and frowned. "Edmond, we are not going to quarrel about this."

"I am our father's heir, not you, so you can't order me!"

"He's right, Allis," Isabelle said. "You're always telling us what to do."

She took a deep breath. She didn't want to have a family squabble in public. "I know what my place in the world is, Edmond. Now come along to mass." She turned to leave.

"I'm old enough to be a page, and if you won't let me, I'm going to ask Father!"

She whirled around and glared at him. "No, Edmond, you will not—"

He stuck out his tongue at her, then ran toward the castle, as fleet as a deer.

Calling for Isabelle to follow, Allis hurried after her brother, while Sir Connor went to pat Demetrius again, a thoughtful expression on his face.

Neither of them noticed Isabelle looking back over her shoulder with every step she took.

Allis hustled Edmond and Isabelle into the solar, then shoved the heavy door closed, setting the tapestry on the wall beside the jamb rippling. "Don't you dare go to our father and bother him with this!" she ordered Edmond.

"I want to be a page. There are even some pages as young as nine, and I'm twelve," Edmond retorted as they faced each other. "You probably won't let me be a squire, either. How am I to be a knight if I cannot be a squire?"

Allis struggled to keep her voice calm. "There is plenty of time for you to be both page and squire after I'm married."

"So you keep saying, but you aren't even betrothed!"

"He's right," Isabelle said as she sat in the chair nearest the window. "I know Father isn't well, but Edmond has to become a knight, and I have to—"

"*What* do you have to do?" Allis demanded, arms akimbo.

Isabelle tossed her head defiantly. "Find a husband. I don't want to wait until I'm as old as you."

"Is there anyone you have in mind?"

"Maybe."

"Sir Connor, perhaps?"

Isabelle frowned and crossed her arms.

Allis marched toward her. "Listen to me, Isabelle. That man cannot be your husband. He is poor, and the baron tells me he was sent back to England after quarreling with the king. Clearly, he is not worthy of marriage to the daughter of the earl of Montclair."

Any daughter. In spite of the way he made her feel, or the emotions he inspired. Despite her yearning for him to kiss her, and hold her, and keep her safe, so that she need never fear again.

She turned back to Edmond. "Yes, he was on the Crusade, but that seems to be the best that can be said of him, and there are other things about him that make him unsuitable."

"What things?" Edmond demanded.

"Percival says he's very skilled in the arts of war," Isabelle offered defiantly.

"That may be, but he has no land and no money, and he has quarreled with the king. Now, as to the matter of my marriage, that you are both so keen to have me make," she said, looking from one to the other, "yesterday I agreed to become the baron's wife. He will formally announce it when he has chosen the day."

Her brother and sister exchanged surprised looks.

"After that, I will try to find a suitable knight for you to serve as page, Edmond, and Isabelle, I will try to find a husband for you."

"I want to find my own husband."

Her self-control, stretched to the limit, finally snapped. Her hands balled into fists. "Then do it," she cried, bringing her fists down as if striking an imaginary table, "just as long as it is not Sir Connor of Llanstephan!"

Edmond and Isabelle stared at her, as well they might. She looked and sounded like a peevish child, not the chatelaine of Montclair. "I'm sorry. Forgive me.

I'm tired." She rubbed her temples. "It's the strain of the tournament."

Isabelle hurried to embrace her. "No, I'm sorry. I know you've been putting off getting married because you hoped Father would get better."

"I'm sorry, too," Edmund said, taking her hand. "I won't bother Father, or you, about becoming a page or squire anymore."

Allis pulled them both into her arms and hugged them tight. This was why she was marrying Rennick DeFrouchette—for Isabelle and Edmond, and their father, too. When Edmond started to squirm, she moved back and smiled at them. "I promise I *will* act upon these things. You two go to the chapel. I'll be along in a moment, after I see how Father is."

They nodded their acquiescence and departed.

She did not immediately go to their father. She needed a moment alone to restore her equilibrium, if that were possible, or at least calm herself. Although she loved her father dearly, it was difficult to see him so different from the father she had grown up adoring, a man of strength and power, yet good humor, too.

Last night he had paced around his chamber like a caged beast. Then, as always, the footfalls ceased, to be followed by the sound of his crying. He wept for their mother every night, and every day, he prayed to die.

Edmond and Isabelle didn't know that. She made sure of it. How could she explain that he wanted to leave them and join their mother in heaven when she didn't understand it herself? Were they not worth staying on earth for?

Last night, when she had told him of her agreement to become Rennick's bride, he had immediately started to weep, bemoaning the fact that her mother was not alive to see her daughter become a wife. No questions for her about her feelings for Rennick, no wishing her happiness.

She quickly forgave him, because his questions or his blessing wouldn't have made any difference. She was destined for misery when she became Rennick's wife.

Connor stood in the dim shadows at the back of the chapel, watching Lady Allis and her family. The quarrel with her siblings had obviously been resolved, and happily, for they stood close and intimate, not as if they were still angry with one another. Her father knelt on the stone floor throughout the whole of the mass. Lady Allis was quietly attentive, but he ignored her and kept his head bowed in silent and fervent prayer.

Connor had seen grief, had known it himself, but never had he witnessed a man more broken by it. Yet, as unsettling as it was for him to witness it, it must be a hundredfold worse for Lady Allis.

Also unsettling was the way Baron DeFrouchette loomed over Lady Allis. With his hawklike visage and long black robe, he reminded Connor of the vultures who circled battlefields, waiting.

One day she must marry, and someone other than he. He knew that as surely as he knew his disgraced name, yet he could not bear to think of her married to a man who would do cold-blooded murder. He must discover if his suspicions about his lance had any basis.

The mass concluded, he tore his gaze from Lady Allis and left the chapel. Outside, the sky had cleared, promising a fine day for the squires' melee, which would take place when all had broken the fast. Then the squires serving the knights who had been in yesterday's melee would face each other. They, too, would try to win ransoms and prizes, and begin to build a reputation for themselves, perhaps hoping for a place in the king's service or to please a father's pride, just as he had done all those years ago.

"Sir Connor? Sir Connor of Llanstephan?"

Halting at the sound of his name, he turned to look at the older man who addressed him. He didn't recall seeing the plump, pleasant-faced man at the welcoming feast, but he looked slightly familiar nonetheless. "Yes?"

"What a delightful surprise! I am Lord Oswald of Darrelby. I believe you knew my brother in the Holy Land."

Knew him? Why, Osric of Darrelby had been with him through the worst of the fighting, steady and truer than even Demetrius, and had saved his life more than once with a well-aimed blow or warning cry.

What he had thought was familiarity was a family resemblance. Osric had had the same nose and the same wide mouth as Lord Oswald, but he had been skin and bones when he died. "I am very glad to say I did."

Lord Oswald surveyed his injury. "I arrived yesterday after the tournament and heard you had been wounded, so I didn't wish to trouble you last night. You are feeling better, I trust, since you came to mass."

"Yes. I had excellent care. I am delighted to meet you, my lord. My father spoke of you often, too, when he returned from his visits to Wessex."

"Your father and I were great friends, and how he bragged about you! He thought your elder brother a fine fellow in his own way, he always said, but when he spoke of you ... well, I never saw a man more proud. A great pity he died while you were away from home. And your mother, too, I understand?"

"Yes, my lord, he died shortly after she did."

"Truly unfortunate."

"Yes, my lord."

Lord Oswald clapped a beefy arm around Connor's shoulder and steered him toward the hall. "Osric was lucky to have you for a friend, especially at the last. He said so in his last epistle. We thought it must have been written on his deathbed."

Connor nodded, and wondered if he should tell Lord Oswald the particulars of Osric's death, when he had been sick of fever and starved because of the neglect of his king. Richard took every care to make sure he himself was comfortable; he spared considerably less thought for his men. "I was with him when a priest wrote the letter at his behest."

"I am glad he was not alone among foreigners."

"There were many Normans sick and dying with him."

Before reaching the hall, Oswald turned him toward a corner of the courtyard which was relatively secluded. "I would speak to you in private a moment."

Once in the alcove, Lord Oswald dropped his arm and faced him, his brow furrowed with concern. "I have heard that the Crusade was not conducted as one might expect, given the amount of money raised for it. I also heard that you said as much to the king himself, and suffered for it."

How many other people believed that had been the cause of their quarrel, as if he were some kind of miser keeping watch over coins? "It was not of money I spoke, my lord. It was the massacre of the unarmed prisoners at Acre that caused me to criticize my king."

"As a man of honor, you could do no less."

Although he was delighted to have someone agree that he was right, this was dangerous ground, as he well knew, for such talk could be accounted treason. "Many would say it was not my place to upbraid our sovereign."

"Then they mistake the duty of a knight. Sometimes a man of honor must speak to those above him who lack it." Lord Oswald slid him a glance that was at once shrewd and curious. "There are many of us who do not believe our king and his military adventures should be paid for by exorbitant taxes or by making bargains with our enemies. Why, he undid the treaty with the Scots king, a just punishment for their rebellion, in exchange for ten thousand marks. And he has said he would sell London, if he could, to finance his grandiose schemes."

"I am a loyal subject of my rightful king."

"Despite what he has done to your family?"

"My family?"

The nobleman's brow furrowed with puzzlement, as if he couldn't believe Connor didn't know something of vital importance.

His chest constricted. It had been two years since he had left his home a second time, and he had not written or heard from them since. Surely Caradoc wouldn't be stubbornly silent about anything serious. He would have sent word—if he had known where to find his roving brother.

"The taxes on your family's Welsh estate are three times that of similar estates in England."

Not death. Not illness. Not arrest or imprisonment. Thank God.

Then the significance of Lord Oswald's words struck him. "Three times?"

"No other Welsh estates are taxed as your family's has been since you were sent from the king's presence."

He had ascribed Caradoc's barely controlled rage during their final argument to anger about his banishment from the king's retinue because of the disgrace to the family, as well as the old conflict about the cost of his knightly equipage, but nothing more.

Connor slumped back against the wall. It wasn't like Caradoc to spare his younger brother's feelings—unless he had not had the chance. He had walked out during the argument and departed Llanstephan immediately. Perhaps Caradoc had not had time to get to the taxes.

"I am sorry, Sir Connor. I thought you knew. I also assumed you knew that Richard can be vindictive. This kingdom would be better off if someone would rid us of such a ruler."

Was he talking about assassination?

"Perhaps God will take him sooner rather than later, eh?" Lord Oswald said with a chuckle as he once again put his arm about Connor's shoulder and turned toward the hall.

Not assassination, but only wishful thinking.

"Enough talk of Richard. I would rather hear about the Crusade. Osric never spoke of it in his letter, except that he was glad to be out of the fighting."

He didn't want to discuss Richard or describe the Crusade. He wanted to ride home at once and find out for himself from Caradoc if what Lord Oswald said was true.

He would be a long time in the saddle getting home, and he knew from experience that could make a healthy man's body ache. Perhaps the holy brother could supply him with a salve or ointment to lessen the pain. "If you excuse me, my lord, I believe I should seek out Brother Jonathan for something to ease my aching shoulder."

"Of course I excuse you, and I am sorry to hear that your injury troubles you, Sir Connor. I hope the good brother can be of assistance."

"As do I, my lord, as do I."

Connor headed across the courtyard toward the dispensary. He would go to the king's justiciar and demand . . . ask . . . request . . . that something be done. He could not go to Richard, even though the king was in England for only the second time in his reign.

For Richard had sworn to charge him with treason and have him executed if he ever saw Connor's face again, and he didn't doubt Richard meant that as much as anything he had ever said in his life.

Yet he must do *something*.

If there was anything to be grateful for in Richard's vindictive vengeance, it was that he had given him even better cause to leave Montclair, before his feelings for Lady Allis grew any stronger, weaving tendrils of desire and hope about his lonely heart.

Chapter 9

As he stepped through the tent flap, Connor hoped Lady Allis wasn't there waiting to help with any of the squires' injuries. Just seeing her would tempt him to linger in Montclair, and that he could not do.

Thankfully, Brother Jonathan was alone, muttering as he took account of the items on the long trestle table before him.

He peered at Connor as he approached. "Ah, the shoulder out of joint," he said, as if that were his name. "How do you fare today?"

"It is not too painful, unless I move it, but since it is my intention to leave as soon as I can pack up my things, I was wondering if there was a salve or ointment you could provide to dull the pain. I can pay you, of course." *If it is not too expensive.*

"I see. Give me your right hand, please."

He obeyed and Brother Jonathan felt his pulse. "Payment will not be necessary, for you should not ride."

"I must."

"Make a fist, please. Urgent business calls you elsewhere?"

"Yes, extremely urgent."

"Ah. Now with the left." Brother Jonathan pursed his lips. "Although I can perceive no serious damage at present, I would urge you to wait at least a fortnight before traveling."

Impossible.

Brother Jonathan let go and regarded him gravely. "By God's grace, there is no damage to the flow of your blood, or lack of sensation. However, if you do not let the joint and muscles around your shoulder heal properly—and that means gradually—you could do lasting harm, and the ball is much more likely to slip out again. Every time that happens, it will mean more trouble, until you may be permanently crippled."

Crippled. He forced away the images of knights missing eyes or limbs, wracked with pain, barely alive. "I can grip with my knees for a very long time, Brother. I have been hours in battle, when I held on only with my knees."

"You may be able to stay upon your horse, Sir Connor, but have you considered that an injured man will be a target for every outlaw and thief along the road?"

Never having traveled alone while injured before, he had not. He could not help his family if he was dead.

Brother Jonathan seemed to realize he had made his point. "Beginning tomorrow, you may slip the sling from your arm and move it upward a little. Then a bit higher the next day. By the Sabbath, you can lift some small objects."

It sounded like a species of slow torture. "As gradual as that?"

Brother Jonathan's hazel eyes softened with sympathy. "Yes. I say this not out of some urge to do you further harm, Sir Connor, or to cause you any difficulty. I want you to heal as fully as possible, God willing."

He resigned himself to the inevitable, and told himself that since Caradoc had been paying exorbitant taxes for two years, one more fortnight couldn't make much difference. "I understand and I shall do as you say. I shall stay until you think there is little chance of the injury happening again, and I can hold my shield. I also thank you for all the help you have already provided."

The little man blushed as if unused to gratitude, then bustled over to his table. "You need have no concern about prevailing upon the earl's hospitality," he said as he fussed about with his pots and potions. "I have Lady Allis's assurance that no one injured during the tournament should leave unless I think they are fit."

"She is most generous."

"Indeed, she is. A true example of Christian virtue."

"Especially honor thy father and thy mother, I think," he suggested as he strolled closer, ostensibly examining the objects on the table.

"The Ten Commandments are from the Old Testament, my son, but yes, she is a fine example of how a child should care for an infirm parent."

He wondered if a man could go to hell for cajoling information from a holy man, then ignored any qualms. "I gather she has had some help managing the estate from the Baron DeFrouchette. Have the earl's other friends also been as generous with their assistance?"

"No, but they did not need to be."

He made a shocked face. "They *did* offer, did they not? Surely they did not abandon the earl's family when they realized he was not well."

"No, not at all. The baron assured them he was taking care of everything."

Or taking *control* of everything?

"Sir Connor, is there some reason you are pestering Brother Jonathan about my family's affairs?" Lady Allis demanded.

He wheeled around and found Lady Allis glaring at him, her eyes shooting veritable daggers of righteous indignation at him and he flushed with shame.

Allis was glad to see him blush, which proved he had some notion of the insolence of his questions.

"I meant no harm, my lady."

He could apologize all he wanted, and look at her with those eyes all he liked, but he still had no right to inquire about such things. After all, it was not as if he could change anything.

She addressed Brother Jonathan. "I came to tell you the melee is about to start. Bob and Harry are already in the field with the litter."

Brother Jonathan's eyes widened as if he had forgotten why he was in the tent. "It is? They are? By Our Lady, I must go!"

He ran out, leaving her alone with the inquisitive Sir Connor, whom she should chastise for his impertinent nosiness.

Except that the words stuck in her throat.

"Forgive my curiosity, my lady," he said in a deep, gentle tone that sent warmth spiraling through her. "I was wrong to ask such questions."

"Yes, you were." She held her breath, waiting for him to explain. Then she realized it might be better if he didn't. Either he was interested in her because he liked her or else he had other, less benign reasons for asking about her situation, and if that were so, she would prefer never to find that out.

"May I be admitted to the armory to examine what is left of my lance?"

He sounded so calm, so logical, while her heart fluttered and danced just from being near him, in spite of all her vows and resolutions.

"Of course," she said, trying to be as cool and self-possessed as he.

Their discussion, such as it was, was now at an end. He should be leaving. Or she should be leaving.

Neither one of them moved and the silence seemed to stretch tight like a line with a great strain upon it. She remembered being alone with him in the garden. The pleasure and freedom of his company. The way his smile made her feel, and his words. His lips upon her wrist.

How much she yearned to reach out and touch his face. She might have, had she been free.

"Brother Jonathan says it will be at least a fortnight before my shoulder will be healed enough for me to leave. I greatly appreciate your hospitality, my lady."

Drawn back to reality, and away from winsome thoughts that could only bring her pain, she said, "It is my father's, too."

He shifted closer. No, he was not as coolly aloof as

he acted, for in his eyes, she saw an echo of her own turmoil.

Joy and sadness, bliss and sorrow, contended within her, and beneath it all, as the bedrock beneath the sand, was burning, fervent desire. Longing— intense as the flames of a conflagration—unfurled and surged through her body, and she was powerless to move away.

"You have a fine family, my lady, one to be proud of. One worth sacrificing for."

He knew. He understood why she was marrying Rennick. Why she had no other choice. "Sometimes love demands such sacrifices from us."

She had never spoken of love of any kind to Rennick, or any other man. She had never wanted to, or thought they would understand if she did. Only here and now, with this man, did that word pass her lips.

"Which does not render it the less impressive." He looked at the ground. "Not everyone is so unselfish."

He glanced up at her, and the questioning, humble look in his eyes nearly undid her. She would never have suspected he could look so vulnerable.

"I have been selfish and unthinking. I have acted without regard to my family or how my words and deeds might affect them." She realized he was trying to smile and it was all she could do not to caress his cheek. "I have also been impetuous, as you know, my lady."

"I do not mind that you kissed me," she whispered, flushing beneath his steadfast gaze, feeling again the gentle, wondrous pressure of his lips on her wrist, and remembering the restless thoughts that had kept her awake that night.

Relief crossed his features. "I feared you would think me a lascivious lout, and that would have given me pain as great as my injury."

There was no false note in his words, but only sincerity.

She wanted to embrace him, to feel his arms around her. She wanted to hold him close and tell him how hard it was for her, that she wished time and time again that there could be another choice for her. She wanted to assure him that it took every morsel of her determination and self-control to do what she felt necessary, and there was not a moment that very same determination and self-control did not seem about to waver and disappear.

But she dared not, or she knew, just as surely as she drew breath, that her resolve would finally crumble into dust and blow away in the wind.

She could not allow that. She had to be strong, always. On her shoulders alone rested her family's security.

Even calling on all the inner strength she possessed, she could not bring herself to leave, although this would be the wise thing to do. Yet she could retreat to safer ground. "My brother finds you quite fascinating."

He blinked, obviously unsettled by the change of subject. "Because I have been on the Crusade."

"He hopes you will tell him all about it."

"If I did, he would be sorely disappointed. There was little glory in the East."

"Then you will not fill his head with exciting tales of great battles and daring?"

He grimly shook his head. "Not I, my lady. Indeed, I would rather not speak of those days at all. They hold little but memories I would prefer to forget. Perhaps you can tell him that for me."

She should have talked of something else. "I am sorry for raising such a painful subject."

"There is no need for you to feel sorry. You did not tell me exciting stories so that I was fixed upon going, no matter the cost to my family. I will not set another young man's feet on the supposed path to glory knowing that it more often ends in pain and sorrow."

She moved away from him and his anguished eyes. "I have heard of your quarrel with the king. Did that cause you pain and sorrow?"

"In part, but we also suffered from deprivation because of his enthusiasm and his vow to take Jerusalem at any cost."

"Which he did not accomplish, despite the cost."

"Which he did not accomplish," he confirmed, coming toward her. "There were many times I wished I had not gone."

"You did what you believed was right."

"Yes, my lady," he whispered, so close to her now, his words seemed like the prelude to his kiss.

She wanted his kiss, his lips upon hers. Already she felt more affection for him than she did for Rennick and probably ever would. Surely it was no wonder, then, that she yearned for his touch, to be caressed as if she were cherished and not bought. More, she wanted him to possess her completely, as she would him. She longed to discover what it was to be intimate with a man she desired with every fiber of her being, the need burning in her like a fire burning out of control in the high summer.

If such dreams were a sin, she would sin. What harm did it do to picture him holding her, sharing her bed? Instantly, that image—and more—burst into her mind. His naked body over hers. The expression of desire on his features, blatant and hot. She beneath him, anticipating his thrust, so eager for him it was desperation.

Then she realized why it was wrong to have such thoughts. She did not want to let them remain a maiden's fantasy.

As if God Himself felt the need to interrupt, voices raised and anxious sounded nearby. Flushing as if she had discovered Sir Connor had shared her lustful vision, she backed away. "Somebody must be hurt."

Although he could do little with his shoulder injured, he might be of some use fetching bandages or medicines, so although Connor inwardly cursed himself for an impulsive cur, he did not leave the tent.

Once again, he had been too forward, too inappropriately intimate. She had only done him good and looked at him with gentle sympathy, but God save him, he had almost kissed her again, even though she was betrothed to another. It didn't matter that she was, without question, the most tempting woman he had ever met his life. He must be more careful. They were separated by rank, by wealth, by duty—by all the barriers society erected.

Bob and Harry, panting hard, ran in with their litter. On it, deathly pale and sweating, lay a young, red-haired squire. Connor saw no blood, but that didn't mean the youth was not seriously injured. His wound had not bled, either.

"What happened?" Lady Allis demanded.

"He was fine in the melee," Bob answered. "Not hit or nothing."

No broken lance, then.

"He got off his horse," Harry continued, "and then

he staggered and fell. Fainted, we thought, and so he had, but it looks a sight worse than just that."

Connor had to agree. He had known men who had trouble bearing the weight and heat of their armor, but this was the worst he had ever seen anybody suffer who had not been wounded, too.

"Let me see him," Brother Jonathan cried as he rushed into the tent.

Connor quickly stepped out of the way to let him pass.

Brother Jonathan bent over the young man, examining him.

Then, suddenly, everything stopped. Brother Jonathan, Lady Allis and the two soldiers formed a tableau of shock and dismay as they stared at the youth.

Connor knew what that meant. The squire had died.

Lady Isabelle ran into the tent and halted confusedly. "Percival?"

With a stricken expression that tore at his heart, Lady Allis went to her sister. "Come away, Isabelle."

Too stunned by the sight before her, the young woman didn't move. "What has happened? What's wrong with Percival?"

"Isabelle, please, come with me."

Nearly as pale as the squire, the girl still stood motionless, staring with disbelieving eyes at the body on the litter and the other three men averting their gaze. "No, I want to stay and help."

Death was never easy to look upon, and his heart filled with pity for her as he stepped forward. "Please, my lady, go with your sister. You cannot help him."

Isabelle's mouth formed the silent word.

"Yes," he gently confirmed. "He is dead."

With a loud cry, the girl fell sobbing to her knees. Lady Allis put her arms around her, trying to help her stand even as she glared at him over her sister's head.

"She is old enough for the truth." Although he believed that, he felt a stab of regret. He should have left that truth for her sister, who knew Isabelle far better than he did.

Lady Allis helped the sobbing Isabelle to her feet. "Come, Isabelle, come with me."

"I should have given him my scarf," she wailed. "I didn't and now he's dead."

"Yes, I know. Come away, dear. There is nothing we can do here."

Slowly, with Isabelle crying and Lady Allis supporting her, the two women left the tent.

Brother Jonathan covered the body with a blanket, then wiped his anxious, perspiring face, while Bob and Harry shuffled their feet awkwardly. "You two may go."

"I pray there are no more serious injuries today," he muttered to himself after the soldiers left and he sat heavily on one of the cots.

"What happened?"

With a heavy sigh, Brother Jonathan scratched his chin. "Young Edmond, who was watching with us, did say that Percival had not been feeling very well this morning, but felt fit enough to be in the melee. If I had heard that beforehand, I might have stopped him."

"You think it was an illness than killed him?"

The little man slowly shook his head. "Not an ague or similar malady. I think it was his heart. Or apoplexy."

"Surely he is too young to die from such a thing."

"It is rare, but it does happen. With the excitement

of the melee, the heat from his armor and clothing . . . it is possible, especially if he had a weak heart before."

"Did he?"

Brother Jonathan spread his hands in a gesture of helplessness. "He may have. Often men have no idea of the weakness lurking within their own bodies." He got to his feet. "I had better go tell the baron, if he doesn't already know."

"The baron? Lord Montclair is the host."

"Percival was the baron's squire, and the earl must be told carefully. He will surely be upset and agitated." Brother Jonathan ran his hand over his tonsure. "Oh, sweet heaven. The burial."

The church frowned on tournaments and had decreed that those killed in them should be denied ecclesiastical burial. Participants were supposedly condemned to suffer eternal torment in hell, including wearing armor nailed into their flesh, unremovable.

Despite his skepticism over these stories, Connor shivered. He had managed to subdue such fears for a long time, for no one had died in a tournament in which he had participated, but what if they were right, and he was killed? Would God take his reason for being in a tournament into account? Would He remember that he had tried to do good by going with the king on Crusade?

"Percival did not die fighting in the tournament, but afterward," he noted.

Relief flooded over Brother Jonathan's round face. "Yes, that's true. So there is no reason he cannot be buried with the necessary rites. Or maybe the baron will decide to send the body home to his family for burial. His father is the earl of L'Ouisseaux."

The earl of L'Ouisseaux was one of the most powerful men in the kingdom, and one whose exact loyalties were a mystery, even to the king and his brother John. It was an interesting alliance for the baron—now broken.

Brother Jonathan turned toward the entrance to the tent. "If you will excuse me."

"May I walk with you, Brother? I am going to the armory."

The little man nodded his acquiescence, and together they went to the castle. Once past the gate, Brother Jonathan bade him farewell and headed toward the hall, while Connor swiftly crossed the courtyard, noting as he did that all seemed quiet and subdued. The death of a man in a tournament was a serious matter; the death of one like Percival, from an important family, was even more momentous.

He glanced at the hall, wondering how Lady Allis and her family were faring. He hoped she did not assume any blame for what had happened. She already bore so much upon her slender shoulders.

He reached the keep of the castle and pushed open the door. Inside, it was like a combination carpenter's shop and smithy. It smelled like both—and something else besides. A long wooden bench covered in tools and bits of wood stood in the center. A hearth was at the far end and glowing hot. Near it lay metal for fashioning arrow tips and swords, and a pile of kindling. Plain shields and two painted lances leaned against the wall. Several swords, used by the garrison no doubt, were in stands near the door, held in racks by their hilts.

The man working at the bench was huge, the tallest man he had ever seen, and perhaps the most filthy. His dark, greasy hair hung lank about his shoulders, and his clothes looked as if they had never been washed.

The man's body odor explained the unusual scent of the room.

"Ya?" he growled in a German accent as he continued to repair the hilt of a sword.

"You are the armorer?"

"Ya."

"I have come to find my lance, which was broken in the melee yesterday."

"Ya?"

This was not going to be an easy conversation. "I understand the broken weapons are brought here."

"Ya." The man nodded toward the opposite wall.

The two lances there had broken ends. "Mine was shattered."

"Ah. Ya." This time, the man stopped working and gestured at the pile of kindling.

"The pieces are there?"

The man shook his head, then pointed into the hearth.

"You *burned* them?"

"Ya," the armorer confirmed, going back to work.

Connor tried to keep calm and not betray any rancor. "On anyone's orders?"

The German glanced up, puzzled, as he shook his head before once more returning to his task.

Connor stalked out of the armory. Perhaps the armorer's fire was the usual fate for broken lances at Montclair, or perhaps someone was cleverly covering his tracks. Either way, now he would never have proof that his lance had been tampered with.

Lost in his rancorous thoughts, he walked right into Lord Oswald. "My lord! Forgive my haste!"

Lord Oswald reached out a broad hand to steady him. "You look upset, as we all are today."

Connor forced away his frustration. "Although I didn't know the young man, a death in a melee is always disturbing."

"The baron plans to take the boy's body home to his father. He says it is the least he can do."

Connor tried not to betray any emotion, and certainly not even a hint of pleasure at the news that the baron would be gone from Montclair. "That is good of him."

Lord Oswald nodded at the armory. "You had business with the talkative Attila?"

"He never said his name."

"No, he wouldn't."

"I was asking about my lance. It was broken in the melee yesterday."

"Ah, yes. Can it be repaired?"

"It was burned." He thought of telling Osric's brother what he suspected, but since he had no proof, he would pay heed to Lady Allis's warning and hold his tongue. After all, it had cost her something to caution him. He had seen the struggle in her beautiful eyes. "It was little more than tinder anyway, I suppose."

Lord Oswald was obviously shocked. "Tinder?"

"Yes, it shattered when I struck the baron's shield."

"How unfortunate! I have heard of such things happening, if the wood is old. Still, between your accident and the lad's death, I am beginning to think this tournament is cursed."

Chapter 10

Late that night, Rennick looked around the chapel, assuring himself that only he, Oswald and Auberan were there. Oswald stood near the statue of the Virgin, his large bulk partially in shadow.

Rennick's gaze lingered a moment on the Madonna, her hands folded in prayer and her head bowed. She looked like Allis, only much more submissive. Of course, Mary submitted herself to God, while Allis would have to submit to him.

Auberan hurried toward him. "How can you be smiling? This is terrible. Had you no notion the lad was weak?"

"Of course I didn't know he was ill. Otherwise, I would have prevented him from participating," Rennick replied evenly.

"Albert L'Ouisseaux was a valuable ally," Oswald remarked.

"There is no reason he cannot continue to be an ally," Rennick said. "Brother Jonathan does not suspect foul play."

"Then you . . . then you . . ."

Rennick glared at the stammering Auberan. "Are you accusing me of something?"

"No, not at all. I meant . . . then you think L'Ouisseaux will still be with us?"

"He hates the king as much as anyone, although he hides it better than most," Oswald said. He smiled as he looked at Rennick, and it was not a pleasant smile. "He was not chosen to be in the king's retinue or given any position at court, either."

Auberan stared at him, understanding dawning on his stupid face.

"Yet all have to pay to finance Richard's quests," Rennick said. "That is our complaint against the king."

"Oh, yes, nothing personal about it," Oswald said with only the slightest hint of a sneer. "Still, a great pity about Percival. I had hopes for him and young Isabelle. If he married your sister-in-law, Rennick, that would have allied you with L'Ouisseaux even more. Now we must find another husband for the charming Lady Isabelle, and another alliance." He looked pointedly at Auberan.

Rennick could barely keep a scowl off his face. Oswald wanted him united in a family alliance with Auberan de Beaumartre? Having that dolt, even though he was a rich dolt, chained to him by matrimony was not a pleasant prospect.

Auberan, however, fairly beamed at the suggestion.

No doubt the fool saw himself hitching his cart to Rennick's horse and being pulled along to power, just as he was using Oswald.

"The poor girl was naturally very upset," Oswald continued. "Perhaps she is in need of comfort, Auberan. Why don't you go and see if you can speak to her? If you can, be sure to say nothing of yourself— only Percival. This is no time to make your goal clear, do you understand me?"

"Yes, my lord," he answered, fairly running to the door.

After he had gone, Oswald turned toward Rennick. "So tell me, how is it a man dies in the prime of his youth?"

He regarded Oswald steadily and lied easily. "His heart was weak and gave out. Or it was apoplexy, according to Brother Jonathan."

Brother Jonathan was clever and learned, but he was young and the drug Rennick had obtained, made from foxglove, was not widely known to affect the heart. Indeed, he hadn't even been sure himself that it would have the desired result despite the assurances of the apothecary in London, a man who had made his reputation by experimenting on the destitute.

Unfortunately, he had not considered that perhaps Oswald knew something about substances that would mimic a natural death.

Oswald strolled back toward the statue of the Virgin Mary. Bending, he blew out one of the votive candles, then smiled with mischievous satisfaction. "I am likewise glad to think that Sir Connor's visit to the armory this afternoon did not produce embarrassing results. I understand he was asking about his lance."

Although his heart raced, Rennick kept his expression as innocuous as Oswald's. "Surely he cannot believe he can fix it. It was shattered to pieces."

Oswald blew out another candle before replying. "Yes. Whatever he wanted it for, it was not there. It was smashed into tinder, and as tinder it was used." He slid Rennick a condemning glance. "I think it is time you stopped taking matters into your own hands, Rennick. I will not have my plans disrupted by childish schemes." He sauntered toward his companion. "It is a lucky thing for you that even I cannot prove Percival's death was murder. We must be above reproach, and if there is any shred of proof that a man allied with me is guilty of a crime, I will cut him loose without hesitation. Do you understand me?"

"Yes, my lord, I understand."

"As for Auberan, I know better than you that he is a stupid fool who will soon prove to be more of a liability than an asset. I will see to him. In the meantime, we shall keep him happy by dangling pretty little Isabelle of Montclair before his nose."

Two days later, Connor walked through the courtyard of Montclair Castle shortly after the evening meal had concluded, heading back to the ward where he was encamped.

Since Percival's death, Lady Allis had not appeared again in the great hall, nor had her father. The baron, who was to leave tomorrow to take the squire's body home, had taken the place of host in the interval. He acted as if Montclair belonged to him and seemed to forget it was his squire's death that had temporarily put him in the earl's carved chair.

Connor paused, looking up at the wall walk and the

sentries patrolling there, a habit born of long years at war. Clouds, thin and dark, raced swiftly across the moon, and the breeze was chill enough to make him shiver. Wrapping his right arm about his left in the sling, he hoped Lady Allis was taking a few moments for herself at this time, or she might become ill, too, from fatigue and worry. He had seen it happen thus. Perhaps there was some way he could suggest—

He walked briskly toward the wicket in the gate. He was in no position to suggest anything to the chatelaine of Montclair and had troubles of his own to deal with.

Nevertheless, as he went past the chapel, he paused once more and looked back at the hall. He had no doubt that Lady Allis was a competent, strong-willed woman, yet it must be difficult for her, with a father incapable of leading the family, a future husband she despised, and having to be a parent to two younger siblings. She had responsibilities the like of which he had never known. No one depended on him for their security or happiness. No one came to him for comfort when they were in pain, or to share their joy.

To be sure, Cordelia had begged him to stay at Llanstephan, but she didn't need him. The king had not needed him; he had cast him out as he might dismiss an unruly servant. Nobody needed him, except to earn money, like a common laborer, and only then because he himself had vowed to do so. Caradoc had not even asked that of him, probably because he could not believe his headstrong, selfish little brother could change.

Caradoc was wrong. He *could* change. Since his return from the East, he had done all he could to help, with the one exception of going to Richard himself, and given what had happened between them, that was impossible. Yet what had he to show for it?

"Oh, God," he whispered as wave after wave of desolate sorrow washed over him. What good was he to anybody? If he died tomorrow, who on this earth would miss or mourn him?

Cordelia, and his horse.

Humbled and ashamed, a great wave of loneliness and despair washed over him as he leaned against the wall, his head bowed with the weight of his pain. The last time he had felt truly needed or wanted was when he held Osric dying in his arms. And perhaps a little that night in the garden, when he had tried to make Lady Allis smile. Or maybe he had been deluding himself about that, too. Maybe she had just indulged him, as she might a child who amused her. Perhaps she had warned him not to accuse the baron, but simply because she had enough to deal with and didn't want an irate future husband on her hands, too.

On the wall walk above, two sentries exchanged greetings. His pride rebelled at being seen in such a state by even a sentry, so he slipped inside the chapel, where he tried to conquer his despair and regain his self-control.

Two candles burned upon the altar, and the votive candles beneath the Madonna added to the feeble light. A hint of incense lingered in the air.

He came farther inside and realized he was not alone.

A woman knelt before the Madonna, her back to him. Her head bowed, her hands covered her face and her shoulders shook as she wept, the sobs wracking her slender frame.

Who was it? Lady Allis? It was difficult to imagine her strength giving way to such heart-wrenching sobs, but not impossible.

Intending to offer some words of comfort, he took a few swift steps forward. Then he hesitated.

As he dreaded being seen in his moment of weakness, so would she. She was as much a warrior in her own right as he ever was or would be, and her battles were as terrible as any he had ever known. He must respect her as he would Osric, if Osric were in her place. He must not speak to her of her pain unless she gave him leave to do so.

The woman raised her head and glanced over her shoulder. It wasn't Lady Allis, but young Isabelle, her cheeks wet with tears and her eyes red with crying.

She jumped to her feet like a startled deer. "What do you want?"

As it was wrong to be alone with Lady Allis, it was wrong to be alone with her younger sister. "Forgive me for intruding—"

"It's . . . it's all right," she stammered, coming toward him. "You don't have to go."

"I must, my lady," he said, turning.

"Please, I would like to talk to you a moment, if I may."

"Your sister will not—"

"Allis is busy with our father. He took Percival's death very hard. She'll be lucky if she can get him to sleep tonight. She thinks I don't know how difficult he can be sometimes, but I do." She sniffled and wiped her nose on her long, dangling cuff as she came closer. I thought . . . I thought I would come and pray to the Holy Mother to look after Percival."

She looked very young and vulnerable, and very much in need of comfort, and he suspected she needed to give voice to her feelings. "And I will pray that he be taken into the glorious company of St. Michael the

Archangel. For an honorable young knight on the verge of manhood, that does not seem too much to ask."

She made a tremulous smile. "Percival wanted to go on the Crusade, as you did, but he was too young. I suggested he ask you about the Crusade and being in the king's retinue."

"You are a very wise young lady."

She looked at him another moment, then burst into tears and buried her face in her hands. "I'm a fool. A selfish, stupid fool," she wailed.

"You could not know he was going to die," he said softly.

"But I might have been nicer to him. I was so horrid!" She began to cry in earnest, her shoulders shaking, her whole body trembling with sorrow. She reminded him of Cordelia, crying when he quarreled with Caradoc.

So he did what he should have done with Cordelia, instead of riding off like a pigheaded fool. He put his right arm around her and let her lay her sobbing head against his shoulder. "He was better off in England."

"But he's dead!"

"He didn't suffer much, though. He might have suffered a good deal on the Crusade, and been dead just the same."

"He would have died in a glorious cause," Isabelle sobbed. "He would have been with the king, too."

Connor clenched his teeth. This was not the time or place to tell the truth about Richard.

"Take your hands off my sister!"

Isabelle pushed him away, the sudden movement sending a pain shooting through his left shoulder. "Allis!"

The chatelaine of Montclair stood at the door of the chapel, her hands on her hips and ire in her eyes.

He stepped away from Isabelle, holding out his hand in a placating gesture. He could guess how their positions looked to her.

"I was crying and he—" Isabelle began.

"Go to bed, Isabelle."

"Don't be angry will me, Allis," the girl pleaded. "We weren't doing anything wrong."

He stepped forward and spoke before there was another quarrel. "No, we were not."

Paying no heed to him, Lady Allis's expression softened. "I'm not angry with you, Isabelle. Please go on to bed."

"Sir Connor was only being nice to me. We were talking about Percival. You've been so busy with Father, I didn't want to disturb you, so—"

"I understand. Please leave us."

With obvious reluctance, Isabelle obeyed. She glanced over her shoulder at Connor before she slipped out the door.

While Lady Allis might excuse her sister, he feared she would not be so quick to forgive him, so he hurried to explain. "I only sought to comfort her in her grief. Death is never easy, especially if you are full of remorse for things left undone and unsaid, or regret those things you have done and said. I merely offered her a shoulder to cry on."

Unappeased, Lady Allis frowned and crossed her arms. "And a very broad shoulder it is, as I'm sure you know. Were you going to kiss her wrist, too, or do you save that for older women?"

"I've only done that once."

She raised a skeptical brow.

"Whether you believe me or not, it's true. And I certainly don't try to seduce distraught girls."

"Only older, betrothed women?"

"I wasn't trying to seduce you." He had certainly wanted to kiss her and he wouldn't have refused had she indicated she was willing to do more, but it had not been his intention to woo her into his bed.

"Perhaps you think to win my love and marry an heiress of Montclair. Exactly which one makes no difference."

Pride and indignation roared through him as he strode toward her. "I am not a harlot, willing to sell myself for gain, not while I have even one good arm to fight with."

"So you say."

"It is the truth."

It was the fierce defiance in his eyes, the firm conviction of his voice and the very way he stood that made her believe him. He did not see her as a means to reduce his poverty. He did not crave her body only to assuage his lust. He had no evil designs on Isabelle.

She turned away, ashamed of the jealousy that had seized her when she saw him holding Isabelle. There had been nothing lascivious in the way they stood, but hot anger had surged through her nonetheless.

That foolish jolt had to be merely another sign of the strain she had been under the last few days. Her father's reaction to Percival's death had been even worse than she had feared. He had moaned and wept, and only Brother Jonathan's sleeping draft had given him any peace. Unfortunately, it was potent, so she had to use it sparingly, which meant she had spent hours in his chamber, trying to soothe him with her voice and

happy stories of the past, to little avail. She had realized Isabelle was grieving, and Edmond upset, but her
father's demands took almost all her time.

The night after Percival's death, she had stolen
away to the wall walk, where the breeze blew cool and
fresh. She looked at Sir Connor's tent, off by itself,
alone and apart, like the man himself. Like her.

She had let herself imagine going to that tent while
he slept and wordlessly joining him in his narrow cot.
She had almost felt his firm, soft lips upon hers, his
kiss demanding a response she would eagerly give.
His strong, lean hands would caress her, and his light-
est touch would send thrills of exquisite delight
through her.

He was too tempting. She must force him away
from her, for the sake of what had to be, and her own
heart, which already ached because of what could
never be. She must be harsh and firm, strong and absolute. "Whatever you were doing, stay away from
both of us, Welshman."

Dismay and confusion flitted over his features for
the briefest of moments before anger returned.

"As you command, so I will do, my lady," he
growled, "as long as you understand that while I may
be poor, I am not yet desperate enough to use a
woman in so mercenary a way. I confess that first your
beauty stirred me, but now it is the bold, spirited
woman I admire. And I assure you, there is only one
woman in Montclair I would like to take to my bed,
and it is not your sister."

He pulled her hard against him. Before she could
move or speak, he kissed her, his mouth searing hers
with hot desire, his arm in the sling pressing against
her body. Her head spun, her knees softened . . . she

was powerless against the onslaught of sensation and need he aroused. She wanted to melt into his arms and ride upon the waves of passion he created, to become a creature of these exquisite sensations and never think of anything again. Never to be responsible again. Never to have to put duty before pleasure again. To be with him, only him, in a world alone and apart.

As she held onto him as if he were saving her from plunging to her death, his kiss gentled. It became more seeking than demanding, tentative and tender. Putting her arms about him, she gave him an answer.

Slowly, his tongue slid inside her parted lips. Questioning still, but when his touched hers, a jolt of raw excitement shot through her body.

She wanted more of this touch, these thrilling new sensations, this incredible excitement.

His kiss made her feel free—free to make some demands of her own. Giving herself up to that heady sensation, she leaned into him so that her whole body pressed against his virile one. Desire blossomed and grew, threading along every limb, as if she could soften and melt into him, melding her flesh to his forever.

Now she was the seeker, as a tense desperation rose when she felt his arousal through the fabric of her clothes.

His kiss was no longer tender and tentative. He kissed deeply, hungrily, demanding her response. Like a wanton, she ground her hips against him, inciting his passion as he did hers. A low moan sounded in her ears, and only vaguely did she understand that it came from her own throat, brought forth by her primitive need. Her grip on his broad shoulders tightened.

With a gasp, he broke the kiss. "A moment's pain,

no more," he assured her in a sultry whisper as he took her mouth again.

His wounded shoulder. Of course. Wounded by Rennick.

Reality slammed into her mind and she lurched back. "I am betrothed!"

His gaze searched her face. Then he smiled not with conquest or even blatant desire, but a tender wistfulness that seemed to reach out and grab her soul. "I have been selfish again. Forgive me." He touched her flushed cheek with the tip of his finger. "I cannot help myself."

Nor could she, and yet this must end.

He knew it, too, for he turned on his heel and left the chapel.

And her.

She ran her fingertips over her slightly swollen lips. She was betrothed to Rennick DeFrouchette, and for her family's sake she must become his wife.

She would repeat that to herself a thousand times if that was what it took to purge her desire for another man from her heart, and she would pray Sir Connor's shoulder healed quickly. When he was on his way, she would feel no more passion and no more yearning for something she could not have. In one way, she would be free—as the dead are free.

These thoughts were unworthy of her. She was a highborn lady who understood that with wealth and privilege came duty and responsibility. She must not be weak. She could not be selfish. Her father depended on her. He needed her to be strong, lest he give in to the melancholy that weakened him.

Today, when he had once again begged God to end

his sorrow and let him die, she had joined him in that prayer, asking God to call her father home to heaven.

She fell to her knees, clasping her hands so tightly, they hurt. She didn't want her father to die. She wanted him to live and be as he was. Yet if he couldn't be as he was, if death were truly a release . . .

Who else would be released? Whose freedom was she really praying for?

But oh, to have a strong arm about her offering her comfort, to be able to lean her head against the broad chest of a man who truly loved her . . .

"Dear Father in Heaven," she whispered, her eyes upon the stone altar, "is it wrong to pray for that?"

Putting her hands upon the floor, she slowly slipped downward, until she lay prone upon the cold stone floor.

And then she prayed for just one thing: the strength to do her duty.

Chapter 11

Standing beside his tent in the ward, Connor watched the grim and silent procession of soldiers led by the Baron DeFrouchette, the only noise that of the soldiers' jingling harness and the rumble of the covered cart's wooden wheels as it carried away a shrouded, myrrh-sprinkled body. They were taking Percival L'Ouisseaux home for the last time.

The ward itself was deserted except for Connor and Demetrius. Beginning the day after Percival's death, most of the visiting knights and their retinues had packed up and gone on their way, even the wounded ones. After all, they had homes to go to, and ones that would not be so mournful.

Sir Auberan, unfortunately, had remained behind, as had Lord Oswald. Like the baron, they had accommodation in the castle.

He was glad Lord Oswald had stayed. Lady Allis needed a friend at this time, and he could not take that place, no matter how much he wanted to. He had even made things worse by kissing her again.

God help him, was he never going to learn to subdue his impulses? He thought he had, but when he was alone with her, he could not. He had never felt this way about a woman before, as if when he was with her, all would be right with the world, and he could do anything. Solve any problem. Conquer any enemy. Mend any trouble he had caused, knowingly or unknowingly. As if he could be again what he was in the flower of his youth, only better, because he would have her to guide him.

Perhaps that was why he was so compelled to take her in his arms and taste her sweet lips. To feel her relax into his embrace was to feel worthy of her desire, her affection, her love.

Yet when he was alone, he feared that her passion was roused only because he was young and virile, and not the man she was fated to marry for duty. That she saw him not as Connor of Llanstephan, both good and bad, but simply as the means to assuage her desire and pent-up emotions. That he was a convenience as much as anything, and to think there was anything more between them was self-delusion.

With that in mind, he had avoided the hall except for meals. He had stayed near his horse and tent, and his only company had been a group of boys from the village who had appeared, watching him as he fed and brushed Demetrius. He invited them to come closer, and it was obvious they were very impressed by his war horse, as well they should be, for he was the best one Connor had ever encountered, too.

Then, half shy and half bold, they had asked about the king and the Crusade. He told them a bit about the journey and the battles, and because they were village boys, he made sure to talk about the grooms, the cooks and foot soldiers, and their valor under duress, which often surpassed that of spoiled rich men's sons. Yet he never made war sound like a glorious adventure, because it was not.

Now, out of respect for the dead, he bowed his head and stood motionless until the cart was past. When the last of the soldiers had disappeared through the barbican, Connor sighed and slipped his left arm out of the sling. Slowly, gingerly, he raised it.

"Still hurts like a spear's been thrust through it," he muttered to Demetrius, who was regarding him with what appeared to be compassionate sympathy.

He tried raising his arm again, and once more the pain shot through his shoulder and along his arm. "*O'r annwyl,*" he muttered through clenched teeth.

"I've never heard that word before."

Connor looked over his good shoulder and saw young Edmond of Montclair a few feet away, watching him.

"It's Welsh," he replied, carefully putting his arm back into the sling.

Edmond came closer. "What does it mean?"

"Oh, dear me."

"Really?"

"Near enough," and that was true enough. He was glad he hadn't said anything more colorful.

"Do you mind if I stay a bit?"

Connor thought of the grave and silent atmosphere in the hall and didn't blame the boy for wanting to be somewhere else. "Not at all. I will be glad for the company. Demetrius is about as talkative as Attila in the armory."

Edmond grinned, then pointed at Connor's shoulder. "Does it still hurt a lot?"

"More than I would like."

"Did you hear it pop out?"

"No, thank God," he said, amused by the lad's grisly curiosity. In that, Edmond was no different from the village boys. "I didn't even know what had happened until your sister told me."

Demetrius lifted his head and whinnied.

"Ah, he recognizes you and expects another apple. I've got another one in my tent you may give him."

Edmond nodded and eagerly got the fruit. As Edmond fed Demetrius his treat, Connor stroked the horse's neck.

"Would you like to try sitting on him?" he offered when the apple was gone.

Edmond turned to him with wide, excited eyes. "May I? I've never been on a war horse before."

"Then it is about time. Under other circumstances, I would gladly hoist you up there myself. As it is, you can use my camp stool to stand on."

Once more Edmond hurried into the tent, and he brought out the stool.

"I'll hold his bridle while you climb on." He saw Edmond's hesitation. "Remember what I said? Steady as a rock, he is, so he won't fidget."

With a determined nod, Edmond stood on the stool, put his arms over Demetrius's broad back and climbed on, struggling a bit to get his leg over. He grinned with delight when he was successful. "Steady as a rock," he confirmed.

"Your legs need to grow a bit."

"I'm tall for my age."

"Perhaps, but you are still short to sit comfortably on a destrier. But you've plenty of time to grow. And you must learn to control a smaller animal in the beginning anyway, or you might hurt yourself."

"I won't! I'm a good rider. Everybody says so."

Most people would tell a lad who stood to be an earl someday that he was good at anything he attempted. "Riding a destrier is different from other kinds of riding."

"How different?"

"You do not direct a war horse so much. A slight touch of ankle or knee—and no reins at all. You need to be free to move your arms. You have to learn to trust his instinct in battle, to turn when he turns and go where he will, once you are engaged. I have seen men crushed beneath another horse's hooves because they fought their own mounts."

"Why, that sounds simple, letting the horse do all the work."

"Wait until you are in a battle—in the thick of it, with the sweat running down your face and back, half blind in your helmet, deafened by the noise. Fear will strike you like you wouldn't ever have believed possible, no matter how ready you think you are, or well trained."

"I won't be afraid!"

"Aye, you will. Every man is, and that is not wrong. Fear will save you from foolhardiness, but it must not dominate you. In your fear, your instinct will tell you to try to control the horse, as you wish to control the battle, yet you must not. You must trust your horse while you fight and protect yourself. A good horse is worth his weight in gold, and more. He will be your trusted friend, the ally you have absolute faith in, and he may save your life."

A subdued Edmond stroked Demetrius's neck. "What about the king's horse? Has he saved Richard's life?"

"Richard has had many horses. He does not value them any more than he does his men."

"What do you mean?"

Connor wished he had not spoken that thought. Edmond was a little young to know how a king could use and discard his own men as if they were chess pieces on a board. "Let's walk a little."

He untied Demetrius and led him at a slow pace toward the inner curtain wall. He glanced back at the boy, who was swaying as if aboard a ship—and looking a little green about the gills, too. He immediately turned and led Demetrius back to the stool.

"When you are broader in the beam, it will be more comfortable," he said as the boy got down.

Edmond nodded, and for a moment, Connor feared he was going to throw up. He didn't, but he was obviously very grateful to get back onto the solid earth. Watching out of the corner of his eye as he tied Demetrius again, he saw the boy sit on the stool. "You have a horse, I assume?"

"Yes, a mare. Her name's Firebrand."

"She sounds tempestuous."

The boy shook his head. "Not very. She's a roan. I wanted a stallion, but Allis said no."

He was not about to get drawn into a discussion of Lady Allis and her restrictions. "If you like, I could teach you some things. You can learn many things on a roan's back that will stand you in good stead when you acquire a destrier. How to ride without using the reins, for one. How to balance with a shield on one arm and holding a lance in the other."

Edmond frowned. "I don't have a shield or lance."

"I saw some old shields in the armory. We can have one of them trimmed to better fit you, and so that the weight is right for your body. A spear will do for a lance. I promise you, young lordling, that will be plenty enough to get you started."

"I wish I could be your squire."

Connor wished he could, too, for he liked the young lad with his proud bravado and bright eyes so like his elder sister's. "You will be a lord's squire in good time."

"I would it could be soon. Allis treats me like a babe."

Connor smiled. "Ah, now there is a feeling I know too well. I thought the same thing of my elder brother, Caradoc."

"That's a funny name."

"It's a Welsh name, and the name of kings. It was a Caradoc who, although a captive, so impressed the emperor of Rome that he set him free, in a manner of speaking."

"What manner?"

"He wasn't enslaved, but he wasn't allowed to leave Rome. For a Welshman so far from home, that must have been a torture."

Edmond slipped off the stool onto the ground and gestured for Connor to sit. "Why a torture? Rome was the greatest city in the world."

"It was not his home. And I imagine he didn't much like the heat."

"I love the summer."

"As do I, but heat gets tiresome."

"You found it so in the East?"

"Aye, I did. I thought of ancient Caradoc often during those days. I imagined him pining for the cold winds of the mountains, or the gentle mists of the valleys, as I did."

"You were homesick?" Edmond asked incredulously.

"Yes. At first, it was an adventure, but then . . ."

"Then?"

"It is dry work, all this talking."

"So let's get something to drink."

"I have nothing in my tent," Connor noted with regret.

"I can ask Merva to get us something if we go to the hall."

Lady Allis would probably be in or around the hall. Surely she would be less likely to be in the kitchen at this time of the day. "Do you think we could go to the kitchen and see if the cook will spare us a little buttermilk?"

"Wouldn't you rather have wine?"

"It was buttermilk I dreamed of in the East, young lordling," he answered honestly. "Not wine or ale, but buttermilk."

Edmond got to his feet. "Then buttermilk it will be, for both of us."

"I see you have already learned one of the most important lessons for a knight."

"What's that?"

Connor ruffled the lad's blond hair. "Courtesy."

"I would do anything to make Lady Isabelle smile," Auberan whispered to Allis as the three of them sat near the hearth.

You could go away. She and Isabelle had embroidery

to busy their hands, if not their thoughts, while Auberan apparently had nothing better to do than hover about them like an annoying insect.

She didn't want to have to think about playing the hostess. She wanted to give Isabelle some attention. Her father was having a nap, thanks to Brother Jonathan's sleep-inducing draft, and Edmond had asked to go to the dispensary to see about a potion for a hound with a sore foot. Lord Oswald was with the men of the garrison, probably playing draughts and speaking of weapons and battles. As for Sir Connor, she didn't know where he was at present. If he was avoiding her, she could not fault him. Indeed, he might be showing more evidence of wisdom than she.

"Would you like something to drink, Isabelle?" she asked. "Some wine, perhaps?"

"Yes, I would."

"Sir Auberan, will you be good enough to go to the bottler and ask him to bring some?"

"It would be my pleasure to bring it myself," Auberan said with an elegant bow and a meaningful glance at the pale Isabelle.

She gave him a smile as weary as Allis felt. Auberan, however, apparently lacked the perception to see that he was being dismissed, for he smiled and hurried away as if on a vital mission for the king himself.

Allis sighed with relief, then regarded Isabelle with sympathy. "You look tired, Isabelle. Would you like to rest in our chamber?"

"I'm tired of Auberan, that's all. And I'm tired of everybody staring at me." She flushed and looked away. "Especially you," she finished in a murmur.

"I am concerned about you."

"Isn't it natural that I be upset? It's terrible that Percival is dead." Isabelle's lip trembled as she jabbed her needle through the fabric in the frame before her. "It doesn't help that I am being studied as if I were . . . as if I were Father."

She flinched, because Isabelle was right. "I'm sorry."

"Or a stupid girl. Sir Connor was only being nice, and you had to spoil everything."

Yes, he was a nice man, kind and generous. She had seen him with the village boys in the ward. They were crowded around his war horse, probably the most important and expensive thing he owned, yet he was allowing them to touch it. The boys were laughing and several talked at once, pestering him with questions, but on his face there had been a patient smile as he answered them. She couldn't think of many warriors who would react that way. Certainly Rennick wouldn't.

"You obviously offended him. Sir Connor hasn't said one word to me since, or lingered in the hall, or anything. He'll probably leave before his shoulder is healed because you were so horrid," Isabelle complained.

What could she say? Those things were all true, and as for the last, Allis thought he might leave too soon, as well, but for a different reason. "He has no cause to stay. He has to earn a living, and he won no prizes at the tournament because of his injury."

"You should offer him a place at Montclair. He would make an excellent commander of the garrison."

"I think not."

"Why?"

"He could win a place in a lord's service and an estate of his own. We certainly cannot offer him that."

"Oh." Isabelle thought a moment, then brightened. "Doesn't the baron have a small manor he could offer after you are wed?"

Allis bit off her thread and knotted it. While she was pleased by this small burst of vigor on Isabelle's part, she was not pleased by her suggestion. "No, and I will not ask him. Neither will you."

"Allis! Isabelle!"

Edmond ran to them from the kitchen entrance. His eyes shone with joy, and there were traces of buttermilk on his upper lip.

"Wait until I tell you!" he cried, skidding to a halt in the rushes. "Sir Connor let me sit on Demetrius today. That's his destrier. And he is going to teach me how to ride without holding onto the reins. With a shield and a spear, too. Not a lance, of course, because that would be too long and heavy for the first, but a real shield, cut down to my size. He's at the armory talking to Attila about it now."

She didn't hide her surprise. "Sir Connor let you sit on his destrier?"

"Yes, and he's going to teach me how to ride like a knight!"

"I thought you were going to see Brother Jonathan."

"I did, and he's going to tend to Bruno's foot. Then I thought I'd visit with Sir Connor. That's when he let me sit on Demetrius. *He* doesn't think I'm too young to learn about being a knight!"

She could easily imagine Edmond pestering the man. "Edmond, I don't think—"

Isabelle rose.

"Where are you going?" she asked.

"I don't know what you're going to do, Allis, but I'm going to thank him. I think it's wonderful of him to offer to teach Edmond, especially since you aren't letting Edmond be a squire."

Hiding her dismay at the accusing tone of Isabelle's

voice, she got to her feet, too. "I never said I was against this. I am simply surprised a knight would let anybody mount his horse."

"Demetrius is steady as a rock. We even walked all the way to the wall and back."

She was very glad she hadn't witnessed this. It was a long way from a war horse's back to the ground. "He doesn't intend you to ride without reins on his war horse, does he?"

"No!" Edmond declared as if she were simple. "On Firebrand. Demetrius is too wide for me, but one day, after Sir Connor has taught me how to balance and when I am broader in the beam, it will be easy for me to ride a destrier without holding on."

Her lips twitched. "Broader in the beam?"

"That's what he said."

"He is in the armory now?"

"Yes."

"Where are you going?" Edmond demanded as she started for the door.

Allis glanced back over her shoulder. "Why, to the armory to thank him, of course."

Isabelle gathered up her skirt and hurried after her. "Me, too!"

"Me, too. I want to see my shield," Edmond cried.

Bearing a tray with goblets and a carafe, Sir Auberan appeared at the door leading to the kitchen and buttery. "Lady Isabelle, Lady Allis, where are you going?"

"To the armory. We shall return shortly," Allis called as the three siblings hurried out into the courtyard, leaving Auberan gaping.

Chapter 12

At the sound of a commotion at the entrance to the armory, Connor and Attila turned to stare at the door.

Edmond ran inside first, crying, "I won! I won!"

Lady Isabelle, panting, came next, and finally Lady Allis, who came to an abrupt halt just inside the studded oaken door and took a deep breath as if trying to restore her dignity.

Connor suddenly realized that despite his vow to stay away from her for both her sake and his peace of mind, he should have asked if Edmond could spend time with him.

"Edmond makes everything a race," Isabelle declared with a bashful smile and blushing cheeks. "Doesn't he, Allis?"

"Yes," she admitted easily and without rancor.

Relief filled him and made him nearly giddy. If she were annoyed, he was quite sure she would make it plain. "I like ladies who are not afraid to run. Indeed, I have known several that moved so slowly, I feared they would be trampled to death even by the pigs if they ever got loose. And as for a cow . . . absolutely fatal."

Isabelle giggled, but he was more pleased to see Lady Allis smile. "Edmond tells me you are going to teach him some riding techniques," she remarked.

"Yes, if you are amenable."

Lady Allis's smile blossomed. "I am."

He grinned like a fool, but he didn't care. Her affectionate smile seemed to reach into his heart and warm it from within. If there could be nothing between them than this genial harmony, he would accept that, and gladly.

"Is that my shield?" Edmond asked eagerly, looking at the wooden object on Attila's work table.

"Ya."

"Is it ready for me?"

"Ya." Attila held it up. It was broad at the top, then tapered to a point at the bottom, and was just the right size for a twelve-year-old boy.

Edmond wiggled his slender left arm into the straps. He stuck out his chest and struck a pose. "How do I look?"

"Very manly," Lady Allis observed, her voice grave but her eyes dancing with merriment. Once again, she was the charming, delightful woman who had been with him in the garden that first night, the heavy burden of her duties and responsibilities blessedly absent, if only for a little while.

He admired the chatelaine, he appreciated the beautiful lady, but the smiling, joyful woman charmed him utterly. This woman he could imagine being both friend and lover, helpmate and haven. She could bring happiness back into his life, and add so much more—if only she were free, and he were worthy.

Isabelle giggled. "You don't look quite like a knight yet."

"I do, too!"

"A miniature one."

"I'm not small!"

"Isabelle," Allis warned. "Enough."

"That shield will do for now," Connor said. He went over to a group of spears leaning against the stone wall and picked one up. "I think this one will be appropriate. It is about the right length. It will be the same size in relation to his weight and height as a lance would be to a grown man."

"I'm nearly grown!"

Connor walked toward Edmond. "You will not reach your full growth for at least four years. That is nothing to be ashamed of." He looked at Isabelle. "A lady should not make sport of those younger than herself. You have the advantage of him in age and beauty so it really isn't fair, is it?" he continued in a gentle way that made Allis's legs suddenly seem soft-jointed.

"No," Isabelle murmured, as obviously affected by his soothing tones as she was.

God save her, she should not have come, not even to thank him. Lit by Attila's hearth, the flames made his skin look like it was fashioned of burnished bronze. To watch him surrounded by the weapons of war reminded her how strong a warrior he was. To hear his kindhearted voice, gentle even in admonition, was to know the wonderful father he would be.

But most of all, to compare the way he looked at Isabelle and then at her was to realize that he did feel something deeper for her. It roiled in the dark depths of his eyes, compelling and fascinating.

"I will bring the shield and spear with me, young lordling," he said, brisk once more. "Go you now, and have the groom saddle your horse. I will meet you at the stable."

"May I watch?" Isabelle asked, as enthused as Edmond.

"If Edmond agrees."

Nearly out the door, Edmond looked back and shrugged. Isabelle smiled her delight and hurried after him.

"May I speak with you outside a moment, Sir Connor?"

"Of course, my lady."

"Good day, Attila."

The armorer nodded, and she swept from the armory into the fresh air of the courtyard, acutely aware that Sir Connor was right behind her.

"There, better this air is and no mistake," he observed as she led him across the courtyard. "Has Attila bathed since birth?"

"I doubt it, but he is the finest maker of swords in this part of England."

"Where are we going?"

Where were they going, indeed?

Rennick was assured of her. Soon enough he would return and claim her for his bride. She would take this one small risk to speak to Sir Connor alone, for what should be the last time. "The garden."

Her throat tight, her heart thudding so loudly in her chest she believed he could hear it, she opened the gate and waited until he was inside, then closed it behind him.

"About Edmond," he began immediately. "He's a bright lad keen to learn, and since I have nothing better to do because my shoulder is hurt, I saw no harm in teaching him a few things. I should have asked your permission first, and I'm sorry I didn't, but glad I am you agreed. Otherwise, I fear he will grow bitter and unruly, and channel that vitality into something else—something you may not like."

Why, this bold, brave knight sounded as tense and anxious as she was. Suddenly, the most outrageous urge to giggle bubbled up inside her and only with a mighty effort did she stifle the undignified impulse. "You sound very sure of your opinion."

He laughed. "I do, don't I?"

He was so attractive when he laughed! "I want to thank you. The past few days have been difficult for Edmond—for all of us—and I appreciate the kindness of your offer."

"I am happy to be of service. Besides, I like him." His voice dropped to an intimate whisper. "He reminds me of you."

She had never had a compliment that pleased her more. As the daughter of the earl of Montclair, she had always been accorded a measure of respect. As she grew in beauty, many men had been fulsome in their praise of her face and body, but no one had ever told her that they liked her.

Then his eyes brightened, and his lips curved up into a delighted smile. A dangerously appealing delighted smile.

A cry of alarm sounded in her mind, as loud and

insistent as a call to arms. She was betrothed. She had given her word. Her marriage ensured her family's security.

Her mind urged her to flee, but her heart asked what harm there could be to any but herself if she allowed herself the chance to savor one last morsel of liberty. "I am curious, Sir Connor. Do you speak from personal experience? Were you a bitter and unruly boy?"

She was sorry to see his smile fade. "No, I was spoiled. I was not denied much of anything in my childhood when it came to the arts of war. Since I showed a talent for them early, my father was proud of my prowess and encouraged me. Too much, some would say."

She sat on a bench and gestured for him to sit beside her. He did and, clasping his hands, he leaned forward, his elbows on his knees. He kept his gaze on the wall opposite as he spoke. "I think my elder brother Caradoc was denied what he most craved. I always assumed his bitterness stemmed from jealousy of me, but perhaps it is something else."

Tempted to touch his tense shoulder, she folded her hands in her lap. "You don't sound certain."

"Because this has just hit home to me. It would explain many things, though."

"You spoke of him the day you were injured. You said he would enjoy seeing you in pain."

He raked back his hair. "Aye, my lady, I'm sorry to say he probably would, because of the quarrels we've had."

His dark hair was as luxuriant as any she had ever seen, and her fingers itched to run through it, gathering it back and exposing the ticklish nape of his neck.

If she grazed his nape with her lips, would that tickle him, too? "Is it as bad as that between you?"

He glanced at her, then looked away. "It has been." He sighed, his regret nearly palpable. "I have always thought Caradoc preferred studying. Training can be difficult, and on the worst days, when I was tired, wet and cold, I would see him in the window of the solar, warm and dry, and begrudge him those comforts."

"But not the learning?"

"No, not the learning," he admitted with a rueful chuckle. "I hated my time with the priests sent to teach us and was a very poor student."

She heard the pain beneath his soft laughter. This could not be easy for him to talk about, and she was pleased and proud to think that he would reveal these things to her. "While Caradoc . . . ?"

"Caradoc excelled." He rubbed his right hand over his angular jaw. He did it absently, unaware of how fascinating she found his hands, or how much she wanted to follow his action and stroke his chin herself. Or trail her lips over the rough stubble, sliding toward his tempting mouth. "But now that I think back, I cannot recall my father ever saying one word of praise for all his efforts. And Caradoc would often ask my father about accompanying him to Winchester or London. My father always promised, but they never went."

Sympathy overcame her desire. Not imagining kisses or passionate caresses, but only wanting to take him in her arms for a comforting embrace, she inched closer.

"When I was preparing to go on Crusade, it was terrible between us. Caradoc accused me of bankrupting the family with the cost of my equipage. I thought it was envy of my skill, but perhaps it wasn't. Yet my father never spoke of the cost, so I assumed it was not excessive."

"Maybe your brother envied you the freedom to go anywhere," she suggested quietly.

"Yes. I think now he did not enjoy his duties and responsibilities as the heir to the estate as much as I wanted to believe because it suited my purpose to think he was merely jealous of me." He turned to look at her and the remorse in his eyes touched her lonely heart. "All these years, and only now do I begin to see that I might have been mistaken. You and your family help me to see my own. And my own mistakes."

As if she had made none! As if she were some kind of angel or perfect being, free of sin and sinful, selfish desires. As if she did not have to struggle against the attraction she felt for him, in so many different ways. "We are none of us perfect."

"As I know too well." He took her hand. His was rough and callused, warm and strong. "Your relationship with your brother might suffer like mine if you don't give him some vent for his dreams and energy."

She forced herself to pull her hand from his, before she begged him to take her in his arms. "Yes, I see that now, and you are probably right. I am grateful for your insight, Sir—"

"No title. Just Connor."

Once again his voice enveloped her in an unfamiliar, wonderful intimacy. How easy it would be to surrender, to give herself up to the passion swirling, burning, coiling within her, and beg him to kiss her.

She fought back the urgent, unspoken wish. "You mentioned a sister, too. What is her name?"

He grinned, roguish and appealing, yet the intimate spell was mercifully broken. "Cordelia. And if I have a temper and act without thinking, I am a model of placidity and careful consideration compared to her. She used to bite, too. Hard."

"She sounds like a hellion."

"A brat she was, but she is older and wiser now."

"How old is she?"

"Sixteen. She was thirteen when my parents died."

"Death makes children old for their age."

"As well as wise and responsible before their time. It must be difficult managing this estate with your father . . . as he is."

How different was his tender and genuine sympathy from Rennick's! Rennick always made it sound as if her father's state were a defect of character. He would never understand how a love's loss could break a man's spirit as well as his heart. But she had no doubt that Connor could, and did. "Brother Jonathan says he suffers from a melancholy brought on by grief, which disturbed his humors. Time often corrects such disturbances. Unfortunately, in my father's case, he fears the imbalance might be permanent."

"I am very sorry, my lady. I have heard many tales of your father in the past, so I have some notion of how he has changed. It must be very difficult, and the responsibility for the estate and your family must be a great burden."

"Sometimes."

"And the loneliness hard to bear."

Oh, God help her! He sounded as if he could indeed see into her heart. "I have my family. And the baron, too, of course. He is eager to help." She tried, but could not hide, her disgust for Rennick. Her emotions were too raw, too near the surface, as if buoyed by the promise of Connor's understanding.

"Does he help, or does he rule?"

Only days ago, she thought no man could breach the walls she had built around her heart to separate her feelings from her obligations. How wrong she was! "Not yet."

"While I would not begrudge you a happy marriage, I would not like to think of you miserably wed, any more than I would Cordelia."

Oh, God, oh, God, give me strength! She had underestimated the risk of being with him and the power of wanting to be loved by him. "I am no relation to you."

"I know that."

"I can be nothing to you."

"You already are far more important than many things to me," he murmured as he put his right arm about her and drew her close.

She knew this was wrong. She must not kiss him. She belonged to another.

Another who was not here. Who cared for her family's property, not her. Who did not—could not—kiss her like this man did.

She took his face between her palms and kissed him with fervent need and growing desire. She wanted him, and the freedom he promised with merely the touch of his lips upon hers.

Leaning closer and wrapping her arms about him, she let her mouth taste his in a slow, sensuous dance. He even smelled better than Rennick, of fresh air and plain wool and leather—simple, comfortable things.

She reveled in the sensation of being held in his powerful arms. Her hands moved slowly up his back, and the taut muscles roiled like waves upon the ocean as he pulled her even closer to him. The ends of his long, waving hair brushed her fingertips. She ran her hands through the thick, marvelous mass of his hair and relaxed against him, as if her bones were butter, melting beneath his passionate touch.

He abruptly broke the kiss, startling her as much as a pinch would have. "My lady, forgive—"

"I do not want to forgive you," she whispered. "I do not want to be forgiven. I want to be with you. I want to kiss you. Please, Connor, kiss me again."

"Allis," he whispered, making her name a caress as he moved his left arm, slipping it out of the sling. He did not raise it, but put it gingerly about her waist before he kissed her as she yearned to be kissed, with desire and tenderness, with equal passion and need, as if he, too, found what he was seeking in their embrace.

So different from Rennick, who took her mouth possessively as a sign of conquest, not love, or even affection. Rennick groped her body to assuage his own desire, not to inflame hers.

She must have more of Connor. Feel more of him. Taste more of him. Her whole body shook with primitive need as she plunged her tongue between his lips.

He wanted more of her, too, his kiss growing more demanding, just as hers was. But he did not seek rough conquest. As he lifted her onto his lap, he requested her willing surrender.

She was very willing.

He was hard beneath her, and she knew what it meant. He wanted to make love with her. His body was ready. So was hers. This moist heaviness was startlingly new, yet every instinct told her what it meant.

He grunted, a small sound of pain deep in his throat, and she instantly drew back, looking at him questioningly.

"A little pain is a small price to the pay for the pleasure you give," he murmured as he pressed light kisses along her throat.

She tried to focus on his injury and not the delight of the whisper of his lips against her skin. "You may be doing lasting harm."

"I will risk it."

And so would she, for never had she felt this way, as a woman in love must feel. As if she must be with him, or she would wither and die, and that death would be welcome, because she was alone.

His right hand slid beneath her skirt and, splayed against her skin, traveled slowly, slowly up her leg. Gingerly she wrapped her arms about him and surrendered once again.

His left hand spread along her waist, before meandering along her ribs, then moving with tormenting leisure to cup her breast. His thumb brushed across her pebbled nipple. Ripples of passionate excitement expanded and she squirmed, anxiously pushing forward to increase the pressure.

There was pressure lower, too, and when she moved, she felt him respond. She yearned to feel that virile length inside her, to be joined with him and feel the power of his passion as he thrust.

"Have you seen Sir Connor?" Edmond called from somewhere beyond the garden wall. "I've been waiting for him."

They both went perfectly still, like a statue of two lovers in the garden.

"Not today, my chick," Merva called from further off.

Flushed and breathless, ashamed and still excited, Allis pulled away. "You have to leave."

Connor's blushing, gasping frustration was a mirror of her own. "Aye."

Neither one of them moved. She had never wanted to stay anywhere as much as she wanted to linger on Connor's lap, his arms around her, making her feel cherished and safe, and no longer alone.

With a gentle tenderness and a sad sigh, he tucked a stray lock of her hair back beneath her scarf. "I had best go before your brother calls out the guard to search for me."

"Yes." As she looked into the dark, shifting depths of his eyes, it was like that first night when she had believed he could see into her heart. But this time, she could see into his. He wanted her with a passion equal to her own, yet beneath that, like the strong rock that withstands the surges of the ocean's waves, there was something more. Something stronger. Something better. Something eternal, like the rhythm of the sea, or the beating of two hearts in unison. Even if they were not together, that bond would still be there.

She wiggled off his lap and got to her feet on trembling legs. "People might start looking for me, too. If they found us together . . ." If they were found together, nobody would care about her feelings, least of all Rennick DeFrouchette.

"It would not go well with you," he confirmed. "Go you through the hall, my lady, and I out the gate. I will be careful."

Yes, he would be. She could trust him. She knew that as if it were carved on that sturdy rock in the midst of the crashing waves. "I know."

He rose and began to ease his arm back into the sling. She lightly touched his left shoulder. "I didn't hurt your shoulder more, did I?"

His grin was as sudden and delightful as the first spark from flint and steel on a cold day. "If you did, I would not complain." He raised his arm a little. "No, not more hurt. In fact, you might have helped."

Once again, his charming, rakish grin nudged away her sadness and made her smile. "I doubt that."

He stepped close and leaned toward her, whispering in her ear, his voice low and seductive. "Have you never heard that kisses have healing power?"

She closed her eyes and let the passionate warmth of his presence flow over and around her. "No, I haven't."

His right arm encircled her. "I haven't, either, but I think somebody should start a rumor."

His soft, moist tongue licked and fondled her earlobe, and she couldn't stifle the low moan that began deep in her throat.

"I must go."

"Yes," she sighed as he nuzzled her neck.

"I don't want to."

"No."

"I must."

A part of her heard his words, and part of her agreed. But another part—stronger, more primitive than reason—anchored her in his embrace.

He moved back and once more his lips turned up, not in a merry grin, but in a smile that warmed her to the tips of her toes and touched her heart anew.

"I really must go," he said firmly, as if trying to convince himself, too. "Until later, my lady."

Yet even then he hesitated and doubt clouded his features.

"Until later," she promised. Until Rennick returned and she must again be the dutiful Allis of Montclair.

Connor paused at the gate and gave her another beautiful smile before he opened it and was gone.

As one day he would be gone forever, and this lovely dream would be at an end. Surely her heart would shatter like his lance when he left Montclair. Would he feel that way, too? Would he curse her for leading him on, or would he understand that she had not been strong enough to conquer her longing and stay away from him?

But duty was bred in her bones and love for her family was the core of her being. She could not ignore that love, any more than her breaking heart could be torn from her chest and she be expected to live. Duty could not be forgotten any more than she could stand without a spine.

When the time came for him to leave Montclair, she hoped he could understand that, and forgive her.

Perhaps she should hope he did not. Let him hate her for giving in to her selfish desire, and let him find another, better woman to love and comfort him.

Let her know his love, his tenderness, his compassion. Let her share his days, and his nights. Let her bear his children and call him husband. And let *her* hear that he was happy, for that would be a fitting punishment for her sin.

As Connor strode across the cobblestoned courtyard toward Edmond, who fidgeted with impatience beside his roan, he tried to climb out of the bliss of passion Allis inspired, and think.

He could no longer delude himself that what he felt for her was something he could conquer. It was too strong, too powerful, too all-encompassing.

And she cared for him, too. He saw it in her eyes, felt it in her touch. When she was in his arms, there was no coyness, no sense that this was merely a game to her. She wanted him as he wanted her, and when they were together, that yearning became potent and overwhelming. Yet for the sake of her beloved family, she had pledged herself to another and he knew her well enough to believe that even if she loved him, her sense of honor and duty would demand that she do what she must to protect them. Could he expect less of her than he would demand of himself?

So when Baron DeFrouchette returned, this pleasant dream must come to its inevitable end. To make that moment bearable for both of them, he should try to loosen the ties of longing and affection already binding them, no matter how much it tore his heart.

"Where have you been?" Edmond demanded as Connor halted beside him.

He had heard that tone of voice before, from a certain king he had once admired. Did this boy have any idea what sacrifices his sister made for him? Or was he already like Richard, taking with no thought of what it might cost the giver? "That is no way for a squire to address a knight."

The lad had the grace to blush. "I'm sorry."

No, not like Richard yet, and with such a sister, perhaps never. He ruffled the lad's hair. "Apology accepted. Come now, let's get that shield and spear."

He gave no explanation for his tardiness and told no lies to Edmond. Nor, as the next few days passed, did he find the strength to stay away from Allis, or loosen the bonds that already wrapped about them like the strongest rope.

Chapter 13

❦

"You're a marvelous teacher, Sir Connor," Isabelle enthused from her place on Connor's camp stool in the inner ward.

"Thank you," he replied, barely glancing at her as he watched Edmond riding while holding his shield.

She had come again to watch Edmond's knightly lessons, or so she claimed, but he knew she spent more time watching *him*. He had not said or done anything about that so far, yet perhaps the time had come to speak to Allis—another excuse, perhaps, to be alone with the woman he was fast falling in love with.

His affection and desire grew stronger every time they were together. Sometimes, they were brief, intensely passionate encounters, like the time he waited for her in the pantry after hearing her speak of getting some bread for her father to eat before he slept. His

loins tightened as he remembered the feel of her body
against his as he pressed her back against the shelves,
fervent longing exploding within him. Softly moaning,
stroking and caressing him as her mouth took his, she
arched back, thrusting her hips toward him, as bold in
her passion as she was in everything. Love, need, heat
exploded and careered through him like sparks from a
forge. If they had not knocked over a basket of leeks,
he might have made love to her then and there, with
no heed to the consequences.

Once she had invited him to join her and Lord Oswald at the high table, as coolly and calmly as she
might any other guest. Only the flash of affection in
her eyes betrayed her, and only, he was sure, because
he knew to look for it.

After the meal, Lord Oswald had excused himself
and disappeared with the accommodating Merva.
There was nothing untoward in Connor's remaining at
the table, and under the eyes of the servants, they
talked. She spoke of the birth of Edmond, and the
great rejoicing that had followed, not hiding that she
had felt distinctly snubbed. Her mother found her
weeping in her chamber, and told her she must not
take the celebration of her brother's birth as meaning
she was less cherished or beloved. Indeed, her mother
had confided, her father indulged his daughters in a
way he never would a son, so in fact she should pity
little Edmond. Allis clearly had not completely agreed
with the last, but Connor heard the love for her mother
in every word she spoke. It was not only the earl of
Montclair who had been heartbroken by her death.

He told her of his parents, and then the Crusade. He
talked of things he had never told anyone, of the misery and horror, and his growing despair. Even then,

and despite the undercurrent of compassionate understanding, he could not bring himself to describe his final humiliating meeting with Richard.

Nor could he help reaching for her slender hand beneath the table. He had done no more than touch her,
and yet that was enough to set his heartstrings singing.

Firebrand whinnied. With a guilty start, Connor
came out of his reverie. Fine thing for a teacher to do,
daydreaming! What if the lad had fallen or been hurt?

Then he realized why Firebrand had whinnied.
"Not too tight with the knees, Edmond, or you'll break
his ribs."

It was an exaggeration, but the boy was gripping
with his knees so hard, the horse looked annoyed.

Edmond relaxed a little and Connor smiled with approval. "I think that's enough for today."

Edmond nodded at the spear leaning against the
pole at the entrance to Connor's tent. "Won't you let
me try it once with the shield and spear both? I won't
fall. Firebrand is being very good."

"No. Not yet. Walk the course first before you run.
Study the battleground before you engage."

"You did better than I thought you would," Isabelle
called out.

"He's doing very well. He has a very good seat, and
his balance is excellent."

"You hear that?" Edmond demanded. "I'm very
good."

"A knight truly skilled and confident has no need to
brag. Now take Firebrand to his stall and rub him
down well, and make sure he has plenty of food and
water. He has worked hard today, too."

Edmond slipped from the saddle. "We have grooms
to tend to the horses."

"No," Connor said firmly. "*You* must do it. Remember what I said about a knight and his horse? Granted, Firebrand is not a destrier, but you must begin to understand horses, especially your own. What do they like to eat best? Where do they prefer to be stroked? Do they like you to whisper in their ears, or does that make them anxious? Horses are like women, Edmond. Every one of them different, and every one needs to be treated differently. It is your task to find out what pleases them most."

Abashed, Edmond nodded, and Connor noticed that Isabelle was blushing to the roots of her hair. He should have thought of a better comparison.

"One more lesson." He got the spear and gave it to Edmond. "Stand to the right of Firebrand. Good. Now, take his reins in your shield hand and the spear in your right."

Edmond did as he was told, resting the butt of the spear on the ground, the tip in the air.

"Tilt the spear so that the tip is pointed at the ground, the shaft under your arm, most of it above and behind your shoulder. You will have to let the shaft slip through your fingers to do that."

Connor took hold of the back of the spear and gently guided it. "Good. Now you are ready to leave the field."

Edmond's face broke into a grin as understanding suddenly dawned. With pride in every step as if he just defeated twenty knights, he headed for the stables.

Which left Connor alone with young Isabelle.

She rose and came toward him, twisting the end of her long blond braid about her fingers. "I wish I could be a knight," she said bashfully. "Even though it is dangerous."

A lighthearted approach would, perhaps, be best with her. "Where would knights be without lovely ladies to impress?"

"I suppose you've known many beautiful ladies?"

"A few," he allowed.

"Were they as pretty as . . . as pretty as Allis?"

He suspected this was a roundabout way to ask if he thought her pretty, too. It might not be wise, but he didn't have the heart to deny her a little compliment when she still seemed so sad and fragile. "Very few are as pretty as your sister, or you."

"Then other men will ask to wear my scarf in tournaments, and I will let them." Her eyes flashed with sudden fire, and he thought that something of Allis's spirited vitality might lurk within her, after all.

"While you regret not letting Percival wear your scarf, speaking as a man and a knight, I would rather have a lady refuse my request than give me reason to believe she feels more than she does."

She slid him a coy and questioning glance. "I daresay you've worn lots of ladies' scarves."

Time to end whatever fantasies this girl was entertaining. "I have never asked a lady for her scarf."

She stared at him, dumbfounded. "Why not?"

"There has never been one I cared enough to ask."

"Not ever?"

"No, not ever."

"Some day you might."

He shrugged. "It is possible, I suppose."

She blushed and looked at the hem of her gown. "I would be very honored if you asked for mine."

"My lady," he said not unkindly, but firmly, too, "I am too old to be asking for your scarf. You should hope to win the affections of a younger man who has his whole life ahead of him. However, I am very aware of the great compliment you have paid me, and I shall cherish it always."

Isabelle planted her feet, and took a deep breath. "If we were to have a tournament today, would you ask Allis if you could wear her favor?"

"No."

There could be no doubt of his sincerity, because he meant what he said. He could not, no matter how much he might want to.

"Because she is betrothed?"

"Yes."

"What if she were free?"

He did not wish to discuss that possibility with anyone except Allis. "Lady Isabelle, the hour grows late, and my shoulder is aching. I think I had best seek out Brother Jonathan and see if there is something he can do. Please excuse me."

With that, he took the wiser course and quit the field.

Allis hurried toward the dispensary. Her father's head was aching, and she needed more of the potion Brother Jonathan made out of willow bark for that complaint.

When the new cathedral, cloisters and chapter house were completed, Brother Jonathan would be moving there, along with his medicinal paraphernalia. She was going to miss the busy little physician and having his medicines so close by, but her father had promised to build a hospital near the cathedral, and on this one point, he had remained absolutely firm, much to Allis's delight and the baron's dismay.

She would also miss the dispensary, a homey place with its strange jars and strange smells from the herbs drying overhead. In the corner was a small hearth Brother Jonathan used to heat his remedies as necessary, and that cozily warmed the chamber in winter. In front of that was the scarred, stained table where Brother Jonathan did the mixing. A variety of dishes, pots, mortars and pestles stood there, along with a bottle of ink, quills, glue and small pieces of parchment for labeling the jars and clay pots lining the shelves.

Hoping Brother Jonathan would be alone and therefore able to prepare the draft quickly, she entered the dispensary.

The little man was not alone. To her surprise and secret delight, Connor was there.

She took a moment to survey his naked back, and the dark, waving hair brushing his wide shoulders. His left shoulder was still very bruised, the skin an angry purple, red and yellow.

Her gaze drifted lower, to his trim waist and narrow hips. Memories of the time he had surprised her in the pantry burst into her mind, and her body warmed as if he were once again kissing her passionately against the shelves.

Brother Jonathan peered at her. "Lady Allis?"

"I'm sorry to interrupt, but my father's head is aching."

"Ah. One moment, and I shall prepare his medicine."

She strolled closer, and spoke as matter-of-factly as she could. "Have you hurt your shoulder again, Sir Connor?"

"I have a bit of an ache," he replied in much the same manner, and only the flare of emotion in his eyes betrayed that there was more than mere courtesy between them.

"He has been doing too much," Brother Jonathan

said with more than a hint of disapproval as he went to his work table.

She wasn't the only one reddening at the particular moment, and she turned away from Connor and his roguish grin. She studied a pot labeled *Tincture of Wormwood* as if fascinated.

"I do not know why men will not listen to my advice," Brother Jonathan muttered, his head bent over his work. "It is not as if I give these warnings out of spite, you know."

"Yes, I do know, Brother," Connor said. "I am very sorry. I have been distracted of late."

It was a good thing she wasn't looking at Connor's face. She could well imagine his contrite expression belied by his merry eyes. If she met his gaze, she would surely start giggling like a besotted girl.

"Fortunately, I see nothing terribly amiss with your shoulder—yet. There is no sign of infection, and the swelling is reduced."

"The bruising still looks terrible," Connor said.

"That is a nasty injury, and you must be patient."

"I shall try."

Believing she had her emotions under more control, she looked Connor in the eye. "And you mustn't think of leaving until Brother Jonathan gives his approval."

"Very well, my lady, and again, I thank you for your generous hospitality."

"We are happy to have you stay."

"You could lift a little weight with that arm, Sir Connor," Brother Jonathan noted. "A bucket with some water in it to begin with will be sufficient. Only about a quarter full, and no more. Once that becomes easier, you can add a little more water, and so on.

Again, however, let me counsel patience, or you will do more harm than good."

"And again, good brother, I shall try. Now I fear I need some help me with my shirt and tunic." He glanced at her in a way that made her heartbeat quicken even more.

"I'll do that, Brother Jonathan," she offered, unable to resist such temptation.

Brother Jonathan hesitated.

"I promise I shall be very careful of his shoulder," she said, not sure if the reason for his hesitation was fear that she might further injure Connor's shoulder, or fear of impropriety in the dispensary.

"Yes, I'm sure you will, my lady," he replied, obviously reassuring himself. "I shall be only a moment."

It was on the tip of her tongue to tell him to take his time, but she refrained. For one thing, her father needed the medicine; for another, what would Brother Jonathan think? Clearly she could be granted a certain leeway with a half-naked Sir Connor because she had nursed him before, but she dared not sound too keen. That was very difficult when Connor grinned at her.

"I am grateful for your assistance, my lady," he said, his tone one of absolute respect and deference which might fool Brother Jonathan fussing with his pots, but not her, not with that devilment in his eyes and the fires of passion lurking below their dark surface.

"I am going to put your shirt over your head," she explained, taking it and standing in front of him, inches from his body. The tendrils of delicious tension between them expanded, wrapping around them in coils of yearning.

He leaned forward as if inexorably pulled toward

her. She eased the shirt over him, taking her time and letting her hands slide over his warm skin. "I shall try to be gentle with you."

First the top of his head reappeared, then his face. "And I with you," he whispered.

For a moment, she both hoped and feared he might kiss her right there in the dispensary, until he gave a barely perceptible shake of his head and pouted, as if he read her mind and replied, "Not here, unfortunately."

She pressed her lips together, trying to calm herself. "If you will put your left arm in the sleeve . . ."

"That would be which one, my lady?"

"The injured one, of course," she whispered. "If I didn't know better, sir knight, I might believe you were trying to delay the proceedings."

"You might be right."

He slipped his left hand into his sleeve and she slowly—very slowly—pulled it up. "My lady, I think *you* are deliberately taking a very long time getting me dressed."

"You wish me to hurry?"

His eyes darkened and his chest rose and fell as his breathing quickened, like her own. "Not at all."

"Then don't complain." Leaning tantalizingly closer, she held the right sleeve for him and he eased his arm into it. "We are not alone." She should remember that, too.

"I am damnably aware of that fact, my lady." He inched back a bit and spoke in a louder voice. "It is a good thing this shirt has big sleeves. And here I grumbled that the seamstress must have been thinking of a giant when she made it."

Although it was necessary, she regretted the loss of intimacy. "It does seem very large for you."

"Actually, it wasn't made for me. It is my brother's shirt. I, um, borrowed it."

"You mean you took it without asking."

"One could say so."

"I get very angry when Isabelle does that."

"Well, he made me angry first. I'll take him a new one when I go home."

When he left her, as he must. Her hands shaking, she picked up his tunic.

The door to the dispensary opened. Lord Oswald sauntered inside, his gaze sweeping over the room, the medicines and the people in it. She froze as he bowed to them in greeting. "My lady, Sir Connor."

Deciding she should not act as if anything were amiss or unusual in what she was doing, she helped Connor put on his tunic.

"What may I do for you, Lord Oswald?" Brother Jonathan asked as he stoppered the small vial of medicine for her father. "I hope you are not ill?"

"A touch of indigestion today, nothing more," Lord Oswald replied with a genial smile that made Allis breathe easier as she stepped away from Connor. "Knowing that such a clever physician was nearby, I thought to avail myself of your services."

"As well you should. I shall be happy to give you something. What are the symptoms? Gas? Burning?"

"Burning. Well, and belching, too, if I am to be completely honest," he replied, winking at Allis.

She returned his smile, liking him. Indeed, she wished he were their neighbor, rather than Rennick. For one thing, he was a man one could trust. For another, he was already married, to the very wealthy heiress of a Norman duke.

"I, too, hope you are soon feeling better, my lord. If Lady Allis will help me with my sling, I can be on my way," Connor said.

"I trust your injury is healing well," Lord Oswald inquired.

"Brother Jonathan tells me it is, although he warns me I must take care a while yet. I shall endeavor to obey."

She deftly slipped the sling over his head and maneuvered it into position, taking care not to touch him more than strictly necessary. He carefully put his arm through it.

"Good day, my lady, my lord, Brother Jonathan," he said as he strolled toward the door. As always when he left her, she thought of the moment he must do so for the last time, and a little bit more of her died.

"Here is the draft for your father, my lady," Brother Jonathan said, handing her the vial.

"Thank you. Good day to you, and to you, too, my lord."

"I look forward to seeing you at the evening meal, my lady," Lord Oswald said, bowing again as she passed him by. "Perhaps we can persuade Sir Connor to give us a song."

She stopped. "A song?"

"Oh, yes, my lady, he is a most excellent singer, or so his father used to say. I assumed you knew this about him."

"No, I did not." Fear skittered along her spine. They had been too careless, too wrapped in their own desire. Lord Oswald wasn't blind; perhaps he had seen . . . guessed . . .

And what of Brother Jonathan? To be sure, he had seemed to be absorbed in his task, but they should have been more careful. She shouldn't have stayed. She should have asked Brother Jonathan to bring the potion.

"He's Welsh, is he not? They are all fine singers, or so I understand."

Her alarm lessened. "Yes, I've heard that, too."

"So we shall ask him, shall we?"

"You don't think he will be offended? He is a knight of the realm, after all, not a minstrel."

Lord Oswald smiled broadly. "Oh, I think if a pretty woman asks him, he might do almost anything, especially if he hopes to impress her."

Another chill of dread spread outward from her spine. "What makes you think he hopes to impress me?"

"Come, come, my lady!" Lord Oswald cried jovially. "Surely you cannot be ignorant of the way he regards you?"

"It matters not how he looks at me," she said, drawing herself up as she lied through her teeth. "I am a betrothed woman."

"Yes, but not yet married, and he is poor and handsome. A man in such a position might try to improve his lot by marrying a lovely heiress. If I were young and unmarried, I would be pursuing you myself."

She thought of time she had shared with Connor, moments of genuine affection as well as passion. His feelings were sincere, and honest. She believed that to the core of her heart, where her own love lived. "You flatter me, my lord," she said with a cool smile. "And now you must excuse me, for my father is waiting."

"Of course, my lady," he said, watching her leave.

Chapter 14

A s they dressed for the evening meal later that day, Isabelle glanced at her sister's reflection in the small mirror in the bedchamber they shared. Isabelle sat at their dressing table brushing her hair, while Allis changed her gown from a plain woolen one to something finer. Isabelle had already donned a very pretty gown of pale blue embroidered about the round neck and cuffs with red and yellow flowers.

"Sir Connor is wonderful with Edmond," Isabelle remarked.

"So I gather. Edmond is very pleased." Allis drew on her blue velvet gown with the satin-lined, green cuffs that reached nearly to the floor. "His voice was almost loud enough to raise an alarm when he told Father about his 'training.'

"His excitement did not help Father's aching head, I'm afraid," Allis finished with a sigh.

Isabelle rose and came behind her to tighten and tie the lacing at the back of her bodice. "I think he's wonderful."

"That's a nice thing to say about your brother."

"I was talking about Sir Connor. Don't you think he's wonderful?"

Mindful of Lord Oswald's possible suspicions and not wishing to raise any in Isabelle's mind, she carefully replied, "I like him, and I am certainly very grateful for the time he has spent with Edmond."

Her task finished, Isabelle came around to face her. "You should come and watch with me tomorrow."

She wanted to very much, but she feared she couldn't mask her feelings well enough. Indeed, it was difficult to mask them now. To hide her face, she reached for the green girdle lying on the bed. "I have too much to do—and I think you shouldn't bother them."

"I'm not a bother. I sit on Sir Connor's stool and do not say a word. If I were a bother, surely he would ask me to leave," Isabelle said as she sat again and began to braid her hair.

"You are the daughter of the lord of a castle where he is a guest."

"I still think he would ask me to leave if my presence was interfering."

That was likely true. A man who would upbraid his king surely wouldn't hesitate to ask Isabelle to leave if she was a nuisance. "I cannot take the time." Which was also, regrettably, true.

"He's very handsome, isn't he?"

Allis reached for her pale green scarf and forced

herself to speak with a nonchalance she certainly didn't feel. "Who?"

"Why, Sir Connor. Who else are we talking about?"

"Yes, I suppose."

"Granted he's not as handsome as the baron, but he's very good-looking."

In the process of lifting her scarf over her head, Allis stilled. "You think Rennick is better looking?"

"Of course! You needn't sound so shocked. Everybody thinks he's very handsome. Why, Merva says—"

"I can guess what Merva says." As she continued to put on her scarf, it crossed her mind that she should try to limit Isabelle's exposure to that particular maidservant and her loquacious tongue. Unfortunately, that was an edict that would probably prove impossible to enforce. "I am surprised that you think so."

"Well, I do. And more importantly, the baron is rich."

"You sound as if you think that of supreme importance."

"I do. So does every noblewoman."

"I don't."

Isabelle swiveled on her stool and stared at her sister incredulously. "That's not what you said before."

Pretending to be absorbed in adjusting the girdle about her waist, she said, "I cannot deny that wealth or lack of it is an important consideration—"

"What else is there? Connections and alliances, I suppose," Isabelle replied, answering her own question. "I think the baron has everything one could hope for in a husband. He's good-looking, rich and our neighbor and ally. He's been very helpful since Mother died. What more could you ask for?"

There were so many things Isabelle didn't know, or

she would never say such a thing, or believe it, either. She would understand why a woman who hoped for an honorable, kind and faithful husband would never wish to be his bride. But she was young yet to have her mind polluted by the vile nature of what some men could do in the name of their rights and the rule of law. "I am surprised you have not talked of love."

"You have never talked of love, either."

Of course, when it came to the baron, that was true. Even now, she could hardly bring herself to talk of love and Rennick DeFrouchette at the same time.

"It is a great pity Sir Connor isn't rich," Isabelle said with a sigh as she tied a bright blue ribbon around the end of her braid. "Otherwise, I would be doing all I could to compel him to ask for my hand."

She couldn't fault her for her taste. "You are too young," she said, picking up the barbette.

"I wonder what his kisses are like."

"Isabelle!" Allis snapped as she adjusted the barbette. To speak of his looks was one thing; to imagine his kisses was . . . something else.

"It's not a sin to wonder about kisses, is it?" Isabelle demanded. "That's not exactly lust, I don't think. It would be a sin if I imagined more, I'm sure, but not a kiss. I'd wager he kisses very well indeed, and I'd be willing to bet that Merva knows. I think I'll ask her."

"You will do no such thing!"

Isabelle rose and gave her a smile. "I'm only teasing, Allis. I won't ask—but I still think he's likely a marvelous kisser."

He certainly was, but she had better not think about that, or let Isabelle's jests trick her into displaying more emotion.

She began to tidy the brushes and pins on top of the table. "Just as long as you don't intend to find out."

Isabelle turned back her cuffs. "He wouldn't kiss me even if I wanted him to. I asked him if he would wear my scarf in a tournament and he said no, he's too old for me."

"Isabelle, you should not have asked. It was inappropriate and unbecoming a lady."

Even as she spoke, guilt tweaked Allis's conscience. Once more, she was playing the hypocrite, for if anybody in this chamber was acting inappropriately and unbecoming a lady these days, it was she.

"He said he wouldn't ask to wear yours, either."

Although that was wise, she felt disappointed nonetheless. "Of course he could not. I am betrothed."

"Which apparently means you cannot even think about kissing anybody else. Really, Allis, what is so wrong with talking about Sir Connor? It's not as if you or I were going to propose marriage to him." Isabelle took Allis's hands and looked at her beseechingly. "You're not angry with me, are you?"

"No, I'm not." As Connor lightened her dark days, so she should seek to keep Isabelle happy. After all, she had been upset by Isabelle's mournful sadness and guilt after Percival's death, so she should be glad to see evidence that she was recovering, even if she would prefer a different subject. "Come now, it's time to go to the hall."

She went to the door and held it for Isabelle. "In the hall I will hear no speculations about kissing," she warned as they went down the tower steps together, smiling to show she was not completely serious.

Isabelle's eyes gleamed mischievously. "What if I whisper?"

"Are you trying to make my hair go gray before its time?"

"What about Sir Auberan?" Isabelle mused. "I cannot even picture kissing him. His lips are too moist. It would be like kissing a toad."

"Have you ever kissed a toad?"

"No, but I can imagine."

"So can I—and I imagine Auberan would be worse."

They laughed genially, as they had not done in a long time.

"We shouldn't be making sport of one of our guests," Allis said with a touch of remorse.

"Why not? I mean, his face when he tries to look manly, like the morning of the tournament—it looks like he has indigestion."

"I was thinking cramps." They both started laughing again. "Oh, we must stop, or I'll never be able to look at him without grinning like a jester," Allis said.

"I . . . I'll try," Isabelle said, gasping and giggling at the same time. "To stop laughing, I mean. I don't think I'll be able to face him ever again. That would be asking too much, especially if he wrinkled his forehead the way he does."

"But maybe if we laugh at him enough, he'll finally go home."

"I'm delighted I am the cause of so much merriment."

His face red with rage, Auberan stood at the bottom of the steps.

Horrified at being caught making sport of a guest, Allis flushed with embarrassment. "Sir Auberan, I—"

He held up his hand. "Say nothing, my lady. Since I am not deaf, I comprehend you perfectly. I will pack my baggage and be gone in the morning."

He turned on his heel and marched away in high dudgeon.

"By the saints," Isabelle breathed.

Allis leaned back against the curved stone wall. "That was most unfortunate."

"At least he's leaving."

"Under terrible circumstances, and he'll tell everybody about our rudeness, too."

Isabelle put a sisterly arm around her shoulder. "Do not take this so much to heart, Allis. He's not worth worrying about."

"I don't want anybody to feel unwelcome at Montclair." *Except Rennick DeFrouchette.*

"Why don't you let me see if I can help? Auberan likes me. Maybe he didn't hear everything and I can persuade him to stay."

"He certainly heard the last thing, and that was bad enough."

Isabelle got that mischievous gleam in her blue eyes again. "Ah, but you said it, not me. That may make all the difference."

Allis slanted a suspicious glance at her sister. "And just how do you intend to persuade him to stay?"

"I certainly won't kiss him, if that's what you're wondering about."

"Good."

"I might imply that I would consider it, though."

"Isabelle!"

"Would you rather he spread vicious tales about the rude chatelaine of Montclair?"

Isabelle had her there. "Very well, but don't make any promises you don't intend to keep."

Her sister's expression hardened a little. "I won't. I wouldn't let poor Percival wear my scarf, would I? And I hold my honor as dear as you do, Allis," she said before she hurried after the disgruntled young nobleman.

"Better, I hope," Allis whispered as she followed.

All through the evening meal, Connor was sure something was wrong. Sir Auberan behaved like a sullen child and Lady Isabelle treated him most solicitously, as if trying to soothe wounded feelings. Allis looked as she had in the hall that first night—solemn, cold, unapproachable—even when she glanced his way.

Perhaps that was because of the arrival of Lord Oswald in the dispensary. He had been taken aback, too, and worried about what the man might think. Fortunately, Lord Oswald's words and actions had not given him cause to fear that the man might misinterpret—no, correctly interpret—their feelings for one another.

Could it be she was reconsidering their growing bond? If so, why should he be surprised? She had much to lose.

"Sir Connor!" Lord Oswald called out as Merva cleared the last of the fruit from the high table where he sat in the earl's place. "I have heard you sing well, like all your countrymen. Would you favor us with a song?"

He didn't want to sing. He wanted to be alone with Allis and find out what had happened, yet he could hardly stand and make that pronouncement. "It's not true that every Welshman can sing," he answered genially enough, despite his worry.

"That is not what we hear."

"Perhaps I should be more specific," he replied with a smile. "Not every Welshman can sing well, but most Normans can't carry a tune at all."

"Oh, surely you are being modest! Your father used to brag of your voice, along with your other attributes. Will you not grace us with a ballad?"

"I haven't sung anything in a very long time," he demurred. That was true enough, and there were only three kinds of ballads he knew: one kind extolled the past glory of Wales before the invasion of the Norman pirates and brigands, not something the Normans were likely to appreciate; another was about the glory of battle, not something he wanted Edmond to hear; and the last was about love.

"Maybe he's just being careful and doesn't want to risk being insulted. *Somebody* might say he's showing off, or sings like a dog howling at the moon," Auberan muttered, glaring at Allis.

Obviously, she had somehow insulted him, or he thought she had. As upset as he was, Connor couldn't imagine Allis purposefully insulting anyone, not even Auberan.

"Will you please sing for us, Sir Connor?" Allis asked, and there, in her eyes, he finally saw a hint of affection and tenderness. She wasn't asking him as she might a servant, but as she would make a request of a friend. Or a lover.

Maybe whatever had caused Allis to be so different had to do with the sulky Auberan and not him, which was a comforting thought. "I will gladly sing, as long as you all bear in mind it has been a long time and my throat is likely rather rusty."

Edmond's eyes widened, and Connor gave him a

conspiratorial grin as he got to his feet, the better to breathe for the long notes. "Not real rust. More of a croaking I'm afraid of."

"I'm sure the Welsh would say even one of them croaking is better than a Norman's singing," Auberan sneered, as he crossed his arms and looked away, as if determined not to listen.

"Well, a Welshman might, at that. Shall we let the ladies judge if I croak, or do somewhat better?"

He didn't wait for an answer. Instead, he filled his lungs and began to sing a song in Welsh that was not a ballad about Wales, or battle, or the love between a man and a woman.

It was the lullaby his mother had sung to him, a soft, delicate tune of sweet spring days, the ewes and their lambs on the hillsides at dusk. He closed his eyes, thinking of his mother and the way she would brush the hair back from his brow at night before she kissed his forehead and bade him good night.

When he told her he was too old for kisses, she never did it again—but she always brushed back his hair, and he never asked her to stop that small, loving caress.

When he was in the Holy Land so far from home and lonely, he would have given anything to have her kiss him once more, or brush the hair from his forehead and bid him a gentle good night.

He sang the last notes low and tender, as if bidding her the farewell he never got to say.

When he finished, Allis sat with her head bowed so that he couldn't see her face.

Lady Isabelle wiped her eyes and exclaimed, "Oh, that was lovely! It was about ill-fated lovers, wasn't it?"

"No. It's a lullaby my mother used to sing to me."

"It was wonderful, quite wonderful, even if I couldn't understand a word," Lord Oswald declared. "What do you think, Auberan?"

"I suppose he sings well enough," Auberan grudgingly conceded. "I've heard Norman minstrels who are better."

Allis still had not looked up.

"What does my lady say?" Connor gently prompted. It was the weakness of vanity, but he very much wanted to hear her opinion.

She didn't reply. Instead, she shoved back her chair and ran toward the stairway leading up to her father's bedchamber.

Connor sat heavily, too dismayed to do anything but stare at the steps.

Edmond sat beside him, putting his arm companionably around Connor's shoulder. "I didn't think it was so *very* bad. If you like, we can play chess."

Connor stopped looking at the stairway and gave the boy half a smile as he ruffled his hair. "If you like."

That would take some time, and he wanted to stay in the hall until he had a chance to speak to Allis and apologize. Of all the things he had been trying to do with his song, he hadn't meant to upset her.

As the evening wore on, Connor began to fear Isabelle and Edmond were never going to go to bed without Allis telling them to. Even Lord Oswald's weary assertion that it was time to retire had little consequence. Auberan lingered, too, yet he eventually departed, so that at last, only Connor, Isabelle, Edmond and those soldiers who slept there remained in the hall.

When Edmond's head was nearly lying on the

chessboard and he could hardly speak for yawning, Connor decided that, guest or not, he had no choice but to take command. "Lordling, go to bed, or you will fall off your horse and break your neck tomorrow."

Edmond raised his sleepy eyes. "One more move and I shall have you."

"One more move and you will fall into my clever trap. The game is over, and it is time for you to go to sleep."

"Everybody always orders me about," Edmond complained, rubbing his eyes.

"If you are to be a squire, you had best get used to that. Being a squire is like being a servant, only with better food. Now *off to bed*."

Reluctantly, Edmond finally stood and went toward the stairs leading to his bedchamber.

Now only Isabelle remained, seated near the hearth and doing her embroidery. The question was, how could he get Isabelle to her room without leaving the hall himself?

She moved her embroidery stand to the side of her chair and rose. "Is the game so truly decided? If not, I will take Edmond's place and finish the match."

"The hour grows late, my lady."

"But not so very late. After all, Edmond is but twelve years old, and I am nearly sixteen. Many ladies of my age are already married, so I should not be bundled off to bed like a child."

She was right, so all he could do was shrug and say, "The game is perhaps not as decided as I led Edmond to believe. If you would care to take his place, you are welcome."

She smiled and sat opposite him.

If she was going to be there, he might as well try to

discover what had happened that afternoon. "Tell me, Lady Isabelle, why was Sir Auberan so sour at the evening meal?"

Isabelle chewed her lip as she studied the board. "He was annoyed with Allis."

"So I gathered. Why?"

"She said she wished he would leave Montclair."

"To his face?" he asked incredulously.

"No, to me, but he overheard. He was very angry and she was very upset." She raised her eyes to look at him. "Allis cares too much what people think of her. She has always been that way, but it's been worse since Mama died. She expects Edmond and me to be perfect, too."

He recognized that grudging tone of voice, for he had used it himself when Caradoc criticized him. Now, as he listened, he heard the childish petulance and regretted that he had spoken so to his brother, who had been right to question the cost of what Connor had desired.

As for Allis, she was not wrong to be wary of the criticism of society. He had lived as an outcast long enough to know it was lonely, sad and difficult. Neither was she wrong to ask Isabelle to be careful, too. "I don't think she asks more of you than she does of herself."

Isabelle moved her queen. "I don't care what people think of me."

He studied the board, then shifted his bishop. "Perhaps because you have your sister to worry about that for you, and to smooth over any mistakes you make."

"It was I who smoothed over Allis's mistake today," she replied with a hint of pique. "I went to Sir Auberan and persuaded him to stay."

"May I ask how?"

"I told him Allis would be very upset if he left, which is quite true."

"Was that all?" he asked with his most persuasive manner.

"Well, I cried."

Connor hid his knowing smirk. No doubt Isabelle's tears were a valuable weapon.

While Allis . . . It would take a great deal to make her weaken enough to cry, especially in public. She would hate revealing that much vulnerability, as would he. "It might have been better to let him leave, given the way he was behaving tonight."

"That's what I think, too, but Allis wouldn't agree. She's afraid he will tell everybody how rude she was and our family honor will suffer."

"It might."

Isabelle tossed her blond head. "Well, what if it did?"

"A family's lost honor is not something to be treated lightly, my lady, as I well know."

She moved another piece. "Not even if it is lost in a good or just cause? Not even for love?"

He wondered what she meant by that, then decided this was a subject best avoided, and this conversation must come to a close. He could not stay in the hall all night, no matter what he wanted to do. "Who can say when a motive is purely unselfish?" he queried as he shoved back his chair and got to his feet. "When you see your sister, will you please tell her I meant no harm with my song?"

"Yes, of course. Checkmate!"

Connor stared at the board. She was right. Good God, she had snatched victory from him without him seeing it coming.

He raised his eyes, to see her grinning, her eyes gleaming with triumph. "I see I underestimated your skill, my lady."

"A lot of people do."

"I give you good night, my lady."

"Good night, Sir Connor," she replied as she watched him stride from the hall, a triumphant smile still on her face.

Chapter 15

In the still, dark hours of the night, Allis sat beside her father's bed watching him toss and turn. He mumbled and muttered, and sometimes wept, too. She held his hand, hoping that would quiet him. Often that simple thing seemed to bring him comfort. Or perhaps it only pleased her to think that her loving presence made a difference.

When he finally fell into a deeper sleep, Allis sighed wearily and leaned forward, laying her forehead on the bed beside his thin, frail arm. Once, together with her mother, he had made the world a safe and secure place. Once, he had been as strong as Connor.

When she had watched Connor sing tonight, his eyes closed and a peaceful smile upon his face, love in every note and syllable, she had remembered a better time, when she had been happy and carefree. She had yearned for those blissful, innocent times, then realized that in truth she didn't really long for the past to return. She craved a different present, one that allowed her to be with him, as his wife.

When she was with him, she felt so much more than secure and happy. Then, it was as if there were a whole new realm of joy awaiting her, full of peace and security, as well as the excitement of a passion that made her heart sing and her blood throb and that titillated her whole body. The thrill of mutual, fervent desire poured through her, where before there had been only the bleak despair of an arranged marriage to a man whose touch repelled her, and the cold comfort of duty done.

She didn't want Connor to leave Montclair. She wanted him to stay and be part of her family. To be her friend, her lover, her husband.

"Please, Father," she softly prayed, "show me a way."

The earl lifted his trembling hand and laid it on the top of her head. "Allis?"

She had not been talking to him, but he must have roused and thought she was. "Yes, Father?"

His face shone in the moonlight, and worry knit his brow. "Are you crying?"

"I was thinking about a song I heard today, that's all."

"What song?"

He sounded tender, concerned—almost like his old self, in the days when he would comfort her after she had hurt herself, or been upset over some little thing like a missing toy. "A song one of our guests sang. It was a lullaby, and very sweet."

"Did I hear it?"

Her chest constricted with dread. "No, Father, you were not in the hall tonight. You took your evening meal here in your chamber."

"Oh, yes, just so. Who sang the song?"

"A Welshman, Sir Connor of Llanstephan."

"A Welshman? He was a fine singer, then?"

"Very."

"Good enough to make you weep over his song, eh?" her father asked with a hint of gentle humor.

He sounded so well, so happy. "Yes, but not just then. I was resting."

"Perhaps he will sing it for me tomorrow."

"I shall ask him. How is your head, Father?"

"Much better. It doesn't hurt at all. Indeed, tonight nothing aches."

"Oh, I am so glad!"

"But I'm tired. Very tired. I was having a strange dream, Allis, about your mother and me. We had quarreled over something—I can't remember what—and she left me all in a huff, the way she used to sometimes. Do you remember?"

"She never stayed angry for long."

"No, because I would find a way to make her laugh. I always could, you know, Allis. I could always make her laugh."

"I remember."

"Marry a man who gives you laughter, Allis."

Another knot of dread balled in her stomach. "I am already betrothed, Father, to Baron DeFrouchette."

He didn't appear to hear her. "Ah, I loved Mathilde so! There is not a moment I do not miss her."

"I know, Father."

"Now I am tired, and I must sleep. Good night, Allis with her mother's eyes," he murmured, smiling, as his eyes fluttered closed. "I hope I shall dream of Mathilde again."

His hand slowly slipped from her head, and his chest rose and fell with peaceful sleep. She pressed a gentle kiss upon his thin hand. How good it was to hear him speak thus! Perhaps everything was going to be all right now. Perhaps the worst was over.

Her father would rest soundly for the rest of the night provided he was not disturbed, so she rose and bent to press another soft kiss upon his forehead before leaving his chamber.

She hurried toward the curved stairway leading up to her bedchamber. She had no candle or rushlight, but she knew the passage well, and there was a little light from the moon.

Before she reached the stairs, a man stepped out of the stairway, as if he had been hiding there. Shock and fear sprang to life, and she gasped and stumbled back, prepared to run.

"It's me. Connor."

At the sound of his deep, gentle voice, her shoulders slumped with relief. Now she recognized his broad-shouldered silhouette. "What are you doing here at this hour?" she asked quietly as she walked toward him, scarcely able to make out his features in the dim moonlight.

"I was going to wait until tomorrow to try to speak to you, but I couldn't. I couldn't rest until I apologized for upsetting you with my song."

"Oh, Connor," she said with a sigh as she took his hand and led him back into the shadowed stairway. "You don't have to apologize."

"I didn't mean to distress you so. If I had known—"

"That your gentle song would touch my heart, you would not have sung it?" Moved by his concern, she caressed his cheek, his stubble rough against her palm.

He nodded his head.

"But touching your listener's heart is nothing to be ashamed of."

He put his hands on her shoulders, the light pressure comforting as his gaze anxiously searched her face. "Then you are not angry with me?"

"No, certainly not. In fact, right now," she murmured, sliding her hands up his powerful chest as wondrous desire warmed her blood, "I am happier than I have been in a long time. My father seems better tonight, almost as he was before my mother died." Or so she hoped.

His hands slipped down her arms, gently stroking her. Her breathing quickened as the familiar, intoxicating excitement of his touch took possession of her. "For your sake as well as his, I am glad to hear it."

"This is not the most convenient place for us to meet."

"No." His lips brushed along her cheek. "But I was not thinking of anything except the need to apologize."

She shivered at the delightful sensation and relaxed against him as her hands glided around his waist. "How did you get back into the castle?"

"I told the guards I forgot something." His mouth crept gently down her neck.

Every tantalizing touch of his lips seemed more exhilarating than the last, and, with a moan, she arched back. "You cannot stay the night here. You must go back."

"Yes," he whispered.

"You had best go, Connor."

"I will," he mumbled before his mouth captured hers in a fervently passionate kiss.

Excitement, raw and primitive, fired within her. Snared by the heady feeling, she forgot where she was, and everything except him—his lips and his body— and her own burgeoning need.

Still kissing her, he maneuvered her back against the curved wall. The stone was hard and cold against her, but in the next instant, that, too, was forgotten. He slipped his arm from the sling and laid his left hand flat against the wall beside her before leaning closer, pressing his body full against hers.

Wrapping her arms about him, she returned his kiss, passion for passion, heat for heat. Her tongue plundered his mouth. He was her love, and she gave herself up to him and to the feelings he brought to such intense life within her.

His hand fumbled with the lacing of her gown and the bodice loosened. The cool air touched her skin as his hand slipped inside her gown to her breasts. Her flesh burned as his strong, callused hands roved over her heated skin and an exquisite tension grew.

She had to feel his skin and glory in the sensation of his nakedness beneath her fingers, so she slid her hands under his tunic and shirt.

"Sweet heaven," he gasped as her hands stole over his bare flesh and the ridges of his scars, reminding her that this was a warrior who held her, a man powerful enough to wear eighty pounds of armor as if it were linen, who knew what it was to lose people he loved. Who had dared to speak his mind to his king, and suffered the consequences. And who could surely have any woman he wanted, but who wanted *her*.

He took his hand off her body and out of her gown.

She vaguely wondered why, until his palm cupped her between her thighs. The pressure he exerted made her writhe and gasp for breath.

"I want you, Allis, so much," he murmured hoarsely. His fingers moved and new vistas of need opened. A hunger, powerful and primitive, surged hot and demanding.

Above, in the tower, a door opened. "Who is there? Allis, is that you?" Isabelle called out.

She wanted to groan with frustration and keep kissing him, but Connor abruptly let go and stepped back. His chest heaved as if he had run all the way from London.

"Go back to bed, Isabelle. I'm on my way."

"Heaven help me, your family has a damnable habit of interrupting," he whispered, sounding as frustrated as she felt.

"Yes, I know."

Yet even though she regretted the interference as much as he, they could not stay where they were. If they were seen . . . !

She reached back to do up her laces. He saw what she was doing and, putting his strong hands on her shoulders, turned her so that her back was to him and began to tie them for her.

The light brushes of his fingers against the nape of her neck made her weaken with longing to be alone with him and damn the consequences.

Isabelle's voice drifted down the steps. "Are you ill? You were making a very strange noise."

"I stubbed my toe. I have no candle to light my way."

"I've been waiting for you, so I have a rushlight still burning. Wait there and I'll bring it."

"Now you really must leave," Allis whispered to Connor.

"Aye, I must," he agreed as he backed away. "But I am not wanting to."

Then he disappeared into the dark as if he had been a phantom lover.

Taking deep gulps of air, she pressed her cool hands to her flushed cheeks. She was not being wise about Connor. Not wise at all. But when she was in his arms, she didn't want to be wise. She wanted to be wild and wanton, reckless and free.

To care for Connor was folly. She was only heading toward misery and heartbreak, and perhaps disaster.

Yet she could not help it. She could not ignore how Connor made her feel, as if she were utterly alive. She could not stop herself from wanting him. She could not help loving him.

But as Isabelle appeared on the stairs above, clad in her white shift and illuminated by the flickering rushlight as if she were a messenger of heaven, one thing remained clear and immutable: whatever happened, she must protect her family, and that she could never forget.

The chapel was as dim and cool as always, yet Auberan perspired anyway. "I don't care about your plans and schemes. I won't take her. I won't stay and I most certainly won't marry Isabelle. Didn't you hear what I said? They were *laughing* at me!"

"Auberan, Auberan, Auberan, calm yourself," Oswald soothed, laying a placating hand on the young man's arm. "It is women's nature to make sport of men. You take it too much to heart."

"Wouldn't you?"

"No," Oswald replied, moving away toward the statue of the Virgin Mary.

As before, she looked down serenely at them, head bowed, hands piously folded, her cares not of this world, but of the world to come. "I wouldn't take their jests to heart if I had more important things to consider, like the woman's dowry and social position. Besides, once she's your wife, you can make her pay for every insult."

At the sight of Lord Oswald's cold smile, Auberan swallowed hard. "Isabelle doesn't want me. She wants that Welshman. She's always with him, supposedly watching her brother, but I know better. I'm not a fool."

"So what if she finds him attractive? What better than some competition to make the game that much more enjoyable for you?"

Auberan looked at Oswald as if he were spouting absolute nonsense.

"Why didn't you leave Montclair immediately, if you are that insulted?"

"Isabelle was so distraught, I thought tomorrow would do just as well."

"She cried, didn't she?"

Auberan studied the toe of his boot. "Yes."

"So you see, she cares for you. It would be a mistake to leave now, and when you seduce her," Oswald patiently explained, "your triumph will be all the greater if there is another man competing with you for the prize."

"*Seduce* her?"

Oswald strolled over to the votive candles. He bent down and blew five out in one puff.

"Why do you do that?" Auberan demanded peevishly.

Oswald turned to him, and the flicker of the remaining candles gave his face a ghastly glow. "Because it pleases me to ruin someone's heavenly petition."

Auberan paled. "As pleased as I am that you believe I can seduce Isabelle," he began, stammering slightly, "I don't think I—"

"You *will* seduce her, to ensure she marries you. When you are wed, you will be united by marriage to Rennick. Between the pair of you, you will hold all the Montclair land and all the power and respect that goes with it."

"I do not think I'm so repulsive that—"

"It's not a question of whether or not you're attractive, Auberan, and it's not as if I'm asking you to do something repugnant, is it? We must guarantee that there will be no refusal, for any reason. If you take her maidenhead, she will not dare say no."

Auberan hesitated for another moment, but as Oswald's stare turned into a stern glare, he finally nodded. "Very well. I shall do my utmost to seduce Isabelle."

"Good."

"I've never seduced a woman before."

Oswald's thick lips pressed together in aggravation for a moment; nevertheless, his voice was calm when he replied. "It is not that difficult, if you try."

"Say what you will, she likes the Welshman better than me," he muttered.

Oswald's brows lowered. "Are you as stupid as you sound at this moment? Have you not seen the lay of the land? Isabelle may like him, but he prefers her sister."

Auberan gasped. "Lady Allis?"

"Lady Allis?" Oswald mocked. "Yes, Lady Allis. He practically salivates when he looks at her."

"But she—"

"She wants him, too."

"What of Rennick?"

"He will find out soon enough, if he doesn't already suspect."

"He'll be furious." Auberan's eyes widened. "Is that why Sir Connor's lance—?"

"The wood was old."

Auberan looked unconvinced. "If Rennick didn't want to kill him before, he will now."

"We need the Welshman, and Rennick understands that."

"What about the betrothal? Surely he won't want to marry Lady Allis if she's not a virgin."

"Did I say she would not be a virgin when she marries Rennick?" Oswald sighed and shook his head. "Good God, Auberan, you have no understanding of women, especially women like Allis. She will yearn for him, and perhaps accept a kiss or a caress, but she will never sully her honor, not when she is betrothed to another. She would rather die."

"You sound very sure, my lord."

"I am. I have known her since childhood, and she is the epitome of dutiful women who hold their honor dear. Sir Connor may sniff about her all he wants, but he will inevitably be disappointed. However, he may not be aware of that for some time. Until he does, he will stay and that will give me a chance to enlist him in our cause."

"I don't think Rennick will applaud this plan."

Lord Oswald drew himself up to his full height and regarded Auberan with indignant majesty. "I do not require Rennick DeFrouchette's permission for anything."

Auberan humbly backed away. "Yes, my lord."

"As for the seduction of a fifteen-year-old girl, it isn't so difficult. Compliment her on her beauty. Tell her she is sweet and charming. Entertain her. Treat her as if she were a grown-up, and for God's sake, be more agreeable, Auberan. Nobody likes a man who sulks like a baby."

Auberan nodded like a studious disciple. "Yes, my lord."

"And bring her presents. All women like presents." He strolled to the door. "One thing I suggest you do not do, Auberan, and that is try to sing. You will only suffer by comparison. Now good evening. The night is young, and Merva is waiting for me." He glanced back at the younger man. "Pray for success, Auberan, for remember, the rewards will be great, especially when Richard is no longer on the throne."

Chapter 16

The sun was still low in the morning sky as Connor made his way toward the main gate of Montclair Castle. During another restless, sleepless night, he had come to a decision. Things could not go on as they were. As much as he wanted to be with Allis in any way possible, subterfuge and secrecy made him feel soiled and sinful, and he abhorred the taint it gave their relationship. Something must be done, and soon, to clarify what was between them and what the future might hold, for good or ill.

In one way, it was already too late. He was in love with Allis. She had become the center of his world and the person most important in his life. Her affection and good opinion were the means by which he measured himself and his worth, which was both bane and blessing: blessing, because she made him feel that his past could be overcome and overlooked; bane because if they could not be together, he would always feel an emptiness in his heart.

Wrapped in such thoughts, he almost didn't realize something was not right as he approached the gate. Years of warfare had honed his senses sharp, however, and a part of his mind realized something was amiss. He halted, and scanned the wall walk. Thank God, the sentries were still there, pacing the walk as they should be.

But it was too quiet. Much too quiet. A castle always bustled with soldiers and servants, even at dawn, and so there was a constant low rumble and rustle of movement and voices. Today, he might have been standing in the vast confines of an empty cathedral all by himself, or on a battlefield, surrounded by corpses.

He anxiously hurried on to the gate. Two guards— Bob and Harry—stood deep in discussion, their heads bowed and their expressions grim. In other parts of the courtyard, small groups of servants stood huddled together, whispering, and many of the women were crying.

When Bob and Harry caught sight of him, they stopped talking.

"What's happened?" he demanded.

"The earl is dead," Bob mumbled.

Oh, sweet heaven. Poor Allis!

"Last night," Harry continued. "In his sleep and without pain, Lady Allis said, thank God. My old mam suffered terrible, and I'm glad to think he was spared anything like that."

Bob sighed as he leaned on his spear. "Aye, he was a good master."

"And Lady Allis? How does she fare?"

Bob and Harry exchanged sorrowful looks. "Not weepin' and wailin' like some," Bob offered.

No, she would not do that. She would bottle it up, as she did so much, and keep it to herself. She would be strong for her brother and sister, and her people, but the pain would be just as bad as if she rent her clothes and screamed to the heavens. No, it would be worse, for she would carry it alone. "Isabelle and Edmond?"

"She woke them and told them herself, poor thing. Merva's with them. She was their nursemaid when they was little. That's why they let her take the liberties she does."

"Aye," Harry confirmed. "She's right tore up, too. I ain't never seen Merva cry, but she's a-cryin' now, all right." He sighed. "She and the earl used to get teasing each other in the old days. Not that he ever touched her—never like that. He loved his wife too much, and she knew she was well off and smart enough not to risk it."

"Where is Lady Allis?"

They both nodded at the hall.

Thinking only of Allis and her sorrow, he hurried toward the hall, past the little knots of mourning servants. He threw open the door, then came awkwardly to another halt.

Lord Oswald, Auberan and Allis stood together on the dais, speaking with a priest Connor had never seen before. To judge by the man's majesty and the quality of his robes, he was a high-ranking member of the church. He was probably the man who stood to preside over the future cathedral.

All three turned to look at him. Oswald cocked a curious brow, Auberan sneered, the priest looked as if he thought Connor must be a servant, and Allis . . .

He hoped he would never again see in her eyes that look of unshed tears and anguish.

She came toward him, her face pale, but her back straight, and never did he admire her more, for he knew that she was maintaining her self-control with a strength few men possessed.

Yet they were being watched, and he was merely a guest in this hall, so he didn't even dare to touch her fingertips. "I am very sorry about your father, my lady."

"Thank you, Sir Connor."

He glanced at the men, who were clearly waiting for her and begrudging the interruption.

"We are planning the funeral mass and temporary interment of my father," she explained, her voice dull and flat. "Later, when the cathedral is built, we will move him there, of course."

He nodded. He wanted so much to tell her how truly sorry he was, and even more to gather her into his arms and hold her close, to offer her the comfort of his embrace. "My lady—"

She put her hand on his arm and looked up at him, tears threatening to fall until she blinked them back. "I know," she whispered, her lips trembling as she tried to smile for him. "Leave me to do what I must, and there is much. I will come to you when I can."

She was being so courageous, so strong, yet he knew her heart must be aching and full of pain, as his had been when he learned of his parents' death. Regardless of the others, he took hold of her cool, quivering hand and brought it to his lips. Very gently and tenderly did he kiss it.

Then he bowed and left her.

* * *

Panting and perspiring, Connor set down the half-filled bucket of water and wiped his brow. He flexed his left hand and raised his arm again, this time without lifting the bucket.

"My shoulder is definitely getting better," he said to Demetrius. "Today, perhaps I can even take you on something more than a walk, eh, my friend?"

Glancing at the wall surrounding the courtyard of Montclair, he slowly expelled his breath. "Something to pass the time."

Four days had passed since the death of the earl of Montclair, and five since he had had an opportunity to be alone with Allis. Those days had seemed unbearably long, yet he thought it best to wait for her to come to him, because that was what she wanted.

On the third day, he had joined in the solemn funeral mass and witnessed the temporary interment of the earl beside his late wife. It had been painful watching Allis and her family as they stood through the whole of the rite, only kneeling to receive the host. Isabelle's face was puffy from crying, her eyes red-rimmed, and she leaned upon Auberan as if she would swoon without him.

As befitting a young noble, Edmond was stoic. Despite his lack of expression, though, his whole body trembled with suppressed emotion, and once he surreptitiously wiped his eyes.

Allis stood as motionless as a marble statue. Wearing a severely plain black gown and equally severe white scarf and barbette, she looked like a nun who had been serving a heavy penance. He doubted she had slept or eaten much since her father had died, and it was very likely that what vitality she had went to comforting Edmond and Isabelle.

The baron still had not returned. The main estate of the earl of L'Ouisseaux was over a hundred miles away, and it would take time for a messenger to reach there.

Not that he was in any rush to have the man return, although the necessary secrecy weighed upon him like a blot upon his character.

"Well, let me try this one more time, Demetrius, and then I shall stop," he muttered as he bent down to pick up the bucket again. "Enough is enough."

The hem of a woman's black gown came into view. He quickly straightened and found himself face to face with Allis. He quickly and carefully drew on his shirt, surreptitiously studying her.

The strain in her pale, weary face and the dark circles beneath her eyes smote him. She had already endured so much and had so many obligations. Surely she deserved an end to pain. He yearned for something—anything—he could do to ease her sorrow, but all he could offer was his compassion. "How are you faring, my lady?"

"Everyone has been kind, Lord Oswald especially. Very kind and very sympathetic, very willing to do things for me."

He caught the edge that crept into her voice as the sadness in her eyes gave way to annoyance. "But you don't want pity or condescension or people taking charge over you, not even now—or perhaps especially not now?" he suggested.

She thrust her hands into her long cuffs and began to pace as if she couldn't bear to keep still. "I do not want to be treated like a child. I know my father is dead. I know what needs to be done. I would have sent for the baron eventually, given the situation between the baron and my family, but Lord Oswald took it upon himself to do so immediately. It will probably be worse when Rennick gets here. I hope his horse throws a shoe every mile of the journey back!"

She sounded so angry at the last, he didn't know what to say. At least she felt free enough to speak her mind to him, and was no longer trying to hide or subdue her feelings. It would be better for her to let them out, or like a festering infection, they would do more damage over time.

She stopped and as she regarded him, seemed to shrink. "I shouldn't be saying such things. I must be a sinful woman. My father is dead, and right now, all I feel is anger."

He ached to hold her, to feel her head resting against his shoulder, but he could not forget the sentries on the walls above. "My mother said once that when someone dies suddenly, you mourn them afterward. When they die slowly, you have already mourned them by the time God takes them into heaven. Your mourning time is past, and it is no wonder to me that you feel as you do."

Her eyes softened as her pale cheeks bloomed with pink. "It was like I was holding my breath all the time, Connor," she confessed softly. "As if I could never loosen the bindings that seemed wrapped about me, of duty and responsibilities, and that if I did, I would break apart like a broken jar.

"Well, that isn't quite true," she said, shaking her head and giving him a tremulous smile. "When I was with you, I felt free. Since that first night in the garden, you have made me feel happier than I have been in a long, long time. You brought joy and hope back into my life." She put her hand lightly on his arm. "It was as if I started to breathe again when I met you."

In all his life, he had never been so thrilled as he was by her simple, heartfelt words. Despite the soldiers on the wall walk who might see, he could not resist the impulse to gather her into his arms. She stood stiffly for a moment, then slowly relaxed and laid her head on his chest.

He longed for the privilege of always holding her secure in his arms, protecting her from any hurt or harm. And how he longed to kiss her—not with passion and desire now, but with tender affection. He yearned to press his mouth gently upon her cheek as a sign of his devotion.

How long they stood thus, he didn't know, but he appreciated every moment, if this was all he could do to ease her pain.

At last she drew back, gently extricating herself from his embrace. Clasping her hands in front of her, she raised her shining eyes to regard him steadily. "My brother is the earl of Montclair and head of the family now."

He nodded. Being more concerned with Allis's sorrow, he had not considered all the ramifications of the earl's death, but this was certainly one of them.

"As such, he has the right to confirm or deny the decisions of our father. There has been nothing officially signed or sealed regarding my betrothal to the baron."

Her simple words, spoken plainly and with firmness of purpose, sent his mind reeling.

Suddenly, that vista of heaven on earth with Allis by his side sprang back to life. If there was no formal legal document, Edmond could easily break any verbal betrothal between Allis and the baron. "Does this mean what I hope it does?"

"While Edmond admires the baron," she said, her smile blooming, "he admires and *likes* a certain Crusader more."

If the heavens had parted and angels appeared to offer him a place with St. Michael himself, he would have happily refused. Heaven on earth was almost in his grasp. "How soon can the betrothal with De-Frouchette be broken?"

"I see no reason it cannot be done as soon as he returns." She took hold of his hand and caressed his fingers, increasing the tension in his body that made him long to pull her into his arms. "I'm sure Edmond will agree, and I am willing to risk the gossip."

Another impediment arose in his mind, threatening to blight his hope again. "Edmond is a minor child. He will have to have a guardian. King Richard is a greedy man, Allis, and many men would pay him well to have the right to oversee Montclair, I suspect the baron most of all."

"I know. That is why I have already decided who should be Edmond's guardian. As soon as it can be arranged, Edmond and I must travel to London to speak with the king about it. Thank heavens Richard is actually in England, so that we can petition him ourselves."

"Who would you ask to have made Edmond's guardian?"

She ran her fingertips along his arm, the sensation delightful and incredibly arousing. "I would *like* to suggest you, but I think it best if we ask Lord Oswald. He is well known and well regarded."

Even in his joy, the past came again to haunt Connor. "And he has no quarrel with the king."

"Yes," she admitted. "He is also older and presumably wiser."

"There is that, I suppose."

"I am glad you are not older, or wiser. I like you just as you are, Sir Connor of Llanstephan with the barbarous hair. Besides, Lord Oswald likes you, too, so he will surely not disagree with Edmond's choice of husband for me."

Connor brought her hands to his lips. "Edmond's choice, is it?"

She twisted her hands so that she held his firmly, her grasp both a confirmation and a promise. "The night my father died, he said I should marry a man who gives me laughter." Her voice dropped so that it was as subtle and sultry as the surreptitious caress she gave his hand. "You give me laughter, Connor, and so much more. I would have you with me always. I want nothing so much as to be your wife."

"Allis," he whispered, pulling her close. "Nothing would give me greater joy."

She glanced upward at the surrounding walls, reminding him that they were not alone. "As much as I would like to stay, I am afraid I have been too long as it is. I had best get back, or Isabelle will make herself ill with crying. Coming so soon after Percival's death, when she was just beginning to recover from that shock, this has been an even worse blow."

"Thank God she has you. Thank God they both do."

She looked at her feet and shrugged her shoulders. "Words seem so . . . useless . . . at such a time."

"It is your presence alone that they most need, my lady." His hand itched to take hers but, cautious once more, he restrained the impulse. Instead, he looked off into the distance and remembered. "I don't know what I could have said or done to be of any help if I had been at home when my parents died, but it is to my everlasting regret that I was not." Her eyes misted and he spoke gently, wanting to do more for her now, if he could. "Is there is anything I can do to help, Allis, anything at all?"

"As a matter of fact, there is."

Her incredible, unconquerable spirit amazed him anew. Allis, weak? Allis, vulnerable? Not for long. How could he not love such a woman?

"It's one reason I've come, and the explanation I gave Lord Oswald for speaking to you. I want you to keep training Edmond. He needs to be doing something."

"It would be my great pleasure, my lady," he answered sincerely.

"I thought you would agree. Thank you." Her soft eyes glistened. "For everything."

"I think I am up to riding today. If you will allow us, perhaps we can leave the castle for a little while? The day is fair, and I assure you we will not go far."

"I see no reason to refuse. Now, if you will excuse me, I really should go, even if I do not want to."

She smiled another, wonderful smile before she hurried away, her black gown swishing over the grass.

Blissfully dumbfounded, he watched her go. "Did you hear that, Demetrius?" he muttered.

Then he laughed softly so that no one would hear, pure joy and merriment and delight thrilling through him. He would gladly spend the rest of his life giving Allis laughter, and anything else it was in his power to bestow.

* * *

Allis ran into the buttery, closed the door, made certain that she was indeed alone, then leaned back against the cool wall and put her hands over her face. What had she just done?

She had made it absolutely clear that she wanted Connor, and not Rennick—to Connor, not just herself. She had brazenly told him she wanted to be his wife.

Beneath her hands, she smiled with delight, and would have laughed aloud if the buttery didn't echo. She hadn't intended to tell him that then, or so bluntly, but when she had seen his surprise and his delight, she did not regret it.

No one on this earth cherished her as he did. She believed that to the depths of her heart, for she had seen it in his eyes, felt his tender and genuine concern when he had embraced her.

Let people say what they would about him, and about her. She didn't care. She wanted to marry Connor of Llanstephan. Edmond would gladly give his approval and Rennick . . .

Rennick would make trouble.

It was obvious Lord Oswald liked Connor, and Lord Oswald was more important and powerful than Rennick DeFrouchette. If they had Lord Oswald's support at court, Rennick wouldn't dare to complain, at least not publicly. Perhaps they could even do something about the taxes on Connor's family's estate.

Her worried expression disappeared, replaced with a broad smile. With Lord Oswald's friendship and Connor by her side, loving her as she loved him, they would surely triumph over any obstacle Rennick De-Frouchette tried to put in their way.

Chapter 17

❧

After the noon meal, Connor waited expectantly as one of the grooms sent from the castle saddled Demetrius for him. The man could have been Attila's Saxon twin, for he was nearly as tall and equally silent. He was different, however, in that he was sandy-haired and relatively clean.

Since this morning, Connor had felt light, joyful—as if he could race the wind itself around the mountains of Wales.

Demetrius tossed his head and stamped his feet, obviously anxious to go. "A gallop it shall be, my friend," he said, "if Edmond can keep up."

"I shall!" the lad cried, and Connor looked over his shoulder to see Edmond coming toward him, leading Firebrand.

His heart soared when he saw Allis behind him

217

with a fine-looking mare saddled for riding. No one had said anything to him about Allis accompanying them, which was probably a good thing. Otherwise, he would have been grinning like a gargoyle all through the noon meal, although they should not show any overt affection until the betrothal between Allis and the baron was broken. Hiding their feelings was going to be even more difficult now, but it would be the wisest thing to do.

Then his happiness diminished, for behind her came Isabelle and Sir Auberan, and their horses. Auberan's black stallion pranced about like a high-strung dancer, despite being weighted down with fancy trappings of scarlet and gold. Auberan obviously believed the more the better when it came to accouterments.

"Allis asked to come along," Edmond explained when he reached him. "And then Isabelle and Sir Auberan."

Allis made a little frown and surreptitious shrug. He understood. After the way she had inadvertently insulted Sir Auberan, she didn't feel she could refuse his request.

"The ladies may need protection. It is no secret that several dishonorable men have come back from the Crusades and turned brigand," Auberan declared.

Allis didn't want her guest to be insulted, so for her sake, he would restrain himself. "I can still use my right hand if the need arises," he said genially, patting the sword hanging on his left. "Fortunately, I understand the Montclair lands are very safe."

"Indeed they are," Allis confirmed, looking as if she was reconsidering the necessity of keeping Auberan's good opinion.

"May we go now?" Edmond demanded, fairly dancing with suppressed impatience.

Ignoring the lad, Auberan sauntered closer and ran his insolent gaze over Connor. "I'm very curious to see how Sir Connor is going to ride with a damaged shoulder."

"You know how, don't you?" he asked Edmond.

Edmond grinned. "With his knees mostly, of course. A good knight with a good horse doesn't need to hold his reins."

Not surprisingly, Auberan appeared a bit peeved. "How are you going to mount?"

"More of a problem there, I grant you," Connor agreed. "If you will give me a hand," he said to the groom, "we can be on our way."

The groom laced his fingers together. Connor placed his boot on his hands, and then carefully mounted Demetrius, who didn't move. He was, as he had told Edmond, steady as a rock. "I'm sorry I can't assist the ladies."

The groom went to help Allis, and Auberan hurried toward Isabelle. "Allow me, my lady."

She did, and Edmond mounted Firebrand while Auberan clambered on his horse's back.

Allis brought her mare beside Connor. "Shall we?"

"With pleasure, my lady," he replied, giving her a warm smile, simply happy to have her company as they led the others out of Montclair.

They rode through the village beyond the castle, and several people called out their sympathies on the death of the earl to Allis and her siblings. She paused in her progress and bent down to speak to the villagers who didn't hesitate to approach. Clearly touched by their words, she answered sincerely and with familiarity, knowing them all by name. The villagers also offered their sympathies to Edmond and Isabelle, but with more reserve.

As they rode out of the village, Edmond took the lead, riding several yards ahead as if he were the standard bearer of an army. Isabelle and Auberan stayed nearly as far behind, leaving them as alone as it was possible to be under such circumstances.

The air was warm for spring, with only a hint of wind, and the sun shone as if blessing their outing.

"I hope both your sister and brother noticed how the villagers spoke with you, and you to them. You are a fine example of what a noble should be," Connor said, breaking their companionable silence.

"I try."

"And succeed."

She flushed with pleasure in a way that delighted him. He enjoyed giving her the praise she was due, especially when her reactions told him that was rarely done.

"An overlord can be treated with respect while he lives and holds power over people's lives," he continued. "It is how his death is received that shows how he was truly regarded. Obviously your tenants thought highly of your father, too."

"Yes, they did," she replied, giving him a smile tinged with sadness and regret that made him realize anew how grieved she had been by her father's death. "He was an excellent overlord, until my mother died. In fact, when I look back, he began to change when he first realized how serious her final illness was." She sighed. "I think my father has been slowly dying of a broken heart for six years."

"At least he had you to comfort him," he said, voicing what he was certain was a truth.

"I did my best, but sometimes it was so hard."

For the first time since he had watched his friend die, he spoke aloud of his days of despair, when it seemed death would be a blessed relief. "Sometimes I wanted to kill Osric myself to end his misery, and he was my best friend, one of the finest, truest men I have ever known. His death, though—his death was something no man should suffer."

"You were with him at the end?"

He did not mind her questions, for he heard her gentle concern. She was not like others, who merely sought to gratify their morbid curiosity. "Yes. He died in my arms."

"I'm sure he was eased by your presence, as I have been."

No one had ever said such a thing to him, and he was deeply gratified. "I am pleased beyond measure to hear that, my lady. But I dared not come near you, although I wanted to very much."

"I did not need you by my side. I could feel your sympathy every time you looked at me, and even when you were not there."

"I wish I could have done more."

"It was enough," she murmured.

His heart took wing as a pride such as he had never felt filled him. He could think of no words to express his feelings, nor did he wish to end this moment of blissful contentment.

They passed through a short band of forest, dark with shadows. The only sound was the jingle of their harness, the wind in the trees and Auberan, quietly chattering to Isabelle behind them.

When they came to a brighter part of the forest, he noted Allis's expression and sought to bring her out of her mournful reverie. "Sir Auberan seems very taken with your sister."

Allis slid him a wry, sidelong glance. "So he does. Poor fellow. He's bound to be disappointed."

"She doesn't seem to dislike him."

"It isn't so much that she doesn't like Auberan as that there is someone else." Her expression told him that she meant him.

"I was hoping we wouldn't have to speak of this, that her interest would wane."

"I know you haven't encouraged her at all, but she is young and impressionable and very firm in her opinions. They are slow to change."

"Does she know?" He gave Allis a significant look, as if to add *about us*?

"No, not yet. I would rather wait until things are more settled."

He nodded. How Isabelle might feel then, he could guess, and he couldn't blame Allis for wanting to delay that confrontation for a little while.

The forest ended, and the road continued through a large meadow. Hills rose gently on either side, and on the other side of the meadow, bushes and willows indicated the meandering river. With the sun shining, it was like being in a warm bowl of light, the soft scents of grass and greenery surrounding him. Nearby, some grazing sheep ran a short distance off as they approached, just as the girls around the village well would scurry away when he and a group of his young friends would saunter past in the days of his youth. Unlike the sheep, though, the girls would giggle and watch them pass, and the boys would swagger a little more, feeling very well pleased with themselves.

He smiled at the memory and glanced at the woman beside him. Doubtless she would not have giggled and run away. He could easily imagine a younger version of Allis standing her ground by the well and regarding them with one brow cocked in challenge, as if to say, "You boys will have to do more than that to impress me."

By God, he would have tried, in the days of his youth, when all the world seemed as young and eager as he.

No, he shouldn't have met Allis then, when he was as arrogant as Auberan, and vain of his battle skills. Better to meet her now, when he had lost his youthful arrogance, and could appreciate all that she was, and all that she had to bestow upon the man lucky enough to win her love.

Demetrius lifted his head and snorted, pulling him from his reflections. "He wants to run," he translated.

"Let's all race to the river!" Edmond cried. "I'll win!"

Before he could respond, Edmond kicked his heels and Firebrand leaped forward, sending the bleating sheep nearest them dashing away in alarm.

"I'm not letting Edmond win!" Isabelle cried, and she spurred her horse to a gallop.

Auberan rushed by on his stallion. The young nobleman looked sick, but determined.

Connor turned to Allis, whose expression he couldn't read. "Riding hard won't further injure my shoulder, will it?"

"No, if you can really ride mostly with your knees."

Anxious to feel the wind in his face himself, he said, "My lady, I have ridden into a horde of infidels loaded down with lance and shield and armor, so have no worries about that."

"Nevertheless," she mused aloud, a pensive expression on her face, "you may want to reconsider. It might be better to rest. In the forest. With me."

Suddenly, any desire Connor had for the wind rushing past his face completely disappeared, vanquished by a different kind of desire. But despite his heart hammering in his chest and the hunger to be with her surging through him, his conscience urged caution. "Will we not be missed?"

"When they reach the river and realize we are not there, they will come back. We will only be alone a little while."

"Long enough to start some tongues wagging, particularly Auberan's. He looks the sort to gossip."

"I'll take that risk." She cocked her head to regard him, her eyes shining with merriment and something more that made the blood throb through his body. "Will you, my bold, brave knight?"

His conscience instantly muffled, he carefully slid from Demetrius's back. "I'll have to find a stump or fallen log to mount again," he noted, leading Demetrius toward her. "And no gallop for my destrier, poor fellow."

"If you would rather ride . . ."

He took her hand in his and gloried in that simple action as he led her into the forest. "Not I, my lady, not I. I'll give him his head tomorrow morning, for as long as he likes. He can wait that long. As I told Edmond, he is a patient beast."

She laughed softly, and the sound added to his

pleasure, just as holding her hand made him happy. They followed a narrow path, probably used by hunters. The light dimmed, and the odor of damp foliage and dead leaves beneath their feet scented the air around them. It was as if they were leaving the cares of the world behind them and entering a forest of enchantment, where everything and anything was possible.

At last, when they had gone far enough to be invisible from the meadow, he draped Demetrius's reins over a bush, then tugged the mare's reins from Allis's hand and likewise looped them over the bush. His body warmed with anticipation as he faced her and pulled her into his arms. "I must confess, my lady, I am not nearly so patient."

She thrilled to hear his words, and even more to be alone with him in the quiet stillness of the wood. As he embraced her with his strong and powerful arms, a rush of heady excitement shot through her. She had thought merely to enjoy a morning's ride in his company, until Edmond galloped off, followed by the others. Then the temptation to be alone with him had proved too great to resist, especially after the conversation they had shared about the sad death of his friend. He tried so hard to hide his pain, despite what he had already revealed of his troubled past, but now she knew him well enough to see beyond his words to the lasting sorrow deep in his eyes and to hear the hidden anguish in his voice.

He kissed her deeply, tenderly, passionately. Heat tripped along every fiber of her body as she eagerly responded, wrapping her arms about him as if she never wanted to let go. She had dreamed of being in his embrace so often these past few days, when the loneliness and heartache of her father's loss and the strain of offering continual comfort to her brother and sister had threatened to overwhelm her. Then, she would remember every look and touch, every tender moment and word, and be comforted herself.

As his firm, soft lips captured hers and teased forth her burgeoning desire, she knew she wanted to be loved and cherished by this man who had suffered and grown strong, who could offer her the solace and strength she so desperately craved. With whom she did not have to hide her fears, and who gave her freedom from them.

She parted her lips for him, then boldly thrust her tongue inside the warmth of his mouth, offering him an intimacy she had not known existed until he came into her life. Moaning softly, she relaxed against his hard, lean body, needing his strength as passion made her limbs soft. The place between her thighs swelled, like a rose about to blossom, hinting at the natural end of this growing, desperate hunger, an end she would share with him if not now, in some glorious future. Or perhaps now, for the titillating tension was too exquisite to ignore, or fight.

With fevered hands she reached inside his tunic, touching the hot flesh of his muscled chest. His right arm about her, his left slowly slid up her bodice to cup her breast. Through her plain woolen gown his thumb lightly stroked her nipple, sending wave after delicious wave of sensation through her. Her nipples tightened, and a low murmur of longing rose in her throat. She wanted to be naked, or clad only in her silk shift which grazed her body like his touch.

"Oh, sweet Allis," he murmured as his lips traveled from her mouth along her jaw.

When she had first seen him, he had seemed a savage, a primitive outsider who had no place in her ordered world. As he grabbed her scarf and tore both it and her barbette off, he seemed again savage, primitive in his passion. But now she gladly fled her closed and constrained world where she was imprisoned, and as she embraced him, so she embraced her own primal urges, free to express all the savage need he roused in her. He was man, she was woman, and here in the forest, they were in their own paradise, alone and apart from the world, at liberty to love.

Her hair, loose and free, tumbled about her shoulders. "Oh, God, your hair," he whispered into her ear. "I love your hair. I love your eyes. I love everything about you, my love. My love."

She arched back, giving herself more fully to him, letting him know she was his to love. His knee slipped between her legs and instinctively she pushed against it, driving her pelvis forward. She reveled in the incredible sensation of pleasure and desire that created. His arousal pressed against her and that inflamed her even more. Determined to share this, to ensure that he felt all that she did, she brought her hand around to stroke him.

His breath caught in his throat as he took hold of her hand and held it still. "Allis?"

Panting, restless, not wanting to stop, she looked up into his desire-darkened eyes.

"I want you, Allis, but not now. Not here," he murmured, letting go. He was as aroused as she, yet there was something else lurking in his dark eyes, a caution that she did not share.

Her body grew warm not with passion, but with the sudden realization that he possessed more self-control than she, that he could have done with her whatever he wished, and she would not—could not— have refused.

But then he said, "I want more time to love you the first time as you deserve to be loved, and in the finest, plumpest featherbed in all England."

Her dread disappeared. He was not stopping to force her to see that he was more in command than she, but only to voice a sincere wish.

His brow furrowed. "I should not presume—"

"That I want you?" Feeling suddenly and wonderfully free, she boldly caressed him again. "Bed or no bed, I am already yours forever, Connor." Emboldened, she grabbed his tunic and tugged him to her. "Your kisses are very potent, sir knight, and I would have more of them."

His smile began in his deep brown eyes, then encompassed the rest of his face. "Would you, my lady?"

"Indeed." She leaned against him, wanton and demanding. "Shall I beg?"

"Never." He kissed her tenderly, but she felt the underlying passion waiting for liberation. "I will gladly give you all the kisses you desire."

He brought his lips to hers for another long, leisurely kiss, as if they had no cares in the world save pleasing each other, and she once again caressed the evidence of his desire.

"Stop that, you brazen wench. We have not the time," he growled as he slowly lifted her hand away. Still holding her hand, he grinned with wry delight. "*O'r annwyl*, I sound just like Caradoc. Perhaps he is frustrated, too, and that's why he sounds so annoyed all the time."

"Are you frustrated?"

"My lady, you have no idea."

She ran her fingertips along his length. "I believe I do."

"If you do not stop this touching, it may be most humiliating when the others return." He held her hand in place, as if daring her to continue. A heady mixture of excitement and daring possessed her that proved irresistible. "How so, sir?"

His eyes dark with unassuaged longing, he raised her hand to his lips. "I am not about to explain."

He didn't immediately kiss the back of her hand. Instead, his tongue flicked out and tickled the tender flesh between her fingers, jolting her to the soles of her feet. "By the saints!"

"Not the place I would most like to do that," he remarked with another devilish grin that seemed to say two could play her arousing little game.

So they could. She grabbed his right hand. Slowly and deliberately, not taking her gaze from his startled and flushed face so she could watch his reaction, she sucked his forefinger into her mouth.

His eyes widened and his color deepened. "Where did you learn to do that?"

Triumphant and delighted, she let go. "Brother Jonathan."

"Brother Jonathan?"

She wrapped her arms about his neck. "I didn't mean it like that."

"Thanks be to heaven!" His arm circled her waist and held her wonderfully close. "I was beginning to think I was totally mistaken in the man."

"He's a priest!"

Connor's expression grew serious. "Allis, I met some supposedly holy men in my travels whose behavior would shock you to the core of your being. I was fairly certain Brother Jonathan wasn't of that ilk until you said that."

She took his hand again and kissed his fingertips one by one. "Brother Jonathan says a person's fingers are very sensitive."

His chest rose and fell rapidly. "He's right about that."

"He taught me to use my sense of touch when it came to healing. Remember how I felt your wound in the tent?"

"Yes," he replied in what was more a sigh than a word.

Seeing how her actions affected him, a new and awesome sense of power came over her. She suddenly felt that with just the touch of her lips on his body, she could be as powerful as any man. And as he became tenser and tenser, as her power seemed to increase, she realized that this incredible power made them equals.

The tree branches rustled above them as they kissed again, their mouths joining in a slow, languid union. Parting their lips by silent mutual consent, their tongues entwined sinuously in a lithe, lazy dance.

"Alllliiissss! Sir Cooooonnor!"

Edmond's voice seemed to come from very far away, outside the walls of their momentary paradise. Nevertheless, their time alone was obviously at an end, and she reluctantly withdrew from Connor's arms. "Edmond must have decided to race back, too." She raised her voice. "We're coming!"

She leaned her head against his chest. "Alas, I fear we must go back."

His expression told her he was as sorry about this as she. "Alas, you're right."

She began to put her hair back under her scarf, but as she did, Connor caught a stray lock and pressed it to his lips. "I wish you would wear your hair loose."

"I couldn't start to do that. What explanation would I give? That Sir Connor of Llanstephan prefers it that way?"

He leaned forward and kissed the side of her neck. "No, I suppose you couldn't do that."

Sighing with both pleasure and frustration, she twisted away. "At least, not yet," she said as she attached the barbette.

That finished, she tilted her head to study him. "Would you cut your hair if I asked you to?"

"Only if *you* asked me to." He frowned. "Are you going to ask me to?"

She studied him another moment. "I think not. I think I prefer you to look like a savage."

He crossed his arms. "A savage? Is that how I appear to you?"

Unable to resist the tantalizing temptation, she ran her hands along his upper arms, her fingers gently gliding over the rise of his muscles. "To me, and to a lot of other people, and I would not be at all surprised to learn you know that and count upon it."

"Whatever for?" he demanded with an indignation that was completely undercut by the blush creeping over his cheeks.

She tried not to show how much that blush, and the masculine vulnerability it revealed, delighted her. "To frighten them, of course."

All pretense of annoyance fled as he smiled with sly devilment and tugged her close again. "Does it work?"

"I must say, it certainly makes you seem quite . . . virile," she admitted as she wound her arms about his neck and looked up into his dark eyes, which twinkled with merriment.

"Then I will not be cutting it off?"

She ran her hand through his wavy locks. "Not for my sake, anyway."

He began to nuzzle her neck, moving with delicious little nibbles toward her ear as her whole body shivered with anticipation and excitement. "You know, I fear I may soon have no secrets from you, my lady." He held her even tighter. "Are you cold?"

"Are you lost?" Edmond called out.

With even more reluctance, she backed out of Connor's wonderful embrace.

"No!" she shouted. She gave him a mischievous look. "No, I'm not lost, and when you hold me, I am anything but cold." She went to the shrub and picked up her horse's rein. "Alas, sir knight, we must return to the others."

"I believe I shall have a little word with Edmond about all this racing," he remarked as he grabbed Demetrius's reins and hurried after her, once more taking her hand in his. "It's not dignified . . . or something."

They both laughed softly as they quickly headed back toward the meadow. She gloried in the simple act of holding his hand for as long as she could, as if they were any young couple in love, and without a care in the world. "I've tried. Besides, we weren't exactly being dignified ourselves."

"We're older." He chuckled. "God's wounds, that's what Caradoc always used to say when he got to do something that I didn't. I fear I'm turning into my older brother."

"Is that so bad?"

"I suppose not—but he's not much fun. Very grim and serious, Caradoc."

"You were very grim and serious when you first came here."

"Well, I was here to win a good ransom in the tournament."

"Losing cheered you up?"

He halted and pressed a quick kiss to her forehead. "Not exactly," he said with that wry self-mockery that charmed her. "By some miracle, I have won something far better."

"You have won my heart, at least, Connor," she said, grave despite his smiling eyes, "but that is no miracle to me. You are the finest, truest knight I have ever met. Or if there is a miracle, it is that you came into my life and brought an end to my sorrow and loneliness. My love is a small recompense for that, but all I have, is yours forever."

He gently took her by the shoulders and looked down at her, love shining in his eyes. "Allis, if we had all the time in the world, I could not begin to tell you how happy you make me, and how blessed I feel."

"Where *are* you?" Edmond demanded peevishly.

"Sadly, we don't have all the time in the world," she said as, the spell broken again, she once more started hurrying toward the sound of Edmond's voice.

"There you are!" Edmond declared when they reached the meadow and found him waiting.

Puzzled, he looked down on them from the back of Firebrand. "What are you doing in the woods? I thought Demetrius wanted to gallop."

"I decided against it," Connor said.

Edmond's eyes narrowed. "You look all red." He studied Allis. "So do you."

A moment's awkward silence ensued, until Allis suddenly realized Edmond was alone. "Where are Isabelle and Sir Auberan?"

"Oh, back there," Edmond replied with a dismissive wave of his hand. "Isabelle wanted a drink from the river. Sir Auberan stayed with her."

She trusted Auberan as much as she would any vain young fool around her pretty sister. "You shouldn't have left them alone."

"Why not? You were alone with Sir Connor."

"I'm older." She swung herself into the saddle. "I'm going after them. Edmond, help Sir Connor find a way to get on his horse."

She dug her heels into her mare's sides and set off at a gallop across the meadow.

Chapter 18

"**N**o, Auberan, I do *not* want to kiss you," Isabelle protested as she gently shoved him away.

Around them, willows bent over the water, and the slender branches of the trees dipped into the river.

Auberan put one foot back into the ferns along the river bank to steady himself. "Isabelle, please, let me," he pleaded, wrapping his arms around her again. "Once. Just once, that's all I ask."

"No!" She pushed harder.

As he let go of her, his feet slipped on the bank. His arms flailing helplessly, he stumbled backward into the river, then splashingly struggled to stay on his feet. The river was very shallow here, so there was no danger of him drowning, but it was rocky, so it was not easy for him to regain his footing.

"Perhaps that will cool your ardor, Sir Auberan," Allis declared as she drew her horse to a halt.

Despite her stern tone and expression, she wasn't angry, at least not at Isabelle.

"How long have you been there?" Isabelle's sodden would-be lover demanded, looking more like a damp dog than a knight.

"Long enough to see my sister push you into the river, as you deserve."

"I didn't mean to push him into the river," Isabelle said. "He slipped and fell."

Allis had seen enough of the altercation to know that she most certainly had pushed Auberan in, and he deserved it, too.

Mounted on Demetrius, Connor appeared on the river path beside her, Edmond behind him. "An odd time to bathe, isn't it, Sir Auberan?"

"Isabelle pushed him in."

"Why?"

"He was behaving improperly."

"Ah."

"I was merely attempting to express my affection for Lady Isabelle," Auberan retorted with affronted dignity.

"Yes, that's all he was doing. I don't think every-body needs to make such a fuss," Isabelle declared. She gave Allis a pointed look. "Especially people who have been off somewhere themselves."

"What I do or don't do is none of your business, lit-tle sister," she replied, feeling a moment's regret that she had given in to the impulse to be alone with Con-nor. A quick glance at him, so tall and regal beside her, banished that regret.

After all, Isabelle was just a girl, and whatever she

said could be easily dismissed as a sibling's annoyed gossip. As for Auberan, given his embarrassment, she was quite sure he would not be keen to explain the circumstances of his soaking.

Her sister moved toward the edge of the bank and offered her hand to Auberan. "Let me help you."

"Be careful he doesn't pull you in, too," Allis warned.

With a sour glance over her shoulder, Isabelle muttered, "I will." Then, smiling at Auberan, she grabbed his hand and helped him clamber, shivering violently, out of the freezing water. "We had better get home at once, before you catch a chill. Perhaps Edmond would ride ahead and ask Merva to warm some chicken broth."

"All right," Edmond readily agreed, turning Firebrand and spurring him into a gallop.

Isabelle shot Allis another pointed glance. "Sir Auberan is our guest, after all, and we should always take good care of our guests. Isn't that what you are forever telling me?"

With that, she took Auberan's hand just as Allis had taken Connor's and walked with him to their horses. Although dripping, Auberan helped Isabelle to mount, then clambered onto his own horse.

"I believe she is upset with me," Allis noted as they began to follow them.

"And I think I have been supplanted in your sister's affections. I'm glad of that, but I must say it's a little humbling to be replaced by that particular fellow."

"You may retain your pride. I know Isabelle, and she's angry, so she's making it *look* that way." Which unfortunately meant she could still be harboring fantasies about Connor.

As distressing as that was, Allis couldn't blame her. Connor was the sort of knight who inspired maidenly dreams. "I'm hoping it's just a youthful fascination that will soon pass."

"Has she had other 'youthful fascinations'?"

She felt a twinge of dismay. "No."

He gave her a comforting smile. "She's a sensible girl, then. When she understands how we feel, she'll probably be upset for a while, but then find a more suitable young man to admire. She's pretty and sweet, and soon enough knights will be flocking around her like bees to honey."

Once again, he lifted a burden from her shoulders. "Although I think you're right, I have to say the prospect of being under siege by an army of young knights intent upon winning Isabelle's affection is a little daunting."

"Be of good cheer, my lady. You won't have to endure it. You will be in Wales, with me."

She saw that he was absolutely serious and, feeling a shadow on her happiness, pulled her horse to a halt. "I cannot leave my family. They need me."

He caressed her hand and a winsome smile crossed his face. "Forgive me another selfish speech, Allis. I have been thinking of a little piece of land where I have dreamed of building a home. But that can wait until Isabelle is well married and Edmond comes of age. Or if you never want to live in Wales, I will make my home wherever you choose. I will be with you, and that is the most important thing."

Her heart filled with gratitude as well as relief. "Oh, Connor, I would go to the ends of the earth with you if I had only myself to think of. But I promise you, once

Isabelle is wed and Edmond of age, we will live in the place you have dreamed of. All I dream of is being your wife, and after all your travels and hardship, you may choose where that will be."

His smile beamed, a delightful reward for what would truly be no sacrifice.

"Besides," she continued merrily as she nudged her horse into a walk again, "I think I should get to know your family. You are certainly coming to know mine."

"And I'm liking them very much, but not so well as the eldest."

Exchanging smiles, Allis and Connor continued to follow the sodden knight and the proud young lady back to Montclair as if they had nothing but happiness before them and all the world was young.

Auberan and Lord Oswald stood in the dark chapel. Clouds covered the moon, so all was dark, save for the dim illumination of the votive candles.

"She herself helped me from the river," Auberan bragged as he finished describing what had happened.

He left out the part about her refusing his kiss, making it sound as if he had slipped when he had been about to embrace her and that she had been very willing.

"Indeed?" Oswald muttered as he strolled toward the candles. He bent forward, glanced up at the statue of the Virgin, then straightened without blowing any out.

"Yes, and she was most concerned about my health afterward. She ordered chicken broth for me, and stayed by my bedside while I ate it."

"I see. Like a mother tending a sick child."

Auberan blinked. "I suppose so," he stammered, "but she held my hand as we walked to our horses."

Oswald barely refrained from rolling his eyes and his hands itched to draw the jeweled dagger stuck through his belt, and do with it what it was made for: to deliver the coup de grâce—a quick and merciful death. This bungling fool really didn't deserve to live. If *he* had been in Auberan's place, he would have had Isabelle of Montclair flat on her back on the riverbank, half naked and begging for him to take her.

He adjusted the wide leather belt around his long, dark blue wool tunic and thought of her fresh young beauty. Maybe he was wrong to give her to Auberan. It might have been wiser to seek her for himself. There would have been the matter of his present wife, but she could be disposed of with little trouble. A bribe to a bishop, and an unfortunate blood tie making the marriage illegal in the eyes of the church could be discovered.

Well, he had not, so he would simply have to stay with his original plan. At least Rennick could be counted on to do as he was told without making a mess of things. To be sure, he had taken longer than he had expected in the matter of the recalcitrant chatelaine of Montclair, but only because he seemed to have some genuine feelings for the girl, try as he might to hide or ignore them. Fortunately, he had finally succeeded before he had to be replaced.

"Do try to make her see you as a lover, not an invalid," he chided the incompetent would-be seducer.

"I almost kissed her before I slipped."

Almost kissed her. Good God, the fellow was truly pitiful.

Rennick might be right. Family connections or no family connections, Auberan could indeed prove to be more of a liability than an asset. "Then hopefully next time you are alone with her, you will not be near a river and so have more success."

"I'm sure I will."

Oswald strolled around the altar, taking note of the costly embroidered cloth covering it. What a waste of money. "Where were the others while you were with Isabelle?"

"Edmond had gone back to join Allis and Connor."

Oswald smiled like a teacher watching a slow pupil finally catch on. "And where were they?"

"They stayed . . ." Auberan finally grasped an important point. "Are you going to tell Rennick?"

His footfalls loud in the silence, Oswald sauntered toward Auberan, who had not moved from the middle of the empty chapel. "I don't think I'll have to."

Auberan frowned. "Shouldn't he be back by now?"

"He had other business to attend to before he could return."

"What other business?"

"That is not necessary for you to know, my young friend. What is necessary for you to know is that you should not be *trying* to kiss Isabelle. You should be kissing her—and more."

Auberan didn't meet his gaze. "I'm doing my best."

"Do better. We have not got an eternity for our plans to mature." *Or you.*

"When do you expect to take action?"

"When the time is right." Oswald circled his nervous young companion, happily intimidating him some more.

"Richard is in England now, for once."

"Yes, but if the time is not yet right, we must wait."

"For what?"

"As I said before," Oswald growled as he once more faced Auberan, "we must be certain we have the support of many before we move. Besides, if Richard is not in England, we can always pay one of his own men to do the deed and make it look like a wound received in a battle far from here."

That was not at all his plan, but he was not about to tell Auberan the truth. "I sometimes thank God Richard is not a peace-loving man. Arrows go astray so easily."

"Arrows are the weapons of peasants and foot soldiers."

He stifled a long-suffering sigh. "What does it matter, as long as it does the task required and from a safe distance?"

"I had not thought of that."

"No, I didn't suppose you had." He had no more patience for dealing with Auberan. "Go back to the hall and Isabelle, and do try to be more of a warrior and less of an invalid."

Auberan bowed and obeyed, leaving Oswald in the chapel to contemplate not his sins or the grace of God, but the destruction of Richard and his own rise to power.

Connor had nearly forgotten how good it felt to have the wind in his hair and the freedom of cantering on Demetrius across an open meadow. The day was not as fair as yesterday, with low gray clouds promising rain later, but he didn't want to make Demetrius wait another day.

He had been selfish enough already. Not that he

was feeling particularly guilty. He had been too happy being in the forest with Allis, holding her in his arms and kissing her sweet lips.

On the other hand, both he and Demetrius needed the exercise. In his case, sleep was long in coming these days as he envisioned a future with Allis to love and cherish. And other things, too—especially Allis in their bed, naked and waiting.

She was everything he could want in a lover, responding with fierce enthusiasm and exciting him beyond anything he had ever felt. Glorious, wonderful Allis, so serene and wise and dutiful, those qualities masking a passionate nature that perhaps he alone fully knew and appreciated.

Yet she was so much more! Wise, patient, loyal, tender, she would not make merely a wonderful wife. She would be a wonderful mother, too. Indeed, in many ways, she already was, for she was as much a mother to her brother and sister as she was their sibling.

At last he slowed and turned back toward Montclair. Perhaps when he got back, he would see Allis and have another chance to speak with her. Perhaps he would have another chance to be alone with her. Yesterday, as soon as they had arrived back at Montclair, she had been summoned by the cook over a question of the meats for the evening meal, and had to leave without much of a farewell.

He glanced at the sky, noting that the clouds were thickening. A storm was definitely brewing.

Then, suddenly, at the edge of the forest, he spied Allis mounted on her horse. She wore a cloak of rich green wool, the silk-lined hood pulled up over her head, yet not so fully that he couldn't see her face. Beneath the cloak, the black skirt of her gown peeked out.

She was like a dream, the embodiment of hope and happiness.

As he spurred Demetrius into a trot and rode toward her, he saw Bob and Harry. They were behind her, mounted on the sort of horses common soldiers were generally assigned.

"Good morning, my lady," he called out as a low rumble of thunder sounded in the distance. "Not the best day for riding, perhaps," he noted as he reached them.

"I wanted to nonetheless. I am merely going to the river and back again. Would you care to join me?" Her eyes sparkled with mischievous delight.

"I would be delighted." He turned Demetrius, so that their horses were side by side. They began to walk toward the river, Bob and Harry dutifully following behind. "You have an escort with you, I see."

"Of course. A lady does not ride out alone. A lady generally does not go up on the wall walk and search the ward for a guest, either, but if she does, and she sees her guest going out riding all by himself, she may decide it is her duty as hostess to join him."

"Her guest is very grateful for her company." He could almost feel the gaze of Bob and Harry on his back. "Will Edmond be coming for another lesson today?"

"Unless it rains."

"We may get caught in a storm."

"Does that thought trouble you?"

"Not at all."

"I understand it rains even more in Wales than it does here."

He laughed. "Aye, there is that. I hated such weather in my childhood, when it meant being confined indoors. I only came to love the rain after my years in the East. There I learned never to take water for granted again. Since then, I have thought every shower a blessing, every downpour a cause for jubilation. I love the sound of raindrops on leaves, the scent of the rain-wet earth, the feel of the water on my skin like a lover's caress."

He glanced at her blushing face, then, mindful of the men behind, continued without any hint of any hidden meaning, "I think I love a good thunderstorm the best of all—the rough roar of thunder and the flash of lightning. It's alive and fierce and wild all at once, like the gods at war."

"Which is why I prefer not to get caught in a thunderstorm if I can help it."

"Yet you rode out this morning."

"To ensure that my guest was not lonely."

There was another rumble of thunder, closer this time, and he looked up at the rapidly scudding clouds. "I think we had best abandon the notion of getting to the river."

The words had no sooner left his lips than fat raindrops began to fall. Lightning lit the sky and a loud roll of thunder followed almost instantly.

"Bob, Harry, ride back to Montclair," she ordered, twisting in her saddle to address them. "Tell them that Sir Connor and I have taken shelter from the storm in the shepherd's hut in the river meadow." She gestured to a hovel at the far edge of the field. "Otherwise, I will be soaked through before we can get back. I have no wish to fall ill."

Another bolt of lightning flashed as the two men exchanged wary glances. Connor was just as taken aback by her suggestion.

"Go, now, before the storm breaks in earnest," she commanded. "I would not have you two sick, either."

The rain began to fall harder, and they obeyed, turning their horses and galloping off.

"Allis, I don't think this is wise."

"They are wearing *gambesons* and helmets, so they are better protected against the rain. I have only a thin woolen cloak."

With that, she spurred her horse and made for the small shelter.

He really had little choice but to follow. He couldn't leave her alone. And if he were being truly honest, he didn't want to.

Chapter 19

As Allis hurried inside the hut, Connor tethered the horses beneath a sheltering oak as quickly as he could. The wind came up, lashing the rain against him. His task finished, he threw his arm over his head, ran to the hut and ducked under the low lintel. The ancient leather hinges creaked in protest as he shoved the decrepit door closed. It took a moment for his eyes to adjust to the sudden darkness as he breathed in the odor of straw and damp wool.

Allis sat on a pile of straw, with her back against the far wall. She had thrown her cloak over her shoulders and had her legs drawn up, her arms wrapped around her knees. "It doesn't leak as much as I thought it would, and we're alone." She smiled and patted the straw beside her.

As he joined her, he couldn't share her levity. "I

don't think it was wise to send Bob and Harry back while we stay here. Furtive meetings in Montclair are risky enough."

"I truly would have been soaked through before we could return." She took off her wet scarf and barbette and laid them on her other side, then shook out her marvelous hair. "I thought you would be pleased, although apparently you are not."

He forced himself to remember why being here with her was not a good idea. "Of course I'm pleased to be alone with you, but this is too reckless. What will people think?"

"That the lady of Montclair didn't want to get wet through and catch her death of cold." Grabbing her scarf, she began to get to her feet. "If you would rather I risk being ill, Sir Connor—"

He pulled her down onto his lap. If she, the dignified lady of Montclair, was willing to risk gossip, he would not gainsay her. Besides, every impulse within him urged him to stay.

"Don't be angry, Allis. Please." He kissed her lightly and pulled the scarf from her fingers. He tossed it away, then reached up and toyed with a lock of her luscious hair, tucking it back behind her delicate ear. "It just seems so impetuous."

Of all the things for him to say! He laughed at the incongruity of it. "The times I've been chastised for acting without thinking, and now here I am chastising somebody else!" he explained as he caressed her cheek.

Then he recalled that too-often, the criticism had merit. "Usually I've gotten into deep trouble when I acted without thinking."

"If you believe this is so wrong, we can go back,"

she suggested, winding her fingers in the lace at the neck of his tunic. Suddenly vulnerable, she tilted her head to look up at him questioningly.

The pace of his beating heart quickened. "I thought you were the responsible one in Montclair, always worried about what people will think and say."

A look of sadness came to her eyes, and he instantly wished he had not said that. "Yes, I have been, for a long time. But when I'm with you, I don't want to worry about such things, at least for a little while. I want only to think of us."

He stroked the silky skin of her cheek and brushed his thumb over her full lips, the softness of them enticing and tempting. "I just don't want anything to go wrong. I don't want to lose you."

"I don't want to lose you, either," she murmured, turning her head slightly. Her lips skimmed over his palm as butterflies flutter over a flower, and the delicate, yet sensual, act fired his blood. "A few tongues may wag, but what of that if we are to be married?"

"Are we, Allis?" he whispered, wanting to hear it from her own lips as he lifted her hand and grazed her wrist with his mouth while looking intently into her glistening eyes. "Are we to be married? Would you agree to be my wife, even though I have nothing to offer you?"

She cupped his face and regarded him steadily as she spoke with undeniable conviction. "You offer me your love, Connor. You offer me a life such as every woman dreams of, beloved, secure, as your equal, not your servant. You can imagine my life as the bride of Rennick DeFrouchette, or another of his ilk. Compare that with the love you offer me, and then tell me which is the better choice." She smiled gloriously. "It is not such a hard decision to make."

Joy, pride, hope, wonderment all burst forth within him at her words. What had for so long been a future dark and bleak as the windswept moors with night upon them was suddenly ablaze with hope and happiness. All the mistakes, anger, despair, fear and regret that had gone before in his life were washed away by her, and he was newly made, re-created and free of the past. Free to begin again, with Allis by his side. Here, now, in this simple hut, he did not envy any king in his palace, or sultan on his throne. He no longer cared what the world thought of him, because Allis's love was all, and she was giving it to him.

He undid her cloak and slipped it from her shoulders. "Allis, my Allis," he whispered as he nuzzled her wonderful soft and smooth neck, then trailed his lips to her mouth, capturing it for a long, luxurious kiss.

She wanted him, he wanted her; they were to be wed. There had been no doubt in her voice, and certainly there was none in her kiss, or when she lifted his tunic. Her graceful hands moved over his naked flesh as if they were dancing a slow, luxurious dance of seduction. He gasped as they wandered over his nipples, then moaned as she tugged his tunic upward and let her tongue do the same dance.

Caution and concern fled as dry leaves in a sudden blast of wind. He could no longer fight the desire throbbing through him. He did not want to struggle against his desperate yearning anymore.

Palming the warm weight of her breast, he brushed her aroused nipple with his thumb. His lips pressed against the throbbing pulse of her neck, and he felt the tempo increase—although her ragged breathing told him all that he needed to know.

"I'm going to make love with you, Allis," he whispered, his voice hoarse with need.

She nodded.

"Now."

"Please," she sighed.

Tenderly, blissfully, he ran his hands up under her skirt and along her bare and shapely legs, letting his fingertips linger ever so slightly at certain places as her breathing suggested. The curve of her knee. The hollow where thigh met hip. There her breath caught in her throat.

"Is this truly what you wish?" he whispered.

She smiled and brought her hands to the front of his breeches. "I will prove it," she said softly as, with swift, sure movements, she undid his belt and tossed it toward the door.

He held his breath as she stripped him of his tunic and untied his breeches to free him, a look of blatant hunger on her face. He closed his eyes and moaned softly as she stroked him, reveling in the building, exquisite tension.

She truly, truly wanted him to love her. And by God, he would! He already loved her as he had never loved a woman, or even knew he could.

"Sweet heaven, Allis, you are my sun," he whispered as he dragged his mouth along her soft cheek, "bringing light and happiness into what has been only darkness and despair."

"Connor, my Connor," she murmured as his kisses transported her away from the world of duty and responsibility, from pain and fear, into a realm of excitement and desire. This time, there was no hesitation and no dread, no concern for what might happen in the future, because she was sure she knew.

They belonged to each other. They were destined to be together, made for one another, alike in need and understanding. He made her feel young, alive, full of life and joy and hope—and so much more. No man had ever roused such a passionate, exciting desire within her, or filled her with such longing. It was as if she had been encased in ice, waiting for the one man who could shatter it and envelop her in the wonderful, all-encompassing warmth of his love.

Slowly, carefully, he eased her back into the straw, cushioning her with his right arm. The straw tickled her shoulders for the briefest of moments, before his mouth left hers and slipped with almost dainty, devastating leisure down her throat. With his left hand, he untied the laces at the front of her bodice just as slowly and carefully.

She gasped and arched as he cupped her breast, then put her hands on his shoulders and pulled him close, wanting the whole length of his lean, hard body against hers. She captured his mouth with fiery need. His kiss likewise seethed with longing and desire, and her hot blood throbbed throughout her anxious body as his tongue claimed hers.

Long and luxuriously they kissed, as if time stood still outside the hut, or as if they were already husband and wife, and this their home. They kissed lightly, playfully, teasing one another with the merest touch of mouth upon mouth. They kissed like young lovers who had never kissed before, delighting in the discovery of the sensations it could arouse. Finally, they kissed deeply, passionately, kindling the subdued desire they could no longer control.

All the intimate moments they had shared before seemed but a pale prelude to what was happening now, as if their previous embraces were a peck on the cheek compared to their deep, intoxicating, feverish kisses.

Her control slipped and slid away, and she didn't care. She was fast approaching the edge of something vast and mysterious and not without its own danger, yet she hurried onward of her own accord. All she cared about was Connor—being in his arms, his mouth upon hers demanding and seeking, loving him.

She gasped her approval as he tugged her bodice lower, exposing her thin silk shift. She might as well be naked, and her taut nipples pushed against the fabric as if anxious for his mouth to surround them. She would swoon if he did not, and then thought she would swoon when he did. He teased, nibbled and licked her breasts through the fabric in a way that set every particle of her flesh tingling.

Arching, gripping his shoulders and raising herself, she sought more and more of that feeling.

He drew back suddenly, his mouth a grimly painful line, while his eyes were still dark with unquenched desire.

She had been holding onto his injured shoulder too tightly.

But she did not want to stop. Not yet. Indeed, she wanted more and more and more. She wanted to love him, fully and completely, with her body as well as her heart.

"I'm sorry. I forgot about your shoulder. Here, lie back." She pushed him down until he was lying on his back beside her.

"What . . . what are you doing, Allis?"

"Helping." Raising her skirts, she stepped over him, so that she was above him. Then she lowered herself over him, until she straddled his hips. At the contact of his body with hers, she grew moist and thought the tension building within her would kill her if she did not assuage it—or let him.

He closed his eyes and moaned softly. She bit her lip to keep from moaning herself as his arousal, hard beneath her, created even more appetite.

"This is better, is it not?"

"Oh, sweet heaven," he muttered, opening his eyes. A look of concern came over his flushed features. "Better does not begin to describe . . . Allis, we should not—"

She put her fingers against his lips, then kissed him deeply, once more feeling him rub against her in a way that made her ache with yearning. "I told you, Connor," she whispered, "I am weary of being wise and responsible. I want to be young and free. I want you to kiss me, and touch me, and caress me."

"I want to make love with you." He ran his hands up her belly over the bunched fabric of her bodice to her breasts, and gently kneaded them.

She held tight to his upper arms, steadying herself against the welcome onslaught of exciting sensations. "Then make love with me, Connor. Please." Unable to resist the primitive urges building inside her, she began to rock against him. "I want you to make love with me, Connor. I want to belong to you, and you to me, for ever and ever. I want this more than I have ever wanted anything. I need you more than I have ever needed anything. Please don't refuse."

"Allis . . ."

"You make me feel so young. Free." She ran her fingers through his hair. "Happy in a way I no longer believed possible. You have made me live again, Connor." She took his face in her hands and stared into his eyes. "Make me feel even more alive now. Love me, Connor, and make me yours forever."

He did not reply with words. Instead, he put his hands beneath her and gently positioned her. Gazing at her face, watching her, he slowly thrust into her willing body, past the slight barrier, until he was fully enveloped in her warm and willing flesh.

Tremendous happiness and tremendous need struggled within him. Primitive impulses urged him to take her swiftly and put an end to the torment of unassuaged desire. Every element of his being commanded him to move, to act, to thrust hard until he felt the bliss of release.

But not yet. Not yet. Not until she gave him a sign that she was still willing, still certain.

And then she opened her eyes, and smiled.

His embrace tightened. Pulling her hard against him, he kissed her fervently. By heaven, what a woman! Never in all the world had one like Allis existed—bold and brave as any warrior, yet fully a woman, with a woman's softness.

He thrust again, trying to go slowly and move with care, fighting to ignore his own need. As she had been a maiden, he must not rush this. He must take time to let her grow used to him inside her. He must be patient, no matter how difficult that was.

Tempted by her flushed skin, he ran his tongue down her neck, tasting the saltiness of her flesh and feeling her heat.

And then she began to move her hips, rocking against him. He bit his lip and fought to be still. Let her do this, at first. Let her set the pace.

As she moved in that ageless rhythm, he closed his eyes and willed himself to wait as long as he could before he let himself be carried away.

Outside, the storm raged on, but he was oblivious, aware only of the thunder of his own blood in his ears and the pounding of his heart. His injury was forgotten, as was everything except Allis, the center of his world.

She bent forward, so that her breasts brushed lightly across his chest, her nipples teasing his, in a way that made him growl with savage desire. Her hair fell about them in a golden curtain as he slipped her shift from her shoulder, baring it to his lips, his touch. He could not wait any longer.

Looking into her beloved face, he lifted his hips, thrusting deeper within her. Her eyes flew open. "Does it hurt?" he asked gently.

"No, it feels . . . it feels so . . ." She squirmed a little, wriggling in a way that inflamed him even more. "Good."

At that, he could no longer restrain himself. He pulled her down and claimed her mouth as he began to buck his hips.

Breaking their kiss, Allis moaned and put her hands beside his head. The muscles of her body squeezed him as her pelvis rose and fell with his movements, matching his rhythm. He had never known a woman to respond with such wild, unbridled abandon, who loved with all her body and vitality, holding back nothing. Unrestrained. Free.

He wanted this to last forever—or at least until she

knew the joy of release first, but . . . he . . . could . . . not . . . wait.

Her name burst from his lips as he climaxed and wave after wave of euphoria washed over him. As she slowly collapsed against him, he could scarcely draw breath, and it was only moments later, as she lay nestled against him while he was still inside her, that he felt her body pulsating.

Slowly, slowly the world around him calmed. Everything returned to what it had been before—or nearly. The world became a blissful paradise in a shepherd's hut.

She shivered against him and he reached for her cloak. He tenderly tucked it around her, and kissed her forehead lightly. "I don't know what I have done to earn this reward."

"You understand me, and so much," she replied softly as she snuggled closer. "The loneliness I've felt, the weight of my duty and responsibility." He felt her mouth form a smile. "And you are very handsome."

"So you want me only for my looks? Oh, I am wounded to the quick!" he cried in mock despair, but really delighted by her drowsy merriment.

She laughed, the sound warm and domestic and altogether wonderful. "I'm sure you're very well aware of how good-looking you are. And if you were not before you came to Montclair, I daresay Merva told you."

"I paid no attention to Merva," he replied with feigned indignation.

"None at all?"

"No, not a whit." A slow ache began in his shoulder, but he didn't want to move. Holding her close in such wonderful intimacy was worth a little pain.

She twisted a lock of his hair about her finger. "I

knew you were different the first time I laid eyes on you, but I fear even then, I underestimated you."

He took her hand and brushed his lips over her soft palm. "What, because I can ignore a brazen serving wench?"

"That one, yes." The rosy blush on her cheeks deepened. "You have been with so many women . . ."

He put his knuckle under her chin and raised her head, so that she had to look at him. "Allis, I have coupled with other women, yes. But I have never made *love* to any of them, not as I have with you." His lips curved up into the sort of roguish grin he used to make in his carefree youth. "And not as I hope to keep making love with you for a very long time."

She gave him a gloriously happy smile. "Well, sir knight, that is my intention, too."

He chuckled softly. "Kiss me again, my love, and you will see how much I pay heed to any other woman at Montclair."

She gladly did as he suggested. Passion stirred and infused the warmth surrounding them. Lazily he traced the edges of her lips with his fingertip, enjoying the euphoria and slowly building tension.

"Connor?"

"Yes," he murmured as the pad of his finger slipped over her cheek and he studied the curves of her ear, which reminded him of other curves.

She shifted, catching his hand as she looked up at him, the regret on her face belying the desire burning in her eyes. "The rain has stopped."

The quiet confirmed it, and he sighed with regret. "We must go, then."

"Yes." She eased herself away from him and pulled

her bodice back into place and retied the laces. "My gown is a wrinkled mess, but I can blame that on the weather."

As he reached for his tunic, he surveyed the hut. "Alas, no featherbed for my first time with the woman I adore. I hope you are not disappointed."

"Not at all, but I would have been had you made me wait any longer." She shyly looked away, reminding him of the vulnerable woman beneath her strength. "Do you adore me, Connor?"

"Adore does not begin to describe how I feel about you," he assured her as he dressed. "Worship?" He mused a moment as he put on his belt. "No, for I confess that my feelings for you are not strictly holy. To even imagine making love to an angel is blasphemous, and I assure you, Allis, I want to do more than imagine."

"I would not want to be worshipped anyway. Even telling me you adore me makes me nervous," she said as she picked up her scarf. "I am only mortal, after all, and far from perfect."

"So am I—but then, I gather you don't adore me."

She attached her barbette beneath her chin, drawing his attention to her beautiful blushing face. "If adoration means I don't expect you to have faults, you're right. I don't adore you. I love you, faults and all."

"Faults? You've just made passionate love with me, and now you tell me I have faults?" he teased, tucking in a stray lock of hair for her, an excuse to let his fingertips caress her cheek again.

"You yourself keep telling me how unworthy you are, so surely you will not now expect me to believe you have none."

He waggled his finger at her. "I begin to think you are too clever, my lady."

She grabbed his finger and brought it to her lips. "Clever enough not to have forgotten that you like this."

"Have a care, my lady," he muttered as she once more sucked his finger into her mouth, sending a surge of hot desire through him. His body responded instantly, and with surprising strength, given that he had loved her only a short time ago. "Unless you want me to make love with you again."

Her eyes gleamed with yearning, but she frowned. "I think the sun is coming out."

"I think you're right again," he acknowledged as he hoisted himself to his feet. He didn't need to look outside, for the sun shone through the wide crack in the door.

He picked up her cloak and put it over her shoulders, then he held out his hand to her. "Come, my love, we must leave our little palace."

"Palace?" she asked as she took his hand. "I fear something has affected your eyesight."

"Palace," he confirmed as he pushed open the door and led her outside. "Because wherever you are is a palace to me."

She laughed and leaned into him, an action as intimate as a kiss, as they picked their way across the wet grass to the horses.

"You can use that stump to get on Demetrius," she noted, pointing.

"So may you to mount your horse, since I cannot assist you." He smiled down at her with lascivious merriment. "But when my arm is healed, my dearest lady, I intend to use any excuse I can to touch you."

"And I, you," she vowed, her eyes aglow.

They mounted their horses and rode home in silence, needing no words. The branches and leaves dripped from the rain, but the sun shone through, dappling the path. The shadows shifted and danced, as if they were as happy as he.

Soon enough they reached the village. Allis straightened, obviously expecting the people out and about to greet the lady of Montclair.

They didn't. They didn't even look at them.

"I'm not liking the looks of this," Connor muttered, the hairs on the back of his neck prickling.

"Nor I."

"What do you think it means?"

She didn't answer. She didn't have to, as he felt the stirring of his guilty conscience for another hasty act, and knew by her reddening cheeks that she was also reconsidering what they had done, if she was not actually ashamed. Although they were in love and secretly pledged to one another, what they had done was a sin.

Yet that was not the worst of it. The worst came when they entered the hall and found Lord Oswald, Auberan, Edmond and Isabelle waiting for them on the dais.

Along with Rennick DeFrouchette.

Chapter 20

A trickle of dread went down Allis's spine at the way everyone stood on the dais behind the scowling baron, as if arrayed against them—or held captive by him. Servants clustered in small groups around the hall and, like the villagers, they avoided meeting her gaze.

This was Montclair, not the baron's fortress, and he had no right to stand there like he was her sovereign.

She straightened her shoulders and walked regally toward him. Connor followed, and she was pleased he did not hang back, as if they need be ashamed. By rights, they should have waited for the marriage vows before making love, but they had not, and she was not sorry. She was glad—delighted, thrilled, ecstatic—that they had, and she would not regret it. She loved Connor, and he loved her. They would be married, and Rennick would not stop them. "Baron DeFrouchette, you have returned."

"Obviously," Rennick replied, running a scornful gaze over them. "Where have you been with this man?"

He tossed his wet hair off his high brow. He must have ridden through the rain, and had probably just arrived. His long, damp, black tunic was muddy at the hem, and he looked as bedraggled as Auberan in the river. And he could glower all he liked, but he couldn't frighten her anymore, especially when Connor came to stand beside her. "I was riding and happened to meet Sir Connor in the meadow by the river. It began to rain. We took shelter until the storm ceased. I didn't want to get wet through and fall ill, and it would have been dangerous for me by myself. Didn't the soldiers return and tell you where I was?"

"Yes, they did and—" Edmond fell silent at Rennick's sharp and censorious glance.

As if the baron were the master here. Her temper surged, full of fierce vitality, and her hands balled into fists. Out of the corner of her eye, she saw Connor's angry expression. He said nothing, though, and that was the wisest thing to do. For now, he was still but a guest at Montclair.

With arrogant confidence, Rennick sauntered toward them. "The storm did not come up suddenly. I wonder, my lady, why you felt compelled to ride out when the weather was not promising."

She spoke slowly and deliberately, glaring at him, letting him see her anger. She was the head of the family in fact, if not in law, and she would have him understand that. "Because I wished to."

"Baron, my lady," Lord Oswald began placatingly, "this discussion would be better conducted in private."

"I see no need for discussion, unless the baron has a charge to make against me."

Lord Oswald hurried down from the dais. "My lady, let us retire before things are said in haste that may be regretted."

She glanced at Connor and he made a slight nod of agreement. Rennick saw their silent communication, and his scowl deepened.

Let him scowl. Soon he would have little power over them, once she asked Lord Oswald to be Edmond's guardian.

The small fear that had gnawed at the edges of her mind for the past few days crept out of the cage she had kept it in. What if Lord Oswald refused, and another man was chosen in his place? What if this other man favored Rennick? This was the barrier that had kept her from asking Lord Oswald to become Edmond's guardian the day after her father had died. With that dread haunting her, no matter how sure she felt that he would agree, she had avoided the question.

"I don't think Edmond and Isabelle need come, or Sir Connor, either," Rennick said coldly.

She hesitated. He was right that Edmond and Isabelle should not hear this discussion, but Connor . . . Despite her yearning to have him with her, it would probably be better if he were not party to this conversation. Nobody yet knew the extent of their relationship, and although they might suspect, she didn't want to give them confirmation until things with Rennick were settled and done with. "Very well. Please stay here, Sir Connor."

He looked about to protest, then nodded his agreement.

She headed for the solar and the other two men followed. As she climbed the steps, she began to marshal her arguments, for although she was absolutely determined to break the betrothal, Rennick was not going to be easy to persuade.

She entered the solar. The sight of her father's table, bare of parchments or candles unlike when he was well, made her throat tighten. *Marry a man who brings you laughter.* So he had said, and so she was going to do. Energized, she wheeled around and watched Rennick and Lord Oswald enter the chamber. As Lord Oswald closed the door, Rennick strode around the table and stood behind it as if it were his.

"What the devil were you thinking, Allis?" he charged as he splayed his hands on the table and glared at her. "You shouldn't have allowed yourself to be alone with him."

She was the mistress here; he was not the master. She would be calm, serene—and immovable as a mountain. "I do not recall asking your opinion, Rennick."

"Since I am betrothed to you, you will listen to it."

"My father agreed to our marriage, Rennick, and now my beloved father is dead. There is a new head of the family of Montclair, and *you are not it.*"

Rennick slowly and scornfully smiled as he straightened. "I'm not?"

Fear slammed into her at his confident retort. Her stomach twisted and her knees trembled, but she would betray nothing of her dread. "No."

"Who is?"

"Edmond, of course."

"He is a boy and not of legal age. He requires a guardian."

Rennick was so confident, so sure of himself! What did he know that she did not? A horrible trepidation that she had left this matter unsettled too long filled her as she turned toward Lord Oswald, who had stayed by the door. "I would ask Lord Oswald to be his guardian."

"In his will your father named the baron to that position," Lord Oswald replied.

Oh, dear God, not him! Not Rennick! Any man but Rennick!

"Oh, you didn't know?" Rennick taunted.

No, she had not known her father had made a will. He had never spoken of it. Yet how often had he voiced his wish for death? He was not simple in the head, only torn apart by grief, so she should have realized he would plan for that eventuality.

But *Rennick* . . . Suddenly she knew how it must have been. Rennick had suggested that himself. She could see him in her mind, looming over her father at that very table like an evil spirit, pouring his poisonous proposals in his ear.

And her father agreed because he had not known how cunning and ruthless Rennick DeFrouchette was. Because she, who prided herself on protecting her family, had kept too much from him.

Grasping at one hope, she couldn't keep the desperation from her voice as she addressed Lord Oswald. "He did so only because the baron had so much influence over him. You are well known at court. I'm sure the king would approve you and override the terms of my father's will."

"Even Richard realizes there are some limitations on the king's power, my lady." Lord Oswald replied so calmly, it was as if he could not hear her need. Or as if he did not care.

"I have already been to Westminster."

Dismayed, distressed, she faced Rennick again, to see the cold gleam of heartless triumph in his pale blue eyes.

He patted the purse hanging from his belt. "I have the confirmation of my guardianship of not only your brother, but you and your sister as well, in my possession. Did you not wonder why I was so long coming back to my *beloved?*" He infused that word with contempt. "I had important business to attend to while you were entertaining yourself with Sir Connor of Llanstephan."

"I perceive this is becoming a lovers' quarrel, so I shall take my leave," Lord Oswald murmured as he opened the door.

"No, my lord, please stay." She hurried toward him, determined to detain him. His hand was on the latch, and she covered it with hers. She would not be alone with Rennick and his coldly exultant eyes. "It is not a lovers' quarrel. It is a legal one. My father was in no fit state to make a will or name a guardian. You saw him—you cannot deny that it was so."

"I am no man of law, my lady, to answer that charge. Besides, has Baron DeFrouchette not assisted your father these many years? Does he not know the state of affairs in this castle and on this estate better than anyone else? I confess, my lady, I do not see why you are so upset. He is your betrothed. I should think it would be only natural for him to be named the guardian of you, your sister and your brother."

Where had the kind, friendly Lord Oswald gone? Was he not her father's friend, and hers, too?

Then he looked down at her hand as if her fingers were leeches and she had her answer.

She snatched her hand away. This man was not her friend, but Rennick's. This man cared nothing for her, or her family. He had been a snake in their midst, worse even than Rennick, because she had trusted him.

"What has Rennick promised you?" she demanded.

Oswald's small, dark eyes glittered like obsidian jewels. "Why, nothing, my lady. It is the king who confirmed him, not I. Indeed, if I were to speak against the confirmation, perhaps I would be branded a dishonorable traitor." Another look came into Oswald's eyes as he touched her cheek with his plump hand, a look even more disgustingly lascivious than Rennick's lust. "But then, such men seem to hold an appeal for you, my lady, so maybe it would be worth the risk, eh?"

Anger flared, hot and strong, and she slapped his hand away.

Oswald grabbed her by the shoulders. "Have a care, my lady, how you presume to treat me, and your betrothed. Every noble in England will agree that Rennick is the injured party here, given what you have done this afternoon."

They could not know all that she had done. "Do you think the honor of the lady of Montclair is so easily stained?"

Oswald's gaze flicked to Rennick, who stood as silent and still as an effigy. "Does it matter exactly what went on? You have been alone for a considerable length of time with a man who is not your husband, or even your betrothed. Everyone in Montclair knows it. They saw you ride out and they saw the foot soldiers come back without you. They know you returned with the Welshman much later. However, this is none of my

province. This is for the bride and groom to discuss."
He shoved her back, then as calmly as if he was off to
play chess, he strolled from the room.

"You see what you have done?" Rennick asked as
the door banged shut. "You have brought shame upon
your family."

Rennick's taunting words revitalized her. She
glared at him as she marched toward him. "You have
what you wanted, control of Montclair. If you think I
have behaved improperly with Sir Connor, break our
betrothal."

He shook his head.

Resolute and determined, she straightened her shoulders. "I *have* behaved improperly with Sir Connor—
very much so. He is my lover. *Now* will you break the
betrothal?"

She had always believed Rennick DeFrouchette to
be a cold, unfeeling, greedy man without a heart to
break. That he did not care for her except as the means
to Montclair. But as she stood defiantly before him and
watched his pale eyes glitter with warring emotions,
she suddenly realized she might be wrong, and if he
did possess a heart to break, she had just shattered it.

She felt a moment of genuine remorse, until he
came from behind the table to circle her like a great
beast of prey, his eyes cold and cruel.

"You are just like Richard, do you know that?" he
demanded. "He, too, led me on, treating me as a friend
and ally only to tell me when he was preparing for the
Crusade that I had better stay at home. That I was not
good enough to be in his retinue—me, Rennick De-
Frouchette! And now you would pass me over for
some disgraced, impoverished Welshman?" He halted
in front of her and his gaze hardened. "Richard is very

impressed that I have earned the respect of the late earl of Montclair. At last he begins to see that he made a mistake passing me over. I will not have that altered, not after waiting all this time." He grabbed her, pulling her inexorably closer. "I will have you for my wife and in my bed, Allis. There will be no more refusals, of anything I demand of you. With or without your love, which must be a worthless thing if you can give it to that Welshman, you will welcome me into our bed and do whatever I tell you. You will be my chatelaine and a credit to me—or all you do care about will suffer.

"And not just those you love, Allis," he continued in a fierce growl full of rage and wounded vanity. "Connor has a brother and sister, too, does he not? Wales is not so very far away that I couldn't make my vengeance felt there, too."

Oh, dear God. He meant it. She could see it in his eyes, hear it in his voice. She wanted to throw back her head and howl in agony, for Rennick would take out his heartbreak not in mournful sorrow or self-recriminations, but in vengeance. Her pride and confidence fractured, for she had made her family more vulnerable than her father ever had.

His hot, wet mouth slid along her cheek. "But all is not bleak and desperate, my beloved. I am a forgiving man, you see. We will still marry, and everyone will be safe."

She shoved hard against his chest and stumbled back as every instinct, every impulse rebelled again that fate.

Nor would she leave her brother and sister in Rennick DeFrouchette's greedy grasp. Titles and riches were not worth such a life. "We will leave Montclair,

Rennick. Edmond and Isabelle and Connor and me. You may have it."

He smiled with mocking scorn as he slowly, deliberately, crossed his arms. "What will Edmond think of this plan, Allis? Do you think he will agree to give away his inheritance? And pretty young Isabelle—do you think she will relish going off to the wilds of Wales and existing in poverty?"

"They will understand," she declared, desperately hoping it would be so.

Rennick shook his head. "No, they will not. They will hate you and your Welsh lover for your selfishness."

He strode toward her. She backed away, until she was against the wall. Still he came on, halting when he was inches from her. "I am weary of waiting for you, Allis, and you have made a mockery of my patience. I should take you right here and right now. You are no longer a virgin, after all, by your own admittance."

He grabbed her and hauled her close. He kissed her brutally, with anger and hostility.

Desperately struggling to get away from his savage grasp, she found the hilt of his sword. She took hold of it, then raised her knee, striking him hard enough to make him gasp.

He let go and fell back, cursing, while she kept hold of his sword and pulled it from the scabbard. She gripped it tightly with both hands and, as he regained his balance, she put the tip against his chest.

His gazed flicked to the blade, then back to her face. He held out his hands, palms upward, as if surrendering. "What are you going to do? Kill me? If you do, what will happen then? Do you think today was the first time anybody noticed something amiss? Lord Oswald didn't just send a message that your father had died, Allis. He warned me that something was afoot between you and the Welshman. If you kill me, people will say it was to be rid of me because you wanted to marry him. He will not be considered innocent, either. You both will be arrested and convicted, then executed."

"I am protecting myself against a man who would rape me. Everybody knows this would not be the first time you have done that, Rennick. I have heard how you abuse the maidservants in your household."

"Do you think there is a lord in the land who has not done the same? Good God, you are an innocent if you believe there is a noble in the court who will not see that whatever I have done with my peasants, I have treated you with respect—until you did not deserve it. Kill me, and they will convict you for being a woman who does not know her duty."

"What have I ever done *but* my duty?" she cried in anguish, the injustice of his words piercing her to the quick.

"Ah, but there is the rub, my lady. You fell in love with the wrong man, and every Norman lord in England will convict you for that alone."

So smooth, so sure, so certain—because he was right, and they both knew it.

Her arms ached with the effort of holding his broadsword, but she did not lower it as her mind worked feverishly, trying to see another way for them to be free of Rennick forever.

"If I am dead, and you are imprisoned or executed, what will become of your family and your beloved Montclair then?" he charged. "Some other overlord will be named guardian, and I daresay Edmond will be lucky to inherit a stick of furniture or sheaf of wheat in due course. You know such things have happened before."

That had happened to a young heir not far from here. His guardian had stripped the boy's estate bare by the time he was of age. "You will do the same thing."

"Will I?" Rennick demanded. "Have I? I could have stolen Montclair from your father time and time again. Did I?"

No, he had not, but that didn't mean he never would, or that he had not wanted to. "You didn't dare."

The look that flared in his eyes told her she had found the truth. "No, you didn't dare," she repeated, nudging him with the tip of the sword so that he was forced to move back, "because I stood between you and my father. Instead, you hovered about us like a vulture, biding your time."

"And now the time has come. You may have my sword, but I have you in my power. You know it as well as I. Kill me, and Montclair is as good as destroyed. Marry me, and your family will be safe, your brother's inheritance protected."

"Protected?" she scoffed as his back hit the door. "By you?"

Suddenly he put his hand on the flat of the blade and pushed down hard. Her arms were too weak to hold it against his strength and it fell to the floor with a dull clang. Before she could move away, he took her by the upper arms and brought his face, full of anger and frustration, close to hers.

"I don't want this land, this heap of stone," he snarled, his eyes fiercely angry. "I want *respect*, and as your husband and the guardian of your brother, I will have it! Can't you understand, you stupid wench?" He shook her, hard enough to hurt. "I need to be your husband—and because I do, I will do whatever I must to make you marry me. Understand this and understand it well, my proud Allis. I have waited too long, been too patient, endured too much, to be thwarted now."

Someone knocked at the door, loud and insistent.

Connor! Connor had come to save her.

She went to cry out, but Rennick clapped his hand over her mouth and dragged her to the far side of the room. She struggled in his arms, but he held her tight. His back to the door, he kept his hand over her mouth, making it look as if they were in some kind of embrace as the door opened.

Isabelle stepped into the room.

Not Connor. Her young and innocent sister.

"You have no business here," Rennick declared. "Leave us."

"I came to tell you I want to be your wife."

Stunned as she was, Rennick let go of Allis's mouth and looked over his shoulder. When his hold loosened, Allis broke away and ran to her sister, shoving her toward the door. "You don't know what you're saying!"

Isabelle planted her feet and regarded her sister with a steadiness and determination Allis had never suspected she possessed. "Yes, I do. You don't want to marry him, and I do."

"You can't!"

She grabbed Isabelle's hand and tried to pull her away, but Isabelle stood firm. "Did I ask for your approval? Just because you do not consider him suitable for a husband doesn't mean I do not."

"Well, well, well, Isabelle." Rennick strolled toward

them, a half-smile on his face that made Allis sick to see. He closed the door, enclosing the three of them in the solar. Then he circled around them before he leaned one hip against their father's table and insolently surveyed them as if they were on display for his pleasure.

Isabelle had said that she found the baron good-looking, but she did not know how cruel and greedy and vicious Rennick could be. As she had her father, Allis had shielded Isabelle from the worst of the tales whispered about Rennick DeFrouchette, thinking her too young and innocent to hear them.

There could be no more innocence. "Isabelle, there are things you don't—"

Isabelle darted an unreadable glance at her sister. "Be quiet, Allis."

Rennick chuckled, and when he spoke, it was to Isabelle, not her. "I see I am not the only one who seeks to put Allis in her place. However, my sweet Isabelle, what makes you think I will have you?"

"I am pretty, and I am younger than Allis."

Allis stared at them helplessly as they spoke as if she had ceased to exist.

"Allis is the elder sister and has the greater dowry."

"What about passion?"

How could this bold woman be Isabelle? It was as if some brazen changeling had come to take her little sister's place. And how could she speak of passion? Isabelle had no idea what passion—the wonderful, heady passion of true love—was.

His eyes shining with lust, Rennick slowly smiled. "You have certainly given me something to think about, my dear."

Dear Father in Heaven, Isabelle had no idea what

her life would be like as Rennick's wife—how he would use her as he might any whore at night, and treat her even worse during the day. There would be no love, no affection, no respect, no trust.

As she would lay down her life for Isabelle if she were being attacked by an armed warrior, so she would die before she let Isabelle marry Rennick De-Frouchette—or she would marry him herself. "You are betrothed to me," she forcefully reminded him.

"Yet it was only moments ago you asked to break the betrothal. Besides, if I marry Isabelle, you will be free to marry your poor Welsh knight. Of course, you will have to do so without a dowry, but I gather that is of no importance to you."

"Allis, you do not want the baron and I do, so what is there to argue about? You will have your freedom to be with Sir Connor, and I will have what I want."

Allis's gaze darted between the two of them, Isabelle resolved and Rennick looking so very, very pleased. "I would speak to my sister alone."

"Very well, you do that," Rennick said with malicious delight as he sauntered toward the door. "But do not take too long. I am anxious to hear who will have the honor of becoming my lady."

Chapter 21

"**S**it down and stop pacing, Sir Connor," Lord Oswald ordered. "You're making me nervous and upsetting the lad." He nodded at Edmond seated nearby on the dais as they waited for Allis, De-Frouchette and Isabelle to return from the solar. Auberan leaned against the wall, glumly pulling on a loose thread in the tapestry behind him.

Connor joined them on the dais, sitting opposite Edmond, but his mind was far from still. He should have listened to his conscience. He should have stayed away from Allis until the betrothal was broken. Once again he had given in to his impulses, and the results were proving disastrous.

He envied Isabelle, who had wearied of waiting, and announced her intention of finding out what was happening. Not even Lord Oswald's protest that she should not interfere had held her back. She still had not returned, and the time stretched out, unbearable, as every moment passed.

"I don't understand why everybody's so angry," Edmond muttered.

"Yes, do explain it to the boy," Auberan suggested to Connor as he joined them on the dais, his eyes full of derision.

God help him, how could he explain love to a boy? Yet it would surely be better for him to try to tell Edmond before Auberan said much more.

He would start by explaining why people were upset, he decided. "It isn't proper for a betrothed woman to spend time alone with another man."

"Allis didn't want to get wet. What is so wrong with that?"

"We were alone for a long time, and we aren't married." He flushed with embarrassment. He didn't want to lose the boy's respect and admiration, yet that might be the price he would have to pay for his weakness.

"Perhaps you are too young to understand these things," Auberan said with arrogant condescension.

"I am not!" Edmond cried with all the outraged pride of a future overlord.

Connor leaned closer, his elbows on his knees and his hands clasped loosely before him. "Edmond, what your sister and I did was improper because she is betrothed to another man. I should not have been alone with her, for any length of time. It implies that there is more between us than mere friendship, something that should only be between a man and his wife."

Edmond's eyes narrowed as he began to comprehend. "If that is so, then the baron is right to be angry."

"Yes, he has some justification." Wanting to make

things right in some way, Connor reached out to ruffle Edmond's hair.

The boy drew back abruptly, as if he had struck him.

Dismay washed over him. This afternoon, in the shepherd's hut, all his hopes and dreams seemed possible and about to come true. Now he feared that had been but the dream of a deluded man who awoke to find all of society arrayed against him.

"Perhaps you should get something to eat, Edmond," Lord Oswald suggested. "The evening meal may be late."

Edmond frowned, but he obeyed. As Connor watched him go, he hoped that in time, when Edmond was a man and perhaps in love himself, he would understand and forgive them.

"Why don't you leave, too, Welshman?" Auberan demanded. "I'm sure you are no longer welcome here."

Lord Oswald spoke with what sounded like genuine regret. "I think Auberan is right, Connor. This is a fairly delicate situation, and your presence may only aggravate it."

After what had happened, it would surely be better to be honest, and put everything out into the open. Subterfuge had only made things worse. "The situation may get more delicate yet. Allis and I wish to be married."

"Married?" Auberan repeated incredulously. "That's impossible! She's betrothed—and she'd never marry *you*!"

"Under God, all things are possible," Lord Oswald remarked as he sat in the chair Edmond had vacated. He rested his elbows on his belly and steepled his fingers. "However, my young knight, this particular thing may not be. The betrothal has been approved by the head of the family."

"But Allis's father is dead, so now the heir must give his approval for her betrothal. We hope that Edmond will do so."

"Sadly for you, Sir Connor, I must inform you that it is Rennick DeFrouchette who must approve. The baron is Edmond's guardian—and Allis's and Isabelle's, as well."

Connor's vision of paradise started to crack into a thousand pieces. "How can this be?"

"The king has made it so."

Richard, the bane of his life, who had destroyed his ideal of a noble king, who had caused so much suffering for his own glory, who had impoverished his family, who spoke of chivalry and honor, then massacred unarmed men, who had called him a traitor and threatened to execute him if he ever saw his face again—he had put Allis into the hands of the man she loathed.

"Yes, my boy, and the king also approves Baron DeFrouchette's choice of bride. I daresay the baron paid the king well for the confirmation. You know Richard always needs money. However much it cost, I'm sure neither the baron nor the king will ever let you marry Allis."

His hands balled into fists. Of course. The king would do anything for money.

Connor got to his feet, too agitated to sit. Too agitated to stay here, lest he say or do something in his anger that would only make things worse.

His face red with fury, his heart full of anger and hate and bitterness, Connor strode from the hall.

"Well, a fiery temper indeed," Lord Oswald noted

calmly as the knight slammed the door of the great hall so hard, it made the nearby trestle table rattle.

Auberan quickly sat in Connor's place, facing Oswald. "That's true about Rennick being Isabelle's guardian?"

"Yes, it is."

The young man's eyes shone with delight. "He'll give his consent to our marriage, then."

"Unless you do something stupid, I believe so, yes."

Rennick appeared, trotting down the stairs. His gaze swept over the hall, then he addressed his two comrades. "Where's the Welshman?"

"He became upset and left. It seems he's annoyed with our sovereign." Oswald smiled, clearly pleased with his machinations. "Very annoyed."

Auberan peered at the stairs. "Where are the ladies?"

"Having a discussion." Rennick glanced at Merva and the other servants who were exchanging puzzled glances and whispers. "Let us go to the chapel, where we may speak in private."

Oswald nodded his agreement, and with long, swift strides, Rennick led the way.

The chapel candles flickered and spluttered as they hurried inside. Coming at the last, Auberan closed the door, and the dull thud echoed through the stone building.

Standing near the altar, Rennick faced his companions, a sly grin on his hawklike face. "Isabelle has made a very intriguing proposal. She suggested that I marry her and not Allis."

Damn these Montclair brats! Oswald thought as Auberan's face reddened with more than the effort of hurrying across the courtyard.

The baron leaned back against the altar and crossed his ankles as well as his arms. "It's a very tempting offer."

No doubt. So young, so ripe.

Auberan strode toward the baron and halted, his fists on his hips. "I am to marry Isabelle!"

"Yes, you are," Oswald confirmed as he strolled closer, putting aside lust and every other emotion except the desire for power and revenge.

"I said she was tempting. I did not say I intended to marry the girl. She holds few charms for me."

Rennick might be tempted by young flesh, but the girl was not the prize. "It's Allis he wants, Auberan, for more than her family connections and her land, you see," he explained to the furious younger man. "It's always been Allis, so he will have her, whether she wants him or not, and whether she's been alone with that Welshman or not. Isn't that so, Rennick?"

The baron's gaze hardened, his pale eyes flickering with a host of emotions—desire, greed, rage, anguish—warring for supremacy. "We are betrothed. I see no reason to break it."

Oswald slipped his hands into his sleeves. "Auberan, why don't you run along and see if Isabelle has come back to the hall? This has been a very difficult day for her, I'm sure, and she will likely welcome some company. Say nothing of her offer to marry the baron, but you might make mention of his age."

"My age?" Rennick's hands balled into fists. "What about my age?"

"You are several years older than Isabelle, Rennick, and Auberan is not."

Pleasure flashed in Auberan's eyes before he hurried away.

"So, I am too old for Isabelle?" Rennick demanded as Auberan closed the chapel door.

"Calm yourself," Oswald said, smiling to placate Rennick's ruffled pride. "Auberan has little enough in his favor. Let him at least brag of his youth."

"My age does not matter to Isabelle."

"Perhaps it doesn't—but what matters or not to that young lady is unimportant."

Rennick walked toward the statue of the Holy Mother. "She was quite persuasive."

This sounded suspicious, but plans had been made, and he would not have them altered, not by some girl or DeFrouchette.

He followed the baron and moved where he could see the man's face, especially his light blue eyes. "Enough to make you forget Allis?"

"Perhaps."

He laughed softly then, for he had seen the truth in Rennick's gleaming eyes. He might be tempted by Isabelle as a starving man might be tempted by a stale crust of bread. But he no more preferred Isabelle than the man would want the stale crust when a banquet lay before him, too. "You are such a poor liar, Rennick. You've craved Allis of Montclair since the first time you saw her when you returned from France eight years ago. I've never seen a man so besotted at first sight, even though she was just a girl and didn't look at you twice."

"She and that Welshman are lovers," Rennick said, scowling. "She told me so herself."

"She has wounded your pride again, has she? Poor Rennick!"

Rennick flushed as he planted his feet and crossed his arms. "Maybe we should reconsider our plans.

Perhaps I should have Isabelle. She is younger and a virgin, and I would still be allied with the family of Montclair."

Oswald waved his hand dismissively. "What is virginity but an impediment to true pleasure? God spare me a virgin's tears and reluctance! Besides, how many times have Allis and Connor been together? Once, twice, three times? Put it out of your mind. You will have her for the rest of her life."

"What if she bears that Welshman's brat?"

"Do not touch her until she has had her women's time after you are wed. If she is not with child by then, she will not be bearing any bastards."

"And if she does?"

Oswald shrugged. "Kill it. Smother it in the cradle." He slid a glance at his coconspirator and decided to let him know that he was not as clever as he believed. "Or I suppose you could give it the potion you gave poor Percival."

Rennick's eyes flickered with dismay, then he regained his composure. "I don't know what you're talking about."

Too late. He was trapped like a fly in a spider's web, the fool. "Some brew of foxglove, probably from that apothecary I told you of in London, the one who performs his interesting experiments on paupers," Oswald said, his tone making it clear he didn't believe Rennick's claim of ignorance. "He is certain foxglove slows the heartbeat, although no other medical man will listen. Still, he's convincing, isn't he? I've been tempted to try it myself."

Rennick didn't speak as Oswald turned to him, his cold, black eyes glittering like a cat's. "So you put it in the young fool's wine. Between that potion, and the weight and heat of his armor, even a young man's heart will fail. I wonder why you felt the need to kill him."

There was no point to lying now. "He knew too much."

"Ah, I thought so. Did he tamper with Sir Connor's lance, or did you and he found out?"

"He did."

"At your behest?"

Rennick didn't reply. Oswald thought he knew all the answers anyway.

"You have behaved like a spoiled child and not a clever man, Rennick. It is fortunate for you that only I have figured this out. I gather his father has no inkling of foul play?"

"No, my lord."

"Lucky for you, because if he did, I meant what I said before. I would accuse you myself before the king."

He would. That traitorous dog would never be loyal, just as Richard was not. Ah, well, he would have no need for a second thought when the time came to rid himself of Oswald, whose expression grew stern and unforgiving.

"Because you seem to lack foresight, let me explain things to you," Oswald said. "You will listen and if you have any hope of sharing power with me in this kingdom, you will do what I say."

No harm in listening—for now.

"I would say that right at the moment, Connor hates both you and Richard in equal measure. The day you wed the woman he loves, he will be ready to have his revenge on the world—or at least you or the king. I intend to turn that desire for vengeance to our advantage."

"If he hates me, he will not join us."

Oswald sauntered and walked toward the altar. "I no longer intend that he should. After all, he has no idea you and I are allied toward a common goal. So let him hate you, as long as he hates the king, too. He may need very little goading to kill Richard."

A clever plan, if it worked. He, too, approached the Lord's table. "You would trust him to do that?"

Oswald turned toward him and gave him a sly, knowing smile. "Absolutely. He is the perfect assassin, heartbroken, full of righteous indignation, wounded pride and twisted chivalry. Even better, he will believe he is killing Richard for the good of the kingdom as well as personal vengeance. And since he will be acting on his own, he will not be able to name us as accomplices. Besides, no one would believe you and he could be plotting anything together, given what has happened with Allis."

The cunning old bastard. "Did you plan for Allis to meet Connor? Did you foresee them falling in love?"

He watched Oswald very carefully as the older man replied. "No. That was merely a fortunate accident."

Fortunate for him. "So he is to be the arrow while you draw the bow."

"Exactly. Richard will be dead, John will be on the throne, and you will have Allis and Montclair." Oswald smiled. "I, on the other hand, will have more land, and more power from a grateful prince made king, and the proof that you killed Albert L'Ouisseaux's son in my possession, should you ever get any ideas about trying to outmaneuver *me*."

As Rennick struggled not to betray his dismay and his rage, Oswald reached into his tunic and pulled out the small vial the London apothecary had sold him.

"Do not try to change a plan of mine ever again. You will do exactly what I tell you, or I will tell Albert L'Ouisseaux the truth about his son's death. His judgment would be much harsher than the king's court, as you well know."

Rennick swallowed hard, because that was true.

"No need to look so glum," Oswald said as he put the vial away. "You are going to have your Allis, after all. So what if she loves another and has taken him into her embrace? She can hardly fault you should you take a mistress or two, can she?"

That old reprobate would never understand his insatiable need for Allis, not if he lived a thousand years.

Oswald put his arm around Rennick's shoulder in a gesture that seemed more possessive than companionable. "What of Allis in all this? Have you convinced her that it would not be wise to repudiate you?"

He resisted lifting away Oswald's arm. "Yes, she understands what will happen if she does."

"Good, and since she is not a fool, she knows you mean it."

"I do mean it."

Oswald removed his arm and started toward the door. "Ah, Rennick, such an apt pupil!"

Rennick didn't follow. "What of Isabelle? She is too good to waste as a reward to Auberan."

Indeed, she should be in his bed, too, with or without Allis's knowledge. One sister for wife, one for mistress. . . . His loins tightened with that tantalizing idea.

He realized Oswald was watching him closely and made his face a blank.

"Perhaps I should reconsider," the older man said, and Rennick wondered how much of his thoughts he had already betrayed. "But for now, let Auberan think she is destined for him. Trying to seduce her will give him something to do."

Rennick turned the conversation to another matter, and away from the women. "What about the Welshman? He can't stay."

Oswald frowned. "Because you made such a show."

"What was I to do when they were not here?" Rennick demanded. "Look as if I didn't care?"

"You might have tried."

Oswald could afford to sound blasé. Allis wasn't *his* betrothed. "As you keep pointing out, my lord, there is the matter of my wounded pride. I should challenge him to combat for insulting my honor."

"No, you shouldn't. For one thing, he's wounded, so how would that look? For another, although he's wounded, he would probably kill you."

Furious at the implication that he was no match for a wounded Welshman, Rennick started to protest, but Oswald held up his hand to silence him. "That is the truth, and you know it as well as I, so don't bother to say otherwise."

He didn't know it, but Oswald gave him no chance to speak.

"And knowing the lady as I do—although perhaps not so well as I thought I did, for I must confess myself shocked she would make love outside the bounds of marriage—I think you need do nothing. You are forgetting the very real possibility that you will gain more respect if you act the devoted, yet betrayed, husband-to-be willing to forgive his wayward bride."

Damn Oswald for finding the one reason to do nothing.

"Either Connor will choose to leave, or she will ask him to go. The pain of being near each other under these circumstances will be too difficult. However, if it will ease your injured pride, you would certainly be within your rights as guardian of the young earl to order Connor to leave Montclair."

"I will."

"I warn you that I am planning to offer my sympathies to Sir Connor and invite him to my castle until his shoulder is completely healed."

Rennick's anger burned brighter for a moment, until he forced himself to think like Oswald. "Until you have convinced him of the necessity of killing Richard, you mean."

"Exactly." Oswald strolled over to the Madonna, bent over and blew out every votive candle, so that the chapel was lit only by a single candle on the small altar. "Come. Let us see if the ladies have finished their useless conversation. My throat is dry from all this talking. I need some of that fine French wine of the late, lamented earl's. And cheer up, man! You are going to have all that you desired. What more could a man ask?"

Rennick DeFrouchette said nothing, for despite all he said and all he told himself and all he planned, he knew that he would never have Allis's love, and it was the one thing he had wanted most of all.

Chapter 22

After Rennick's departure, Allis and Isabelle stood listening to his retreating footsteps.

"I'm not a babe," Isabelle declared as silence descended.

"No, you are not," Allis retorted. "Nor do you understand the full import of what you have proposed."

"Yes, I do."

"You do not know the kind of man DeFrouchette is."

"I have known him all my life. I know what he does."

"Not everything." Allis readied herself to reveal some of Rennick's more sordid activities.

"I probably know much more than you think," Isabelle said as she crossed to the window and looked out. "You are not with me all day. I hear things."

Could it be that Isabelle had heard the stories about

Rennick and did not care? "Then you know that he punishes his tenants for the least thing, and as harshly as the law allows?" Allis asked as she went to stand beside her. "How he always claims the *heriot* before a tenant's body is barely cool, even if that is the only beast the family owns? How he makes some women 'pay' the taxes on their family's property, or that sometimes he simply takes those he fancies."

Isabelle colored and continued looking out of the window. "Those are only rumors, gossip spread by disgruntled tenants. Every Norman nobleman has such things said about him by his peasants."

How she wished she had told Isabelle the truth sooner! "Isabelle, look at me."

Reluctantly, she obeyed, and she regarded Allis with a steadfast gaze, as if as certain of her purpose as Allis had ever been.

With an even stronger sense of desperation, Allis gently took her by the shoulders. "Isabelle, in his case, the stories are true. I have spoken with Brother Jonathan, and he has tended to the victims of Rennick's justice who weren't put to death, but only had their hands cut off or their eyes put out. He has comforted the sobbing women raped by Rennick DeFrouchette."

Isabelle didn't even flinch.

"He is an evil man," Allis persisted, "who wormed his way into our household when our mother died and our father was sickened by his grief. He has been gradually taking control of our estate, and now, as our guardian, he has it."

Still Isabelle regarded her steadily. "You say he is a terrible man, yet you agreed to marry him."

"To protect you and Edmond, and our father, while he lived. I wish with all my heart I had not."

Isabelle came closer and suddenly, Allis found herself staring into her father's eyes as they had been before her mother's death, sure and determined.

"You wish it because you love another."

Before she could respond, Isabelle clasped her hand tightly, firmly, with a sure confidence. "Although you have not told me, I know how you feel about Sir Connor. You love him and hate the baron. I believe Sir Connor loves you with his whole heart. You should marry him."

"Yes, I do love him," she said, speaking to Isabelle as an equal and not a younger sister, "and nothing would make me happier than to be his wife, but I cannot. If I don't, the baron will take out his ruthless anger on you, and Edmond, Connor and even Connor's family. I have no choice but to marry him, and there is nothing you, or anyone, can do."

"Yes, there is, and I intend to do it. I'm not a stupid child. I know what Rennick DeFrouchette is—and I know what he will do to you, even if you are his wife. *Especially* if you are his wife, because of your love for Connor. He will make your life a hell, Allis, and I will not have that happen, not after all you have done for Edmond and Father and me. I cannot let all your efforts and sacrifice be repaid with more suffering. I will not let you give up your chance for love and happiness with Connor, not while I live." She made a wistful smile and her eyes shimmered with unshed tears. "You taught me better than that, sister, and you taught me well."

Allis put her arms around Isabelle and hugged her tight. Never had she been prouder of her sister, or loved her more. And now, more than ever, she could not condemn her to the miserable life that awaited Rennick DeFrouchette's wife.

Isabelle began to weep. The sound tore at Allis's heart, and strengthened her resolve. "Forgive me for underestimating you, Isabelle. Forgive me for thinking you an ignorant, flighty creature, but I am older than you and so you must do as I say." She gently wiped the tears from her sister's face. "And I will not let you throw your future away by marrying Rennick De-Frouchette. I agreed to be his wife, and I must accept my fate. Still, know you this, Isabelle. By marrying him, I will be keeping the people I love and cherish safe, and that will comfort me, no matter what happens."

"But can you trust him not to hurt anyone, even if he gives his word?"

"No, I cannot," she admitted as the wall around her heart began to rise again, stronger and thicker, like the stone walls of Montclair. She would put her love behind that wall, where Rennick could never go. "But if I am his wife, I will know if he harms those I love, or Connor's family."

"What will you do if he does?"

"I will kill him."

Allis meant that as much as anything she had ever said in her life. "Now I will hear no more of this. I have made my decision." She went to the door. "I will go and tell Rennick that he has made an agreement, and as I intend to abide by it, so must he."

Isabelle followed her and grabbed her hand to make her stay another moment. "Is there no other way?"

For an instant, her resolve wavered. By going to Rennick now, she was giving Connor up forever. There would be no going back. Her heart shuddered and cracked, ready to break, behind the stone walls. "There is not."

"I would marry him, Allis. I would!"

She caressed Isabelle's cheek. "I know, and you have made me proud and grateful, Isabelle. One day, you will make some lucky man a wonderful wife, but it must not be Rennick."

With that, Allis hurried down the steps, determined to speak to Rennick while her resolve was at its strongest, before she weakened and sacrificed her family for the love that lived in her wounded heart.

Connor was not in the hall, or Rennick. Or Oswald or Auberan or Edmond. Only the servants, who once again didn't meet her gaze—except for Merva, who boldly stared while she laid the linen on the tables for the evening meal, although no such order had been given. Who could think of food now?

She marched toward Merva. "Where are the nobles?"

"They left."

Allis regarded Merva with cold, stern command. That was easy to do when her heart was encased in stone. "That is no way to address the chatelaine of Montclair."

The woman flushed and looked away. "Your brother's in the kitchen. I don't know where anybody else went."

She started to go past Merva, then halted abruptly when the woman's murmured words met her ears. "What did you say?"

Merva stared at the ground, abashed at Allis's harsh demand. "I said, I never thought you'd disgrace your family."

Allis blushed hotly. Yes, this was how the stories of

what had transpired today were going to go. She would be painted an evil Jezebel, and Rennick would be a good and virtuous man for marrying her anyway.

Too upset to speak, she hurried out the door, as if she could flee rumor and gossip and the mess she had made of her life, and the danger in which she had put her family, and Connor's, too.

She couldn't face Rennick now. Not yet. There was time for her to tell him what must be. First, she would find Connor. She needed to see him, to be with him. To ask him to leave and say a last farewell.

She slowed to a walk. She had cast aside honor to be with him, and dared to hope. Honor and hope were dashed; the least she could do was try to maintain her dignity.

But she didn't want to be dignified. She wanted to throw herself to the ground and wail and rend her clothes, screaming her anguish, demanding that God take pity on her and smite her enemies—

The door to the chapel opened and Auberan came out.

She could not bear to see or speak with Auberan. She ducked inside the garden and closed the gate.

Turning, her breath caught in her throat as she saw Connor. The walls around her heart quivered, then shook, and a great breach opened and her love for him poured out and through her, burning fierce and bright when he saw her and jumped to his feet.

She ran to him and threw her arms about him, holding him as if she would never let him go. She didn't want to let him go, now or ever. Only the safety of their families could come between them, and it had.

Slowly, reluctantly, she stepped back, her gaze searching his face, determined to memorize his features so they would always be in her mind. Cold comfort, but better than none.

"I know what has happened, that the baron has been given guardianship of you and Edmond and Isabelle." He gently pulled her into his comforting embrace. "Come away with me, Allis," he whispered, his breath light and warm on her cold cheek. "You and your brother and sister. I've been sitting here thinking about it, and that is what you must do. It is the only way we can be together and your family safe."

Even as she held him as if her life depended on it, Rennick's threat sounded in her ears and she shook her head. "I cannot. We cannot."

"You must!"

"If we do, Rennick will hunt us down and destroy us—and your family, too, Connor."

His embrace tightened. "He can't!"

"He can, and he will. There is only one way to keep everyone I love safe, Connor. I have to marry him, as I have already pledged."

He drew back and the pain in his eyes was like her own. "No! I won't let you throw yourself away on that dog. As you love me, you must come away with me. I will protect you and both our families with my last breath, if need be."

She reluctantly shook her head. "Against Rennick your martial skills will not be enough. He will not come at you directly the next time, with a lance or sword, but he will find a way."

"Poison?" he suggested. "Such as something to make a young man's heart fail?"

Of course! She should have seen this, too! She had truly been a blind fool.

"I know the kind of man he is," Connor said, his deep voice full of confidence as he rested his hand on the hilt of his sword, "and that knowledge means we can protect ourselves."

How she wished it could be so simple! "Against the assassins his money can buy? He will stop at nothing to be avenged."

"You fear him that much?"

"I know him that well."

"He is not above the law, Allis. He is not above the king and the king's court."

"What good will the king's justice be to any of us if we are dead?" She took her beloved's face between her hands and as she looked into his wonderful eyes full of love for her, she willed him to understand. "My love, my dearest love, nothing but the threat of death against all those I care about would make me give you up and marry Rennick DeFrouchette."

Connor gathered her into his arms. "There must be another way," he murmured fervently, his lips against her cheek.

"Not without risk to everyone we hold dear."

"Then you will not come with me?"

"Oh, my love!" she cried, her voice breaking with grief. "If it were only the two of us I had to consider, I would not hesitate. But I have to think of Edmond and Isabelle, as you must think of your brother and sister— four other people, Connor, who have done nothing to deserve trouble except be related to us. I cannot put them in jeopardy because of what I want. Can you?"

Hurt and dismayed, he twisted away from her. "I have done it before, have I not? I have spoken and acted with no thought to anyone but myself, and my wounded feelings and betrayed ideals. You stand here telling me what I must do, as if I cannot make a sacrifice. Is that what you truly think of me, Allis? That I do not comprehend duty and sacrifice?"

"No, that is not what I think. You are chivalrous, and understand duty and sacrifice better than many a man, for you have tried to repair your past mistakes. If you were selfish, you would not be risking your life in tournaments to pay your family's debts. But there is one more sacrifice you must make, Connor, for your family's sake, as I make it for mine."

A sob caught in her throat, and the sound ripped into him like a dagger.

"And I hope you may yet be full of dreams, and hope. That someday you will know love and happiness again, Connor, because I never will. When you leave, you will take my love and happiness and all my dreams with you. We have had a time in paradise on earth, however brief, and that is more than most people will ever have. But now it is over. You must leave here and never come back."

As he enfolded her trembling body in his arms, he knew that he would never break her resolve. The strength he had so admired was now marshaled against him, and she would never yield. She would do what she must to protect others, no matter how much she loved him or the cost to her own happiness.

He could not make her be less than she was.

"Never is a very long time to stay away from you," he whispered, his own voice breaking.

"For my sake, it must be so. Please do not come back. I couldn't bear to see you and be reminded of what I have lost."

"Isn't this touching?" Rennick slammed the gate

shut. "Let go of my bride, Welshman." Connor kissed his beloved's forehead. Then he faced their enemy and smiled his dangerous smile as he drew his sword, ready to kill for her freedom, or die in the attempt. "Make me."

"No," she commanded, stepping between them. She turned to him, her eyes blazing with passionate determination. "Connor, if you kill him, you will be brought before the king's court—before Richard. It will not go well with you, not after what we have done. People already suspect we are lovers, and they will believe you killed Rennick to have me."

His blood boiling with the longing to do battle, he did not care what happened to him, as long as she was free of this parasite. "They would be right."

"The charge would be *murder*, Connor, and you would be executed."

"I would be saving you from this blackguard and defending myself."

"Is that how it would look to Lord Oswald and other Norman nobles, or like you killed the man I was to marry for our own selfish, dishonorable desire? Can you expect them to sympathize or understand?" She clasped her hands together in supplication. "Please, Connor, put up your sword and go. Do not risk a disgraceful death for me. The only thing that will give me any happiness in the time to come is knowing that you live."

"Listen to her, Welshman," Rennick sneered, "and take the opportunity to leave while you can. I am a patient man, as Allis well knows, but even mine eventually wears thin."

Allis looked at Connor with love and blatant yearning, as well as hopeless despair. "Go, Connor, and live for me."

Their gazes met and held as they had that first night. But this moment stretched into an eternity of regret and longing. She could not be his, not while Rennick DeFrouchette stood between them, yet he must do as she asked—or seem to. Regardless of Rennick, he pulled her into his arms and kissed her passionately. His kiss was a promise and a pledge, even if she did not know that.

But as he had sat in the garden where they had first kissed, he had made a plan. He would save her by going to the king and seeking his help, even though doing so would be risking his life. Richard might make good his threat to have him charged with treason and executed for daring to come into his presence again, but that was a risk he was willing to take.

"Good-bye, my love," he murmured as he broke the kiss.

"God go with you," she whispered, choking back a sob. "My love, my heart."

"Since I am willing to be merciful, Welshman," Rennick growled, "I will give you until the noon tomorrow to be gone from Montclair."

As Connor stepped away from Allis, he smiled once more—coldly, deliberately. He knew as well as DeFrouchette that great harm could be done without raising a weapon. "I go now because Allis asks me to, but I swear before God, His Son and all the host of heaven, that I will not forget you and what you have done. Do not sleep too soundly. You are not the only one who knows how to bring death swiftly, before a man's proper time."

Rennick colored and his hand moved toward his sword. "If I die unexpectedly before my marriage to your lover, you will be suspected."

Connor walked slowly toward him. "You assume *I* have no patience, do you? That I am still that impetuous young man who dared to upbraid his king? Well, perhaps I am, and so if I ever hear that you have harmed the woman I love, or any of her family—if you render her sacrifice useless—I may impetuously come for you and just as impetuously kill you."

"Get out!"

Connor bowed insolently, then he gave Allis one last, longing look before he strode from the garden.

The gate slammed shut, like the thunderclap of heaven, ending her paradise on earth with a blow that smashed her heart.

But then, as Rennick crept toward her like an upright snake, so different from Connor, the broken remnants of her heart shifted and reassembled into something stronger, bolder, more resolute than before, forged in the heat of her passion and tempered by the elements conspiring against them.

Before, she had been a coward, despite all her words about duty and sacrifice. She had feared not what Rennick DeFrouchette would do, but what he *might* do.

Connor was right. She had doubted his ability to protect her and her family. She had not trusted him, or been willing to count on anybody except herself, despite all that he had said and the love she claimed to feel for him. Instead she had renewed her promise to marry this odious blackguard standing before her now.

What a fool she had been not to accept Connor's love and protection! But it was not too late. He was still here in Montclair and she could go to him, and bring Edmond and Isabelle, too. Let Rennick have Montclair; he would not have them.

Rennick continued to ooze toward her, sly and slick. "So Allis, now we will have no more foolishness."

Blatant, greedy lust gleamed in his cold blue eyes, but she was not afraid of him anymore, not even when he grabbed her and hauled her close. "Let go of me, Rennick."

He eyed her, wary and surprised. "You are mine, Allis, to do with what I will."

"The chivalrous Baron DeFrouchette! Do you think to rape the lady of Montclair?"

The lust glimmered in his eyes as he shook his head. "Rape? No. I am not going to put my seed in you until I am sure you're not with that lout's child."

He shoved her away so hard, she fell to the ground. He put his foot on her back and pressed her body down. "There are other ways you can pleasure me that will not get you with child, Allis, but not now. Still, it's nice to see you groveling at my feet, where you belong." He pushed down harder. "Remember this position, Allis. As my wife, that is where you had better imagine yourself, or it will be all the worse for your brother and sister. Now go and change your gown. That is no fit way for a lady to look."

He left the garden, and after the gate closed behind him, she slowly got to her feet.

Rennick believed he had won.

More fool he.

Chapter 23

Careful not to wrench his left arm, Connor tore out the pegs holding down the sides of his tent, then tossed them into a leather pouch on the ground nearby. In the diminishing daylight, Demetrius whinnied as if shocked by the violence of his actions, but he ignored his horse as he started to haul the fabric off the poles. They were leaving as soon as he could take down his tent and gather his things, for he couldn't let Allis marry that disgusting, loathsome, greedy nobleman and he knew what he must do. His pride, his honor, his life—he was willing to give anything for her freedom.

Out of the corner of his eye, he realized someone was approaching. Begrudging any interruption, he looked impatiently over his shoulder to see Lord Oswald sweeping across the grass of the ward.

"I have heard that you have been ordered to leave by the noon tomorrow. You do not look to be waiting even that long."

Connor let go of the tent fabric. "I want to be on my way as soon as possible," he said, in too great a hurry to couch his words in the mantle of calm politeness.

"I think that is for the best. Where will you go? Home to Llanstephan?"

He saw no need to tell anyone his plan, not even Lord Oswald. If Allis learned what he intended to do, and he failed, he would be adding to her despair. "No, my lord."

"Ah. Too difficult, eh? Your justified denunciation of the king has caused them much suffering. In that case, I invite you to stay at my home in Wessex until you are healed."

This offer was completely unforeseen, unexpected and unusual enough to raise his suspicions. "What will the baron think? You are his friend, and you invite his enemy to your home?"

Lord Oswald smiled. "The baron doesn't have to know about it, does he? I certainly won't tell him." The nobleman clapped a beefy arm about his shoulder. "I am saddened by all that has happened to you at our greedy sovereign's hands."

Connor's mind urged caution as Lord Oswald removed his hand. "It might have been better for me never to have left my home in the first place."

"Oh, a fine warrior like you would never have been content to stay in Wales! Yet you could have avoided the Crusade and fought for a better cause. I'm sure many a king or lord would have paid well for your services."

To suggest that he should have been enriching himself instead of freeing the Holy City from the infidel added to his doubts about the man before him, for it was not with the purpose of the Crusade he quarreled, as least in the beginning. It was the leadership of the army that first caused him to question the supposedly holy mission. "What better cause, my lord?"

Oswald leaned closer. "A better king for England."

Maybe this was a test of his loyalty—a notion that filled him with ire. He had spoken the truth to Richard's face out of outraged ideals, not thwarted ambition or greed. "Such talk is treason, my lord."

"After all Richard has done, you would still be loyal to a man who has robbed and wronged you? Aye, and England, too?"

If Oswald blamed Richard for his brother's death, that could drive him to vengeance, yet to plot against God's anointed king was heinous treason. "I am a loyal subject of my king, my lord."

"But in your heart, you agree with me, I think," Oswald prompted. "And the man who would rid England of this blight of a ruler who is bleeding it dry could be sure that there are those who would reward him, perhaps who would even see to it that he be given that which he desires most."

This was an offer, plain and simple: kill Richard, and Allis would be his.

Temptation, hot as fire, strong as a desert whirlwind, flashed through him. Kill Richard, the vainglorious bane of his life, and he could have Allis for his wife, to love and cherish always. It sounded so simple, so easy.

"You need make no decision today, Connor. Go to my estate in Wessex and consider. But if you do decide to help England, you will be rewarded, that I promise."

"Yes, my lord. I understand, and I thank you for the offer of your hospitality."

His eyes glittering with pleasure, Oswald smiled. "The least I can do, my boy. Now if you will excuse me, the dew is not good for my old bones. This invitation is, of course, between the two of us, so say nothing to anyone as you go."

"I will not, my lord."

Edmond rubbed his sleepy eyes and nearly tripped as Allis led him to the bedchamber she shared with Isabelle.

"It's the middle of the night," he protested, yawning. "What are you doing?"

"Hush until I've got the door closed. I'll explain when we're alone," Allis whispered, and the intensity and tension in her voice silenced his whining. They had to be quiet if they were to succeed.

Once in the bedchamber, Edmond blinked in the bright moonlight, then stared at Isabelle who sat upon her bed, fully clothed. He was dressed only in his long shirt and stockings.

"What's going on, Allis?" he demanded, more awake now as he faced her. "Haven't you made enough trouble already?"

"Yes, I have. And I'm not finished yet." She saw their uncertainty and smiled to reassure them. After all, she had never roused them in the middle of the night before to take them from their home and all they knew.

Edmond looked at Isabelle. "What's she talking about?"

Isabelle shrugged her shoulders, puzzlement on her face. "I have no idea. She woke me up and told me to dress, then said she was going to fetch you. Before I

could ask questions, she was gone. What *are* you doing, Allis?"

"We are going to go away with Connor, and we
must leave before dawn, so you must dress." She
pulled some clothing from a large leather pouch she
had hidden beneath her bed. In it she had put some of
their clothing, and all their jewels, leaving room for
food they would get from the kitchen as they fled.
"While you were eating, I was gathering some of our
things to take with us."

"What?" Edmond cried as Isabelle gaped. "Go
where? Why? I don't want to go anywhere."

"Please be quiet. Sit beside Isabelle and I'll explain."

"We can't leave Montclair. I'm the earl now and—"

"Sit down, Edmond, and let me explain," she said
firmly, still in a whisper but determined that he understand. From now on there would be no secrets or hiding the truth from them.

Despite her determination, she was relieved when
he obeyed.

"I have kept many things from you both," she began. "Ever since Mama died and Father became as he
was, the baron has been slowly, carefully taking command of Montclair. I truly believe that Rennick De-
Frouchette will never give Montclair up."

Again Edmond started to protest, but she held up
her hand to silence him. "Please, hear me out. For
some time I have also been learning about his evil
deeds on his own estate. He is a vicious, greedy brute,
yet I thought that if I agreed to be his wife, I would be
able to protect you from the worst of his machinations.
As his wife, I would have the right to question things,
and to learn some of his dealings, either directly or by
subterfuge of my own.

"Now I think otherwise. I have come to see that he may be more evil and more determined than even I believed. And the situation has grown worse, because Rennick has been made our guardian, confirmed by the king himself. Any restrictions he may have felt are gone. In fact, his threats are no longer implied. When I asked him to break our betrothal because I have fallen in love with Connor, not only did he refuse, he told me to my face that if I do not marry him, he will have his vengeance not just on me, but on you both, and even Connor's family. I believe Rennick is capable of harming anyone, for any reason. Although Connor offered his protection, I asked him to leave for his own safety." Her voice softened as she remembered those last poignant moments. "And he finally agreed."

Then her resolve and her voice grew in strength. "But afterward I realized that was a terrible mistake. If we stay, we will never be free. Not me, not you, Isabelle, or you, Edmond. We will be Rennick's prisoners. Nor do I believe that Rennick will let Connor and his family escape his wrath. He will move against them whether I marry him or not."

"What about Montclair?" Edmond asked, jumping to his feet. "This is my estate."

"Montclair is yours in point of law, and nothing Rennick can do will change that. But if we stay here, we will be little more than hostages. He will rule, not you."

"When I come of age—"

She gazed at him steadily, willing him to see the truth of her words, to suddenly understand that the world could be a vastly different place from what he knew. "*If* you come of age."

"He wouldn't dare to kill the earl of Montclair!"

"He may dare." Holding onto his slender shoulders, she bent down so that they were eye to eye. "Either way, we will never know what he might do, should we cross him. That is what I'm trying to tell you, Edmond. If we go with Connor, we will have a measure of safety and freedom. If not, we are condemned to be Rennick's prisoners, for as long as he decides."

"You just want to be with your lover!" Edmond declared with disgust as he twisted away from her.

"Yes, I want to be with my lover," she agreed quietly as she straightened. "And I will make no apologies for that. I have done all I could to keep you safe, and it has not been enough. Now I will accept his offer of help."

"Then go with him and leave us here in our home!"

Resistance from her proud and stubborn brother didn't surprise her—but she could be stubborn, too, especially when she feared for their lives. "I won't abandon you."

"I won't go!"

Isabelle looked from Allis to Edmond and got to her feet. "She's right, Edmond. We have to leave. The baron is an evil man."

"You just want to be with Connor, too! I've seen the way you look at him!"

"I don't want Connor. He loves Allis." She clasped her hands together and spoke with insistent fervor. "Allis has always put our needs and our safety before her own, and if going with her means she can be happy, we should not begrudge her that. You are not the only one giving up something, Edmond. You at least will be able to reclaim the estate. Who can say what dowry might be left for me? But I will give it up, and gladly, because of all that Allis has done for us. I would go with her now simply because she asked it of me, even if I didn't know the kind of enemy the baron is to us."

"Father didn't think he was bad, or he would never have made the baron our guardian."

Again her past reticence rose up to haunt her. If she had told Edmond even a part of what she suspected, he would be more willing to believe her now. He had to believe her now, and come away. "His grief made Father no fit judge, especially at the end, and I did not voice all my concerns to him, to my regret. Besides, you like Connor. He can continue teaching you how to be a knight. Think of the day you ride back into Montclair and claim it, wearing armor and on a fine war horse."

"I'm not a little child to be bribed with fairy stories," Edmond grumbled. "I understand what you are saying."

But still he did not agree.

Sweat trickled along her sides as her desperation mounted. They could not linger much longer. They had to leave before first light.

She knelt in front of Edmond and took his hands in hers. "As I love you, I beg this of you. You must leave Montclair. It is the only way we will ever be free. You will still be the earl of Montclair, and one day, the estate will be yours. Will you come with us?"

He looked at her for what seemed a lifetime before he nodded his head. "If I must."

Weak with relief, she got to her feet. "Believe me, Edmond, if I thought we could stay here safely, we would."

He began to dress, while Isabelle helped Allis tie the leather pouch. "How are we going to leave without the guards seeing us?" she asked. "And when the baron realizes we have gone, he will surely search for us."

"We shall go to the kitchen, and from there to the stables. I shall saddle the horses, while you and Edmond go to Connor and tell him we are going with him after all."

Isabelle straightened abruptly. "He isn't expecting us?"

She shook her head. "I realized my mistake after he had gone and didn't dare risk trying to speak with him. It was too late for him to be on his way before dusk, or he would have been benighted on the road. Rennick gave him until the noon to go, but we should slip away before first light."

"What if he refuses to take us?"

"He won't," she replied, believing that to the very core of her soul.

"How will we get past the guards?" Edmond asked warily.

She blew out the candle, so that only the bright moonlight illuminated the chamber. "There is a way to the inner ward beneath the wall in the stables," she said as she picked up the pouch and slung it over her shoulder. "Originally it was an error in the building, and some stones fell away. Father showed it to me once, shortly before Mama died. As a temporary measure they had piled some old beams in front of it. I made sure they are still there, so it was never repaired. I don't think the baron knows about it. I have certainly never heard him mention it, or anything about fixing it. You will go to Connor and rouse him, and I will bring the horses."

"How are you going to get three horses past the guards at the gatehouse?"

"I am still the lady of Montclair, so I hope they will not try to stop me. If they do and you hear the alarm being raised before I can reach you, go without me. She took off the crucifix of gold and rubies she wore around her neck and pressed it into Isabelle's hand. "Sell this if you must, for food or horses. Connor will watch over you, and I have every faith that he will keep you safe."

Isabelle's lower lip started to tremble. "We won't go without you."

"Tell him that I said you must, and make him take you away from here. Otherwise, all my planning and concern for you will be for naught. Either way, I expect an alarm to be sounded as soon as we are discovered to be missing, but it takes time to mount a troop of men. Then they will expect us to ride for Wales, and I have another plan."

Traveling by lesser roads, they would head south for the coast and drop hints that they intended to take their quarrel with the baron to the king. After laying a false trail, they would sail to the Welsh coast and land in one of the isolated bays, and go to Connor's home. She hoped that a brother's love would overcome whatever animosity Caradoc felt toward Connor and then, if Connor's brother was anything like her beloved, Rennick would find himself facing not just one dangerous opponent, but two.

If Caradoc refused to help, they would live however they could. At least they would be together, and they would be free.

She took one last look around her chamber, her heart sorrowing for the home they must leave behind, before she went to the door and listened.

All was silent. "Come along now," she whispered, herding Edmond and Isabelle out into the corridor.

Hurrying down the stone steps and into the hall, they made little noise. The soldiers sleeping in the hall were not disturbed, and although the dogs awoke, they raised no cry. These were friends, after all, not enemies.

As they passed by, she imagined the uproar when they were found to be gone. Rennick would rage and send out patrols searching for them. He would question the servants close, but none of them knew anything. Surely he would realize the reticent lady of Montclair was quite capable of planning an escape on her own.

Nevertheless, as they continued into the dim kitchen, a pang of sorrow and regret struck hard. She might be putting her people in danger, and it was possible that her brother might never see his inheritance again.

The cooking fire was banked, and more dogs slumbered by its lingering warmth. Although the cooks were the first to rise, she paused a moment at the storeroom to snatch a loaf of bread and some apples before sneaking into the courtyard behind her brother and sister. The night was clear, the stars twinkling in the heavens unobscured by clouds, and over Montclair hung the silver orb of the moon to light their way.

And to shine down into the courtyard. "Stay in the shadows of the walls," she whispered, pointing at the sentries. Although their watch was over the outer walls to the area beyond the castle, figures surreptitiously moving about the courtyard would be cause for them to raise an alarm.

Mercifully, it was but a short way to the stables and they reached them without being seen.

As they crept inside, she inhaled the scent of hay, horse and leather. For a moment, it was like being back in the hut with Connor, and a reminder of the joy of that afternoon.

The eyes of a cat, there to keep the mice under control, gleamed in the darkness before it slowly padded away. Disturbed, the horses made some sounds, but again, not enough to wake the stable boys or grooms slumbering in the loft above.

She led her brother and sister to the pile of old beams. Moving as quickly and silently as they could, she and Isabelle and Edmond shifted them until they could see the small opening, barely big enough for Isabelle to squeeze through.

"Go to Connor," she whispered. "If there is trouble—if I am not there by the time you see the first light of dawn—go without me."

Isabelle looked about to protest again and Allis turned to Edmond. "As the earl of Montclair, you must see that she does."

His expression was enigmatic as he nodded his agreement.

She was asking so much of him! She silently vowed that one day, she would see him in the great hall of Montclair, enthroned on the dais as the earl, with all his land, rights and privileges restored. "I shall see you in a little while."

Sniffling, Isabelle nodded and crawled through the small space. Without a word or backward glance, Edmond did the same.

It was enough that he had agreed to come with them, she thought while she struggled with the heavy saddles. She truly didn't know what she would have done if he had refused.

She tied the pouch to her saddle, then led the three horses into the courtyard. The noise of their hooves was loud in the silence, and they would be easily seen in the moonlight, but there was nothing else to be done, so she boldly—and swiftly—walked toward the gate.

"My lady?" one of the two guards asked as he moved to block the entrance. It was Bob, and he was clearly puzzled, as well he might be.

"Yes, it is I."

"Where are you going?" the other queried, and she realized it was Harry. "It's night."

"I know that." She drew herself up and spoke in her most imperious manner. "I am the lady of Montclair, so what I do or when is none of your concern. Now let me pass."

Exchanging uncertain looks, they were about to step aside when the sight of something behind her made them hesitate.

Then Rennick DeFrouchette's voice echoed through the courtyard, loud and mocking. "Where are you going, my lady of Montclair?"

Chapter 24

Caught. Caught like a criminal at the gate of her own home. Caught by Rennick, the man she hated. Caught, perhaps never to be with Connor again. Never to feel the bliss of his embrace and the warmth of his love.

As despair settled over her, she slowly turned and saw Rennick marching toward her, a torch in his hand that he must have taken from one of the sconces in the hall. It illuminated his rage, and his sword dangling from his belt slapped against his thigh. He wore a cloak, but no tunic, just a shirt, breeches and boots, as if he had dressed in haste.

A swift glance at the wall walk showed the watchmen moving about, kindling torches and rushing to see what was afoot in the courtyard below.

Please, God, she prayed as Rennick bore down on her. *Let Isabelle and Edmond see and take flight. Do not let them wait or try to rescue me.*

"I asked you a question, my lady. Where do you think you're going?" Rennick repeated as he came to a halt in front of her.

She must be as courageous as Connor and as strong as her father had been in the prime of his life. "Obviously, I am going out of Montclair."

"At this time of night, and with three horses? I think not."

The door to the hall opened and more soldiers, as well as servants, came out, curious to see what was going on.

Let them look. She didn't care. All that mattered was buying time for the others to get away. "I don't particularly care *what* you think. I can do as I wish. I am not a prisoner here, am I?"

"Ah, Lady Allis, you are indeed a spirited creature, like a pretty bird," Lord Oswald remarked as he sauntered toward them. He, too, had obviously dressed speedily, for his long indigo tunic was not fully laced. He had on his cloak, and like Rennick, a sword belt and scabbard. His tone changed, to one cold and unfriendly. "A bird who needs her wings clipped."

She didn't hide the scornful curl of her lip as she looked at the man who had betrayed her trust. "My lord, this is just another lovers' quarrel, so I suggest you retire before you get a chill. The night air is dangerous for one of your age and girth."

Oswald's eyes flickered in the torchlight and his expression soured. "My lady, have a care—"

"No! *You* have a care, my lord. As I am still the lady

of Montclair, you would be wise to let me leave."

A dumbfounded Auberan joined the small crowd. "What's amiss?"

Rennick ignored him. "Why do you have three horses, my lady? And perhaps it has escaped your notice, but it is the middle of the night."

"Since I am not yet your wife, I do not have to answer your questions or explain myself to you—or Lord Oswald, either."

"Yes, you do, for the king has made me your guardian." He came close, smiling cruelly. "You cannot escape the law, Allis. Not you, or your brother or sister. So where are they, eh? It would be better for you, and for them, if you tell me quickly and do not try my patience further."

He was right; she was bound to him by her father's will. But she would say nothing.

Lord Oswald's lips turned slowly up into a smile even more cruel than Rennick's as he looked past her. "Calm yourself, Baron. Here they are."

Agony drowned her as she turned.

Their eyes wide with fear, Edmond and Isabelle stood just outside the gates, Rennick's soldiers behind them. Rennick must have ordered some of his own men to watch the gate, lest she try to run away.

She had left this too late, seen the truth too late, changed her mind too late, had faith in Connor too late. What remaining hope she had disappeared like the morning mist in sunlight, leaving only dark despair, as Edmond and Isabelle were marched into the courtyard.

She took a step toward them, but Rennick grabbed her and pulled her back. Although his grip tightened on her arm, he could have wrenched it off before she would give him the satisfaction of crying out in pain.

"Sir Connor has already departed, my lady," Oswald announced. "He rode off before nightfall. Indeed, he was most impatient to be gone. Perhaps he decided you were not worth the trouble, after all."

She straightened her shoulders and raised her brow haughtily, every inch proclaiming her unbeaten and unconquered.

"Traitor" was all she said, but never had she infused a single word with such scornful derision.

Oswald's fat hand struck her cheek with a slap that resounded through the yard and sent her staggering back. She tasted blood, hot and coppery, as she struggled to regain her balance.

"You can't do that to my sister!" Edmond cried as he broke away from the men holding him and ran toward them.

Rennick took hold of her again and tugged her back, and she collided hard with his chest.

"Shut up, boy," Oswald thundered, stepping between them. "You will all do as you're told."

Edmond skittered to a halt. "I won't! I'm the earl!"

As she struggled in Rennick's grasp, Oswald moved with surprising speed. He grabbed Edmond by his tunic and lifted him up, until they were nose to nose, Edmond gasping for breath.

"What arrogant pride did those parents of yours breed in you all, eh?" Oswald snarled. "Your sisters do not know their place, and you, boy, had better learn when to keep quiet!"

"Take your hands off him, you . . . you Judas!" Allis shouted, twisting and turning and trying to get free.

"Judas, am I? So accuses Jezebel," Oswald jeered. "The whore dares to upbraid me? At least when I make a plan, it *works*."

He let go and Edmond fell to the ground. Still gasping for breath, he rubbed his throat. She watched, full of rage and hate, despairing and helpless, as Isabelle ran to him and put her arms around him.

While Isabelle helped him stand, Allis's gaze darted to the servants and Montclair soldiers, silently pleading with them to help. They muttered among themselves, upset and uncertain, and Merva started to cry, but they did nothing.

Were they all traitors, too?

Then, as she glared at them, dark anger on her brow, she realized with guilt and dismay why they did not come to their aid. It was the example she had set for them. For too long, she had only observed what was happening between her father and the baron, and rather than make trouble, she had stayed silent. She had even acquiesced to the baron's plans, agreeing to the betrothal, rather than fighting him by going to the court and the king. If they did nothing now, it was because that was what she had taught them.

"Connor's gone, just like you wanted," Rennick growled in her ear as he turned her to face him. One hand still clamped around her, he cupped her chin with the other, squeezing hard and forcing her to look at his loathsome face. "Gone for good. But I'll find him. By God, I swear it. I'll track him down like the cur he is, and I'll kill him."

"The day he dies will be your last, Rennick," she vowed in a low, determined voice. "Kill him, and I will kill you, even if I am drawn and quartered for it."

His eyes flared with burning anger as he let go of her chin. "You are both mad, the pair of you."

She smiled, for her love made her strong, and not afraid of his rage, or his lust. He could do what he willed with her body, but he could never destroy what she felt for Connor. "We love each other, which is something you will never understand, and for that, I pity you, Rennick."

"I don't need your pity anymore than I need your love," he snarled. "And have a care how you speak, my fine lady, for your brother's and sister's sake."

"It is for their sake that I do. I was silent too long, and let you work your way into our household. I should have spoken long ago and told my father—nay, anyone who would listen—what a despicable varlet you are."

Rennick raised his hand as if to strike and she stiffened, awaiting the blow and the taste of blood, when Oswald's voice cut through the air. "Enough! Inside. Now!"

"Take the young earl and his sister to the hall to await my orders," Rennick commanded his men as he began to drag her there. "Auberan, I leave you in charge."

She fought him every step, across the courtyard, through the hall and up the stairs to the solar, but it was no use. He held her too tight, and although he didn't strike her, it was only because he needed both hands to hold her.

Once in the solar, he hauled her in front of the table while Oswald closed and bolted the door. Then, as she stood before the trestle table, Oswald took the seat behind the table as if he stood in judgment over her. Rennick went to stand at his right hand, the place of a lackey waiting to serve his master.

She was lost. Those marshaled here against her had too much power—but she would not simply submit. Her pride and her honor and her love demanded otherwise.

"That was a very foolish thing to do, Allis," Oswald began.

"*Lady* Allis." She curled her lip as she looked at Rennick. "So, you cannot even be evil by yourself. You must latch onto someone more wretchedly clever, like the leech you are."

"My dear, you really are too hard on him. He does care for you in his own way, and many women would be grateful for that."

"I'm not."

Oswald leaned back in the chair and folded his arms over his broad stomach. "What were you going to do, take to the road and live a gypsy life? You and your brother the young earl, and your sister, too?"

"You have no right to question me."

"I do," Rennick reminded her, glaring. "As your guardian, I have every right to question you, and to punish you for this, too."

"Punish me for what, Rennick? What have I done? Nothing except lead three horses to the gate to meet my brother and sister to go riding. Other than that, what evidence have you of anything else?"

"You would go riding in the dead of night, with baggage tied to your saddle?"

"We planned to be riding all day."

Rennick strode around the table and raised his hand again. Instinctively, she shrank away, then wished she had not when she saw the flash of pleasure in his eyes.

"There is no need to beat her—yet. Like any creature of spirit, she continues to fight the bit," Oswald said. Rennick lowered his hand, like the trained dog she now knew him to be.

"However, Allis," Oswald continued, "it is time to

surrender. Be grateful your betrothed doesn't draw a sword and kill you. I certainly wouldn't accuse him of murder if he did. You have utterly disgraced him with your misbehavior."

She glared at them, all vestige of demure lady gone, consumed by rage. "You would chastise me like a child?"

"Would you rather we denounce you for a whore?" Rennick demanded.

"I love another man, and it is he I want to marry. That does not make me a whore."

"All this talk of love," Oswald scoffed. "We are the nobles of Norman England, Allis. We do not marry for love. Whatever fairy stories your parents fed you— along with tales of honor and chivalry—forget them. They are not reality. Reality is marriage for gain and power. Has your lover not gone just as he was ordered? Has he stayed to fight for you? No. He has run off like a thief in the night."

"He did so because I asked him to."

Oswald raised his heavy brows. "So why were you going after him? Really, my dear Allis, you lie even more poorly than Rennick.

"Here is the way of things. Because you have dared to choose another man who is not your betrothed, because you have given another man your body, Rennick could kill you, and not a nobleman in England would speak against him. They have sisters and daughters to dispose of, and marriage for anything but alliances and gain will not sit well with them."

"Then let him kill me if he dares, the coward!" she cried, quaking with rage at the injustice of a world ruled by men.

Oswald shook his head. "He will never kill you, Allis. You make so much of love, you should be pleased that Rennick dotes on you like a besotted boy. Indeed, I have long considered his affection for you a great weakness on his part, but you see, my dear, he simply cannot let you go. Nor should he, now. I told you, his coming marriage into the family of Montclair has already garnered more respect than anything else he has ever done."

Allis swiveled on her heel to glare at Rennick. "Do you hear how he speaks of you, this *friend* of yours? Where is the respect you crave by marrying me?"

Rennick's face reddened as his gaze darted to Oswald as if he half agreed with her—but in the next instant, he had her pressed painfully against the wall, his furious, impassioned face inches from hers. "I am going to have you, Allis, one way or another. Only then will my blood cool! Then I will be free of this spell you have cast over me. Afterward, when I am no longer enthralled by you, you will be nothing more to me than a well-born brood mare, the mother of my sons."

His lips took hers, cruel, domineering, in what was lustful possession, while his hands roughly pawed her body.

Fear and loathing gave her strength. She splayed her hands on his chest and shoved him back. He stood staring at her, but with a different look on his face from any she had ever seen before, as if he were suddenly lost and alone. Vulnerable.

She seized the moment. "We both want the same thing, Rennick—freedom. Let us go. You will have Montclair, and you will forget me."

That moment of vulnerability might have been a trick of the light, so quickly was it replaced by the familiar cold-blooded deliberation in his cold blue eyes. "No."

"I will not marry you," she declared. "I will refuse to take your hand, or say the vows, or wear your ring. I will spit in your face instead."

"You seem to forget we hold your bold brother and charming sister, too," Oswald observed.

The fiery blood throbbing through her chilled at those words, and cold spears of terror stabbed her. Here was *her* vulnerability, made of flesh and blood.

Oswald gestured at her while he addressed Rennick. "You see how easy it can be, Rennick? No violence, no rape—find the weakness and there will be submission. She will do anything for her family."

"If you harm them in any way, you will answer to the law!"

"Oh, Allis, Allis," Oswald sighed. "How tiresome you are! You will marry the baron, and Rennick will have the young earl for his squire, to train him in the ways of knighthood. As for pretty young Isabelle, she will marry Auberan. There is nothing you can do to stop it."

They had the fate of her family all planned. Yet there must be something she could do. There had to be!

"I grow fatigued and it is nearly dawn," Oswald said as he hoisted himself to his feet, "so do with her as you will, Rennick, to ensure her cooperation. Just take care not to leave any visible marks."

Rennick stood stiffly, as if he were not a human being at all, but a blue-eyed marble statue. "I know a way, my lord."

Oswald eyed him as he sauntered to the door. "I thought you might."

As the door closed behind Oswald with a dull thud, Rennick lunged for Allis and shoved her hard against the tapestried wall. His wrathful, icy blue eyes bored into hers. And although he held her pinned against the wall as he had before, there was no lust in his eyes—and that frightened her even more.

His eyes glittered like hard blue diamonds as he pressed his body against hers. His knee slid between her legs. Panic seized her, but she forced it back. She must think, and remember Connor, and not be afraid.

"Why do you make me do this?" he murmured as he put one hand on either side of her head and leaned closer. "Why do you goad me?"

Her throat parched with dread, she swallowed hard. "I am not goading you, Rennick. I did not fall in love with Connor to spite you."

He kissed her neck and the feel of his wet lips disgusted her. "You wanted to inflame my desire, and you have."

Oh, why had she ever said that to him? she silently cried as she willed herself not to move. "If I were not sincere, would I abandon Montclair, and take Edmond and Isabelle with me?"

He abruptly drew back. "Then you do give me no choice. Hear this, my lady, and remember it well: you will do as I say, or your lovely little sister who spoke of passion will pay." He boldly caressed her breast. "Do you understand how?"

Oh, Connor, Connor, I need you! I need your help and your strength. The words keened through her mind as she numbly nodded her head. She looked up into Rennick's face, and his eyes told her that he saw her surrender. "I believe you understand me, Allis, but just to make sure you know that I can and will punish you in other ways, you will come with me."

Weakened, distraught, not sure how or if she could fight him anymore, she put up no resistance as he hauled her to the door. "Now take my arm, my lady, as if we are going for a walk in your lovely garden."

The garden, where she had kissed Connor. At least he was well away from here, and safe. Yet even that knowledge couldn't silence the wail of misery that seemed to swell within her, trying to burst free, as Rennick led her from the solar.

They passed through the hall, past Merva and the servants and soldiers who looked confused and fearful, but made no move to intervene. They went out through the courtyard and toward the armory. Was he going to rape her there? Her steps faltered, so that he was all but dragging her by the time he pushed open the door with his foot.

"Attila?" he called out.

There was no answer. Was that good, or bad?

He roughly pulled her into the workroom. "He's getting drunk in the village, I expect. I don't suppose the clever chatelaine of Montclair knew that about her armorer, did she, or that the man will do anything for pay? He will burn the pieces of a broken lance, or ignore a woman's cries for help."

Allis tried to breathe, to think, to stay calm as he forced her down the steps. A scuttling sound told her rats were the usual denizens of this horrid place. At the bottom, he shoved her into a small, dank, windowless room.

Was this where he was going to rape or beat her?

Rennick stood in the doorway like a hellish gatekeeper, watching her.

She crouched, almost afraid to disturb him, because at least he was not touching her.

She dared to hope a man of honor lurked in him somewhere. "Rennick, it is not too late. Show yourself a chivalrous knight of the realm and let us go! You know what you do is wrong. I have seen it in your eyes. If you truly care for me at all, you will let me and my family go."

He started to close the heavy wooden door, shutting out what little light there was.

"If you do this, Rennick—if you treat me and my family as pawns for your gain and ambition—you will live to regret it."

She could no longer see his face, so his voice seemed to come only from the darkness, like that of some grim spirit.

"My father used this method of correction on me, and it always worked. And my only regret is that I didn't try it sooner."

Chapter 25

Tired and hungry, his knees aching and his shoulder throbbing with pain, Connor approached Westminster, that area outside London dominated by the great abbey and the palace built by William Rufus, where Richard would be.

He had been on the road for two days, ever since he had left Montclair as night fell. Determined to get to London as quickly as he could to see the one man with the power to change Allis's fate, he had ridden hard and rested little.

It had been so difficult to leave her in the garden with that blackguard. Only the conviction that he had to go to Richard enabled him to do it, not her pleas, or her belief that she could save him and her family by sacrificing herself. He had known too many men, greedy, self-centered men like DeFrouchette, who would do whatever suited their own purposes. Men like Richard, and himself, in the days of his youth, before he had seen what selfishness could do. Once more he silently vowed that if he did nothing else with his life, he would do whatever was necessary to save Allis and her family from their enemy.

The people made way for him, and as they did, many pointed surreptitiously at his surcoat, his shield and his helmeted head, for he had dressed to show all, and especially the palace guards, that he was a knight of the realm.

He passed the abbey, the large hulking building built for the glory of God. Only slightly less impressive was the palace, built to remind people of royal power. The sense of awe he had felt the first time he had seen them returned, but muted. He had learned that men of God could be as fallible as men of power, and men of power could be as vicious and unchivalrous as any brigand.

He dismounted and approached the soldiers guarding the entrance.

"Who are you?" one of them demanded, stepping out to meet him.

"I am Sir Connor of Llanstephan and I have come to see the king."

"You and half the nobles of England," the guard replied with a smirk.

"If our sovereign spent more time in England, he might not be so besieged."

The man frowned and glanced at his fellow guard, obviously not sure what to make of Connor. "Who did you say you was?"

"I am Sir Connor of Llanstephan, and I was in the king's retinue on the Crusade."

"That's what they all say," the other guard scoffed. "The king'd be a poor man if he had as many in his retinue as claim to be."

Frustrated to be so close and yet kept at bay by two foot soldiers, Connor spoke sternly. "The king *is* a poor man. Is my surcoat not proof that I was on the Crusade? Are my armor and my destrier not evidence that I am a knight of the realm? Is not my manner? Or would you care to test me by combat? If not, go to the king and tell him who awaits."

"You might have stolen those clothes and that horse," the first guard charged.

"Here, Bert, I'll go. What'll it hurt? And what if he be a knight?"

The first guard gave a reluctant nod, and the second one trotted off.

"So, you were with the king, eh?" the first guard said as he slowly surveyed Connor. "You don't sound Norman."

His jaw clenched, but it would not be wise to push his way past or fight his way inside, despite the temptation. "I am from Wales."

"Ah." The guard leaned on his spear. "You were a good friend of his, were you?"

Although he would have thought it impossible to be more anxious, he tensed. "Not that good a friend."

The second guard strolled back toward the gate.

"What did he say?" Connor asked, trying to keep the impatience from his voice.

"You're to come inside and see him," the guard replied, eyeing him as if not at all sure what to make of him. "The king laughed and said you had some gall."

Richard's laughter could mean so many things, not

all of them pleasant. Still, he was going to the king, and that was what mattered, Connor told himself, as he led Demetrius through the gate.

The moment Connor saw Richard enthroned in a chair in the great hall of Westminster, he knew he was not forgotten or forgiven. Suspicion shone in his sovereign's eyes beneath his slightly lowered brows and anger flared his nostrils. A hint of grudging curiosity resided in his face, as if he could not quite believe a man he had threatened so specifically would dare to come into his presence again.

Still the same Richard—haughty, arrogant, fearless, a warrior king for all that meant, and despite all that had passed, admiration rose in Connor's breast. But never again would he stand in blind awe of his king and obey without question. Never again would his hands be stained with blood shamefully shed.

He strode forward, his booted footsteps loud in the silent chamber, and he surreptitiously noted his surroundings. As always, Richard was not alone in the large room, but accompanied by several of his close— and sometimes intimate—friends. They varied in ages, and some might have been courtiers who handled affairs of state. Chances were, most gathered here were not, for Richard was casually attired in a plain red velvet robe.

Surprisingly, it seemed a fairly civilized gathering and not a drunken, noble version of soldiers' barracks. A chessboard stood nearby. Wine and bread were laid out upon a nearby trestle table, and a minstrel sat in the corner, idly strumming his harp. The only thing missing was women, whether to serve or provide company, but it was always thus with Richard.

Connor halted while he was still several paces from the king, then went down on his knee and bowed his head. "My liege."

"Sir Connor," Richard replied as he rose with the considerable majesty he commanded. He was taller than his companions, and they fell back as he strolled toward Connor. "Why are you dressed in your surcoat and armor?"

"To make my request to see you easier, sire. I wanted the guards at the gate to believe that I was a knight of the realm and that once I had been in your retinue."

"That once you had been my friend, until you saw fit to call me—what was it?" Richard's voice hardened. "A disgrace to my name, my throne, my countrymen and my God. So, Connor, have you forgotten what I vowed to do if you ever dared to come into my presence again, or have you finally come to beg my forgiveness?"

He had not forgotten, and he still believed that every word he had said to Richard as he faced him at Acre had been completely justified. Richard had acted without mercy. Without justice. Without honor.

And he had silently vowed to die before he would beg his king's forgiveness for telling the truth. But now, his heart commanded him to do what he had sworn he would never do, what his pride and righteous outrage demanded he must never do—until his love for Allis became stronger than his pride and indignation, and her life more important to him than his own.

Sir Connor of Llanstephan lay face down on the floor, his arms wide, prostrating himself in a gesture of complete surrender and humility. His shoulder screamed in agony, but he ignored it. He must regain

Richard's trust and save Allis. Nothing else mattered. "I most humbly beg your forgiveness, sire."

There was a long moment of silence like the quiet that had descended upon Acre when the last of the slaughtered Saracens fell. That silence had seemed as if Judgment Day had come and gone, and this heavy quiet was much the same.

Richard's feet came closer. "Is that all you have to say to me, Sir Connor?"

He knew that tone of voice, and his heart began to beat anew. He had opened the door, but now he must do all he could to get Richard inside, and the best way was to appeal to his self-interest. Richard would never go out of his way for Connor of Llanstephan, but he would certainly act if he felt threatened—and swiftly, too. "No, sire. I have also come to warn you. Some of your lords are plotting against you."

"I daresay they are. Dissatisfied noblemen always plot against their king."

Although he spoke as if this did not disturb him, Connor knew Richard well enough to hear the subtle change in his voice. "Send these others away, sire, and I will tell you all that I know."

"What, do you think I wish to be alone with you, a man I very nearly accused of being a traitor? And you are armed, too."

Connor raised his head to look at Richard. He recognized that shrewd, calculating gleam in the king's eyes and his hope increased. "If you had truly believed me a traitor, sire, you would have killed me the day I denounced you at Acre, or had me accused of treason and executed upon my return to England. You know that I am, and have always been, your loyal subject."

"Rise, Sir Connor."

Pressing his lips together to prevent himself from crying out in pain, he put his hands on the stone and pushed, heaving himself upright. "I am still your loyal subject and would never harm you. However, if you doubt me, one of these men may take my sword when they leave the room."

Richard gestured to the others. "Leave us."

"But sire!" one protested.

Richard whirled around to glare at them and spoke in the voice that had commanded men in battle countless times. "Leave us!"

As Richard strode toward the large carved chair near the hearth and sat, they scurried from the chamber like sheep being chased by a dog.

Richard gestured for Connor to come closer, but not to sit, and made no mention of his sword. "Well, what is this conspiracy you have come to warn me about?"

"It concerns the Baron DeFrouchette, whom you have just confirmed as guardian of the children of the late earl of Montclair."

"You think he plots against me?"

"Yes. And if he has Montclair—"

"He does not have it. He is merely the guardian of the young heir, and was named as such in the earl's will. I saw no need to go against Lord Montclair's wishes."

Not completely surprised, Connor absorbed the revelation. Oswald had not been truthful about how the baron had come to be named guardian. After their last conversation, his doubts about Oswald's loyalty had grown, and now he was sure he was to have been a pawn in the man's schemes. "The late earl was in no fit state to agree to anything, sire."

Rubbing his strong jaw with an even stronger hand, Richard regarded him skeptically, but he did not contradict him. "How do you know this?"

"I saw the earl shortly before he died. It was quite obvious he was very weak and suffered from melancholy. DeFrouchette preyed upon his weakness, because he wants Montclair for himself."

"The will was not made shortly before the earl died. It was some time ago."

That was unexpected, but according to Allis, the baron had been influencing the earl for at least six years. "Be that as it may, the baron has been slowly taking control of Montclair ever since the earl's wife died six years ago."

"You sound very sure of this, although you were with me six years ago."

"Lady Allis, the late earl's elder daughter, told me."

"Isn't she the one Rennick DeFrouchette is going to marry?"

"Yes, sire."

"Yet she told you this about her future husband." The king studied Connor, then he smiled. "One can only wonder why."

Richard was vain and selfish, but he wasn't stupid. If Connor was less than completely honest now, the king would be suspicious, and surely DeFrouchette and Oswald would use his relationship with Allis against them if they stood accused before Richard. "She told me because she trusts me and because we are in love."

The interest fell out of Richard's face, to be replaced with scorn. "So now you come rushing to me to tell me your beloved's betrothed is involved in a conspiracy. Very convenient for the two of you."

Connor fought to maintain control, to sound reasonable and not the slave of his feelings. "Do you trust him, then, sire?"

Richard tilted his head and regarded Connor with that coldly measuring stare he used to such great effect. "I don't trust any of my nobles." He got to his feet and started to pace as he always did when he was upset. "I do not trust you, especially when you tell me how you feel about Lady Allis. However, it is a long way to go from mistrust to an accusation of treason." He halted in front of Connor, and his eyes gleamed fiercely, like a wolf's in the dark. "As you know, Sir Connor, I do not make such accusations hastily."

He met his king's gaze steadily, and although he forced himself to use a deferential tone, his voice was firm and sincere. "Lady Allis has never wanted to marry the baron. The baron is the insistent one, because he would gain much by marrying her."

Richard's eyes flared. "So would you."

"Yes, I would, because of the woman herself." Richard would not care what Allis was like, so he altered his course back to the king's safety. "I warn you that not only DeFrouchette is plotting against you. Lord Oswald of Darrelby is, too."

Another look passed across Richard's face. Oswald was a powerful man. Richard might be able to ignore treachery on the part of DeFrouchette, or put an end to it with relatively little trouble. Oswald was another matter entirely.

Connor pressed on, sensing that the king was yielding. "They are combining forces against you, sire, and trying to convince others to join them. They tried to convince me. Lord Oswald was trying to make me so angry at you that I would kill you."

Richard's glance darted to Connor's sword. "No,

sire, I will not. And there is yet more, Richard. Have you heard of the death of the son of Albert L'Ouisseaux?"

The king nodded and returned to his chair. Gesturing for Connor to sit near him, Richard sat heavily, as if burdened by his cares and the weight of his years, no longer the dashing figure of his youth, but a man who had been in power, with its attendant woes, for a long time.

Connor might have pitied him, save for Acre and the taxes on his family's home. "I believe the death of Percival L'Ouisseaux was no accident, but murder. I think DeFrouchette poisoned him because the boy knew that the baron had tampered with my lance at the tournament hosted by the earl of Montclair, which caused me to be wounded. Or else the lad had done it at his bidding. If the baron will kill a boy for that, he will do anything to have what he wants, even kill his sovereign." He leaned forward and infused his words with every ounce of conviction he could muster. "You must believe me, Richard. Those two are planning to kill you and I have come to warn you."

"Even if I did believe you, what proof have you?"

They had come to it at last—the one thing that could make Richard disregard all that he had said, or spur him to action if his offer was accepted. "I have no proof except my word, and my willingness to put my accusations to a test in a trial by combat, my sword against DeFrouchette's."

Richard frowned and Connor could scarcely breathe as the king spoke. "If you triumph, you will have the lady, and all the wealth that goes with her—and that means power. I may be exchanging one enemy for another."

Dismay and desperation overcame the need for

caution. "Yes, but sire, if I do not speak the truth, surely God will let DeFrouchette be the victor."

"Let me finish!" Richard snapped, his eyes blazing with a fire all too familiar.

Flushed and remorseful, fearing his impulsive outburst had been a disastrous error, Connor sat back in his chair.

"God's ways are mysterious, Connor, or we would be having this conversation in Jerusalem. You come to me with no proof save your own conviction and ask me to trust you, even though you admit you want the bride of one of those you accuse. What am I to make of that?"

Connor slipped from his chair and knelt before his king. There was one more thing he could offer to prove that he spoke honestly. One more chance to save Allis from DeFrouchette.

"My liege, I have always been a man of honor and integrity, not greed and ambition. I think that in your heart, you know this to be true. I beg you to let God judge the truth of my accusations. If you do, and if I live and Rennick DeFrouchette dies, I give you my solemn promise before God that I will not marry Lady Allis of Montclair."

Rennick regarded Oswald warily as the older man rode beside him at the head of their cortege. Oswald had suggested it would be a good idea for the people of Montclair to see him in public with that sullen brat, Edmond, to reinforce his position as guardian of Montclair.

But it was now clear that Oswald wanted to speak with him in relative privacy, away from the castle with its disgruntled servants. "What do you mean, he isn't there?" he asked.

"He didn't go," Oswald answered. "He never arrived. How much plainer can I make it? My estate steward hasn't seen hide or hair of that Welshman, and he's had more than enough time to get there."

"Maybe he hurt his shoulder again. Or maybe he decided to go back to Wales after all. Maybe he's lying dead somewhere—God willing."

Oswald shook his head. "You really must learn to look beyond your own wounded vanity, Rennick. Connor could be a very valuable weapon against the king."

"He's such a hotheaded fool, maybe he's already gone after Richard. Maybe he's on the road to Westminster right now."

"I would like to hope so, yet I would rather be certain. A bit premature for my other plans, but Richard dead is Richard dead. Now or later makes only a little difference."

"And if he hasn't?"

"Then we'll have to find another man with a grudge against the king. That shouldn't be too difficult." Oswald glanced back at Edmond riding between two of Rennick's personal guards. "What do you make of the young earl's silence?"

"He's sulking, like a babe. Once I have married his sister and he is my squire, he'll come around."

"Or he could be nursing a fierce bitterness, like your son in France, that could prove very harmful to you one day. Take care it is not so."

Rennick clenched his jaw. "I didn't think you knew about Alexander."

Oswald chuckled, a most unpleasant sound. "Oh, come, come, Rennick! I make it my business to find out things about my friends as well as my enemies. Naturally I have learned all about you and the young lady you seduced and abandoned once she was with child. I know you have seen the boy but once, although he is nearly twenty. I also know, Baron, that he hates you with a passion."

Rennick really didn't care. "He's only a bastard."

"Bastards have a very inconvenient habit of causing trouble. I would get rid of the fellow if I were you. One less thing for you to worry about." Oswald eyed Rennick with a sly, malicious glee. "He is the spitting image of you, you know."

No, he didn't know, but he didn't care about that either, any more than he did about the boy's mother. She was no proud, disdainful beauty like Allis, whose conquest would be an exciting victory.

Allis in his bed. He had thought of little else these past three days as she lay in that dark cell in the armory. Soon, she would be freed to take her place in his bed, where surely she would be very willing to please him, in every way. A victory indeed, and the just reward for all his patience.

"I would also suggest you take care how you deal with Edmond de Montclair. He is, after all, the heir to a great estate."

Edmond the brat, who looked at him with Allis's eyes and hateful expression. He cared even less about Edmond than he did about his bastard. "If he lives to inherit."

"I've been giving that some thought, Rennick, and I believe he should. You can strip the estate of what is valuable between now and then. I would also suggest you educate the lad in the finer points of debauchery, which I understand you know so well."

Yes, he did, and Allis was going to learn all the

ways he liked to be pleasured, whether she wanted to or not.

"If he is a drunken, lascivious lout and an embarrassment to the other nobles, no one will care very much what happens to him, except his sisters. A few years of patience, and then Montclair may be legally and truly yours."

At last. At last.

Oswald slid Rennick another sidelong glance of malignant merriment. "Of course, Allis remains a bit of a problem. I think you were wise not to invite any guests to the wedding. Who can say what a woman like that, driven to desperation, might do?"

"She will be tamed, my lord."

"You sound very confident."

Rennick thought of the dark, dank hole in which she had been imprisoned. "I am."

Chapter 26

Footsteps. Boots coming down the stairs. Her legs weak and trembling from hunger as well as fear, Allis tried to stand. She braced herself against the wall, determined to stay on her feet and face whoever came to fetch her.

The door opened, and Rennick stepped into the chamber.

Rennick the cruel. Rennick the wolf, the snake, the rat, the worm. Rennick the fool, who had left her for days with nothing to do but think. To compare him to Connor. To decide what she must do.

He coughed and held his hand over his face. "Time to go, my lady. The priest awaits to make us husband and wife, once you have washed and put on a clean gown."

Keeping her back against the stones for support, she

swallowed, trying to wet her throat to speak. "Does he know that the bride is unwilling?"

"Father Duncan is a very ambitious fellow determined to build a new cathedral on my estate. I have agreed to give him land for the cathedral, and he has agreed to marry us."

Filled with hate and scorn, she curled her lip. Of course a man like Rennick would find someone willing to do what he wanted for the right price. Men like her beloved and honest Connor were an even rarer breed than she had suspected.

Rennick held out his hand to her. "Now come. I should think you would be ready to leave this place."

She crossed her arms. "I would gladly stay here for the rest of my life than marry you."

He laughed harshly and the cold, heartless sound echoed off the slimy walls. "No, you wouldn't. A few more days starvation, you would be glad to do anything for me, with or without benefit of clergy, if it got you out of here."

If she could have, she would have spit in his face. As it was, she stood her ground and glared at him.

"If you try anything to prevent our marriage today, my lady, I will lock you in here and I will not return until I am good and ready. So come along, Allis. You need to prepare to be married." He yanked her forward, making her stumble. "Do I have to carry you?"

She drew herself up and, with what strength she could muster, pulled her arm from his grasp. "Don't touch me."

"Proud even now," he sneered as she passed him. "Proud as a highborn lady should be, but more foolishly stubborn than most. Very well, my lady, hold your haughty head high. We shall see how long it takes to break you—and I *will* break you."

She didn't reply to his boastful words. Let him talk all he wished, or strike her. She had her plan, one that would free all those she loved. And all it would cost was her life.

Despite her firm resolve, her steps faltered. She didn't want to die. She wanted to live—to be Connor's wife, to bear his children in peace. What had she said to Connor that first night? That we all had burdens to bear? Right now, hers seemed like the weight of the world.

But she must bear it, and not weaken, even if she could never be with Connor again. If he heard of what she had done, she hoped he would be proud of her, and their love.

Rennick behind her like the shadow of death, she made her way up the steps, into what seemed light as bright as heaven would be. A strange euphoria took her, like a contentment. Soon, everyone would be free, and that was worth her life.

They reached the main floor of the armory and Attila was not there. There were so many weapons, and so close by! If she could but get hold of one, even as weak as she was—

Rennick anticipated her thoughts and walked close beside her as they went outside. With frightened expressions, the servants surreptitiously watched as they passed. They could not help her, for if the baron could make the lady of Montclair suffer as he did, it did not take much to imagine what he would do to servants who tried to interfere.

The strange sensation of being in the world yet not

of it lasted as he took her through the hall and up to her bedchamber. A tub of water for bathing stood ready. Her finest gown of white silk lined with gold and a girdle of gilded leather lay upon the bed.

Rennick shoved her into the room. She fell forward, putting her hands out to break the fall; her palms slapped the hard, unyielding stone with nearly the same force as her kneecaps. Pain leaped and bit, but she ignored it as she struggled to her feet. She would not be on her knees in Rennick's presence. "Make her ready."

Who was he talking to?

Rennick slammed the door behind him. She raised her head, and only then saw Isabelle and Merva, who hurried to help her.

"Oh, Allis!" Isabelle cried, tears coming to her eyes.

She patted Isabelle's arm gently as her gaze anxiously scanned her sister. She was well dressed, and although she was pale and upset, did not look ill treated. "You are well?"

"In body, yes, but we have been so worried about you! He wouldn't tell us anything, that viper, and only Attila was allowed in the armory. Are you hurt?"

"A little. Is there water? Or bread?"

"Not here, my lady, my lamb, but never you fear," Merva said. "I'll fetch some right quick. That blackguard never said nothing about that, and the cook likes me right well, so orders or no, I'll get it." She hurried to the door and put her hand on the latch, then looked back over her shoulder, contrite and sad. "Forgive me what I said before, my lady. About disgracing your family. You're the finest, bravest creature on God's good earth." With a sob, she opened the door and ran out.

Although Merva's condemning remark had been

far from her mind, the woman's words pleased her, and made her feel a little stronger as Isabelle led her to the bed.

"Can you sit, or do you want to lie down?" Isabelle asked gently.

"I can sit. Indeed, I shall stand, and you can help me out of these clothes. Then into the tub. The warm water will help ease the aches in my limbs."

With a nod, Isabelle began to help her remove her soiled scarf and barbette.

"Edmond—how is he?"

"He is well."

She caught the hint of fear in Isabelle's voice, and another dread slid into her heart. "Has the baron hurt him?"

"No, no, nothing like that," Isabelle hastened to assure her as she untied the lacing of her gown. "It's just that he barely says a word, even to me."

She was not surprised by that. "Much has happened, and he is young to comprehend it all."

"It's more than that, Allis. He's changed. He hardly seems like a boy anymore."

"As you are not a girl anymore. I did my best to spare you, and instead only made things worse."

"You mustn't think like that! I shouldn't have told you, but Edmond's almost . . . almost like Father."

Oh, God help her, she had hurt them both, far more than she had ever imagined she could. And they were not the only ones. "Has there been word of Connor?" she asked, voicing the other great worry that had haunted her all the long, dark hours of her captivity.

"No. We have heard nothing."

"Thank God!" It was as she had hoped and prayed.

Rennick would surely have come to gloat if they had him in their power.

"Do you know where he might have gone? We could send him a message—"

"No, I don't, and it is better if we do not. Otherwise, Rennick and Oswald may discover his whereabouts, too, and harm him. I have already caused enough trouble to my loved ones. I will prevent what I can. Is Oswald here still?"

"Yes, but something happened yesterday that upset him. A messenger came, and he was obviously displeased by whatever news he brought. Auberan says he thought the messenger was from Lord Oswald's estate."

"I dearly hope some part of his clever plan has gone awry!" As she removed her shift, she slid Isabelle a questioning glance. "And Auberan?"

Isabelle's eyes flashed with anger. "Still here. Still trying to convince me that he cares for me, but he doesn't. He's just doing what Lord Oswald tells him, like a child."

Relieved that Isabelle knew not to trust that young man, she walked to the steaming tub and carefully slid into the warm, soothing water. It surrounded and embraced her, and made her feel almost human again. Closing her eyes, she leaned her head back and let herself enjoy the sensation, for it was almost like being in Connor's arms.

Merva barged into the room like a force of nature. " 'Ere I am, back with food and some nice cool water."

"Give it to me here," she requested.

With a nod, Merva obeyed.

Allis ate and drank, feeling the life returning to her

limbs, energy to her body, and strength to her determined heart. When she was finished, she rose from the tub and wrapped a large square of linen about her body. "Merva, please leave me alone with my sister."

Merva's brow furrowed at the calm tone of Allis's voice, then she glanced from sister to sister, and left when Isabelle nodded her acquiescence.

She put on the clean silk shift Isabelle gave her, then the gown. "What are you going to do?" Isabelle finally asked after she had tied the bodice lacings for her.

"I'm going to marry Rennick."

Isabelle gasped. "*What?*"

Poor Isabelle . . . but this was how it must be. "I will go through with the ceremony. I will do as he commands me, until the day I get my hands on a knife. And then I will kill him."

How very simple it sounded. How very simple it was.

"You'll be accused of murder!"

"I expect so. And convicted, too, I should think."

"Allis!"

Isabelle was so young. But she had been younger than Isabelle when their mother had died, and Isabelle had the makings of a fine and worthy chatelaine of Montclair. She could die knowing that Edmond would have Isabelle to watch over and protect him, as he would Isabelle when he was of age.

"If I could conceive of another way for all my loved ones to be free, I would do it," she said, certain of her course. "But I cannot. This is the only way I can be sure that you do not have to live in fear of Rennick." She reached out to cradle Isabelle's horrified face between her palms. "So we must be a little patient, but one day, you will be free. I want you to promise me that you will do your best to look after Edmond."

Isabelle fell to her knees and covered her face with her hands. "Oh, Allis!"

She bent down and gently pried them apart so that she could look into Isabelle's eyes. "Promise me."

"I do. Of course I do!"

She let go of her and smiled. "Then I am content."

Yet even as she spoke, they heard the sounds of a mounted party coming through the gate and into the courtyard.

Isabelle rose and ran to the window.

Allis wanted to follow, but fear weakened her knees and she could only stagger to the bed, holding on to the large post at the foot of it.

Despite her prayers, it might not be Connor, or anyone coming to her aid. It might be guests Rennick had invited to the wedding.

Isabelle whirled around and stared at Allis, her eyes wide, her expression both astonished and jubilant. "It's Connor—and the king!"

Joy, relief and hope exploded in her as she stumbled toward the window. Yes, there he was, riding beside a man in a scarlet surcoat marked with three golden lions and wearing the crowned helmet of the king of England. Behind them rode the king's guard, pennants flapping and harnesses jingling, as they entered the courtyard of Montclair.

Wonderful, beloved Connor! He must have gone to Richard, the one person with the power to defeat Rennick's plans. Her gaze lingered on Connor, drinking in the blessed sight of him. He was dressed in knightly apparel, and bareheaded, so that his long, waving, beautifully savage hair fluttered in the breeze.

"Come, Isabelle, we must go to him!" she cried, her voice, like her love and her hope, given new life.

She dashed from the chamber and, hiking up her skirt, ran down the stairs, then through the hall past astonished servants. She came to a halt when she went out the door and nearly collided with Rennick, who had gone down on one knee as the king dismounted. By this time, most of the servants had got wind of the king's arrival and come to the courtyard, where they milled about, curious and uncertain.

She bowed to the king, but she kept her head raised so that she could look at Connor, her love, her life.

How tired he looked! Strain, weariness and pain were etched in his brow and around his mouth. His shoulder probably ached from his journey. Going to Richard had not been easy for him in so many ways, and if she had needed any proof of his devotion, this would have been more than enough. She would gladly return that devotion all the rest of her life.

He stared at her, too, as if equally desperate for the sight of her. But he did not smile.

A quaking sliver of dread touched her happy heart.

Perhaps it was only that he dare not look too joyous because things were not yet resolved. Yet they would—must be, or else why was he here with Richard?

Oswald the betrayer strode out of the kitchen and bowed to Richard. "Greeting, sire."

Attired in his finest clothes, Edmond approached the royal party. There was no longer any hint of boyish innocence or even excitement in her brother's features as he, too, bowed to the king. Only days ago, he would have been fairly dancing with glee to meet Richard.

"I bid you welcome to Montclair, my liege," he said.

Tall and broad-shouldered, handsome and commanding, every inch the warrior king, Richard acknowledged Edmond's obeisance with an inclination
of his head. She could see why a man might follow
him into battle, and how a man would be disappointed to learn Richard was a fallible, mortal man—
even more shocked and disillusioned than she had
been by Oswald's betrayal, for she had not left home
and family to fight with the promise that it was a
chivalrous undertaking for the glory of God.

"You must be Edmond, the son of the late earl of
Montclair."

"He is, sire," Rennick said, stepping beside Edmond
and putting a possessive arm around his shoulder.
"This is my ward."

Enraged by his action, she stepped purposefully
forward, but before she spoke, Edmond shrugged off
Rennick's encircling arm.

She glanced at Connor, seeking his reaction, but his
face showed nothing, and he didn't meet her gaze. It
was as if he was dead inside—and the finger of dread
touching her heart became a fist clutching it, strangling
her joy and confidence that all would now be well.

"And who is the young lady?" Richard's scrutiny
had more than a touch of royal insolence, but she kept
her face as carefully blank as Connor's, taking her cue
from him, for he knew Richard well and perhaps—
please, God, let it be thus!—the king disliked displays
of emotions, save for the hot-blooded rush of battle. If
that were so, she would do well to show nothing of the
emotions roiling within her.

Rennick quickly abandoned Edmond's side for
hers, and answered before she could. "Sire, may I pre-

sent Lady Allis, my bride-to-be. How delightful that you have arrived on our wedding day. This is an honor I had not anticipated."

"It is not an honor at all." Richard gestured for Connor to join him, and her heart raced at the sight. Surely this was a good sign. "Sir Connor has given me to understand that there is conspiracy afoot in Montclair. That you, Rennick, are plotting against me."

Sweet heaven, not only were they in danger, but the whole realm. She should have seen it.

As she gazed at Connor, so honest and noble, and the arrogant man who ruled, she guessed how Connor had convinced him to come here. He had appealed to the man's fear of conspiracy, the price of power every king must pay.

"Your Majesty, that is a blatant falsehood!" Rennick protested. "Surely you don't believe that, or you would never have confirmed me as the guardian of this boy and his sisters."

"Sir Connor had not spoken to me then."

"Sire, perhaps we should retire inside—" Oswald began.

"I have a hearty dislike of secrecy," Richard interrupted, running a scornful gaze over the large man, delighting her. "That is the breeding ground of conspiracy and mistrust. I see no reason we should not air these suspicions in the courtyard and settle the matter."

Oswald's demeanor became smoothly humble. "Majesty—"

She could not even bear to hear him speak. "He is not the man you think he is, sire. Do not trust him, either."

Richard gave her the ghost of a smile. "Oh, I don't."

He darted a condemning look at Oswald. "Sir Connor has raised many questions in my mind, and answered some, too."

"Your Majesty, I am innocent of any conspiracy against you," Oswald said at once. "But, I, too, have had my doubts about the baron, which is why I stayed here. They have been confirmed. I was about to leave for Westminster myself to warn you about him."

"Liar!" Rennick snarled.

She smiled as their evil alliance shattered like Connor's lance. Then relief hit her full force, and she thought she was going to swoon.

Connor rushed to her side, and once again his strong, protective arms enfolded her. "Sire, I fear the lady is unwell. She should not be standing."

She looked up into his wonderful brown eyes—still full of a pain she could not fathom. If Rennick was arrested by the king, they would be free.

"We will all sit out here in the courtyard," Richard ordered. "Bring chairs and benches, and have the horses taken care of."

Nobody moved for a moment, until Allis spoke, for she was still the lady of Montclair. "Do what the king commands."

As the servants hurried to bring benches and chairs, and the nobles took their places, she was aware only of Connor and being with him once more. "You've come back to save me," she murmured, gently caressing his cheek.

As he looked down at her, seeing how thin and pale and weary she was, his heart broke anew. He wanted nothing more than to hold her in his arms forever, yet no matter what happened today, he would never again have that chance.

She could never be his, for so he had promised his king.

As for DeFrouchette—he was going to die today. That was the only thought that had lightened his despair all the way back from Westminster. Even if he didn't know exactly what DeFrouchette had done to Allis, one look at her altered state would have sealed the man's doom if he had not already determined it.

Holding her close, he stroked her glorious hair, and gazed over the assembly at Edmond and Isabelle.

Mercifully, they looked in better health than Allis, and Isabelle seemed little changed, except for the dignity of her carriage, so like Allis's the first time he'd ever laid eyes on her. But Edmond—he was different, and he could guess why. The lad had been forced over the threshold of manhood by all that had happened.

Merva brought a chair. "For my lady," she murmured, her eyes full of pity for her mistress.

Allis must sit, but he hesitated nonetheless, not wanting to let go of her.

Yet slowly, slowly he helped her to the chair. Then, unable to bear the sight of her loving eyes, knowing that she was still blissfully ignorant of his promise to Richard, he turned away and went to face DeFrouchette.

"What exactly are the charges this Welshman brings against me?" DeFrouchette demanded, his eyes full of hate, his stance outwardly confident—but only outwardly.

Connor had fought too often, against too many men, to be fooled by mere bravado. "That you have obtained your current position by fraud and deceit upon the earl of Montclair," he declared. "That you caused the untimely death of Percival L'Ouisseaux, and that you tried to kill me by tampering with my lance. That you are unfit to be the guardian of the young earl and his sisters, and utterly unworthy to marry one of them. That you are a foul traitor, plotting against your lawful king."

Fiercely angry, DeFrouchette turned to Richard, who was enthroned on a large and finely carved chair. "He wants to marry my betrothed and has made up these accusations against me to prevent the marriage. What evidence does he have to prove these incredible charges? How did I cause Percival's death? How did I tamper with this Welshman's lance? How do I plan to kill you, sire? If he has proof, let him produce it."

"The matter of Percival's death can be brought before another court another time," Richard said. "It is because of a conspiracy I have come."

Rennick flushed hotly. "Again, I say, what proof?"

"I have none," Connor answered, "but we can put the matter to judgment."

"What, let the king decide?"

"No. God."

Aghast, Rennick stepped back. "You are suggesting trial by combat?"

As Connor had suspected from the first, DeFrouchette was a coward. Without some means to ensure the outcome he desired, he was terrified. "Yes. If I am right, you will die. If I am wrong, I will."

Allis rose, beautiful and proud, lovely and wonderful. "Your Majesty, Sir Connor injured his shoulder in our tournament. It would not be just if he were to fight today."

His poor, beloved Allis, who did not know that even if he lived today, a part of him must die.

Isabelle, surprisingly, also got to her feet. "That's true, Your Majesty. Brother Jonathan can vouch—"

"Here, sire!" the little man called out. He bustled forward, at once deferential and determined. "Sir Connor's shoulder was forced out of joint."

As Connor's heart swelled with gratitude that they cared, the king held up his hand to silence them. "Sir Connor, you did not tell me of this injury."

Nothing would prevent him from freeing Allis, not even pain like the fury of hell. "It is of no consequence, sire. I am ready to fight."

"Good," Richard replied. "I would have this settled today."

"But sire—" Allis objected.

"I would have it settled *today*."

She looked desperately at Connor. This time, he met her gaze, willing her to see that he had to do this.

Her brow furrowed slightly, and then she slowly sank back into her chair.

"This is but another means to try to steal my bride, sire," Rennick protested despite the king's inexorable command. "He doesn't care about God's judgment and your safety. He is only thinking of himself and the woman he wants."

"That may very well be true, Rennick," Richard replied. "However, it may not. Indeed, I think he must be acting out of some concern for me, because he promises he will not marry the Lady Allis if he wins."

Connor heard Allis's gasp and it was like the stab of a dagger in his heart. He did not look at her. He could not. He had to be strong and watching her as the realization of the meaning of his promise penetrated her understanding would destroy him. "Yes, Baron, that is what I have promised my king. I have given my word, as a knight of the realm."

"*Your* word."

"Yes, Baron, *his* word—and that is more than enough for me," Richard said. "Unlike some of my subjects, he has always been an honest man—perhaps too much for his own good, but that only makes him all the more trustworthy."

Out of the corner of his eye, Connor saw Allis rise again. *Oh, God, please,* he prayed. *No more. Let it be done. Let me fight him now and give me victory.*

"Your Majesty," she said, "the conspiracy against you encompasses more than Rennick DeFrouchette and Lord Oswald."

At her accusation, there was a sudden commotion among the spectators. Sir Auberan de Beaumartre had fainted.

Connor realized he should have suspected Auberan's complicity, too.

"Attend to that man," Richard ordered. His eyes narrowed as he scanned the benches. "Where is my lord Oswald?"

He was not there. He had disappeared while everyone's attention was elsewhere.

"Find him!" the king commanded, and several soldiers hurried to obey.

Richard rose and approached DeFrouchette. "This is looking very bad for you, Baron. You and he have been friends for many years."

DeFrouchette's gaze darted from the king to Connor to Allis, then back to Richard. "Perhaps he felt ill, my lord."

"You are looking rather ill yourself."

"I am," the baron said. He unexpectedly squared

his shoulders and looked Richard in the eye, and suddenly Connor saw the warrior DeFrouchette might have been. "I am sick of you, Richard. I am sick of the way you play favorites. I am sick of your taxes and paying for your vainglorious adventures. Nor am I the only one. We are many, Richard, and if you were less arrogant and vain and selfish, you would realize that. England is not your storehouse, waiting to be plundered and made barren."

Then his hand moved toward the dagger in his belt.

Chapter 27

"Assassin!" The word burst from Connor's lips as he lunged forward and shoved the king out of the way. Then he drew his sword in one fluid motion as he faced the baron.

Rennick pulled his sword from his scabbard. They both crouched, watchful, their weapons at the ready.

"You of all people should have let me kill him, Welshman, for your family and your country," Rennick growled as Richard got to his feet.

"Whatever I think of Richard and what he has done, he is my rightful sovereign. He will be dealt with accordingly—by God, who is sovereign of all."

Richard's men had drawn their swords, but Richard held up his hand as he moved back, so that only Rennick and Connor were in the center of the courtyard.

"Sir Connor has offered to discover the truth in a trial by combat, and I agreed."

Happy in a way, Connor smiled his dangerous smile as he circled his opponent. "If I must be miserable for the rest of my life because I must live without Allis, I will have your death to comfort me."

"You are a lying Welsh bastard," Rennick jeered, sweat glistening on his face. "You don't care about Richard. You just want Allis."

"You heard what the king said, DeFrouchette. I will never have Allis." Connor raised his sword. "But she will be free of you."

Rennick moved swiftly out of the way, and once again they faced one another, circling, each waiting for the other to make a move or present an opening.

"Not good enough, DeFrouchette," Connor said. "How long has it been since you faced a man in honest combat—or have you ever?"

Terror and desperation surged in Rennick's eyes as triumph sang in Connor's blood. Finally, all the years of training and fighting, of harsh warfare and death and blood—finally they were going to mean something.

Rennick lunged—not for Connor or Richard, but for Allis. He grabbed her and pulled her against him, his sword at her neck.

"Let me go, or by God I'll slit her throat!" he snarled.

Rage, fierce as a mad dog, hot as the sun, consumed Connor as he faced the coward. He took a step closer, staring at Allis's wide eyes and the trickle of blood running down her neck.

By God, DeFrouchette would pay! But for now, he willed Allis to have faith in him, and as he looked at her, complete confidence in him shone in her eyes, and he was strengthened.

"I mean it, Welshman," DeFrouchette cried like the trapped creature he was. "I'll kill her rather than give her up."

The whole courtyard seemed to hold its breath as Connor replied. "A very strange sort of love, that."

"She would have loved me one day if you had not come, just as Richard was realizing his error in not taking me in his retinue."

"The guardianship of Montclair would have been your second chance, Rennick, as I gave Connor a second chance," the king declared from the other side of the open space. "Had you performed that duty well, I intended to reward you."

Tears of anger and frustration gleamed in Rennick's eyes as his grip tightened on Allis. "I shouldn't have needed a second chance! I had never done anything wrong!"

"Except be too sly, too malicious and therefore, I feared, untrustworthy. I see my fears were well founded."

What in the name of God was Richard doing, goading his enemy while he held a defenseless woman as his hostage? Connor inwardly cried.

He was being Richard—thoughtless, arrogant, with no regard for anyone but himself.

Awaiting his chance, Connor kept his eyes on De-Frouchette and the dangerous tip so close to the vein throbbing in his beloved's throat.

"Only because you rejected me! You play with me even now, Richard. You say you would have rewarded me, but how do I know that's not a lie?"

Connor saw his chance. Making a sudden lunge, he

dropped his sword and grabbed DeFrouchette's arm, wrenching the sword from his grasp. He heard the sound of his own shoulder coming out of joint as he tugged Allis away with his left hand, but paid no heed.

Allis stumbled backward, out of danger. De-Frouchette tried to regain his balance. Not fast enough. Connor grabbed his sword and plunged it into his chest.

His eyes wide, blood staining the front of his tunic, Rennick looked down at his wound as he slowly backed away. He fell to his knees and looked at Allis with pleading eyes, already glazing over with death.

"I did love you," he whispered, panting. "I did. I tried . . ." He looked away from her, to Richard. "Rot in hell, my liege." Then his body pitched forward, and with one last gasp, he died.

The courtyard remained silent as Connor went to Allis and gathered her to him with his right arm, holding her close. Safe from DeFrouchette, she was still lost to him. How he craved one more day to be with her. One more hour. One more moment.

Richard came toward them and put his hand on his shoulder, and he had to let her go. "Well done, Sir Connor. You have saved the lady, and your king."

"No thanks to you, Your Majesty," Allis declared.

Connor stared at Allis, who clutched his hand as if determined never to let him go.

For so she was, as she faced the stupid, arrogant man who could have gotten them both killed. "It is hardly the proper time to upbraid an enemy when he holds a sword at someone's throat."

Richard was clearly as shocked as Connor, but she would not be silent. She had been silent too long, about too many things. She would speak, like her brave, glorious lover, because like him, she was right. "Was the life of the lady of Montclair of so little consequence? I think you owe me an apology, and Connor some sign of your gratitude for saving your life."

"You do, eh?" the king demanded, his brows lowering.

She didn't care. She had just had a sword at her throat—and she was right. "Yes, I do."

Suddenly, the king smiled and bowed regally. "My lady, forgive me for speaking without more thought, as a certain knight once addressed his king." He turned to Connor who, she realized, was pale to the lips. "Sir Connor, of course you must be rewarded for saving my life. You may have the reward you want best, the hand of Lady Allis in marriage."

Joy filled her to hear his words. Now all would be well, and nobody could speak against their marriage if the king approved.

Connor blinked as if trying to clear his vision and began to sway. "Sire, I gave you my word—"

"By my sword, Connor, you are the most stubbornly honorable man I have ever met. You deserve the girl, and the wealth that goes with her. I will not hear another word. I must say you are both the most outspoken people I have ever had to endure, too."

"Sire, I thank you . . . I thank you with all—" Connor began.

Then he fainted.

When Connor opened his eyes, the first thing he saw was Allis sitting on the cot beside him, looking down at him with love and concern shining in her beautiful brown eyes. A single candle burned upon the table beside them, casting a small pool of golden light like the glow of happiness he felt within. From the herbal scent in the air, he knew they were in Brother Jonathan's dispensary. A fitting place, for with Allis beside him, their troubles over, he could truly heal, the wounds of the past as well as his shoulder.

He lifted her hand and pressed a soft kiss to her wrist. The first time he had done that, she had shied like a skittish horse. This time, she gave him a glorious smile. "You frightened me, fainting like that."

Although she spoke cheerfully, the shadow of fear lingered in her eyes. He would once more make her smile, a task he would gladly accept for the rest of his life. "I daresay I should feel totally humiliated, but I don't, perhaps because I'm much too happy." She still didn't smile with her eyes, so he abandoned levity. "And you? How are you? Did DeFrouchette hurt you?"

Whatever the baron had done, no matter how he had abused her, he would cherish her and do his best to make her forget.

"He didn't rape me, Connor." She briefly told him what had happened while he was gone, and it was a good thing DeFrouchette was already dead, or Connor would have taken great delight in beating him with his bare hands until he cried for mercy.

"If I had known what was going to happen—!"

"If you had somehow become a mind reader and discovered I was going to come to you that night," she interrupted, grasping his hand tightly. "I should have sent you a message, but I feared it would be intercepted, and I didn't dare come to you myself. I am as much to blame as you in that regard, so please don't feel any guilt. You saved me, after all." She tilted her head to regard him. "I must say, though, that I never thought you would go to Richard."

"Nor would I have, had I not been desperate," he confessed. "I had to act, and quickly, and the best way was to go to the king. My pride mattered nothing when your freedom was at stake."

She pressed a tender kiss to his lips, and instantly, passion flared. He teased her lips with his tongue, skimming their surface until she parted them. Then his kiss deepened as he gently thrust inside and his hand slid slowly up her bodice to her breast.

With a gasp and a maidenly blush, she broke the kiss. "I think you must be feeling better, Sir Connor."

"I am." He went to raise himself, until a pain stabbed his shoulder and he fell back. "In heart and mind, at least."

She brushed back a lock of hair from his forehead and it became a caress. "You hurt your shoulder again."

He turned his head and rubbed his cheek against her soft palm. "So I gather."

"You will have to be careful and give it longer to heal before you ride for hours at a time."

He continued to move his head until he could kiss her palm. Her skin was so warm and welcome against his lips, and now that he was free to do so, he enjoyed the wonderful sensations even more. "I had a very important reason for doing that, and I have a very important reason to stay."

"Connor," she whispered, his name little more than a sigh as delightful excitement blossomed as she remembered all his lips and hands could do. "Connor, we are—"

"In love. Lovers." His eyes gleaming with desire, he reached up with his right hand to cup her head and draw her close. "I think there is much more I could do, my lady, if you will join me."

"The dispensary is no place for what you are suggesting, sir," she murmured, letting her yearning take her.

"But I am already half naked."

How much she wanted to kiss him, to feel his mouth on hers, teasing forth passionate delight . . . "Yes, I can see that."

Behind her, Brother Jonathan loudly cleared his throat. "How are you, Sir Connor?"

Allis sat back abruptly, blushing furiously. She had not heard him enter.

Connor, however, seemed not a whit disturbed. "I have never been better."

Brother Jonathan smiled indulgently. "I mean, are you in any pain?"

"My shoulder does ache a little."

"But not worse than before?"

Connor's hand wandered toward hers, and she took it, reveling in that simple act. "No, Brother."

"Excellent."

"Did you set my shoulder? Or"—he glanced up at Allis, his eyes bright—"did my future bride?"

She was going to be his bride! Happiness trilled along her limbs and burst into chorus in her heart.

"I did, sir. It was easy because you were unconscious. And I must say, it's a good thing Richard caught you as you fell, or you might have hit your head upon the cobblestones and done some serious harm. As it is, you will have to take more special care of your shoulder."

"Mercifully I do not think I will be called upon to defend my king or my bride any time soon."

"And no more tournaments, or your shoulder may be permanently injured," she warned. She brushed a light kiss along his wrist. "You don't need to do that. After all, you are going to have your bride's dowry."

Not unexpectedly, for he was a proud man, a small frown creased his brow. "I am not marrying you for your money."

She widened her eyes as if surprised. "Alas, sir knight, Edmond, the king and I have decided the matter and the amount."

He had the sudden sensation that he had been outmaneuvered, like the time Isabelle had beaten him at chess. He looked at Brother Jonathan, but the little priest spread his hands in a gesture of helplessness— and then he grinned. "As a physician and considering the state of your shoulder, I must say anything that keeps you from injuring it again is bound to meet with my approval."

"I don't see why you're looking that way," she said, making the kind of pout Isabelle had likely used with devastating effect on the hapless Auberan. "Most men would be pleased to get a lady's dowry."

Her lip thrust out so temptingly was having quite an effect on him at the moment. He had to shift, lest he be embarrassed by his body's blatant desire in front of the priest. "All I want . . . all I *need* . . . is the lady."

"But the king himself—"

He didn't care if Brother Jonathan was there or not. He wrapped his hand about her neck and pulled her down to capture her lips in a fiery kiss.

"Ahem."

He ignored the priest.

"*Ahem.*"

Allis pulled back, panting, her face red, and her eyes shining with desire. And frustration, too. Grinning, he said, "So you are telling me I have no choice but to surrender?"

"Yes . . . no . . ."

"Then I must agree. Now if the good brother will excuse us, I believe my bride and I have business to discuss."

The priest's brows rose. "Business, you say? I assure you, my son, I was not *born* in a monastery."

He had gone too far. Again.

Then Brother Jonathan smiled broadly. "But as you are an honorable knight, I shall take my leave of you. Do have a care of that shoulder and remember that you are not yet joined by the holy bonds of matrimony."

"We will," Connor gravely answered.

Despite his vow, however, the moment Brother Jonathan closed the door behind him, he drew Allis down for a long, luxurious, passionate kiss.

Her whole body softened and warmed as his mouth explored hers. Pleasure slid outward from there, to move with slow seduction through her. She twined her arms about his neck, spreading her fingers through his hair, and felt him tense as she brushed his bandaged shoulder. "Does this hurt?" she murmured as her lips moved toward his cheek.

"Not as much as not doing it," he assured her. He drew back, a merry grin on his handsome face, but passion smoldering in his eyes. "And I am feeling better all the time," he said before they shared another kiss full of love and the promise of more delight to come.

"Richard says we may wed as soon as we like."

"Tomorrow is too far off," he said with arousing invitation.

Her heart raced and her body yearned for his caress. Excitement bubbled and boiled. "Alas, I am but a weak-willed woman, and I fear you are trying to seduce me."

His laughter surrounded her like a beam of sunlight on a chill afternoon. "You are quite right, but you, my lady, are the last woman I would call weak." He stroked her cheek, his rough palm wonderfully welcome, his low, deep voice a seduction in itself. "Will you let me seduce you, Allis?"

Once more their lips met, their mouths voicing their passion without uttering words. Gingerly, as if this was their first time, their hands began to explore, the fire between them growing hotter with need and desire, and the memories of what they had already shared.

"Apparently both of you are recovering."

With a startled gasp, she pulled back to see Richard, Isabelle and Edmond watching them— Richard amused, Isabelle delighted and Edmond, sadly, enigmatic.

She stood, then bowed. "Sire, we are both feeling very much better, especially since you have given us permission to marry."

The king smiled, and again it was easy to see why men would follow him and women desire him, why minstrels would sing ballads about him and poets praise him—but he was no Connor of Llanstephan.

Connor started to rise, until Richard gestured for him to remain in bed. "Your marriage is a fitting reward for your loyalty, Connor, and for saving my life, but there is still one thing lacking. A man wed to an heiress of Montclair really ought to have his own estate, so I have decided to give you DeFrouchette's."

"Sire!" they cried simultaneously, equally shocked.

"Since the man was a traitor, it is the Crown's to give. Of course, I will expect the taxes to be paid on time."

Connor got a very determined look on his face. "Since we are speaking of taxes, sire—"

Richard waved his hand dismissively. "Yes, yes, I shall speak to the justiciar about lowering the taxes on Llanstephan before I return to the Continent. I gave the order in haste when you first angered me, and in truth, never thought of it again. It was to have been a temporary measure anyway. I do value honesty, when my temper cools. Indeed, I trust you will continue to be honest with me—and I promise I will not be so remiss in future. You have the word of Richard on that."

Allis wasn't convinced the word of Richard was much of a guarantee, but perhaps there were times it was better to be silent, just as there were times, as she had learned, when it was better to speak.

Richard nodded to Edmond, who came forward. "This young man has a request."

"I would like Connor to continue training me in the arts of war." He turned toward the king. "And when Connor is satisfied that I am prepared, I would also ask that you will accept me in your retinue."

Richard chuckled. "By my sword, if Connor thinks you are sufficiently trained, that will be good enough for me. I will be proud to have you in my company, young earl of Montclair."

Like Connor in his youth, once she would have considered this a great honor. Now, having met the king, she was not so sure. Still, it would be years before Edmond would be fully trained to be a knight, and much could happen in that time. It could be, as he thought back on what had happened, he would change his mind.

But for now, Edmond smiled, although she saw that it was not as he had been wont to smile before. In the past several days, he had been tried, and he had not been found wanting, but he had paid a price.

Richard abruptly whirled around and addressed Isabelle, who had been hovering near the door, so quiet Allis had forgotten she was there. "Since your king is in a generous mood, is there anything you request, Lady Isabelle?"

She nodded. "I would ask that you do not execute Sir Auberan de Beaumartre."

Had that traitorous young man managed to obtain Isabelle's affection, after all?

The king's good humor vanished. "It is not my custom to forgive traitors. He would not name any of the others who would plot against me, although all here confirm that he shared in their secret councils. That woman, Merva, was most adamant about that, yet he claims he does not know who Oswald and Rennick were in league with."

"Auberan is a follower, sire, not a leader," Isabelle said. "He is probably speaking the truth when he says he does not know, and I do not ask that you forgive him completely. Strip him of his title and estates and banish him, but let him live."

"You care for him, do you?"

"Not in the way that you think, Your Majesty. Not as my sister loves Sir Connor. I pity him."

"Others might take this for a sign of weakness on my part."

"Or an example of their king's benevolence, sire. Anyone who has met Auberan will understand that he could pose no real threat to a man like you."

Wise Isabelle had realized that the most effective

way to persuade a man like Richard would be to appeal to his vanity.

"I will banish him to the far north, where he can live among the heathen Scots," Richard reflected. "No doubt he wouldn't last the winter anyway."

"You are most generous and merciful, sire," Isabelle said.

So Rennick was dead, and Auberan banished. That left one conspirator unaccounted for, and he was the worst of all.

"What of Oswald?" Allis asked.

"Escaped, the blackguard. But we will hunt him down eventually, now that we know where his loyalties lie. Now, Sir Connor, my lady, I believe we should leave you to discuss the nuptials." The king turned to Edmond and Isabelle. "Come along, you two, and I shall tell you about my campaign in the Holy Land. It was marvelous, I assure you, and we would have taken Jerusalem except for a most foul set of circumstances."

When they were gone, Allis smiled at Connor. "Perhaps you are tired and wish to rest? You were very quiet."

"After all these years, perhaps I have learned the wisdom to hold my tongue."

She again sat beside him on the bed. "Have you?"

He shifted, making more room. "Or perhaps my bride-to-be was talking enough for both."

The heat of a blush warmed her cheeks. Maybe she should have been more circumspect.

His arm crept around her. "And perhaps I was content to listen to her speak and admire her, so proud and happy that such a woman was willing to be my wife."

Proud and happy, too, she lay beside him. He

wrapped his right arm around her and she nestled against him, content. "Is that true, sir knight?"

He brushed her cheek lightly with his marvelous lips and tremors of delight skittered and danced. "Very much so. I still cannot quite believe my glorious dream is coming true."

Thrilling to his touch, she murmured, "We should discuss our nuptials, as the king suggested."

Connor's mouth moved down her neck, heating her blood and making it hard for her to think. "We could discuss your dowry."

"I thought you didn't care about that."

"That is not the dowry I meant." He slowly stroked her breast, arousing her even more. "This is one part I am thinking of." He ran his forefinger over her lips. "This is another part."

His touch sent shivers of delight along her body and her hunger for him grew. "You don't want to talk about it, do you?"

"I suppose I should know how much it is," he muttered as he trailed kisses across her collarbone. "Is it more than a penny?"

"Yes," she whispered as he dragged his hand up her leg, pulling her gown upward, too.

"More than a mark?"

"Yes," she sighed, closing her eyes and giving in to the pure ecstasy of his touch.

"Then I am satisfied."

She opened her eyes. "Well, Sir Connor of Llanstephan," she teased with an undercurrent of blatant desire, "I am not."

She moved her hand beneath the linen sheet. As his touch excited her, so she would excite him, and his low moan and closed eyes told her she was succeeding.

She stroked him and he grew harder under her hand. It gave her a heady sense of triumph as this bold, brave warrior surrendered to her caress.

"Oh, sweet heaven, Allis," he moaned, "what are you doing?"

"Giving you pleasure, I hope. Does your shoulder trouble you too much? Should I stop?"

"Yes. No. I don't know," he said as he pushed against her hand. "Don't stop."

She didn't want to stop, and yet the tension and yearning within her was building to a fever pitch. Carefully, so that she did not move his shoulder, she pushed down the sheet and untied his breeches, freeing him. Then, as he watched, his eyes gleaming and telling her he wanted this, too, she settled herself upon his hips.

"You do not weigh what you did."

"That's good, isn't it—considering?"

His low chuckle filled the air as she bent down to kiss him. "It's very good."

"My dowry is eight hundred marks."

He gasped again, and not with passion.

She pressed a light kiss on his forehead. She had been waiting for a good time to tell him, and this seemed as good as any. "I understand that is enough to pay off the taxes on Llanstephan."

He moved, arousing her even more. "You would do that?"

She kissed his fine, straight nose. "Of course. And it leaves some for new clothes for you."

"I don't need new clothes."

Then she kissed his marvelously masculine jaw. "And for smaller clothes. Children's clothes. *Our* children's clothes."

"Allis!" he cried, going perfectly still. "Are you with child?"

She smiled as she shook her head. "Not yet, but soon, I hope. It may take many tries, of course. With that in mind, my dearest, most wonderful knight of the realm," she murmured, her voice husky with yearning, "the only thing I want to talk about now is how I intend to pleasure you."

He laughed softly, the sound warm and comforting, making her feel happy and beloved, secure and at peace at last. "My dearest, most wonderful lady of Montclair, I am listening."

Dear Reader,

Satisfy your desire for unforgettable, sensuous romance by seeking out these Avon Books—all coming next month!

If you love historical romance, don't miss THE SEDUCTION OF SARA by Karen Hawkins, where you'll meet pert, pretty Lady Sara Carrington. Her brothers want to marry her off to a stodgy old man, so she's determined to find a husband who won't mind her willfull ways. She picks Nicholas, the Earl of Bridgeton—he's England's most notorious rake. He's willing to teach Sara the art of seduction—but marry her . . . never! Until she applies those lessons to him . . .

Cait London is an incomparable teller of tales and her contemporary romances have wowed her many readers. They're dramatic, romantic and filled with twists and turns that will keep you turning the pages. In LEAVING LONELY TOWN she's created her most memorable love story yet—between Sable Barclay, a woman desperately searching for the truth about her past, and Culley Blackwolf, a strong, silent man who just might know the answers to her questions.

Fans of Scotland—and there are many of you!—shouldn't let Lois Greiman's THE MACGOWAN BETROTHAL pass them by. Isobel Fraser is determined not to let Gilmour of the MacGowans steal her heart—even if his roguish ways are so very tempting . . .

And in Linda O'Brien's passionate BELOVED PROTECTOR, a young lady in need of a bodyguard expects to have a boring old man watching over her . . . instead she gets broad-shouldered, lean-hipped Pinkerton detective Case Brogan. Suddenly, Eliza Lowe isn't so sure if she wants him to protect her—or seduce her.

Don't miss any of these spectacular Avon Romances!

Warmly,

Lucia Macro

Lucia Macro
Executive Editor

Avon Romances—
the best in exceptional authors
and unforgettable novels!